WRONG N

Carys Jones

About *Wrong Number*

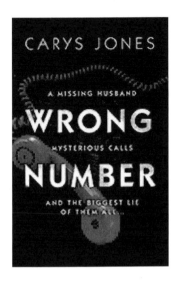

A missing husband. Mysterious calls. And the biggest lie of them all…

Read with caution – you may never want to answer your phone again

Will and Amanda Thorne are living the dream until, one day, their phone rings. Within 24 hours, Will is missing and Amanda's world is shattered. Who was on the phone? Where has Will gone?

Amanda is determined to find her husband and is drawn into a world of drug dealers, criminal masterminds and broken promises.

As the truth becomes clearer, she has to face the terrible possibility that she may never have known her husband at all…

To Sam – for always listening

Prologue

Amanda ignored the metallic taste in her mouth and did her best to focus. Sunlight was bleeding in through the windows in the small kitchen, casting ornate shadows upon the bare wooden floors.

But Amanda didn't notice them. Nor did she smell the heady aroma of fresh heather floating in through the open door, or hear the gentle rustle of the long grass outside as a cooling breeze brushed its way through it.

All she saw was the barrel of the gun looming inches away from her head. There was only darkness in its depths. And possibly her own death. Her fate hung on the twitch of a trigger. Amanda had known fear like this before when she was eight years old and she'd almost tumbled over the edge of the cliffs near her home. The sun had been shining that day too.

Only now her father wasn't waiting in the wings to save her.

'Why did you come here?' he growled the question at her, each word drenched in angry disdain.

Amanda swallowed, using the second to gather her thoughts. She couldn't risk saying, or doing, the wrong thing.

'I had to.' She squeaked out the words like the frightened mouse she had become.

'No,' he was shaking his head but the hand holding the gun remained eerily stoic, like his muscles were well rehearsed in steadily managing its weight. 'You should never have come here.'

The taste in Amanda's mouth grew sharper. Just as it had that day when she had nearly dropped over the cliff edge and saw the sea and jagged rocks swirling beneath her. She defiantly raised her chin to meet his gaze.

'I had to come,' she told him, her voice strengthening along with her resolve. 'I had to find you.'

1

Two Weeks Earlier

Leaning back in her leather desk chair, Amanda Thorn raised her arms up over her head until she felt a satisfying click. Giving a light sigh, she shook out her shoulders and placed her fingers back upon her laptop's illuminated keyboard.

Golden sunlight was pouring in through the window, pooling at her feet. The hot afternoon was preparing to burn into a balmy evening. Amanda shuffled in her chair, her bare legs sticking to the soft leather.

'Damn heatwave,' she muttered as she cast a pained glance down at the denim cut-offs she'd pulled on that morning. Coupled with a loose fitting white T-shirt, the outfit had been perfect for jogging through the woodlands behind her home earlier but not such a wise choice for working in.

Leaning forward, Amanda reached for the tall glass of water that was standing beside her laptop like a solitary crystal guard. Droplets beaded down its sides, allowing the glass to leave a perfect circle upon the oak desk as Amanda lifted the drink towards her lips.

'Urgh,' she crinkled her nose when she spotted the water mark. Not because it bothered her but because she knew it would bother her husband, Will. He was a meticulous man; from the way he dressed right down to how he fastidiously organized the contents of their refrigerator. It was one of the things that had first drawn Amanda to him; the way he always looked so perfect and put together. It was a stark contrast to her own dishevelled appearance. Amanda refused to abandon the jogging bottoms, hoodies and T-shirts she'd lived in as a student. She was the kind of woman who preferred comfort over style although in the current heat she felt less comfortable than she'd have liked.

'Baby, you're such a knockout,' Will was always telling her, even when she'd only thrown on whatever clothes she could get her hands on. In their house he threw around compliments like confetti but Amanda wasn't so sure. When she looked in the mirror she still saw the gawky teenager who'd rather hide behind a computer screen than face the real world.

Putting her glass back down, Amanda focused on her computer screen. The website she'd spent the last week building was almost finished. She ran a critical eye over the various pages, hoping her client, Diowater, would be pleased with the results.

'Designer water,' she muttered to herself with a rueful shake of the head. Her icy blonde hair tumbled into her line of sight. Exhaling deeply, Amanda blew the few strands away and looked at her handiwork. The website looked slick and expensive, just like the product it was advertising.

Diowater was a new brand of bottled water. Even the plastic bottles the exclusive beverage came in had been warped to look like the carefully fractured surface of a diamond. Amanda continued to review the pages. This one job paid enough to cover her for a few months. She could stop working if she wanted to. Not that she'd ever do that. Amanda needed a connection to her computer like most people needed oxygen. She'd be lost without it. Growing up she had more virtual friends than real ones. If she wasn't online playing a game she was in some chat room or teaching herself how to code.

Will didn't share her passion for technology. He was a complete technophobe; his mobile phone still had buttons!

'I don't trust touchscreens,' he'd protested loudly in his thick Scottish accent as Amanda stood with in him in the centre of PC Universe. She was updating her laptop. Again. Will didn't even have a computer of his own.

'We could get you a tablet,' she'd taken his large, calloused hands in her own and led him over to where all the computer tablets were tastefully displayed.

'A tablet?' Will's dark eyes had crinkled at the corners and lit up with a mixture of amusement and concern. 'Honey, a tablet is something you take when you're sick.' He was smiling at her in the way he always did, like she entertained him simply by breathing.

Laughing, Amanda had led him away, accepting that a new tablet for her husband was the last thing she'd be purchasing.

He may not have been technically savvy but Will was an oak tree of a man. He was tall, with broad shoulders and a solid chest. In a storm he was the guy you'd grab on to in order to anchor yourself and save getting blown away. He had a shock of dark hair which filtered down into the whisper of a beard. Hair that had once been as black as night was now flecked with silver. The previous summer Will had celebrated his fortieth birthday; Amanda swore that with each birthday he became even more handsome, more rugged.

She was thirty-four and as slender and elfish as a feather beside her giant mountain of a husband. The only thing the couple shared was their impressive height. Will stood at six feet four inches while Amanda just skimmed the six foot mark.

'You could have been a model,' her mother would cluck at her when she'd had one too many glasses of wine. 'You're so beautiful, Amanda, but you're always hiding yourself away, disappearing into that *virtual* world.' Her mother always said the word virtual as though it stung her thin lips as it passed through them.

Amanda lifted her glass again. The air in her study had become thick and stale. She'd open a window but she knew it would do no good. The air out there was just as still as the air inside.

'Air conditioning,' Amanda muttered to herself as she used her free hand to hastily scrawl the note in her nearby writing pad. It was something Will had mentioned in the past but then decided against as he didn't like the idea of all the dust and debris the installation of air conditioning would cause.

'But he's not the one who works from home all day, is he?' Amanda chirped brightly to herself. Will was currently enjoying the benefits of air conditioning in the lofty warehouse where he worked as a site manager. His job didn't have the time-sensitive pressures of Amanda's, nor the flexibility of working from home, but Will got to do the one thing he loved most: ordering people about. People took orders from him as willingly as a baby receiving free candy. Will never came across as bossy or condescending. He was always warm, kind and friendly. The guys at the warehouse loved him. He'd go out with them a couple of nights a week, leaving Amanda to curl up on the sofa and catch up on all her favourite shows on Netflix.

Will loved shows like *Deadliest Catch*; about real men doing real work. Amanda liked to lose herself in a gripping drama. It was just another area in their lives where the couple didn't see eye to eye.

'You're too different,' her mother had scolded after she'd first met Will.

'I thought you said opposites attract.'

'Not too opposite.'

'Urgh, there's no pleasing you,' Amanda had stroked the tortoiseshell cat who was perched on her knee in a tight ball.

'Now, you and Shane, you had so much in common,' her mother had peered at her from across the cup of tea she'd raised to her lips. The steam briefly misted her thick-framed glasses.

'And look how that worked out,' Amanda had frowned at her. Her mother's preoccupation with her ex-boyfriend had gone from annoying to flat-out intolerable over the past few months. It was like the more time that passed, the more obsessed Corrine became with the past.

'You could be yourself around Shane,' her mother had infuriatingly pressed on.

'I can be myself around Will.' Amanda was grinding her teeth, colour rushing to her porcelain cheeks.

'Can you?' the question had hung in the air and been left unanswered.

Amanda looked at the clock in the far corner of her laptop's screen. It was almost five. Time to switch off and head downstairs to start getting dinner ready. She was still holding her glass of water, the ringed mark upon the desk glaring up at her, daring her to leave it.

'It's my desk,' Amanda told herself as she lowered her glass and shut down her computer. The laptop hummed for a moment and then went silent. 'I'm the only one who should be bothered by anything in here,' she continued as she started to head out of the room.

The entire house was a testament to Will's desire to keep everywhere nice. There wasn't a single item out of place. Even the books on the shelves were neatly arranged in height order. Amanda entertained his desire to keep everything just so, assuming it was some by-product of a past which he'd only fleetingly refer to as 'difficult'. And she knew enough about managing demons to choose not to pry. Will would open up to her when he was good and ready.

The only pictures on the wall of their house were ones from their wedding day. There was no pile of post on the counter in the kitchen, no shoes lined up by the door in the hallway. In many ways the house still looked like the show home they'd originally viewed it as.

In the kitchen, Amanda put a pan on to heat and removed some chilled steaks from the refrigerator before she turned around and powered back upstairs, cloth in hand. She scowled as she quickly scrubbed away the water mark, leaving the oak desk just as perfect as it had been before she sat down to work.

Back downstairs, Amanda swept the back of her hand across her brow. Her hair already felt sticky upon her head even though she'd thrown open both windows in the kitchen. For two weeks the sun had burned down on her county making the grass in the front garden start to singe and burn.

The other houses in their street looked far worse. Their grass had been reduced to little beige curls. Some of Amanda's lawn was still green, thanks in no small part to Will's sneaky visits out after dark, hose pipe in hand. He'd stand in the shadows in his pyjamas, stealthily watering the garden.

'We should just get sprinklers,' he'd moan.

'We can't. There's a hose pipe ban.'

'I don't even know what that is,' Will would scrunch up his nose as his thick eyebrows met together.

The steaks were in the pan and Amanda was busy preparing a bowl full of fresh salad when the house phone rang out in the hallway. Its sharp little bell shattered through the relative silence of the house as it sung out as constant as a heartbeat, determined to be answered.

'Bloody hell,' Amanda put down the cucumber she'd been peeling and briefly wiped her hands on a nearby tea towel. 'Always when I'm getting dinner ready,' she scolded as her bare feet padded softly against the tiled floor. She plucked the cordless handset from its receiver and wedged it between her shoulder and ear as she began to retrace her steps back into the kitchen.

She was fixed for a fight as she curtly greeted her caller. 'Hello?' The only people who called so late in the day were telemarketers. Amanda had been tempted to ignore the call, to let it shrilly ring out until the answer machine kicked in and played the message she and Will had recorded when they'd first

5

moved in: 'Hi, you've reached Amanda and Will. We can't get to the phone right now so please leave a message and we'll get back to you after the BEEP.' In fits of giggles they had both made the sound of the beep. They sounded so happy in their outgoing message. So smug. Amanda almost hated herself whenever she was forced to listen to it now. She made a mental note for what felt like the hundredth time to tone down the message. She yearned for a more subdued greeting, to reflect the calm seas her marriage now sailed upon rather than the tempestuous storms of passion they'd encountered in their honeymoon haze.

But Amanda couldn't ignore the call in case it was Diowater giving some very prompt feedback on her work. There was only an outside chance it was them, since she had a call scheduled with their head of marketing the following morning, but it was a chance she couldn't take all the same.

'Hello?' Amanda repeated more sharply when her caller failed to announce themselves. She could feel her patience stretching out like an elastic band about to snap. She was sick of telemarketers constantly calling, pulling her away from her work.

'Hi,' a male voice suddenly boomed in her ear. 'Is Jake Burton there?'

The caller was Scottish. The accent was as thick and pronounced as Will's.

'Jake Burton?' Amanda repeated the name. It sounded no more familiar when she said it herself. 'Sorry, no. No one by that name lives here.'

She and Will had been in the house for eighteen months, almost the length of their marriage. It had been a new build just a twenty-minute drive from her mother's house. The landline number was the same one Amanda had used at the apartment she'd lived in for eight years. The apartment she'd once shared with Shane.

'No, he lives there,' the caller challenged arrogantly. 'Jake. Burton.' He said the name slowly as though he were speaking to a small child. Amanda blew a sharp breath through her nose, causing wisps of her ice-blonde hair to dance before her.

'Like I said,' Amanda gave what she hoped was a most audible sigh. She liked to convey her displeasure through non-spoken gestures, unlike Will who was always so direct. He'd have already told the caller to get lost by now. 'There is no one here by that name. And I should know since I live here with my husband.'

'I'm certain there's a Jake Burton there.' The caller was so confident, so sure of himself. It made Amanda want to throw her cordless phone at the wall. She didn't have time to deal with a delusional Scotsman.

'Well I'm certain there's not,' Amanda could feel herself bypassing angry and slipping into irate. She'd always shared her father's less favourable quality of being quick to anger. 'You've got the wrong number.'

'I don't think so.'

'Jesus,' Amanda raked her hand through her hair which hung loosely down to her shoulders. She should really have tied it back, especially when the weather was so densely hot both inside and out. But when she'd stepped out of the shower that morning she'd decided to just let it dry naturally. And so it had stayed hanging loosely around her neck for the rest of the day. Her blue eyes darted around the room as she flirted with the idea of just hanging up on the creepy caller. Her British sensibility forced her to hold on. It'd be too rude to just hang up, wouldn't it? Taking a breath Amanda spoke slowly, clearly; 'There is no Jake Burton here. You've got the wrong number,' she dwelled on each word, hammering her point home.

'You're wrong.'

'What?' Amanda squeaked the word in shock. 'I'm... I'm wrong?' she pressed her hand to her chest. 'I'm wrong about who lives in my own bloody house?' she was pacing back and forth across the kitchen tiles. 'Yeah, that's exactly it,' she hoped her voice was dripping with scathing sarcasm. 'Look, there is no Jake Burton here. Accept that you've dialled the wrong number and don't call here again.'

Amanda pressed down harder on the red cancel button than she needed to. The dull drone of the dial tone replaced the caller's challenging tone. Staring at the handset, Amanda froze. She hated getting weird calls, especially since she was at home working on her own all day. If she was in an office or something it'd be easier to brush off.

Jake Burton.

The name danced around her mind. No matter how much she wore it out it remained foreign to her. She truly knew no one by that name. Her mind was drifting to the dinner preparations when the phone rang again. The sound was even more piercing when fired straight out of the device which was still in her hand.

Amanda let it ring once. Twice. Her heart started to race. What if it was the weird caller again? What if they weren't going to take a hint and were intent on harassing her? Would she have to disconnect the landline? Will would be furious. Not at the disconnection of the phone but at someone making Amanda feel like she had to go to such lengths. Will was a traditional alpha male in that sense. He saw Amanda as something he had to protect, something he had to shield from the true ugly nature of the world.

Three rings. Four. Swallowing down a deep breath, Amanda answered. Her hand tightened against the phone.

'Hello?'

She must have sounded a suitably high level of annoyed as the woman on the other end of the call was instantly apologetic.

'Oh, Mrs Thorn, I hope this isn't a bad time. I know I wasn't supposed to call until tomorrow but was hoping I could just catch you.'

Amanda instantly recognized the voice of Marnie Collins, the head of marketing for Diowater. She wilted with relief against the kitchen counter as around her the air became thick with the rich scent of cooked meat.

'Oh, hey, Marnie, no this is a good time.'

As Marnie started discussing the changes Amanda had made to the site in her trademark clipped, formal tone, tyres crunched on gravel outside as Will arrived home from work.

Less than a minute later he was pushing open the front door and stepping inside.

'Yes, uh-huh,' Amanda was nodding along to the call, raising a hand to silence her husband as he walked into the kitchen to greet her. The T-shirt he was wearing fit tightly against his sculpted chest and he was holding the plastic bag he took to work to keep his lunch in. 'I'm glad you liked those changes,' Amanda was saying as she paced once again around the tiles. She was focused on her work call, all thoughts of Jake Burton momentarily banished from her mind.

2

Meeting Will Thorn was like stepping in quicksand. The more you tried to fight against it, the deeper you sunk. Amanda had been in her local DIY store when she first felt the heat of his gaze upon her. In an aisle filled with wrenches and hammers she was doing her best to look like she belonged there. The sink in her apartment's kitchen was leaking… again. Amanda had lost count of the nights she'd had to fall asleep to its militant dripping sound echoing through her small home like a tinny heartbeat.

Apparently she needed a certain wrench to tighten the base of the tap. And Amanda was determined to not only source the item herself but also fix the problem. She still felt the hole in life where Shane had been, especially in these moments. He wouldn't have known how to fix the tap; he wasn't that kind of guy, but together they'd have sussed it out and had fun in the process. Or at least the old versions of themselves would have.

'You look a little out of your depth.'

Amanda's head pivoted to look at the handsome stranger standing further down the aisle. He almost completely filled the space between the two display racks. Grinning at her, he ran a hand through his thick dark hair. His body looked so big, so powerful, as though he'd been carved out of stone rather than flesh.

'Oh, does it show?' Amanda could feel her lips twinging up into a flirtatious smile, which really wasn't her style. She was always the shy, nervous girl in the shadowy corner of the dance floor.

'Maybe I can help?' the great mass of a man took a step towards her, still smiling kindly. 'These stores are kind of my comfort zone.'

Each word he spoke was rounded by his warm Scottish accent that had a slightly guttural edge to it. He sounded exotic and welcoming all at once.

'I'm Will Thorn,' he extended a large hand to her. 'I don't pretend to be some DIY expert. I promise you I'm just offering some honest to goodness help, I'm not some weird billionaire preying on hot women in hardware stores.'

Amanda laughed. The light sound filled the space between them. Had he just made a playful reference to the infamous *Fifty Shades*? Shane had refused to acknowledge that such books even existed; he was so straight-laced.

'So you've read the book?' Amanda wondered teasingly, tilting her head to the side and eyeing him with interest.

'Sorry?' Will's eyes crinkled at the corners as his grin widened, revealing a set of perfect white teeth. He was like a lumberjack who moonlighted as a model on the weekends. He was rugged, earthy, yet undeniably handsome. Amanda could feel her cheeks burning up as she laughed again.

'Or maybe seen the movie?' she added with a flirtatious bat of her eyelashes.

'Book, movie,' Will waved a dismissive hand through the air. 'I'm just trying to help is all. With no creepy undertone.'

'You here visiting?' Amanda had deliberately tucked her chin down and peered up at him coyly through her curtain of blonde hair.

'No,' Will took another step towards her, allowing her to breathe in his oaky cologne. 'I actually just moved to the area.'

A week later they had their first date. Within a month their first sleepover. Being with Will was like being on a rollercoaster that had one speed setting: fast.

*

'Hey, baby,' Will carefully whispered his greeting as he entered the kitchen and stooped down when he reached Amanda to plant a soft kiss upon her cheek.

'That could totally work,' Amanda was continuing her work call as she flashed him a quick smile. 'Yeah, I know what you mean.'

Will placed his carrier bag down on the counter and stalked over to the refrigerator. Reaching inside, he plucked out a cooled bottle of beer and removed the cap using nothing more than the strength of his own grip. Amanda had giggled girlishly when he'd first done that trick for her. Being around Will brought out all the characteristics in herself which were normally dormant. He made her feel feminine and elegant whilst with other men she'd always felt gangly and awkward. He made her want to laugh at his jokes and get tangled up in his powerful embrace.

Beer in hand, Will was pointing towards the living room. Amanda could only nod and turn her back on him.

'A week?' she was saying into the cordless phone. 'Yes, that's doable.'

Half an hour later the couple sat down to have dinner. The French doors to the back garden had been thrown open allowing the heat of the day to filter inside and dance around their ankles as they sat at the small dining table.

Will insisted on always sitting down to eat dinner together.

'It's the proper way to eat dinner,' he'd say stiffly. Shane had been content to sit on the sofa with his dinner in his lap. It was just another way in which the two men couldn't be more different.

'How was your day?' Amanda asked as she used her knife and fork to neatly cut up her steak.

'Same as ever,' Will rolled his eyes and reached for his beer.

'You're too smart for that place. You should look for a job elsewhere.' Amanda felt like a record on repeat as she said the words. She noticed Will clench his jaw before drinking deeply from his beer bottle.

'I'm fine,' he assured her briskly as he put the bottle down.

'You're wasted there,' Amanda pressed on as they became engaged in their usual dance for the evening. Each move had been rehearsed and committed to memory. The night would either end in the slamming of numerous doors or a passionate union between the sheets. It was a romance forged on stormy seas rather than the tranquil waters Amanda had been used to with Shane. But she liked that. She liked how Will sometimes showed flashes of a powerful passion that made her knees grow weak.

'We've been through this,' Will growled the words at her. 'I'm fine there.'

'You're wasted there,' Amanda repeated.

'But I'm happy.'

'How can you be?' Amanda put down her cutlery to stare boldly at her husband. 'You're far too smart for the job. You could be doing so much more with your life.'

Shane had been driven. But it was that drive which had ultimately pushed Amanda away. Last she heard he was doing really well at the local precinct, had even made detective.

'I'm happy with my life,' Will reached across the table and placed a hand over Amanda's. She knew from the pressure in his touch that, this time, they were destined to collide together beneath the sheets. Her skin tingled at the prospect. 'Tell me about your day,' Will was swift in diverting the conversation away from himself.

'I'm still on the Diowater project,' Amanda sighed. 'And it looks set to go on for a few more weeks yet.'

'It's good for your portfolio though, right?'

'Right,' Amanda agreed with a nod. 'As clients go they can just be very... particular.'

'They have a vision for their brand, I get that.'

'Yeah,' Amanda's mind was still racing from her work call. She already had at least a dozen things to do to the Diowater website the following day. There was a time when she'd have worked late into the evening, while the conversation was still fresh in her mind. But Will insisted on ending their working days at a reasonable time which Amanda didn't mind, it helped keep things balanced.

'We don't want to risk getting burned out,' he'd say.

'Anything happen other than work?' Will pressed.

Amanda pushed her hands through her icy hair, banishing it back over her shoulders. She mentally replayed her day, how she'd gone jogging, done some work, made a few calls. And then paused halfway through discussing her call with Diowater, her eyebrows thoughtfully pulling together.

'Actually,' she leaned back in her chair, stretching out her legs beneath the table. The weakening rays of the sun bathed her feet in a pleasant warmth. 'I got a weird call earlier.'

'Oh?' with his plate clear Will drained the last of his beer and swiped the back of his hand across his mouth.

'It was just a wrong number,' Amanda rolled her eyes. 'But pretty annoying.'

'What did they say?' an edge crept into Will's voice. He didn't like to think of anyone annoying his wife in his absence. He was always so protective of Amanda. He made her feel safe not just because of his size but because of his passionate loyalty too.

'It was weird,' Amanda began massaging the back of her neck. 'Like I said, it was a wrong number. They kept asking for this guy and they wouldn't listen when I told him they don't live here. I mean, I think I should know who lives in my own house.'

'Yeah.'

'And his accent, the inflection in his voice was kind of similar to yours. I figured maybe he was from Scotland too.'

'Who did he ask for?' Will asked the question in a steady tone but a blush was creeping up his neck, making his thick ebony hair and deep-set dark eyes look almost demonic. It was a look which he rarely ever wore.

'Umm,' Amanda pulled her lips into a tight line. The name had been right there before. It was still lingering in the house, she should be able to just pluck it out of the surrounding air. 'Jack… John…' the Diowater call had pushed the name out of her mind. 'Does it matter?' she shrugged.

'I just wondered that's all,' Will's jaw twitched as his cheeks remained blood-red.

'I guess I've forgotten,' Amanda began gathering up their plates. She was halfway back towards the kitchen when the name returned to her as sharp and sudden as if she'd just stepped on broken glass.

'Jake Burton,' she blurted, not bothering to look back. 'That was it.' Stooping down, Amanda loaded the plates and cutlery into the dishwasher. 'The caller was proper insistent that he lived here,' she shouted over the sound of the clattering kitchenware. 'It was pretty creepy.'

'What did he say exactly?'

Amanda jumped. She hadn't expected Will to be so close. Normally he dropped down on to the sofa after dinner to catch the evening news or a televised football game. Instead he was standing in the doorway, blocking the way back into the small dining room.

'He, um…' she straightened, relishing the cooling sensation of the kitchen tiles beneath her feet. 'He said he was certain that there was a Jake Burton living here and that I was wrong to think otherwise,' she was talking quickly, hurriedly relaying the facts.

Will's expression hardened.

'It was just a wrong number,' Amanda said soothingly as she

stepped towards him. She pressed her hands against his strong chest. It was as solid as a brick wall. 'You don't need to get all jealous,' she told her husband teasingly.

Will could get frightfully jealous. More than once Amanda had been forced to pull him out of a pub after he threatened to punch out a guy for checking her out. She was pretty certain that he was getting jealous about the call, winding himself up unnecessarily.

'Don't stress about it,' she swept her hands further up his chest. This was usually the moment when he'd cup her waist and spin her around with such power and speed that Amanda felt as light as a feather. She wanted to lose herself in his strength, in his passion. If she didn't she'd only spend her entire evening fretting over the workload Diowater had given her.

'What time was the call?' Instead of scooping her up in his arms Will was staring into space. Both his gaze and his voice were distant.

'I don't know,' Amanda stepped back in annoyance, raising her arms. 'Just before the Diowater call. Don't make this a weird jealousy thing, Will.'

She'd stopped feeling flattered by his jealous nature when he'd shouted at Shane in Tesco's during their first month of marriage. Shane had merely come up to the couple to offer his congratulations, though the smile he wore didn't extend to his green eyes, which had lost their sparkle in recent years.

'She's mine now, bud,' rage had simmered just beneath Will's usually composed surface as he came face to face with Amanda's ex-boyfriend. Shane had been the guy she fell for at university, the guy who had been in her life for years, waiting to be discovered. But as Shane got more drawn towards the police force, he stopped being so enamoured with Amanda's line of work. Back then she hacked via the darknet to support her studies. She operated outside of the law in the virtual world, and Shane had been okay about that, supportive even. But support turned to judgement and judgement turned to disdain as Shane rose up the ranks within the police force. With every barbed comment or cold look the canyon between the couple widened until it reached a point where neither of them could cross back over to the other.

'Hey, I was just offering my congratulations,' Shane had defensively raised his hands. He matched Will in height but like

Amanda he looked painfully slight beside him, as though he could disappear in Will's shadow.

'Well don't bother,' Will's hands had tightened around the trolley he'd been pushing so that his knuckles were bleached of colour.

'He's just being nice,' Amanda had whispered, trying to avoid Shane's concerned gaze.

'He needs to forget about you,' Will had barked. 'You're mine now.'

Amanda blinked away the memory which grew more painful with time. She often reminded herself that they were from different worlds. Will's life up in Scotland had been so traumatic that he couldn't even bring himself to talk about it. So she made allowances for him, excused away his temper. But if Will was getting jealous over a wrong number then they had some serious problems.

'It was just a wrong number,' she dwelled on each word, stretching them out for a beat longer than necessary.

'Did you tell your little cop boyfriend about it?' Will snarled.

Amanda's mouth fell open in shock. *Had she told Shane?* She'd not spoken to Shane since Will had humiliated her in Tesco's.

'Did I tell my ex-boyfriend about a wrong number?' she almost laughed at the absurdity of the accusation. 'No, Will. I did not. Jesus, what the hell is wrong with you tonight?'

Will groaned and began massaging his forehead. 'I'm sorry, baby,' he stepped forward and reached for her. Amanda allowed herself to be folded into his embrace. The musky scent of sweat and toil still clung to Will. Amanda pressed herself against his chest, breathing him in. 'I'm just stressed right now,' he mumbled as he leaned down to kiss the top of her head.

'It's okay,' Amanda closed her eyes contentedly. This was what she'd always wanted; a man who'd come home to her every night. A man who would place her at the top of his list no matter what. And that was Will. He was as loyal and as powerful as a Doberman.

'Jake Burton, you're sure that was the name?' he wondered aloud.

'Uh-huh. Why?'

'No reason.'

Yawning, Amanda lifted the remote and turned off the television. She was stretched out across the sofa, left alone to watch her favourite shows on Netflix since Will had gone to bed an hour earlier with a headache. She'd been disheartened by his desire to go up early but her sadness had quickly been assuaged when she realised that it meant she could indulge in a *Gilmore Girls* marathon.

Being the last one to head upstairs meant that it fell to Amanda to check all the doors were securely locked. She wandered into the dining room and pressed down on the white door handles. The double doors remained firmly closed. Outside, the garden glowed beneath the silvery light of a full moon. Stars sparkled like distant diamonds in the tapestry of the night sky. It was a beautiful summer's evening. Amanda took a moment to dreamily gaze outside at the small strip of green lawn that was slowly succumbing to the burning heat of the summer. No droplets clung to each tiny blade. Will had clearly neglected to water the lawn tonight.

Amanda unlocked the doors and stepped outside. The evening air was blissfully cool as it wrapped around her bare legs and arms. With quick, light steps she headed to the outside tap and the long emerald green hose pipe attached to it. Beneath the watchful gaze of the moon she quickly sprinkled water over the frayed parts of the lawn. Will's desire for the perfect house was rubbing off on her.

Her feet were damp as she hurried back inside, leaving a trail of footprints along the wooden floor as she wound her way deeper into the house. Amanda was grateful to touch down on the soft grey carpet of the hallway. She paused at the foot of the stairs and listened. Usually if Will had gone to bed first she'd hear the gentle hum of him snoring. Now there was only silence. Taking care to move on her tiptoes and make as little sound as possible, Amanda crept up the stairs and quietly carried herself over to their bedroom.

Though the cream curtains were closed, the bright light of the moon burned against them, making the room seemed infused with ethereal light. In the centre of the room was a grand queen-sized bed which took up almost all of the space, barely leaving the required inches for the sleek mirrored bedside tables Amanda had bought with her from her apartment. Will had insisted on a large bed. When he'd first seen the double bed in Amanda's apartment he'd paled.

'Where am I going to sleep?' he'd wondered.

Amanda untucked her side of the bed. The duvet was already bunched at the foot of the bed, no longer needed during the long hot nights of the summer. The linen sheets were crisp in her hands as she folded them back. Will was rolled up on the other side of the bed, his back to her. He seemed so far away. Settling down into bed, Amanda threw her husband one final longing glance. She yearned for him to roll over and grin at her sexily. But instead he remained frozen in place, probably already lost to a dream. She couldn't resent him for getting a headache. In her line of work she suffered from them with an annoying regularity.

'Goodnight,' Amanda whispered to him, feeling every single one of the extra inches their giant bed placed between them. Leaning back on her plump feather pillows, Amanda looked up at the ceiling and sighed. The house was stoic around her, indifferent to her still racing mind, as was the man sleeping beside her.

3

The waves roared like a beast about to pounce as their white tips pounded against the rocks. Amanda could feel herself falling. The ground beneath her gave way and several stones were skittering past her, disappearing into the whipped waves below. She was toppling over the cliff edge, soon she'd be free-falling to her certain doom. Her hair tangled around her, she opened her mouth to scream but the wind buffeted the sound away.

Everything slowed down. Amanda tasted something metallic as her heartbeat echoed so loudly in her head that it almost drowned out the ferocious roar of the waves. She couldn't tear her eyes away from the jagged rocks which were inching ever closer. With a gasp, she imagined how it would feel to crash against them like a piece of debris. She'd break as easily as the pieces of driftwood she loved to source along the beach.

Suddenly something strong was pulling on her legs, reversing the momentum of her fall. As she flailed, she was winched back over the cliff edge as she sucked in frantic, desperate breaths. Her hero was backlit against the sun. Squinting, she prepared to say something, but her breathing was still ragged. Her vision was blurred, her heart still racing—

Amanda's eyes snapped open. Panting, she sat up, drawing her crisp bed sheets up to her chest. The cliff edge was still so vivid in her mind, she could taste the salt on the air, smell the freshness of the sea breeze. Cupping her head in her hands, Amanda took several slow breaths and waited for her body to calm down.

'It was the nightmare again,' she eventually muttered groggily. 'I keep dreaming about that day on the cliffs.'

Amanda paused expectantly, but there came no reply from the other side of the bed. Turning, she noticed that the sheets were already pulled back; the pillows sagged in the centre.

'Will?' she called out for her husband, his absence making her feel even more disorientated. She leaned to glance at her bedside clock. It was a quarter to seven. The alarm wasn't set to go off for another fifteen minutes.

The bedroom was already ablaze with early morning sunlight which pressed heavily against the closed cream linen curtains. 'Will?' Amanda rubbed her eyes and looked around the room. Tilting her head, she remained perfectly still and listened for the whine of the shower coming from the en suite.

Had she tossed and turned so violently during her nightmare that Will had been forced to get up? Lately her nightmares had been worse than ever, going from a weekly occurrence to a daily nuisance. It felt like every time she closed her eyes she was transported back to that fateful day when her twelve-year-old self got to sample a bitter taste of her own mortality.

The white panel door to the en suite was firmly closed and there was no sound of rushing water coming from beyond it. Pulling her eyebrows together, Amanda swept her long legs over the side of the bed and stood up.

'Will?' she was calling for him as her hand pressed down on the door handle. It opened with ease. Inside, the pristine white suite was stark and unoccupied. The air wasn't even clotted with steam from a previous shower.

'Will?' Amanda leaned back out of the small bathroom. Where was he? He was usually such a reliable creature of habit. When the alarm shrieked at seven, he'd grumble, get up and stalk over to the shower. After standing beneath the powerful jets of almost boiling water for a good twenty minutes he'd saunter downstairs and turn on the percolator. As the house filled with the comforting aroma of fresh coffee, Amanda would make them both breakfast, usually something simple like porridge or poached egg on toast. At quarter past eight he was heading out the front door. Amanda always dismissed him with a parting kiss before waving as he climbed into his navy blue van and carefully backed out of the driveway. The routine was always the same. Will wasn't a man who welcomed change.

'Will?' Amanda was out on the landing, still calling out his name. The stony silence of the house mocked her as she wandered towards the staircase and breathed in deeply. She wanted her senses to be relaxed by the oaky aroma of fresh coffee. But all she could smell was the vanilla-scented plug-ins she turned on each night. The plug-ins which kept her house smelling like a show home.

'Where the hell are you?' Amanda asked of the emptiness as

she went down the stairs and burst into the kitchen. Will was not there. The room was empty. The expensive percolator the couple had received as a wedding gift was still flush to the wall.

'Will?' Amanda sighed wearily as she dropped one hand to her waist. Absently, she stepped deeper into the room and gazed out of the large window which overlooked the garden. The sky was already the brightest blue, stretching out above her little house as vast and empty as a perfect ocean.

Perhaps Will had gone for a jog. Sometimes, usually on weekends, he liked to pull on his running shoes and power through the nearby woodlands. Unlike Amanda, who'd run at any time of the year, Will preferred to save his running for the months of the year when the sky was heavy and grey and the ground beneath his feet hard and icy.

Amanda drifted through the house to the hallway. She opened up the cupboard beneath the stairs and peered inside. Will's running shoes were gone. As were his work boots.

'Huh,' she straightened and closed the cupboard. She must have been sleeping so deeply that she didn't even wake when Will left. But why the early departure? He hadn't mentioned anything about working overtime.

Back in her bedroom Amanda grabbed her phone from her bedside table and fired off a text to Will.

> Hey handsome. Woke up to find you gone :(You working earlies
> this week or something? Xxx

Placing the device back down, Amanda returned to the en suite, keen to stand beneath the massaging power of its hot water and wash away the remnants of her dream.

*

Stepping out of the shower, Amanda was immediately enveloped in a thick cloud of steam. She dipped down, grabbing a towel, and flicked her long hair up into it and then secured it atop her head. Her skin glistened from the heat of the shower as she opened the door and wandered into the bedroom, which now felt icily cold in comparison. Immediately she headed for her phone. It was twenty past seven. Will would surely have text her back by now.

Amanda clicked off the alarm clock which had been shrilly bleating for the past twenty minutes. She looked at her phone. She had no new messages. No missed calls.

'Huh,' she tossed the handset on to the bed. It landed amongst the unmade sheets. Now that Amanda was completely free from the fog of sleep she was starting to get annoyed with Will.

On her way downstairs she paused by the window on the landing and looked down at the driveway. Her silver Prius was alone, Will's blue van was gone. If she'd just taken off so early without saying anything he'd be furious.

'*Oh, baby, you had me so worried, don't do that,*' she was mumbling angrily to herself as she went back into the kitchen. She briskly pulled the percolator into the centre of the counter and switched it on. It gurgled to life and began making everywhere smell like a Parisian café.

'*You know how I worry,*' she continued mockingly in a deep tone as she reached into a cupboard for a mug. Like most other things in her home it was uniform white and without a single chip or crack. It was perfect.

'Perfect, perfect, perfect,' Amanda lamented as she dropped a spoonful of sugar into her mug. She paused, teaspoon in hand, before making a snap decision and ladling in a second helping of the sweet white powder.

By the time she'd drank her coffee, ate her porridge and dried her hair, it was eight o'clock and there was still no word from Will. But Amanda couldn't afford to sit around and fret over him. He was blatantly just working an early shift and had forgotten to bring it up.

Nursing a fresh coffee between her hands, Amanda walked up to her study.

Turning on her Mac, she tied her hair back and prepared to buckle down for the morning.

*

Amanda loved to code. She liked the structure she found within the string of symbols and letters, liked how she could manipulate the way something looked with the input of the correct information.

As a little girl Amanda had been the kind of child who'd take apart a toy just to see how it worked. Her behaviour would infuriate her mother, especially when she took apart the Game Boy her parents had bought her one Christmas, which was apparently a very expensive gift. But her dad always encouraged her inquisitive nature. He'd bring home old calculators from the bank where he worked for her to take apart and then methodically put together again. Sometimes Amanda could even repair broken models.

She'd often struggled to understand people. 'Cold' was the term Shane had used during their bitter break-up. Amanda knew he was half right, as painful as that was to admit. People were difficult, unpredictable. Technology never asked anything of Amanda, it always just did as she wanted without question.

And Will was like that. He took the lead in their relationship, happy to give Amanda enough space to be her introverted self. He didn't try and take her to parties or on nights out with his friends. In fact, he'd never actually introduced Amanda to anyone other than his work colleagues. But it was because he respected how she was; that she wasn't a people person. She belonged behind a computer screen, lost in cyberspace.

Amanda's fingers were dancing across the keyboard of her laptop, effortlessly making changes to the Diowater website. A soft smile pulled on her lips as she worked. She was in her element. By nine o'clock she'd forgotten all about the dream which had woken her so abruptly that morning. She was in the zone, working hard and working fast which was always her preferred method.

Something was ringing.

The sound was so sudden, so piercing, that it caused Amanda to audibly gasp. Her gasp deepened into a groan as she realized that it was the phone.

'Great,' she moaned to herself as she twisted round in her leather office chair and reached for the cordless handset which was cradled on the far side of her desk. Before pressing the green answer button she sucked in a breath, praying that it wasn't Diowater calling her to make yet more changes to the website. They'd already changed their mind four times since she'd taken on the project three weeks ago. Marnie had assured her only last night that this last change would be the final one. Now that she was so close to completion she wanted them to just allow her to get on with their job. At the end of it they'd have a beautiful, sleek website and everyone would be happy.

'Hello?' Amanda sounded formal as she answered. She braced herself for what was coming next. She wished she'd opted for a more expensive model of cordless phone which would at least show caller ID. Either her current client would start reeling off a list of newly urgent requirements to her, or worse, she'd hear the clipped greeting of her mother.

Corrine Roberts was usually out in her garden early on a morning, pruning her beloved roses and tending to her azaleas. She normally didn't intrude upon Amanda's work day until at least two in the afternoon, by which time she'd gossiped adequately with all her neighbours and friends and was keen to try and get blood from a new stone. For Amanda never had any gossip. None that her mother and her bingo clique would be interested in. But that didn't stop Corrine calling and probing her daughter on a daily basis.

'Mrs Thorn?' So it wasn't her mother calling.

Amanda pulled her chair back towards her laptop. Her mouth became dry as she considered it might be another wrong number. This voice was softer than the one who called yesterday, with less rough edges.

'Yes,' Amanda coughed uneasily.

'Mrs Thorn, this is Mike from the warehouse. We just wanted to check why Will hasn't shown up for work today. Is he off sick?'

Amanda reached forward and gripped the edge of her desk for support. The slick surface did little to stabilize her. She could suddenly hear the crashing of the waves in her eardrums as her heart's pace quickened in her chest.

'He… um…' she tried to find her voice, to sound decidedly less startled than she was. 'He's not come in?'

'No,' Mike confirmed quietly. Had something crept into his voice that wasn't there before? Remorse? Embarrassment? Amanda couldn't tell. 'His shift started at half eight but he's not here yet.'

'He's not?' Amanda blinked away tears.

'Maybe he's got stuck in traffic,' Mike offered. Could he sense her distress?

'Yeah,' Amanda cleared her throat. 'That must be it.' Only she knew that couldn't be it. Will had been gone since before she got up. Still holding the phone, she stood up and went to the window on the landing. She looked down at the dark tarmac of the driveway. Will's blue van was definitely gone.

'Okay, Mrs Thorn, well can you tell him to get here as soon as possible?'

'Yes,' Amanda was wiping her free hand across her eyes, 'yes of course.'

'Thanks, Mrs Thorn. Sorry for bothering you.'

The line went dead and Amanda leaned towards the window, staring at the vacant space on the driveway. For a moment she froze, allowing her mind to entertain a host of panicked thoughts.

What if he'd been in a car accident?

What if he was currently lying in a pool of his own blood as the life seeped out of him?

What if he never came home?

Amanda's chest was tightening as she headed downstairs, making her breaths ragged. She punched Will's number into the cordless handset and raised it back to her ear. She was in the hallway as she waited for the call to connect. It was taking longer than usual. Each second was painfully drawn out as Amanda was forced to just stand and wait.

'Ring, dammit,' she urged the handset. Why wasn't it ringing?

Finally she heard something click in on the other end of the line. Had Will picked up?

'The number you dialled has been disconnected,' an indifferent mechanical voice told her.

'What?' Amanda raged. That was impossible. She sprinted back up the stairs, running into her bedroom and grabbing her mobile phone. With a few swipes of her finger she was calling Will again. There were the same drawn-out delay and then the clipped voice informing her, 'The number you dialled has been disconnected.'

She tried the number again. And again. There was no way Will's number had been disconnected. She'd spoken to him on his mobile only the previous day during his lunch break. What was going on?

Amanda listened to the automated response eight more

times. Her hands were shaking as she threw her phone back on to the bed and paced anxiously back and forth. Will wasn't at work. He was unable to answer his phone. Where the hell was he?

4

Every ten minutes, Amanda dialled Will's number again, clinging to the hope that this time the call would connect. But it was never her husband who picked up. Amanda knew the clipped monotone response by heart as it echoed in her ear: 'The number you dialled has been disconnected.'

She'd heard the message so many times that she feared it had been forever ingrained on her soul. That years, even decades from now she'd hear the objective words as they became permanently housed in the darker recesses of her mind.

'Come on,' Amanda chewed down on her thumbnail as she paced across the landing. Her mobile phone was held to her ear in the midst of a pregnant pause during which she crossed everything, praying that Will would answer.

Amanda had never been someone to entertain superstitions. She'd put shoes on the table, cross someone on the stairs and deliberately fail to acknowledge a solitary magpie. She didn't believe in fate. But now, as the morning started to creep worryingly close towards the afternoon, Amanda was willing to do whatever it took to find out where her husband was. She'd cross her fingers, never walk beneath a ladder again and throw salt over her shoulder if she had to.

Finally, the call was answered. But not by Will. It was the automated response again.

'Dammit,' Amanda seethed and ended the call with a blunt press of a button. Her mind was racing as she headed downstairs.

Was Will hurt?

Was his phone just broken?

Was he now at work?

Amanda looked at her phone. She needed to call Mike. To check that Will hadn't turned up late for his shift and thanks to a suddenly fault phone just couldn't contact her.

Every surface in the kitchen burned brightly beneath the glorious glow of sunlight which was beaming in through the windows. Amanda reached for the percolator and switched it on before stepping back from its loud gurgles and trembles. She pressed her phone against her ear.

'Yeah?' Mike gruffly answered as though he were annoyed at the distraction.

'Mike, hi, it's Mrs Thorn,' Amanda tossed her hair out of her eyes and wandered over to the French doors at the far end of the kitchen, looking out at her little garden.

'Oh, Mrs Thorn,' Mike cleared his throat and softened his tone. 'Everything okay?'

'I, um,' Amanda sighed, realizing that she was about to risk sounding like a slightly crazy person. 'Did Will show up for work in the end?' she blurted the question, moving hard and fast like she was ripping off a plaster and trying to minimize the damage caused.

Mike paused and Amanda felt her stomach squeeze in on itself.

'No, he didn't.'

Amanda closed her eyes and leaned against the French doors for support. The heat of the day burned against the glass.

'Is everything all right, Mrs Thorn?' Mike wondered kindly.

Chewing her lip, Amanda wondered what to say.

No, everything isn't all right. My husband is missing, his phone isn't working and I've no idea where he's gone.

'I'm fine,' Amanda forced herself to smile as she straightened. 'Will's phone is just broken so I can't check where he is.'

'Okay, as long as you are all right.'

Amanda had never met Mike. From what she'd heard about him through Will he sounded like a decent, fair man who'd take on any new hires at the warehouse so long as they were willing to work hard for him. He wasn't the kind of guy to suffer fools gladly. Amanda knew that Will's sudden absence at work was putting his job in jeopardy.

'When he does surface, tell him to give me a call, will you?' Mike requested.

'Yes,' Amanda was nodding briskly. 'I will.'

The percolator ceased bubbling and rumbling just as Amanda ended her call with Mike. She poured herself a large cup of fresh coffee and then tried Will again. She got the same response.

'Shit.' Tears streaked down her cheeks as she wandered

through the front room. She felt like she couldn't settle anywhere, like the air around her was constantly electrified as if a storm were about to break.

Her front room was a testament to the blandness of beige. At least that's what her mother had said when Amanda had brought her round to the house for the first time. The walls were white, the carpet magnolia and the leather suite a soft taupe. It was all very chic, all very modern just like the rest of the house.

'Where's the personality?' Corrine had demanded as she moved deeper into the room. In her bright purple tea dress she was like a giant inky stain of colour in the middle of the space.

'It's a house, Mum, it doesn't need personality,' Amanda had objected.

'Of course it does,' Corrine insisted. 'Your house is your home, the beating heart of your family unit. It should reflect how special you are.'

Amanda lowered herself on to her sofa. She didn't have to regret the leather in the heat since she'd pulled on loose-fitting jogging bottoms that morning and a white vest top. She placed her coffee down on a mirrored coaster on a side table and let her eyes flicker around the familiar space.

There was a large plasma television on the wall. A white fire surround housing a flame-effect glass fireplace. And above it were a couple of pictures from Amanda and Will's wedding day. In the images, Amanda had both palms pressed against Will's broad chest and was gazing adoringly into his eyes. Her hair looked as light as her ivory chest as it gathered at the nape of her neck in a large bun.

'Think,' Amanda urged herself as she wiped at her cheeks. She kept gazing around the room as though hoping an answer would suddenly spring out from one of the far corners and present itself. She knew that Will wasn't at work. That he'd gone out in his van first thing whilst she still slept.

'Oh, Christ,' Amanda bunched her hands into fists as she steeled herself against fearing the worst. She'd tried Will's phone; she'd called Mike at the warehouse. Her next logical step was to call the local hospitals and make sure someone matching Will's description hadn't been brought in.

Amanda's hands were shaking as she looked up the relevant numbers.

Twenty minutes later and Amanda had successfully called

the two major hospitals in the area. Neither had reports of a car accident involving a blue van or a man matching Will's description being admitted that morning. Amanda took some comfort from that but not much. It still begged the awful question of where exactly was her husband.

Amanda drained the last of her coffee before making her next call. Her heart crept up into her throat with each passing ring.

'Tremwell Bay Police Department, how may I direct your call?' a kind-sounding woman asked.

'I,' Amanda stood up, massaging the back of her neck. 'I need to report that my husband is missing.' Her tongue felt too big for her mouth as she said the words. It felt so surreal, so ridiculous. How was this even happening?

'When was he last seen?'

'Um,' Amanda thought back to that morning. She'd slept beside Will all night but she couldn't be sure what time he had stolen away from their marital bed. 'Early this morning.'

'This morning?'

'Yes.'

'I'm afraid that someone needs to have been missing for a considerable amount of time before the authorities can get involved.'

Amanda coughed but it sounded more like an alarmed squeak.

Considerable amount of time? What did that even mean? How long was she supposed to go on being normal? To eat dinner? To sleep? Hanging on every passing minute in the vain hope that her husband would return.

'I just don't know where he is,' Amanda admitted helplessly. She could hear her own voice starting to break.

'I'm so sorry,' the call handler empathized. 'I know how difficult this must be, but unfortunately there is nothing we can do when someone has only been missing for just a few hours. Most people turn up within forty-eight hours. I'm sure your husband will be home soon. If he's vulnerable or at risk because of any mental issues -'

'No,' Amanda softly cut the woman off. 'My husband is always…' *an oak tree.* 'Fine.'

'Very well then. Just hang in there, your husband will come home.'

Amanda maintained a level of politeness and thanked the woman for her time and ended the call. Even if Will did return, it wouldn't explain where he'd gone. This was so unlike him. You could usually set your clock to Will's rigid routine. He was the very definition of reliable. He didn't go out drinking with friends; he enjoyed doing chores around the house. From the moment Amanda had met him she'd known he was the constant she'd been searching for.

'You've got lullaby eyes,' Will had told her flirtatiously over drinks back when they first started dating.

'Lullaby eyes?' Amanda had playfully batted her eyelashes at him. She loved how deep and rich his voice was, like every word he uttered had come all the way up from his toes.

'Yeah,' Will grinned boyishly, looking much younger than his age. 'Lullaby eyes. Because each time I look into them I just want to go to bed.'

Amanda had almost spat out her JD and Coke.

'For someone so beautiful you really don't know how to take a compliment,' Will had laughed.

The sound of the house phone ringing rattled through Amanda's head, shattering the memory into a thousand pieces. She tensed upon the sofa and grabbed the nearest handset from the seat's plush armrest.

'Will?' she gasped, knowing she'd give anything to hear her husband's velvety voice on the other end of the line.

'Amanda?'

Instead it was the shrill pitch of her mother.

'Amanda, are you there?'

'Yes, Mum,' Amanda pressed a hand to her chest, she could feel her heart fluttering anxiously just inches beneath her fingertips. 'I'm here.'

'Well you should be *here*,' Corrine Roberts announced tightly. 'You said you'd come round for lunch, remember?'

Amanda groaned at the dim light of recognition which illuminated the space around her. She had indeed been due to go to her mother's for lunch. It was one of their many weekly rituals together. But Amanda was also supposed to have spent her morning working on the Diowater website. And her husband was supposed to be at work, not lost. Nothing about her day was going to plan.

'Mum, I forgot, I'm sorry. Something came up.'

'What came up?'

Work, say work.

But Amanda's worry had made her weak. She yearned to share the burden of her concern with someone else.

'Will's gone missing,' she blurted.

'I'll be there in five,' Corrine stated before hanging up. Amanda stared at the phone in surprise as the dial tone droned on at her, wondering if having her mother come round was really the best idea.

*

It was actually more like twenty minutes when Corrine's mint green Fiat 500 pulled into the driveway. Amanda had been loitering at the far end of the front room, intermittently peering through the wooden blinds to glance up the street when she wasn't staring at the screen of her mobile which had become glued to her hand.

Amanda pulled open the door before her mother had a chance to ring the bell.

'Oh, my sweet girl,' Corrine instantly reached for her daughter and enveloped her in a tight embrace. She smelt strongly of vanilla and peppermint tea. 'My poor, poor baby,' she muttered as Amanda managed to kick her front door shut. Corrine eventually stepped back, her hands still resting on Amanda's shoulders. She swept the blue eyes she'd given her daughter over Amanda's long frame and pursed her thin lips together. They'd been painted the same red as her dress thanks to a particularly vibrant shade of lipstick.

'So he's finally left you?' Corrine asked, tilting her head to the right.

'No,' Amanda shook her mother off and stormed towards the kitchen. 'He's not left me, Mum. He's *missing*.'

'They sound like the same thing to me,' Corrine tutted.

'Well, they're not.' Amanda reached for the percolator.

'Ooh, no coffee for me,' Corrine protested, 'it wreaks havoc with my sensitive bowels.'

'I know,' Amanda sighed as she also turned on the kettle. 'The coffee is for me.'

'I imagine you've had enough,' Corrine raised a slender,

dark eyebrow at her. 'The last thing you need right now is to be all wired and twitchy.'

'I'm not—' Amanda abruptly silenced her own protest. Her mother wasn't the sort of person you could reason with. She was far too stubborn to listen to opinions other than her own.

With their fresh drinks in hand the two women drifted into the front room. Corrine neatly draped herself down at the far end of the leather sofa. Her long red dress gathered at her ankles and the array of bracelets she wore up her arms clattered together in a waterfall of sound each time she reached for her cup of tea. As usual Corrine was a blast of colour in the otherwise demure room.

'So, tell me what happened,' Corrine urged. Her bejewelled fingers rested around her ivory mug, each sumptuous gem capturing a sliver of light that was still pouring into the room.

'I got up and... he wasn't there. Wasn't in bed, or the shower. But his van was gone. And he's not turned up for work. I presumed he was on earlies but then Mike from the warehouse rang to say he hadn't shown so I've no idea where he is.'

'Have you called him?'

Amanda swallowed, her mouth suddenly consumed with a bitter taste. 'His phone's been disconnected,' she admitted woefully.

'I see,' Corrine's perfectly plucked eyebrows shot up to her wrinkled brow. While she and Amanda both had eyes the colour of a summer sky, that was where their similarities ended. Corrine Roberts was a stout woman with ample curves and a head of thick curly brown hair. She had dimples when she smiled and a laugh so loud it could surely wake the dead.

Amanda had inherited her father's slim figure and pensive nature. Like her he enjoyed solitude, preferring long walks along the coastline to nights out with friends. He'd had icy blonde hair and dark, brooding eyes. He always looked like he was pondering on some great question; like the true origins of the universe.

'Might he have gone home?' Corrine queried. Amanda could feel a flush rising in her cheeks.

'This is his home, mother,' she said through gritted teeth. Her blood had begun to boil in her veins. She knew she should be searching for Will, not wasting time defending him to her mother.

'He's *Scottish* darling,' Corrine noted with saccharine sweetness. 'This will never truly be his home.'

'Well, it is,' Amanda raged.

'I never did trust him,' Corrine shook her head to herself as she blew into her tea. Her blue eyes had rested upon one of the few wedding pictures in the room. Her gaze narrowed as she scrutinized it with fresh interest. 'I mean, on your wedding day, to have no one from his side there.'

'He had people.'

'From work,' Corrine scoffed. 'But what about his friends? His family?'

'I told you,' Amanda sighed, leaning forward and raking her hands through her hair, 'it was too short notice for them to come over, and he mentioned something about his mother being sick.' The latter was a lie Amanda felt obliged to tell. Will had always been so fiercely private about his family and she respected that but she knew that her mother wouldn't.

'What sort of mother would let a bout of sickness get in the way of attending her son's wedding? And it's not like they'd have had to have crossed oceans to be there.'

'Mum,' Amanda groaned. She was in no mood to deal with her mother's judgemental attitude. In her eyes Will had never been good enough, and her dad was no longer around to give his seal of approval.

'Your dad would never have trusted him,' Corrine declared with authority as though she'd somehow been able to read her daughter's mind.

'You don't know that,' Amanda challenged hotly.

'I do,' a sadness had crept into Corrine's eyes as she looked away from the picture back towards her daughter.

Amanda lowered her head. Whenever they talked about her father she felt her heart breaking all over again and she only had the strength to deal with the potential loss of one man that day.

'Where do you think he could be?' Amanda wondered quietly.

'Will?'

'Yes, Will,' Amanda gasped in exasperation. 'My husband. The guy who is missing, remember?'

'For his sake I hope he's lying in a hospital bed somewhere with ten broken fingers that have prevented him from calling,'

Corrine said bitterly. 'He's got some nerve getting you all worked up like this.'

'I called the hospitals,' Amanda recalled numbly. The events of the past morning felt as though they'd happened to someone else, not her, in a movie she'd been watching. This couldn't be her life. The Will she knew would never just take off without so much as a goodbye. He loved Amanda. He was her port in a storm, her anchor.

'They knew nothing?' Corrine pressed.

'No.'

'Well, he's got to be somewhere. Grown men don't just up and disappear. Though your father and his alien conspiracy theories would have you believe otherwise.'

'He'd be setting up his telescope in the conservatory and monitoring the skies for me,' Amanda laughed. It felt good to laugh. To pretend if only for a second that everything was still normal.

'He loved watching the stars,' Corrine smiled wistfully. 'He'd spend hours gazing up at them, dreaming of distant worlds.'

'But he loved this world too.'

Amanda remembered walking alongside her father on heady summer afternoons. He'd suddenly stoop his willowy frame down and gesture for his little girl to do the same. Together they'd kneel amongst the dry grass as Ivor carefully cupped a rare flower in his long fingers. He had the hands of a pianist though he'd never even held an instrument before.

'Look at the beauty,' he'd urge Amanda. 'It's all around us, just waiting to be found.'

'He loved you,' Corrine's eyes glittered as she looked at her daughter. 'Above all else, he loved you, you were his darling little girl.'

Amanda nodded tearfully. It was hard to imagine what her dad would have done if he was there with them then. He'd only ever known Amanda the girl, not Amanda the woman. Would he be as angry over Will's absence as Corrine was? Or would he just be concerned, sitting quietly in the corner and fretting over what might have become of his son-in-law?

'If he doesn't come back he's a fool.' Corrine reached across the centre of the sofa which stretched between them and clasped Amanda's hands in her own. Her jewellery clattered loudly as she moved like she were a one-woman percussion show.

'He'll come back,' Amanda said with force. If she sounded convinced then perhaps she'd feel it too. Because if Will hadn't returned by the following morning she'd be heading to the Tremwell Bay Police station to officially report him as a missing person. And the thought of his absence becoming so real terrified her.

5

Tremwell Bay Police Station was a faded white two-storey building. The mottled walls were supposed to reflect the quaint personality of the seaside town. A tightly packed, sloped car park led up towards the glass-fronted double doors.

Amanda parked by the outer wall, in a distant corner of the car park, in one of the few remaining vacant spaces. Climbing out, she leaned against her car and took in a deep, salty breath.

The police station was on the edge of town, so close to the shoreline that Amanda could hear seagulls roughly calling to one another overhead. They dove through the air like daring stunt pilots.

A sharp wind blew Amanda's hair into her eyes. She knocked back the platinum strands and smoothed her hands down the khaki shirt dress she was wearing.

The sun had disappeared. It had been blocked out by a curtain of grey cloud which had brought an unseasonal chill to the air. Rain was coming. All the tourists who'd flocked to the Bay in the hope of spending their day at the beach would be sorely disappointed.

Amanda bent her knees and checked her reflection in the side mirror. Her eyes were shrouded in unflattering shadows. She'd barely slept last night. Each time she dared to close her eyes she thought of Will and all the terrible fates that could have befallen him. Every creak outside the window made her heart race as her breath hopefully caught in her chest, every fibre of her being praying that Will's blue van had just pulled up outside.

She imagined his twisted body on the side of the road somewhere, battered and barely recognizable, his handsome features hidden beneath a mask of dried blood and broken bones. Or she imagined him in the arms of another woman, throwing back his head and callously laughing when he considered how worried his wife must be. Either fantasy was heartbreaking.

Twenty four hours ago Amanda would never have

considered that her husband would cheat, would lie to her. Now she was having to accept the possibility that perhaps he would, that perhaps he'd always intended to leave her in such an abrupt way.

'No,' Amanda wiped at her eyes and pushed back her shoulders as she straightened up. Will was missing. That was why she was here at the police station. Her husband loved her, he would never willingly leave her.

Holding her head high, Amanda did her best to look poised as she strode across the car park to the double doors, hoping she didn't look as broken and exhausted as she felt inside.

*

'Not seen you here for a while,' Officer John Morris was behind the reception desk. He revealed a toothy smile when he saw Amanda walk in.

'Hi, John,' Amanda softly returned the gesture. 'I mean, Officer Morris,' she added, cheeks reddening.

'What can I do for you, Amanda?' John asked, resting his hands on the portly belly he was growing.

Amanda had known John Morris since she was five and they were both cherub-faced children running around the playground of their infant school. He'd always been big for his age, chubby even in childhood. He had thick black hair and a kind nature. Back in school it had always been John, Amanda and Shane. They'd pretend that they were the three musketeers. They were the best of friends until they turned twelve and then everything changed.

But college reunited the trio. Shane became more than a friend to Amanda but their holy trinity remained strong. It was John who'd tried so fervently to keep the peace later when things started to fall apart between Amanda and Shane.

Glancing around the familiar reception area of the police station, Amanda's shoulders sagged self-consciously. How many nights had she burst in, face streaked with tears asking where Shane was? John was always on hand to reassure her that he was just out working late, that he'd be home soon.

As the years passed, Amanda stopped turning up at the station, stopped waiting for Shane to come home.

'Amanda?' John was gazing at her expectantly. Amanda blinked and gave him an apologetic smile. She saw that there were new lines on his face and some considerable weight poorly concealed beneath his ill-fitting pale blue shirt. She noticed the silver-rimmed glasses which hung down from his neck and wondered how long he'd needed to wear them. How many years had it been since she'd seen John? The fact that Amanda had to dwell on the question proved that it was too many.

'Sorry,' she tucked her hair behind her ear, feeling nervous. 'I'm a bit out of it. How are Daisy and the twins?'

'They're monsters,' John laughed heartily. 'Well, the twins at least, not Daisy. Tell me we weren't that bad when we were younger?'

'I'm pretty sure we were.'

'Last week Tyler weed on Jackson's bed. *For fun.* They are a pair of little tyrants, I tell you.'

'They sound mischievous. How old are they now? Four?' Her smile was tight, forced. It was taking all her self control to engage in polite chat when all she wanted to do was scream about how scared she was for her husband.

'Six.'

'Six, wow.'

Amanda remembered the night that John had found out he was going to be a father. It was one of the rare occasions that Shane was around. Together, they all sat on the beach and drank beers until the sun came up.

'I'm scared,' John had admitted, looking to the friends who he felt he'd known all his life. 'So much is changing, it freaks me out.'

Shane glanced at Amanda but she couldn't meet his gaze. It was earlier that day she'd told him to pack his stuff up and move out. The three musketeers were officially disbanding like petals blown from a flower; powerless against the winds of change which blew them from themselves.

'As much as I'd like to think otherwise, you've not come here to catch up with me,' John leaned forward, clasping his hands together on the reception desk.

'I... um,' she cleared her throat and glanced around. Uniformed officers passed through the reception area causing a steady soundtrack of footsteps and swinging doors.

'Amanda?' John was frowning at her, looking concerned in

the way he always used to do right before she'd start crying about Shane.

'I need to report a missing person,' she blurted, taking care to lower her voice.

'Oh?' John looked genuinely alarmed.

'My husband.' Amanda wilted as she passed the weight of worry over her missing spouse to her former friend.

'Okay, let's have some privacy,' John stood up and reached for some official papers and a pen. 'Deb, can you watch the desk for me for a minute?' he shouted over his shoulder.

John took Amanda into an interview room. The stark grey walls were painfully familiar to Amanda as she sat down across the table from John. So many times Shane had led her into such a room to explain away from prying eyes why he was going to be late home again.

'So your husband is missing?' John queried carefully. Amanda nodded stiffly and pulled her thoughts back into the moment.

'Yes, since yesterday morning.'

'That was when you last saw him?' John was writing notes as he spoke.

'Yes.'

'Was there anything unusual that happened yesterday morning?'

'No.'

'Okay.' More writing. 'Do you have a photograph? Full name? We'll need all his details.'

Amanda nodded as she unzipped her handbag and pulled out one of her wedding pictures. She slid it across the small white table towards John. He plucked it up with his plump fingers and smiled at the image.

In it Amanda was holding hands with Will and they were seemingly walking through a meadow. Her free hand was clutching a bouquet of daisies.

'Wow, you look beautiful,' John kindly complimented her.

Squirming in her chair, Amanda realized that neither John nor Shane had been invited to her wedding. Barely anyone had been. It had been a small, intimate affair.

'So this is your husband?' John pointed at Will who was immaculate in a dark suit, smiling broadly for the camera.

'Yep, that's him.'

'Woah, he's a real brick shit house of a guy,' John was still looking at the picture. He drew in a breath and opened his mouth to say something and then thought better of it.

Amanda smiled thinly at him. She knew what he'd been about to say; how Will didn't look like her type. He was the complete opposite of Shane who was slender and wiry with eyes the colour of rain-soaked grass.

'He didn't turn up for work yesterday,' Amanda explained. 'And his mobile phone is disconnected.'

John's eyes widened.

'You guys will find him, right? Now that he's officially a missing person?'

'We'll file the report and do everything that we can,' John was stating, his tone suddenly formal and no longer friendly.

'I'm worried sick about him,' Amanda said pleadingly.

'I'll send the report on to the relevant department for you.'

Amanda didn't feel in any way comforted by his words.

'We'll contact you as soon as we hear anything.'

'Right,' Amanda started standing up, knowing when she was dismissed.

'Do you want me to tell him?' John also stood up, firing the question at Amanda when she was just at the door. She turned back around, but not before releasing a pained sigh.

'He doesn't work missing persons, does he?'

The last she'd heard Shane had risen up so high in the ranks of the police force that he was now a DCI on homicide cases, which was exactly what he'd always wanted.

'No, but he'd want to help,' John insisted.

'But he can't if he's the wrong department, can he?' Amanda replied coldly.

'Well then, let's hope his department doesn't get involved,' John raised his eyebrows at her. Amanda wanted to reach across the distance between them, turn back time and go back to when they were the best of friends, back to when she could crash against his chest and be wrapped in a fond embrace. So much had changed since they were reckless, hopeful teenagers.

'Just find him,' Amanda whispered, tears gathering on the ends of her eyelashes. 'Bring my husband back to me.'

*

'I'm not sure this was a good idea,' Amanda turned her cup of coffee in her hands and glanced across the small café table at her mother.

Corrine was draped in a bright red and orange shawl, making her look like a recently risen phoenix. Her curled hair was splayed madly about her head and the heavy purple eye shadow she'd chosen to wear clashed terribly with her outfit. Her dimples were briefly revealed as she threw her daughter a forceful smile.

'A civilized drink in a boutique café is always a good idea,' she insisted, her tone firm.

'Not when my husband is missing,' Amanda hissed, glancing around at the handful of other patrons who were too busy talking amongst themselves or reading their morning papers to eavesdrop.

'No, this is exactly when we should be out and about,' Corrine slapped a bejewelled hand down on to the table, her collection of bangles loudly jangling together. 'This is a time of crisis, Amanda. And in a time of crisis it's important to retain a level of civility.'

Amanda stared into her cup of coffee, watching the milk swirl against the darker contents. She remembered sitting in the same café when she was twelve years old, clutching a giant mug of hot chocolate between her hands even though it was a scorching summer's day outside. Only back then it had been much harder to keep up an air of civility. Amanda had openly bawled her eyes out as stunned onlookers came over to ask if everything was okay.

'I just want to be at home,' Amanda groaned. She regretted answering her mother's call as she'd headed back to her car after reporting Will as missing. The second Corrine discovered that her daughter was in town Amanda could basically hear her firing up the engine of her little car. All Amanda wanted to do was go home and wait by the phone.

'I'll be right there,' she'd blurted, sounding a little too excited. 'Meet me in that little café you've always loved.'

Before Amanda could correct her mother and point out that it was actually Corrine who loved the café, she'd hung up. Amanda had hated the café ever since that day when she was twelve, when her mother had insisted that the world kept turning and that they must be strong.

Corrine had always ridden the wave of despair with grace and elegance, using it as an opportunity to show the world her strength and resolve. Amanda couldn't be more different. In times of strife she wanted to lock herself away in a dark room and disappear into her beloved virtual world. It was there she'd first gone when her heart had been shattered into a thousand pieces. As she learned more about coding, about websites, algorithms and formulas, she began to heal. And as she healed, she learned about the places online that straddled the fine line between what was legal and what wasn't. Amanda loved to play jump rope over that line. It made her heart beat faster, made it feel almost whole again to know she was dicing with danger.

'How did it go?' Corrine enquired gingerly as she raised her dainty porcelain cup of tea up to her lips. She sounded as though she were asking about the weather or a holiday Amanda had just been on.

'John was there.'

'John Morris?' Corrine's eyes widened with delight. 'He was always such a kind boy. Too greedy for his own good, but so kind.'

'Yeah, he said he'd file the report for me.'

'And Shane?' Corrine stared directly at her daughter, unflinching.

'Shane?' Amanda spluttered out the name.

'Did you see him too? I heard that he's a detective now, most impressive.'

Amanda ground her teeth together and bit back tears. 'No, I didn't see Shane,' she seethed. 'He works homicide, Mum, not missing persons. Besides, why the hell are you even asking about my *ex-boyfriend* when it's my *husband* who is missing?'

'Don't get tetchy with me,' Corrine warned, lowering her tea. 'I was merely asking. Shane has always adored you, I'm sure he'd help you find Will if you asked him to.'

'You'd love that,' Amanda pouted, leaning back in her chair and folding her arms across her chest.

'Yes, I would,' Corrine admitted honestly. 'I think you were wrong to banish Shane from your life.'

'God,' Amanda rolled her eyes. Surely her mother wasn't picking such an inappropriate moment to once again cheer for Shane's side. Ever since Amanda had thrown him out of her apartment Corrine had been doing her best to initiate a reunion between the young couple. She clung to a naïve hope that first love could still be the greatest love of all, as her own had been, even in the wake of Amanda's marriage to Will. But then Corrine didn't realize how terribly things had soured between her daughter and Shane. How could she? To most people in Tremwell Bay they were the perfect couple; childhood sweethearts who'd developed into something more, something substantial. Everyone expected them to go the distance, to get married on the beach where they loved to sit and read their books together on lazy Sunday mornings.

'I don't want to talk about bloody Shane,' Amanda raged. Even saying his name was making her agitated. She should be thinking about Will, only Will. Her husband still hadn't come home and she had no idea what, or who, could be keeping him away from her.

'Do you want to find your husband?' Corrine demanded, her gaze unblinking and penetrating.

'Of course,' Amanda blurted. 'What sort of a question is that?'

'Because if you want to find him you need to use every weapon at your disposal. And like it or not, that includes Shane. He's one of the brightest minds in the Police Department. Couple that with how much he's always cared about you and he's the sort of ally you want on your side at a time like this.'

Amanda was shaking her head. The last time she'd seen Shane had been in Tesco's a few months after the incident with Will. She'd accidently bumped into him, literally, during a late-night shop for some essentials. With their trollies between them like a barrier, they'd locked eyes. Amanda was about to say something when Jayne Richards slinked up to Shane and looped her arm into his. Her fire-red bob shone brightly beneath the supermarket lights. She smiled contemptuously at Amanda, stroking Shane's arm as though she were the victor in some war Amanda hadn't even known she was fighting in. Jayne Richards had bullied Amanda in school. She'd labelled her chest an ironing board and called her a loser with such regularity that Amanda had started to believe it.

Making her excuses Amanda grabbed her trolley and turned around, hurrying away from the couple before they had chance to saying anything else.

'I'm not calling Shane,' Amanda told her mother resolutely.

'Suit yourself,' Corrine shrugged. 'But I really think you should.'

*

Amanda watched the clock on the front room wall tick over to nine p.m. On her lap her dinner of a microwaved lasagne lay untouched. She couldn't eat. She also couldn't watch TV or do any of her work. She was living on a knife-edge of anticipation, knowing that at any moment the phone might go and it would be Will calling to tell her he was coming home. Or worse; it would be the police telling her that they'd found him.

Picking up her mobile phone, Amanda started scrolling through her contact list. She'd already called Will fifty times that day. Each time it was the same automated message which greeted her. Mike had left a message on the house phone. He was worried since Will still wasn't in work. Amanda didn't have the heart to call him. Besides, news that Will was officially a missing person would have surely circulated through the Bay by now. People in Tremwell kept secrets as well as they kept colds.

'Damn,' Amanda sighed as she dwelled on Shane's number. She'd not called it in years, yet for some reason she had never deleted his details, even though she probably should have. If Will knew that Shane's name was still in her phone he'd be furious. Maybe the number wasn't even current anymore. But Amanda knew that if he'd changed it she'd know. It was a tenuous link to keep each other's numbers but one they'd both adhered to over the years. She stared at Shane's name as nine became quarter past. Each ticking echoed the steady, nervous beating of her heart. She hated to admit that her mother was right. Shane Perton was the best detective on the force. If anyone could find Will it was him.

Pressing down on the green call button, Amanda held her breath. It rang out three times before Shane picked up.

'Hello?' his voice was tight and surprised.

'Shane?' she began shakily. 'It's me, Amanda. I need your help.'

44

6

Amanda sat in front of her laptop, its blue glow providing the only light in the room. She'd spoken with Shane over an hour ago. He'd been formal throughout their conversation, keeping Amanda at arm's length. But he had offered to help.

Her hands danced across the keys of her laptop. She'd been able to touch-type since she was fourteen. Amanda ran searches on lost people in the local area, searches on Will. But it felt like it was all in vain. She wasn't finding anything concrete, nothing that could give her solace.

This was to be her second night sleeping alone without Will. Each time Amanda thought of her bed she shuddered apprehensively even though her body was starting to ache and her eyes grew heavy. It was within her bed that she felt the pain of her husband's disappearance most acutely. She missed hearing the reassuring rumble of his deep breaths, missed rolling over and being able to stretch out a hand and connect with the warmth of his body.

'Where are you?' she asked of her laptop. In the past there had been few problems she couldn't solve with her laptop.

Amanda shifted in her chair, her legs were exposed in the mint green pyjama short set she was wearing and her skin had become mottled with goose bumps. She knew that she should just head to bed but the lure of the laptop and its endless possibilities for connectivity held her in place, just as it had when she was a teenager.

Corrine would lament that Amanda was going to get square eyes as each time she cracked open her daughter's bedroom door the girl was cross-legged on her bed cradling her computer in her lap, staring intently at the screen as though it were the most wondrous thing she'd ever seen.

'Bed,' Corrine would snap, clicking her fingers as she gave the order.

'In a minute.' Amanda was always vying for another minute, another sixty seconds to spend exploring her beloved virtual world.

'Bed now or I'll take that damn thing off you.' Corrine wasn't the kind of woman to make idle threats. Amanda would swiftly sign off and shut down her computer, pouting as she did so.

Now Amanda didn't have to worry about her mother bursting in and demanding she turn off her computer. She didn't even have to worry about Will moaning that it was late and she should come to bed. She was completely alone in the house with only her laptop for company.

*

There is something about the dense cover of night that calls out to dark deeds. Beneath the scrutiny of the light of day certain ideas might be forsaken. But at night, with only shadows prowling the streets, it was easier for the heart's darker desires to take hold.

Amanda was feeling drawn to such darkness. Or more specifically a dark place; the darknet. It was an area of the Internet away from the prying eyes of government officials, a place where deadly deals were struck and illegal goods exchanged with the ease of shopping on Amazon. It was a place Amanda had found when she was sixteen. She'd heard whispers of it in chat rooms, and one dark night, as the wind made the waves in the bay rise up and crash against the rugged shoreline, she summoned up enough bravery and curiosity to check it out for herself. And from then on she was hooked. Amanda loved the anonymity of the darknet, the way it seemed to exist beyond the fringes of society. That was how she felt as a teenager; always on the outside looking in.

As Amanda became more proficient with her computer skills, she became more present on the darknet. She started to hack. By the time she went to university she was hacking for money. Her hacker ID was Lambchop, a sentimental nod to a television show she'd loved growing up.

Hacking could bring in serious money. Amanda hacked websites, email accounts, even security networks to access their CCTV data. She used to feel empowered as she sat at home in her dingy bedroom conducting grand scale espionage. She felt like Tremwell Bay's very own Batman. When she was on the darknet she got to play at being a superhero.

Amanda now had three windows open on her laptop. They each contained Will's social media accounts. Her fingers hovered just above the keyboard, twitching with anticipation. She could so easily hack into his accounts, see what, if any, secrets he was hiding from her. Chewing her lip, Amanda stared at the screen.

Will's page was sparse. He gave the most basic information about himself and used a profile picture that he'd clearly shot on his phone. The image did little to capture what a powerful, charismatic man he was. Amanda stared into the eyes of the picture, willing it to reveal some secret to her.

'Come home, baby,' she pleaded with the account. 'Argh,' Amanda pushed herself away from the laptop and buried her head in her hands. Thinking about the darknet had opened up a can of rotten worms in her mind.

What if someone had taken Will? What if he was now being tortured? Amanda groaned helplessly as she imagined him in some damp, dingy basement screaming in agony as a grizzly faced man used a rusted knife to hack off one of his fingers.

Was her hacker past catching up with her? Amanda looked up at her laptop in shock. What if the very thing she'd turned to for comfort for so many years had finally turned against her? When Lambchop's online activity was at its peak she was being hired to target big, global companies. Household names. It was Shane who'd encouraged her to step away from that murky world. But still she couldn't resist its pull. Only last year she'd secretly aided a group of hackers in bringing down an exclusive dating site that catered to those who were married and wanted to commit adultery. She didn't do it out of some moral code, she did it for the rush, to feel powerful.

But what if she'd gone too far? What if someone was now punishing Will for Lambchop's past?

Amanda was trembling as she pulled herself closer to her desk. If Will hadn't been taken from her then he'd left of his own free will. And what did that mean? Amanda was staring at his profile again. If she ran a few programs, enabled a keystroke memory search she could log in. The whole process would take less than twenty minutes.

'Your past is going to come back to haunt you,' Shane had warned back when they were together and he'd learned just how deep the rabbit hole for Lambchop went.

'Damn it,' Amanda let her fingers fly across the keyboard. She executed the relevant searches, began the initial sequences which would allow her to access Will's social media accounts. 'What are you hiding, baby?' she asked of the screen as the laptop whirred.

The progress bar was almost complete. Amanda was seconds away from complete, unauthorized access to Will's limited digital world. She licked her lips in anticipation. Maybe now she'd get some answers.

The doorbell rang. It was so loud, so crystal-clear and unexpected that it sounded like someone screaming throughout the house and left Amanda just as startled. Her heart was in her throat as she pushed away from her desk and hurried on to the landing. Just as her feet connected with the staircase she stopped. It was late. Way past ten. Who would be coming by at such an hour? With her hand resting on the painted white wood of the banister she peered down suspiciously into the shadows of the hallway.

Could it be Will? But he had a key, surely he'd just let himself in?

The doorbell rang again.

'Shit,' Amanda nervously powered down the stairs. In the hallway she could see through the front door and beyond its upper glass panel was the unmistakable shadow of a figure.

'Shit,' Amanda repeated under her breath. She glanced towards the cordless phone resting in its cradle on a nearby side table. She edged herself towards it, prepared to call the police if she had to.

'Who is it?' she shouted out, thankful that the quaking in her bones hadn't carried through to her voice.

'It's me. Shane.'

Amanda gasped in shock. Her body weakened with relief but her heart maintained its anxious palpitations.

'Just a second,' she called as she approached the door and unlocked it. Pulling it open, Amanda found Shane on her doorstep. He was in a grey suit, white shirt and black skinny tie. Clearly he'd just come from work. His hair was shorter than it had been when he was with Amanda, but he was still able to style it, flicking it forward with gel. His cheeks were freshly shaved, revealing the impressive profile of his jawline.

'Sorry to stop by so late,' Shane noted apologetically.

Amanda opened and closed her mouth several times as she debated what to say. She hadn't expected Shane to just show up at her house. She figured any interactions they had would be at the station.

Shane's gaze dropped, taking in her bare legs.

'Come in,' Amanda stepped aside, hugging her arms around herself self-consciously.

'Nice place,' Shane commented as he stepped in. Amanda flicked on all the lights, revealing the modern space in all its glory. She reached for a cardigan that was hanging on a coat rack and gratefully hugged it around herself.

'Thanks,' Amanda smiled courteously at him.

'It's very... new,' Shane offered, his tone guarded.

'I like new,' Amanda bristled as she led him into the kitchen. When they stepped inside, she saw Shane sweep his gaze around the room, taking it all in.

'Coffee?' she enquired politely.

'Sure,' Shane cleared his throat. 'Thanks.' He sat down on one of the white plastic stools beside the kitchen counter. The percolator grumbled to life as Amanda drifted over to where he was. She almost wanted to laugh at how surreal it was to see him sitting in her kitchen.

'Were you working late?'

'Yeah,' Shane reached for his tie and loosened it.

'You always were... passionate, about the job,' Amanda chose her words carefully. Shane had offered to help her, she didn't want to be the cause of yet another argument between them. Towards the end of their relationship it felt like all they did was argue.

'Uh-huh,' Shane scratched at his cheek. He looked uncomfortable. The percolator ceased gurgling and Amanda hurried back to it, grateful for the distraction it had provided.

'And you're behaving yourself these days, right?' Shane asked as her back was to him, pouring them both a mug of coffee.

'Me?' Amanda's eyes were wide with innocence as she passed him his drink.

'You, Lambchop,' Shane cracked a smile.

'Oh,' Amanda blushed and leaned against the counter, choosing not to sit down. If she did she'd be on the stool right beside Shane and she'd risk their legs brushing up against each other and that felt too close for comfort. This was still the home she shared with Will; she had to be respectful towards her husband even in his absence.

'So you're not hacking?' Shane raised his eyebrows at her.

'I'm all legit now,' Amanda smirked at him, 'I run my own website design company from home.' Her laptop resting just a few feet above upstairs told a different story but Amanda was always careful to conceal her digital tracks. Shane couldn't uncover the truth about her internet history even if he wanted to.

'Sounds good.'

'It is.'

'So where do you think your husband is?' Shane blurted the question, destroying the friendly atmosphere that had tentatively developed between them.

'What?' Amanda lowered her mug.

'Where do you think he is?'

'If I knew that he wouldn't be missing, would he?' Amanda replied sharply.

'I need to ask some awkward questions,' Shane reached inside his jacket and brought out a small black Moleskin notepad and pen.

'Okay,' Amanda hugged the ends of her cardigan, the garment did little to fight off the cold which made her shiver. So this was a work call after all. Shane hadn't swung by merely to check in on her. Amanda hated herself for feeling disappointed.

'How would you describe your relationship with your husband?' Shane's pen hovered over his notepad.

'Excuse me?'

'Were things good between you two? Or strained at all?'

'Good,' Amanda snapped, wondering what sort of a question that was to ask, especially given her and Shane's complicated history. 'Good, very good. Great even.'

'Okay...' Shane scribbled a note. 'And to your knowledge your husband had never engaged in relations beyond your marriage?'

'Are you asking me if he had an affair?' Amanda was on the verge of tears. She could feel them gathering behind her eyes, hot and heavy.

'Like I said, these questions are awkward,' Shane sighed

apologetically. 'But in a lot of cases like these the missing person has actually just returned to another family.'

Amanda pressed a hand to her chest and breathed deeply. There was no way Will had another wife tucked away somewhere, another life. Was there? But the possibility gnawed at her, came for her in her most vulnerable moments. Every woman who'd ever been cheated on surely felt blindsided, believed that their betrothed loved them. And Will *loved* Amanda. He loved their modern little home. Just last week he'd come out of work to fix a flat tyre for her when she'd gone out shopping. She didn't even have to ask. She'd texted him as she walked into the store, moaning that one of her tyres appeared to be flat and by the time she came out laden down with shopping bags she spotted Will's van parked up beside her little car and him crouched down beside it, tightening the few remaining nuts and bolts on a new tyre. Because that was the kind of man Will Thorn was; decent and reliable. He wasn't the sort of guy who'd be living a double life.

'We just have to explore all possibilities,' Shane stated gently. Amanda wiped a hand across her eyes and stared at him.

There was no denying that all suited up Shane Perton was a devastatingly handsome man. His green eyes permanently sparkled as though he were forever privy to some sordid secret. He had sharp, chiselled features and long limbs which he'd grown into since his awkward days of puberty. But when Amanda looked at him she still saw the boy with the mullet haircut in the baggy Linkin Park T-shirts. The boy who tasted of cigarettes and cider the first time he'd kissed her out on the beach beneath the stars.

'So when did you last see Will?'

'The other morning,' Amanda recalled. She hated that the memory was already growing less vivid in her mind. Like when you watch a film and before you've even left the cinema's car park you're forgetting elements of the plot.

'You saw him leave?'

'No, he must have left while I was sleeping.' Amanda noticed Shane's jaw clench. No matter how heatedly they argued, how many vile words they slung at one another, Shane had always kissed her goodbye each morning, always. He would kiss her as she drifted off to sleep and come the morning she'd wake up to his lips grazing hers and soft sunlight filling the tiny bedroom they shared. To disappear like a thief in the night had never been Shane's style.

He scribbled something in his notepad, not meeting her gaze. 'Can you remember what your last words to Will were?'

Amanda opened her mouth and then snapped it shut. She actually couldn't remember what she'd last said to him. When she'd come up to bed the previous night he'd already been sleeping, tucked away on his side of the bed beyond her reach. Then when she'd woken up he was gone. Amanda gripped the kitchen counter and released a single sob.

'Hey,' Shane was instantly on his feet. He ran around to her and looped a strong arm around her thin waist. 'It's okay.'

He was so close, Amanda could smell his cologne. He smelt like liquorice and oranges. 'I,' she was shaking her head, wishing her memories of that last night with Will were sharper, less dulled by time and an inability in the moment to know how vital they would prove to be. 'I don't remember,' she wilted against Shane. 'I don't remember,' she repeated as tears came tumbling down her cheeks. 'What if those were the last words I ever get to say to him and *I don't remember them*?'

'It's okay, it'll be all right,' Shane whispered soothingly as he guided her on to a nearby stool and handed her a coffee.

'We will find your husband,' Shane told her, his voice strong with determination. Amanda gazed woefully into his bright eyes as he used his warm hands to wipe the tears from her cheeks.

'What if we don't?' she choked out the question.

'We will,' Shane confirmed, still certain. Amanda had always admired his unwavering faith in there being good in the world. But his optimism had been one of things that ultimately drove a wedge between them. Where Shane saw goodness and possibility, Amanda saw only darkness.

'Why...' Amanda sniffed, wishing she could stop crying. 'Why would he leave me?'

'I don't know,' Shane's hands were still on her cheeks. His touch was so warm, banishing away the shivers which had previously gripped her body. 'But I can promise you that he regrets leaving.'

Shane was so close, staring at her like he used to; as though she were the most precious thing he had ever seen. He opened his mouth to speak but before he could get any words out his phone started to shrilly bleat in his suit pocket. Clearing his throat nervously, Shane stepped back from her, straightened up and accepted the call.

Shane lowered his voice but not enough as he headed into the hallway. 'Hey, babe.'

Amanda sighed. She wiped away any remaining tears and hoped that Shane was right, that if Will had willingly left her that he'd come to see the error of his ways, that he'd come home.

*

'Jake?'

The road was an endless parade of cats eyes which glistened away into the darkness. Jake shook himself awake, raking his hand down his face.

'You all right, man? You seemed like you were dozing off there for a bit. Need me to take over?'

In the shadows of the truck, Billy looked young. Too young. Life hadn't hardened him the way it had Jake.

'I'm all right,' *Jake nodded, tightening his grip on the wheel as the truck roared past a sign which was briefly illuminated by its headlights;*

LONDON – 208 MILES

'I was just thinking about McAllister, that's all.'
'What about him?'
'What he said about Ewan.'

Jake thought of the tiny pink bundle back home. Of the blue eyes that shone with joy whenever they reached for his thick fingers. Of the gentle gurgling sounds the boy made as he fell asleep.

'You think he meant it?' *Jake wondered as he looked at the dashboard and checked the petrol level.*

'He said something about babies being vulnerable right?'
'Uh-huh.'

'And how shit it is to grow up without a father. Although in our case it's arguably a lot shittier to grow up with a drunk for a dad. Your old man was as bad as mine.'

'If not worse.'

'Hmm.' *Billy drummed his hands against his thighs. He was so* awake. The coffee he'd downed at the last service station was clearly more potent than the one Jake'd had.

'But he was threatening Ewan, right? Like when he said either we come back with the delivery all signed off or we don't come back at all?'

'The man trades in threats.'

'But he meant it, right?'

'Jake, just try and relax and think about all the sweet, sweet cash which is coming our way.'

'Relax?' Jake looked away from the road to direct a dry laugh at his friend. 'You're so tightly wound I'd swear you were high.'

'I've been clean for months,' Billy replied with a hint of bitterness. 'You know that.'

'Shit man, yeah. I'm sorry. You just seem… kinda nervous.'

'I'm just excited about turning our fortunes around.' Billy smiled in the way that he always did; confident and brazen. It was a smile that never failed to woo women or endear him to his friends. Billy was inherently loved by all those around him. And to Jake he was like a brother.

7

Amanda watched the headlights of Shane's car back out of her driveway and disappear down the street. Closing the front door, she breathed in, noticing that the remnants of his cologne lingered in the house like a stubborn fog. Amanda swept her hair out of her eyes and headed back up to her study.

She was so blinded by rage that her world turned red. She had so many questions for Will. They snapped at the back of her teeth, desperate to get out. Each question started the same way.

Why?

Why had he left so suddenly?

Why had he not come back?

Why had he not called? Or text?

Amanda was chewing on the word as she sat back down at her laptop. With a click of her mouse the screen came back to life, effortlessly banishing the darkness it had momentarily slid into.

An information text box told her that her hack was complete. She now had access to all of Will's social media accounts. Holding her breath, Amanda began clicking through the relevant data. She opened up all of his accounts, checked the private messages, checked the status updates.

The more Amanda searched, the more easily she began to breathe. There was nothing to arouse any sort of suspicion. None of the accounts had been touched in days. The only messages Will had received were spam ones. It seemed that he was as aloof online as he was in real life. Will had never been one for small talk and social niceties. He belonged to a dying breed of men who clung steadfastly to old, abandoned ways.

'Huh,' Amanda reached the end of the entries on the accounts. She frowned at the screen and leaned towards it. She clicked her mouse repeatedly, urging the search to continue but it couldn't. There was no more information to reveal.

Amanda checked the dates of the oldest entries, then cross-checked them across all of Will's social media accounts. Weirdly they all lined up. Clicking back and forth, she searched for more entries but there was truly nothing. All of Will's accounts had been set up just over three years ago. Just before he met Amanda. It had slipped her attention before, mainly because she fought the urge to digitally stalk Will when they were dating. She'd seen her friends do it and it always ended badly. She had wanted to take Will at face value, to let him divulge his secrets to her at his leisure rather than rummaging around online and hauling all of his skeletons out of the closet when they'd just started getting to know each other. She'd known Shane inside out when they dated. Will was a mystery. And she kind of wanted him to stay that way for as long as possible. But maybe that had been a mistake. Maybe she should have searched for the man behind the mask instead of enjoying the fantasy.

'Weird,' she muttered to herself as she began running a more thorough search on Will's name and date of birth. Perhaps he had other, older accounts which he kept from her. The feeling that he might stoop to such duplicitous levels sent an icy sensation trickling down Amanda's spine. She shivered against it. Will loathed technology, she highly doubted that he'd be able to conceal other accounts from her. And to what end? What could he possibly be hiding?

But in a lot of cases like these the missing person has actually just returned to another family.

Shane's warning rang in Amanda's ears, causing her to almost choke on the breath she'd been holding. She was shaking her head as her vision became blurred with tears. Will wouldn't do that to her. There was just no way that he had another family hidden away somewhere. That wasn't his style. He was a good man with an open, honest heart. It was why Amanda had fallen for him as swiftly as she had done.

'No, no way,' Amanda gasped as she wiped at her eyes. She wouldn't believe it. She ran yet another search on Will's name. All of her results kept coming back the same. Up until just over three years ago it seemed that Will Thorn hadn't even existed. Online he'd been a ghost.

'He just hates technology,' she reconciled herself, angrily slamming her laptop closed.

There had to be an explanation for Will's lack of a presence online. There had to be an explanation for everything. But Amanda knew she wasn't going to find it sat at her laptop so late at night. Her head throbbed and her shoulders ached. She needed to rest.

The silence that greeted her in the bedroom was unnerving. It felt like stepping on to an ice-covered lake in the dead of winter. Everything around her was silent, as though the entire world were sucking in an anxious breath. She didn't dare do anything to disturb the peace, because if she did, the ice would crack and she'd be plunged to her dark, frozen doom.

Amanda pulled back the bed sheets and climbed into her side of the bed. Even though it was still mild outside she reached down for the duvet which was usually stowed at the base of the bed during the summer months. Amanda pulled it up tightly to her chin and squeezed her eyes shut. She tried to imagine the sound of Will sleeping beside her, of the steady rise and fall of his relaxed breaths. But instead the silence became suffocating. The emptiness mocked her, reminding her how alone she was. Amanda burrowed herself deeper beneath the duvet as tears trickled out of the corners of her closed eyes.

She felt so afraid, like the world no longer made sense. Softly crying herself to sleep, she didn't feel like the young married woman she was. She felt like she was twelve years old again, weeping for the father she'd lost forever.

*

The phone rang. Shrill bells bounced off the walls, staying silent for only a second before starting up again.

Amanda was in the hallway, staring down at the telephone on the sleek phone stand as though she could somehow see through the plastic of the receiver, right down the line and into the eyes of whoever was calling her.

Maybe it's Will.

She clung to the hopeful thought like a child with a teddy bear. It gave her comfort. Made her feel safe. But Amanda had been burned before.

It had started in the night. At first Amanda had thought she was dreaming the relentless ringing as it dolled in her mind like a set of doomsday bells. But as she stirred and groggily wiped the sleep from her eyes the ringing persisted. Amanda had leapt out of bed, her body instantly buoyed by hope. She'd practically floated along the landing towards her study, seizing the phone, already wearing a smile.

'Hello?'

There was silence on the other end of the line. That and the giveaway crackle which told her that someone was there.

'Hello? Is anyone there?'

Nothing.

'Will… is that you?'

More silence.

'Will… please… come home. Or at least *say something*.'

She pleaded. She cried. The line crackled some more and then went dead. Amanda hammered 1471 into the keypad.

'The caller withheld their number,' an automated voice told her with cool indifference.

'Dammit!' Amanda had slammed the phone back into its cradle so fiercely that the whole thing almost tumbled off its trendy stand.

The calls kept coming through the night. It was always the same; the ringing would pluck her from the safety of a dream and bring her down into the shadowy pit of her current reality. She'd clutch the phone to her ear; plead with her unknown caller whilst trying to decipher any trace of sound she could pick up on their end. But there was nothing. And the number was always withheld.

As the sun rose it was all becoming too much. Amanda stood barefoot in the hallway, a light cotton robe wrapped around her shoulders. She watched the phone as it continued to ring. And still, despite her exhaustion and all the disappointment of previous calls she held on to hope.

On the eighth ring she picked up.

'Jesus, Will, if this is you say something. You're breaking me doing this. You're breaking *us*.'

The line only crackled in response. Tearfully, Amanda wasted no more time on the call. She returned the receiver to its cradle before bending down and yanking out the phone's connecting cable from the wall.

In her heart she knew that the caller wasn't Will. He wouldn't torment her like that. Or at least she hoped he wouldn't. But she had a feeling that whoever was prank-calling her was connected to her missing husband. She knew she should stay at home and do some more investigation but she was too tired, too afraid. She needed to be somewhere she felt safe.

*

Amanda stood waiting on the doorstep of what had once been her family home. A web of yellow roses bordered the bright red front door. The paint had dulled in places to a warm shade of pink. Amanda traced the woodwork with her fingertips as she waited for her mother to answer the door.

The morning sun was already burning down on the back of her neck. There was a weekend bag at her feet, hastily stuffed full of some essentials. It took over five minutes for the door to eventually creak open. Corrine peered out of the darkness, blinking into the sunlight as though it were blinding her.

When people suffer a mutual loss they either forge a stronger bond or drift apart. For Amanda and her mother, it had been the latter. While her mother dealt with being a widow, with the loss of her beloved husband, by disappearing into her garden. As her grief grew so did her attention to her roses. And each time they bloomed Corrine became a little stronger, saw beauty in the world and managed to smile a bit easier. Amanda hid within her virtual world. She spent hours upstairs in her room at her computer, enjoying the distance she felt from everything that hurt. When she played games, when she chatted online, she was no longer the girl who'd lost her Dad. On her computer she didn't have to endure all the stares which shadowed her around school. Online she could be anybody. Nobody. And that gave Amanda a rush. It was a drug she couldn't get enough of. The more time Amanda spent behind her computer screen the less time she spent with her mother. With the rest of the world.

And Corrine had liked Shane. He was the boy from Amanda's past, the link to a world in which Amanda's father used to live. When Amanda ended things with Shane it was like her mother felt that she'd permanently severed that link and resented her for it. Amanda was entering a new stage in her life. She married a man who had never even met her late father, who wasn't even from town. He was a stranger which made her decision to wed him seem strange to Corrine. There was too much alienation for Amanda's mother's taste, too much distance being created between the past and the present.

But Amanda couldn't keep holding on. And beneath the smiles, the hugs and the assurances that everything was fine, she blamed her mother for what had happened that day. It was at her behest that her dad was out on the road. Amanda knew that if the tables were turned and her father had tumbled over the cliffs that Corrine would carry the same resentment in her heart. They both loved him too much not to.

'Hey, Mum,' Amanda tilted her head at her mother. She'd not shown up on the doorstep like this, like a stray, since she was a teenager. Back then, she would often end up on the stone step following a night drinking on the beach with Shane and John. Drunkenly she'd spread herself across the step, gazing up at the stars through the leaves of the rose bushes which grew overhead.

Either her Mum or the milkman would discover her, depending on who was up first. If it was the milkman, then Amanda had time to steal inside and climb back into bed. If it was her mother, then she had to brace herself for a royal telling-off.

'Amanda,' Corrine looked genuinely startled to have found her daughter on her doorstep. She glanced down at the weekend bag and her eyes widened. 'Sweetheart, is everything okay?'

'I just can't bear it anymore,' Amanda admitted as her shoulder began to quake. 'The emptiness of the house. It's overwhelming.' *And this was home once.* The little house held many happy memories as well as sad ones. Amanda had bloomed into a woman there, had shared her first kiss with Shane down on the beach beneath the stars. Her mother's home felt safe. It always had. Somedays Amanda felt like she could still sense her father's presence lingering in the living room or resting beside the kitchen window, staring out to sea.

With every tick of the clock, Amanda knew it was another second passing where her husband was lost to her. Even though her house was minimally decorated she still felt Will in every room. His strong presence endured even in his absence. If the light flickered in the corner of her eye, Amanda would think he'd just walked by. She'd sprint into the next room, breathless and desperate to see him. But he was never there. Will had become the ghost that he was online. His number never connected, his van never pulled into the driveway. Amanda knew that soon people would stop believing that he was ever going to come back. And then it was only a matter of time before they pushed those beliefs on to her.

'Come in, come in,' Corrine quickly ushered her daughter inside. 'You could have just let yourself in you know.'

'Oh no,' Amanda shook her head wildly and dropped her bag down in the hallway. 'Never again, not since I caught you going through that tantric yoga phase.'

'Oh, yes, that,' Corrine's face softened wistfully as Amanda moved past her towards the kitchen.

The home her parents had shared was a small cottage nestled on a clifftop just outside of town. The little house was regularly pelted by fierce winds and rains rolling in off the coast, but it always managed to retain its quaint charm. The small windows were leaded in a diamond pattern and the ceilings were lined with thick oak beams. Local historians estimated the house to be several hundred years old. At night it creaked with the held memory of thousands of footsteps running across its boarded floors.

'Where do you keep the coffee these days?' Amanda asked as she began pulling open cupboards. There was a time when she'd have known her way around the kitchen blindfolded. Back when she lived there, back when it was her home.

'I've had a sort out,' Corrine stated as she gingerly opened a cupboard at the far end of the room, above the microwave, and pulled down a barely touched jar of store-brand coffee.

Every three months or so Amanda's mother would rearrange the entire house. The front room and the dining room were forever switching places, as were the bedrooms upstairs. But there was one room which Corrine never touched, one which remained trapped in its very own time warp.

Once her coffee was made Amanda headed up there, the stairs groaning in protest as she ascended them.

'Stay as long as you like,' Corrine smiled at her as she kissed her daughter's cheek before dashing off towards the bathroom. The pipes were creaking within the walls as Amanda peered into her bedroom.

Everything was just as she'd left it when she'd stormed out at eighteen with grand ideas of what her life would become. She was leaving for university; she intended to never come home again. She intended to change the world.

Leaning against the door frame, Amanda breathed in the familiar, musky scent of her room. The small single bed was still wedged up beneath her window, a faded purple duvet tucked up over it. A smile pulled on Amanda's lips as she remembered how Shane would often climb the trellis of the rose bushes up to her window and struggle to fit his wiry frame through its small opening.

Posters of all Amanda's favourite movies covered the walls. *Edward Scissorhands, Labyrinth, Dark Crystal.* These were the movies she had loved, the movies which had shaped her formative years. Stepping into the room, she carefully sat down on the edge of her bed. She was reluctant to disturb anything; the room was like a shrine. Smoothing her free hand across her duvet, she wondered how many nights she'd spent sat on her little bed, gazing out of her little window towards the ocean. She used to love how its surface glistened in the moonlight.

'If you look real carefully you'll see the flick of a mermaid's tail,' her Dad would tell her.

'No, Dad, I won't,' Amanda would protest wisely.

'Yes,' Ivor would insist. 'You will.'

As a little girl Amanda had stared so hard at the placid surface of the water, desperate to catch a glimpse of a mermaid tail that she feared she may go blind through such intense concentration. But a tail never broke the surface and sparkled in the sun and her Dad was no longer there to tell her to keep searching, to keep believing.

Lifting her gaze, Amanda saw the framed picture on her bedside table. It was in a shell-covered frame. Each one had been collected by Amanda along the beach and carefully glued in place. Picking up the frame, Amanda stared at the people in the image. She was looking at her younger self, smiling and carefree. Her golden hair, unruly even back then, was dancing in the wind and her cheeks were speckled with freckles. Beside her was her dad, his arm hugged around her slim shoulders. They were both smiling and beyond them lay the infinite ocean. The picture had been taken in the back garden of their little house, one week before Amanda had almost gone tumbling into the waves. Snapping her eyes shut, Amanda banished the memory and placed the picture back down. She'd come to her mother's house to heal, not to rip open old wounds.

'So, has there been any news?' Corrine asked as she dolloped baked beans on to pieces of toast. It was lunchtime and Amanda was sat at the kitchen table, warmed by the sunlight which came in through the double doors which her mother had thrown open. She could hear the gentle lapping of the waves close by and the occasional cry of a seagull.

'I called Shane,' Amanda stated as her mother handed her a plate of beans on toast.

'Oh?' Corrine quickly bustled down into her own seat, raising her knife and fork but ignoring her lunch.

'He, um, came round last night to ask questions.'

'Like what?'

'Like could Will have had another family stashed away somewhere?' Amanda stared directly at her mother, goading her to say something against her absent husband. But instead Corrine nodded sadly to herself and looked down at her dinner.

'That's quite something to say,' she sighed. 'It would have broken your father's heart to hear such talk.'

'I know,' Amanda agreed, her chest tightening as though her own heart were slowly breaking.

'He always believed wholeheartedly in the sanctity of marriage,' Corrine continued. 'Since the day we said our vows to one another he was always telling me how much he meant it, that we were bound together forever.'

Amanda reached across the table and grabbed her mother's hand as Corrine blinked away tears. She was wearing a bright green sarong and long emerald earrings. With the light pouring in behind her she looked like some sort of grand peacock.

'Dad was a man of his word. He'd never have just up and left you,' Amanda scowled at her dinner.

She'd thought that Will was like her Dad; a man of honour. A real-life hero. But instead he'd left her dangling when her dad would have risked anything to save her, even his own life.

'He'd be furious at Will, that's for sure,' Corrine clucked, briskly shaking her head. 'But he'd never believe that he had some other family.'

'Then what is it?' Amanda pleaded. 'Why has he left me like this?'

Corrine sighed and dusted her hair out of her eyes. Her curls were tightly coiled together as her hair was still damp.

'Your dad wouldn't have believed it,' she began carefully, 'because he always saw the good in people. Me, I was always the bad cop in our scenario.'

'What are you saying?' Amanda's nostrils flared. 'Do you think Will has left me for some family he's kept secret for years?'

'Maybe,' Corrine pursed her lips. 'Stranger things have happened.'

'We're *married*,' Amanda raged. 'How could he have an entire family that I don't know about?'

'I always said it was suspicious that none of his relatives came to your wedding.'

Amanda rolled her eyes. She was in no mood to listen to the broken record that was her mother's conspiracy theories about her wedding day.

'It was too far for them to travel and his mother was sick,' she snapped bitterly. 'We've been through this.'

'But have you even met them?' Corrine asked with a tilt of her head.

A silence stretched between them and Amanda realized she'd taken too long to answer the question. She wiped at her eyes and focused on her lunch.

'You've not, have you?' Corrine answered for her.

'No, I've not,' Amanda slammed down her cutlery. 'Are you happy now?'

'When you met Will you were so bowled over by him that you didn't stop to ask questions. You just went with your heart.'

'And what's wrong with that?'

'I just let you get on with it, it was just so nice to see you happy again.'

'Mum, you were forever sniping at him, moaning about his aloofness!'

'And clearly with good reason,' Corrine raised her eyebrows.

'Mum, he's *missing*. No one knows why, not even the police.'

'Not even you.'

'What does that mean?' Amanda's voice thundered throughout the kitchen, managing to drown out the distant roar of the waves and call of the gulls.

'It means that you married a stranger.'

'What?' Amanda hissed. She could feel her cheeks getting hot, could feel the pressure of gathering tears behind her eyes. Will wasn't a stranger. He was the oak tree of a man she'd fallen in love with. He was the man who'd mended the fence when it blew down, the man who held her all through the night when she got flu last winter. He was her husband.

'Does he know everything about you?' Corrine challenged. 'Does he know about Shane?'

Amanda had to force down the food she'd been chewing. Suddenly everything tasted bitter.

'No,' she admitted at length. 'I mean, he knows that we dated. Sort of. He doesn't know the depths of it. I felt like he didn't need to know.'

'There you go,' Corrine spread her hands across the table, palms turned up to the ceiling. 'You had your secrets and it certainly looks like he had his.'

'He doesn't have a secret family, Mum,' Amanda raged. 'Whatever has happened to him, wherever he is, it isn't that.'

'Why did you want to come and stay here?' Corrine's voice was soft, kind. Her tone lacked its usual layer of judgement.

'Am I not welcome now?' Amanda challenged hotly.

'You are always welcome, you know that. This will always be your home.'

'So what's your point?'

'I think you came to stay here because you don't think Will is coming back,' Corrine stared at her daughter for a beat and then dropped her gaze to her half-eaten lunch.

Amanda opened her mouth but no words tumbled out in her absent husband's defence. What if her mother was right? What if she'd already given up hope that Will was coming back?

8

'Amanda.'

There was salt on her lips and the roar of the waves in her ears.

'Amanda.'

The ground beneath her buckled uneasily, sending loose stones skittering down into the swirling depths below. Everything spun on an invisible axis. The sky became the ground as she started to tumble, to veer over the edge.

'Amanda,' something roughly shook her shoulders. Amanda blinked her eyes open and suspiciously peered around the room she had once called her own. The air felt warm and heavy and dust danced in the thick thread of sunlight which pressed in through the window. Sitting up, Amanda rubbed at her eyes and looked at the diamonds upon the floor, cast by the pattern of the window. Growing up, she'd always loved those diamonds, how when the sun shone they appeared on walls and floorboards making the entire house feel gothic and magical.

'You were fast asleep,' Corrine's voice was soft, apologetic. She was sat on the edge of the bed, one hand still resting on Amanda's shoulder. 'I didn't mean to wake you but you have a visitor.'

'What? Who?' the questions tumbled from her lips like a knee jerk response. Who would even know to find her here, at the little house on the shoreline with the rose trellised garden?

Could it be?

'Is he here?' Amanda felt light-headed as she imagined her husband waiting patiently downstairs. She'd hurry down to him, her footsteps full of pent-up anger, but the moment she saw him and looked into his kind, soulful eyes, her rage would instantly burn away to relief. She'd run to him, let him open up his arms so that she could once again nestle in the safety of his embrace.

'Shane has stopped by,' Corrine must have seen the hope ignite in Amanda's eyes. Her words were brutally swift in extinguishing it. Amanda felt as deflated as a child finally learning the truth about who left the presents underneath the Christmas tree.

'Shane?'

'He wanted to check in on you. When you weren't at home he figured you were here.' There was something in Corrine's tone which annoyed Amanda, like she was holding something back. In different circumstances she'd probably gush about how well Shane knew her, about how he still understood her in a way no one else could. The unspoken words grated against Amanda as she hauled herself out of bed. Her clothes were crumpled around her but she didn't care. 'I'll leave you to talk,' Corrine left behind a cloud of Estee Lauder perfume as she headed towards her bedroom.

Amanda sighed. The floorboards creaked, loudly announcing her presence as she went downstairs to find Shane sat at the weathered oak table in the small kitchen, nursing a cup of tea. He looked comical in his smart suit clutching a bone-china cup and saucer decorated in ornate ruby red roses. Amanda was surprised to find herself suppressing a smile.

'Hey,' Shane's expression changed from thoughtful to pleased when he saw her. His green eyes glimmered in the late afternoon sunlight.

'My mum said you were here,' Amanda slid into the vacant chair opposite him.

'I thought I'd swing by, see how you were doing. I went by your place first.'

'Yeah, she said.'

It was a good twenty minutes by car between Amanda's home and her mother's, even longer if the traffic was bad. Tremwell Bay was full of twisting, narrow roads which made travel through the town slow-going.

'We've not really heard anything about your husband that can lead us to his whereabouts.'

'Right,' Amanda's stomach knotted in on itself. With each passing day she felt as though she moved further and further away from a joyful reunion with Will.

'But our investigation has revealed some interesting discoveries. He took out some money at a local service station,' Shane reached for his moleskin notebook and began relaying his notes to Amanda.

'How much?'

'Almost a thousand pounds. He hit up a couple of cash points.'

Amanda tightly clenched her hands together. Her knuckles whitened. Will had always insisted on separate bank accounts citing their need for independence. Amanda had thought him liberal and forward thinking. Respectful even since she earned more than he did. Now she started to worry about his true motives for keeping their finances separate.

'It was taken out the morning you reported that he initially went missing.'

'And his van?'

'It was abandoned at the service station. I've got one of my officers heading out to the car depot to retrieve it as we speak.'

'He abandoned his van?' Amanda could hear the wail in her own voice. Why would he leave his van? He loved his van. Except for the gears.

'Stupid stick shift,' he'd grunt as the car spluttered beneath him, the clutch groaning angrily.

'Did Will owe money to anyone?' Shane tapped his pen against the open page in his notebook as he spoke. Amanda could imagine all the theories he'd hastily written down in his tight scrawl.

'Not that I know of,' her voice sounded cold, detached.

'We're still treating this as a missing persons case,' Shane insisted.

'Why wouldn't you?' Amanda demanded tersely. 'My husband is still missing.'

'Yes.' Clearing his throat, Shane reached for his tie and loosened it slightly. 'But eye witnesses at the service station remember your husband being alone. He showed no signs of stress, or a struggle.'

'That doesn't mean anything,' Amanda unclasped her hands to smack them against the table. The wood shook fearfully at the impact. 'Just because someone wasn't shoving him up against the cash point and threatening him doesn't mean that he's not in danger,' she raged. 'Someone must have forced him to take that money out, to leave his van.'

'Or he just didn't want us to trace him. He ditched his bank cards in favour of relying on cash.'

Amanda stared at Shane, feeling as though he'd just kicked her in the chest, knocking the air out of her lungs. She gasped as she tried to compose herself.

'Look, Amanda, we don't know anything for certain yet,' he was reaching across the table, trying to bridge the gap between them, but he'd need more than his slender fingers to create an olive branch. Amanda jumped up, pushing her chair out. It scraped noisily against the terracotta tiles on the kitchen floor.

'My husband is *missing*,' her chest heaved as she said the words. Hot, salty tears began to trace their way down her reddened cheeks. 'I have to find him.'

'Let's look at the facts,' Shane remained sitting, peering up at her with hooded eyes, which told of the sleepless nights he'd recently suffered through. He began listing each fact on his fingers, his voice level as though they were back on the beach drunk on cider and sunshine debating who would win in a fight; Wolverine or Superman.

'His phone has been disconnected; he's withdrawn a chunk of money and abandoned his van. These often signify someone who wants to disappear.'

'That all means nothing,' Amanda snapped. 'It's just circumstantial evidence, or whatever the hell you call it.'

'Like I said, in previous cases that followed a similar pattern, the missing person in question usually didn't want to be found.'

'What do you know?' Amanda hated herself for crying, for falling apart whilst Shane was remaining so annoyingly together. It felt too much like all their old arguments. She wiped her palms against her cheeks and tried to steady her breathing. 'You don't even work on missing persons; it's not your department.'

'You're right, I don't,' Shane agreed. He was standing up now, smoothing down his jacket. 'I work in homicide, which is where I often see people who have been abducted. My professional opinion, for what it's worth, is that your husband hasn't been abducted.'

'Will, his name is Will.'

'I promise you that if your husband wants to be found then I'll find him.'

Amanda sniffed as a few more tears silently bled down her cheeks. There was a time when she held a promise from Shane in the highest regard. Back then, if he'd made a promise, he'd never break it. But in recent years she'd lost count of all the promises that existed between them which had now been shattered into a thousand regret-filled pieces.

They'd promised each other forever.

Amanda refused to let herself think of that night on the beach beside a bonfire when Shane had knelt down in the sand and told her that nothing could ever come between them, that they would forever be two hearts beating as one.

'You just need to stay strong,' Shane was staring at her from across the other side of the kitchen. He was lingering in the doorway as though he were unsure if he should leave. Or perhaps he was caught in a web of all their tangled memories as she was. Amanda swept her gaze around the small room. How many times had she and Shane stood against the oak table and kissed? How many times had he cupped her face in his hands and stared deep into her eyes as though their blue were as vast and infinite as the ocean? Amanda drew her fingers through her hair and swept away her memories of what had once been. She needed to focus on the present, on the man who was missing from her life. The one she could still bring home.

'Bring him back to me,' Amanda pleaded. Her fingertips spun the golden band which was a permanent reminder of her promise to Will. A promise she wasn't prepared to break.

'I'll do everything I can,' Shane nodded briskly and shoved his hands deep into his jacket pockets.

'I just want him back,' Amanda stated tearfully. 'I just want him home.'

*

The breeze held on to the remaining heat of the day as it whipped around Amanda's bare legs. It felt good to feel the sand between her toes. She slowly paced along the beach, the setting sun causing the sky above to burn the brightest shade of red.

'Get some fresh air,' her mother had urged when she'd walked into the kitchen and found Amanda stood frozen beside the oak table, her cheeks flushed and her lips twisted in a grimace. 'It will do you good,' the older woman had said, insistent as she ushered Amanda out of the house.

At the back of the garden there was a small gate and beyond that an overgrown set of steps which precariously led down to the beach. As a little girl Amanda wasn't allowed to traverse the cliff-side path alone, but when she was with Shane and John it was a rule the three of them regularly flouted. Together they'd pick their way down to the shoreline and then race across the sand before letting out high-pitched screams as the icy waves broke against them.

The beach was quiet now. All the tourists had packed up and headed inland. Shielding her eyes against the sun, Amanda could see a few solitary figures walking their dogs as the waves gently lapped at their feet. This was always the time Amanda liked best. When the sun was setting and the world felt serenely still as it braced itself for yet another night. It was on such balmy summer nights that she'd steal down the path with Shane. Together they'd sit beneath the stars and kiss one another until their lips were numb.

Amanda angrily kicked at the sand. It danced up around her like a dust cloud. She shouldn't be thinking about Shane. She tossed a hand through her loose hair, physically pushing any memories of him back into the recesses of her mind. She should be thinking about Will.

He hadn't liked the cliff-side path. He'd peered down at it warily and shaken his large head.

'Now that doesn't look safe.'

'It's perfectly safe, I promise,' Amanda had already taken a few steps ahead. The sun was low in the sky; if they didn't move soon they'd lose what little daylight remained.

'No way,' Will had shaken his head again and folded his thick arms across his chest, strengthening his protest. 'It's too steep and overgrown.'

'It's perfectly fine, you big baby,' Amanda called out, taunting him as she continued to pick her way further down, carefully edging closer to the beach. After several more steps, she heard Will loudly sigh in defeat.

'If I fall and break my back it's on you,' he shouted.

'It's no problem, we're married now, there's such a thing as life insurance, you know,' Amanda had called back, grinning as she teased him.

'That's cold,' Will's voice boomed down to her. She could still only hear him, not see him. 'I never realized my wife could be so cold.'

Eventually they'd reached the beach.

'See,' Amanda had eagerly taken Will's hand and pulled him towards the waves which were idly rolling in. 'Isn't it beautiful?'

She'd watched Will's eyes widen as he took it all in. With the setting sun, everything was tinged with a crimson hue as though they'd stepped right into some majestic painting.

'It's beautiful,' he breathed softly. 'I've never seen anywhere like it.'

'I know, right?' Amanda had eagerly tucked herself up in the crook of his arm, beneath his broad shoulder.

'You're lucky to live here.'

Together they'd walked along the surf. Amanda shivered deliciously as the icy water washed over her bare feet.

'What was your home like?' she wondered, tilting her head to peer up at Will. He stared blankly ahead at the quiet beach, seemingly lost in his own thoughts. 'Will?'

He blinked and looked down at her, offering her an apologetic half-smile.

'Your home,' she prompted, 'what was it like?'

'Nothing like this,' Will sighed. 'It was all steel buildings, busy streets and families crammed in on top of one another. Growing up having your own bed was considered a luxury. Space was definitely a premium back then.'

'You had a big family?'

'I guess,' Will replied vaguely as his gaze became distant.

'Didn't you say you had a brother? Did you guys share a room or anything?'

'Uh-huh,' Will continued to stare into space.

Amanda struggled to imagine it. She was an only child. When she was little it was just her and her parents. The original musketeers. Then she met Shane and John. And then she turned twelve and her family's trio went down to two. Amanda looked at her feet, wanting to talk about Will's family, which were still a mystery to her instead of her own heartbreak.

'So you had a big family?'

'Sure,' Will agreed. He was always doing that; just adapting to Amanda's perception of him without really giving anything away himself.

'It's a shame none of them can make the wedding,' Amanda leaned away from Will so that she could lace her fingers through his. Their wedding date was just a month away. Soon she'd be Amanda Thorn. A thrill of excitement danced down her spine at the thought of it. She felt like a superhero preparing to take on a new identity.

'It's a long way for them to come,' Will replied bluntly. 'Besides, we were never that close.'

'Not even with your brother?'

Amanda imagined the two brothers being thick as thieves. Crammed together in a tiny little bedroom as though they were living in Mother Hubbard's shoe, she thought they'd get up to all sorts of adventures. It would have been like a non-stop playtime. Only Will wasn't smiling wistfully. His face hardened as though his features were cast in stone.

'He was killed,' he stopped walking and looked out to the sea, towards the placid water, which though calm on the surface hid a plethora of secrets in its depths.

'That's terrible,' Amanda squeezed his hand. She wanted to say more but something stopped her. The hair on the back of her neck and arms bristled, warning her that she was close to something terrifying. Looking further up the coast, she saw it; the sheer cliff side where the birds came to nest. At its base there was no sandy beach, only waves scratching against the rocks desperately trying to reclaim the land. Sucking in a breath, she raised her gaze to peer at the cliff edge, but it was concealed in shadows, already lost to the night as the sun had almost completely set.

'I don't talk about my family,' Will told her. 'And I don't want to. Some things are better left unsaid.'

Amanda shakily released the breath she'd still been holding as she kept staring up at where the cliff edge was, though she saw only darkness. 'Yeah,' she agreed tightly, 'some things are better left unsaid.'

*

The sand grew damp and compact beneath Amanda's feet. She ceased walking and looked around. She was half a mile from the precarious little path behind her mother's house. Ahead of her the beach would soon get eaten up by the sea. Amanda turned back before she could look upon the cliff edge which had nearly claimed her life. Crouching down, she stuck a finger into the wet sand and drew two initials, connecting them with a looped &.

A & W

She didn't dare tack on a forever or even an infinity symbol.

Chewing on her lip, she wondered where her husband had gone. Why he was seemingly running away from her. Was he even running? But then why leave the van? Amanda chewed so hard on her lip that her mouth became filled with the coppery taste of her own blood. Scorning herself, she swept her foot across the initials, blurring them so that they became barely readable.

'He's coming back,' she promised herself. Whatever was going on there had to be an explanation for it all. Will loved her. You didn't run away from someone you loved. She began hurrying back towards the steep little path home, her steps sinking into the sand leaving a brief imprint of her movements. Questions pounded in her mind like a relentless hammer trying to break through impenetrable rock.

Why leave? Why disconnect his phone? Why not at least call her from a payphone and let her know he was okay? What had she done wrong to deserve that kind of callous treatment? Didn't he care about her anymore? Had he ever truly cared for her? Had it all been a lie? And where was Will now?

Amanda was panting by the time she reached the base of the cliff-side path. Looking up, she saw only darkness, but thankfully she could plot her way up and down it blindfolded.

I promise you that if your husband wants to be found then I'll find him. She thought of Shane's promise, clinging to it. Shane would bring him back. He was a great detective. If anyone could find Will it was him.

Halfway up the path, Amanda froze. One word in Shane's promise taunted her, undermining all her hopes.

If.

9

The light from within the little house with the leaded windows guided Amanda the rest of the way up the cliff-side path. Stealing her way through the shadows in the garden like a cat in the night, she glanced in through the front room window and saw her mother sat neatly on the sofa in a full-length cream nightie. Her dark hair was loose and tumbled in tightly packed waves down her back. The television wasn't on and the glass of red wine resting on the coffee table appeared untouched. Corrine was focused on something in her lap; a heavy book. The ends of each thick page were gilded in silver and shone as they caught the light. Amanda ground her teeth together. She recognized the book and knew exactly what her mother was looking at.

She entered the house like a tornado; all loud fast movements in a flurry of activity. Amanda bounded into the front room, startling her mother whose head snapped up from the book the second her daughter burst in.

'What are you doing with that?' Amanda demanded accusingly.

'Oh,' Corrine stroked her fingertips across the open page. Her lips were downturned with sorrow and her eyes were red as though she were about to cry. 'I was just reminiscing.'

'No, you were just picking apart my husband.' Amanda was still stood up, she pointed at her mother and then at the wedding album the older woman was cradling in her lap. 'I bet you were sat here ranting on about the lack of guests on his side, like you always do.'

'Actually, no,' Corrine patted the vacant spot on the sofa beside her. Amanda wanted to resist the invitation but she found her legs crumpling as she sat down and peered at the open page in the album. 'I was thinking about how happy you looked on your wedding day.'

In the photograph Amanda was walking up the aisle in her simple ivory dress, escorted by her mother who was decked out in a fuchsia two-piece dress suit. While Corrine's usually cheerful face was pinched with sadness, Amanda's smile was radiant and provided enough light in the image for both of them.

The wedding had been a simple affair. It had been a joint decision since Amanda loathed the idea of being the centre of attention and so few guests were attending that it seemed pointless to indulge in an elaborate celebration. Amanda had worn a strapless ivory dress she'd found in Debenhams whilst Will had rented a suit which miraculously managed to house his broad shoulders. There had been a knot in her stomach as she walked up the small aisle at the registry office towards him. But when she turned to look at him and saw the beginnings of a nervous smile pulling on the corners of his mouth the knot untangled.

'I now pronounce you husband and wife.'

The registrar had finally relinquished her formal demeanour as she gave the proclamation.

'You may kiss the bride.'

Will's kiss had been gentle upon Amanda's lips, lacking the hunger he'd always displayed when they were dating. 'You're my wife now,' he'd whispered as they parted, his voice low enough for only her to hear. 'And I'll protect you. Always.' His hand found the small of her back and they turned to face the applause of their gathered guests.

I'll protect you.

It was easy to feel safe around Will. He was so tall, so broad. The human equivalent of the Titanic; seemingly unsinkable. When Amanda placed her hand in his, she lost the feeling that had haunted her since the day at the cliffs – the feeling that she was falling. She knew that Will's arms would always be strong enough to catch her, no matter what.

But now her steel ship of a husband was gone. And she was lost at sea. Alone.

'I was so nervous about giving you away,' Corrine recalled. She sniffed fiercely and pulled her mouth into a tight line. 'But you were so happy,' her voice cracked as she rested her hand on Amanda's beaming image. 'You told me that you were marrying the man of your dreams.'

Amanda smiled and leaned against her mother, remembering it all so well. On the day of her wedding she'd been all aflutter with nerves. She felt like every part of her was held together with the most fragile of fibres. It was only when she saw Will waiting for her at the end of the aisle at the start of the ceremony did her nerves calm, did her heart start to hammer out a more regular beat. He was the lighthouse in the storm, calling her to safety. He'd turned and smiled at her, a pillar of strength and classically handsome in his suit. He looked as though he'd stepped off the set of some old Hollywood movie. He just oozed that sort of charm and timeless appeal.

'But that's the thing,' Corrine snapped the album shut with such sudden force that Amanda jumped. 'He was always the man of your dreams, Mandy. He never became a reality. How could he when you placed him on such a pedestal?'

Amanda wasn't sure what had annoyed her more – being told that she idolized Will too much or hearing the nickname which she'd insisted had died with her beloved father. He was the only one she ever allowed to call her Mandy and she intended to keep it that way.

'Somehow I knew you'd manage to turn this all around to have a dig at me,' Amanda pushed herself away from her mother but remained sat on the sofa. She didn't have the energy to get up. Her legs throbbed from the long walk to and from the beach. She'd forgotten how steep the cliff-side path could be. Despite her daily jogs in the woods, she wasn't as fit as her teenage self, who could race up and down the path to her heart's content with no concern about growing tired or starting to ache.

'I'm not having a dig,' Corrine's hands were resting on the cover of the album, which was embossed with Amanda and Will's names in silver lettering. 'I'm just wondering why your husband would leave you all of a sudden like this if he was truly the great man you believed him to be.'

'He's *missing*,' Amanda hissed the word. 'The police are looking for him. Shane is looking for him. They will find him.'

'What about his phone being disconnected? And the van? He just ditched it.' Corrine wondered quietly, peering out at Amanda from the corner of her eyes.

'I should have known you'd be lurking somewhere listening in,' Amanda raged.

'Just ask yourself,' Corrine pleaded, 'do you truly believe he was taken, or did he leave?'

Amanda wiped her hands across her eyes and refused to answer the question, even when she asked it herself.

'The phone, leaving the van. What does it all mean?' Corrine pressed, still clutching the wedding album on her lap.

Amanda closed her eyes and wished that her dad was there. Her entire body felt raw from how much the desire for his return burned in her veins. If Ivor was there he'd know what to do, what to say, how to make her feel better. He'd take the little information that they had and make sense of it. But then he'd have read Will long ago with just a simple handshake. Amanda's father had a gift for assessing people. And he didn't waste his time with those he deemed to be unworthy and harbouring a cruel heart. Locals thought him aloof and distant, but Amanda knew the truth; her father was just picky about who he chose to care about. And the fact that he loved her above anyone else made her feel wonderfully privileged and special. No one else had made her feel that way until she met Will. When his eyes met hers she felt as though he'd picked her out in a crowd, had assessed her heart with only a look and deemed her worthy.

It had never been like that with Shane because she knew him. She'd read the darker parts of his soul growing up along with her own. Like two little weeds, they'd grown up together, side by side, vying for the same scrap of sunlight. Amanda got to see all the parts of Shane, including those which he'd usually hide. She knew about the twenty pounds he'd once stolen from his mother's purse, about the badger he accidentally killed when he borrowed his brother's scooter one rainy night. She even knew about all the girls he'd messed around with other than herself.

Shane had never been a book of secrets like Will had been. He'd always revealed his heart to her in its entirety. But it meant that he never got the pedestal

'I don't know what it means,' Amanda sighed, slowly opening her eyes. 'I wish I did.'

'Well it has to mean something,' Corrine deduced contritely. 'People don't go around withdrawing hundreds of pounds and leaving vehicles for no reason.'

'Shane said the police will search the van for clues when they collect it.'

'Do you think they'll find any?'

Amanda looked down at the faded floral carpet in the lounge, ignoring her mother's piercing gaze. She knew what Corrine was getting at; she was now supporting the same theory as Shane.

If your husband wants to be found.

Amanda and Will were happy, weren't they? They loved one another and had a beautiful home. Admittedly they rarely talked about the future, but it was because they were still getting to know one another, still enjoying the last of the honeymoon phase.

'Where would he go?' Corrine was lifting a hand from the wedding album to squeeze Amanda's forearm. 'He has to have gone somewhere, people don't just disappear into thin air.'

Amanda frowned. Where would Will go? She'd spent so long assuming he'd been kidnapped, taken from her, that she hadn't stopped to consider that he'd left under his own volition, that he was actually now en route to another place.

To another family.

The thought made her blood turn to ice in her veins. Amanda shivered.

'You know him better than anyone,' Corrine whispered soothingly.

'Do I?' Amanda wondered aloud.

'Of course you do. You're his wife. Where would Will go? Where did he have family, friends, connections?'

'Home,' Amanda didn't like the way the word instantly popped out of her mouth. It felt like she was betraying herself and the sanctity of her marriage. 'He'd go home,' she repeated. Only she didn't mean the marital home that she and Will legally shared. She meant his original home, the one he rarely spoke of, the one which existed due North, all heather-clad hillsides and vast mist-covered lochs.

'Scotland?' Corrine sounded surprised and a little alarmed.

'Scotland,' Amanda deadpanned. 'It's the only thing that makes any sense even though nothing seems to be making any sense right now. Scotland,' she repeated, her voice low, 'it's all I've got to go on.'

*

Amanda couldn't sleep. She tossed and turned all night beneath the purple sheets of her childhood bed. Each time she closed her eyes she saw Will. Only now his smile wasn't kind, it was menacing. And his embrace wasn't solid and supportive, it was bone-crushingly tight. Amanda sat up, gasping and clawing at her throat. The sheets around her were soaked in her own sweat. Breathing hard, she leaned forward and pulled back the curtain. It was still dark outside. Stars twinkled overhead as Tremwell Bay rested.

Pulling herself out of bed, Amanda flicked on the light and reached for her bag which she'd hurriedly tossed her belongings into when she left her house. After a few seconds of rummaging she located her laptop. She found its sleek surface comforting as she lifted it out of the jumble of clothes she'd packed.

Amanda tucked the laptop under her arm and headed downstairs. She turned on numerous lights as she journeyed through the small house, stopping in the kitchen for a glass of water before opening up the French doors and stepping out into the cooled even air. Her exposed skin prickled against its brisk touch as she sat down on a cushioned bench beneath an outdoor wall light. Amanda opened up her laptop, typed in her log-in details and then headed back inside to fetch her cardigan.

When she came back out to the bench, she found her mother sat upon it, gazing out towards the ocean which glistened beyond the clifftop beneath the silvery light of the moon.

'Mum?' Amanda tightened her cardigan around her. 'Sorry, did I wake you?'

'I wanted to make sure you were okay,' Corrine had thrown on a long turquoise dressing gown. Her slipper-clad feet poked out from the base of it. Like most of her clothes, her slippers were elaborate. They were adorned with feathers and sequins and glistened beneath the outdoor lights as exquisitely as any star.

'I couldn't sleep,' Amanda explained as she picked up her laptop and sat down. 'I keep thinking about Scotland.'

She typed a few searches into her laptop and sat back as the data collected on her screen.

'Your internet here is terrible,' she grumbled as the device loudly laboured.

'You used to spend hours out here,' Corrine recalled with a

chuckle, 'you'd bunch up beneath your duvet in the winter months and drag your computer out on to this bench so that you could chat with Shane.'

Amanda laughed. She dreaded to think how many hours she'd clocked up chatting away to Shane on MSN messenger. They'd type little messages to each other all through the night as though they hadn't just spent the entire day together.

'Will rarely talks about his family,' Amanda said as her fingers gracefully danced across the keyboard of her laptop.

'I remember you saying he lost a brother.'

'He said he was killed.'

'Ah. You felt like that connected you both. Because he understood loss.'

'But he never actually said his name, or age' Amanda continued, talking almost as quickly as she typed. 'And I never pressed him on it because I just assumed it was too painful to talk about.'

She was typing hard and fast, running numerous searches and pushing her mother's limited internet access to its capacity.

'You think that's where he's gone, back to his family?'

'Where else could he have gone?' Amanda shrugged. More typing, more searches.

'If he's gone there, why wouldn't he just tell you?' Corrine wondered logically.

'I don't know. Maybe it was too upsetting for him. Maybe someone else has died.'

She searched for Will's name. For his family. For his hometown up in Scotland. She searched for deaths of any relations with the surname Thorn. All of the searches yielded no results. There was nothing about Will. It seemed it wasn't just on his social media that he was a ghost. Amanda needed to dig deeper, but she couldn't do that at her Mum's. She needed the speed of her fibre-optic broadband.

'I need to go home,' Amanda declared decisively as she stood up, closing her laptop.

'What, now?'

'It's not like I'm able to sleep,' she was marching purposefully back into the house.

'Amanda,' Corrine was calling to her from where she was pulling the French doors closed.

Amanda spun around, keen to act on impulse and carry on

with her search back home.

'Just be careful how deep you dig.'

'Why?'

'Because you might discover something you wish you hadn't found.'

'The only thing I care about finding is my husband,' Amanda replied forcefully.

*

After unlocking her front door, Amanda stood in the hallway absorbing the silence. She held a breath, expecting to hear doors opening upstairs and Will's heavy footsteps echoing across the landing as he peered over the banister and demanded to know why she was wandering about so late. But the house was silent.

Amanda checked every room. Each time she pushed open a door and flicked on a light, she imagined finding Will asleep. But each room was empty. No one had returned there since she'd left for her mother's. Her shoulders dropped in disappointment and she felt foolish for having dared to hope that Will might have miraculously returned.

The percolator gurgled loudly as Amanda brewed herself a fresh coffee. She could already feel her senses starting to dull as exhaustion crept up on her. And she refused to sleep, not yet. She couldn't rest until her curiosity was satiated. With coffee in hand, Amanda took her laptop up to its usual resting place in her study. She switched it back on and felt her body lighten with relief as it accessed relevant searches with lightning speed.

Fuelled by caffeine, Amanda abandoned the regular search methods she'd been using and opened up a new browsing window, one where her search history wouldn't be recorded. She resurrected her Lambchop identity on numerous dubious websites and began a more thorough, less legal search.

She searched for Will Thorn. For his date of birth. For any family members. As Lambchop Amanda could access police records, hospital databases. If there was a single shred of truth in anything Will had told her about his family, then her hacker abilities would find it.

But there was nothing. She couldn't even find Will's birth certificate.

'What the hell?' Amanda propped her head up in her hands. It didn't make sense. How could Will just not exist online? Had someone already tampered with his records, hidden them from even her expertly intrusive eye?

Outside, the darkness had brightened to grey. Soon the sun would be rising. Amanda stretched, pulling out the knots which had settled in her joints. As she stretched, her mouth widened into an epic yawn. She was shattered. Her latest search on her laptop blurred before her tired eyes.

'Okay, okay,' Amanda logged out of her Lambchop accounts and closed her laptop. Wearily she stalked her way across the landing towards her bedroom. She pulled the curtains closed, keen to block out the new day. She could already feel the warmth in the air, signalling that it was going to be yet another beautiful summer's day. How could the weather taunt her so much? Amanda didn't want sunshine. She wanted heavy pewter clouds and rain that bounced off the pavement. She wanted thunder and flashes of bright lightning. She wanted the world to shake.

'Where are you?' Amanda muttered to herself as she climbed into bed. She wriggled over to Will's side, pressing her head into his pillows and breathing in his scent. She closed her eyes, wishing she was running her fingers through his thick hair instead of pressing a pillow against her face.

Had Will really headed back to Scotland? How did he even intend to get there without his van? Was he going to board a train? Had he already left? If so he'd be even harder to find. But she would find him.

Amanda made the promise to herself as her eyes closed and her breathing slowed. She turned and hugged Will's pillow to her chest. She would find her husband no matter what. Even if she had to act outside of the law. Shane wouldn't stop her; he'd turn a blind eye like he always used to do.

As Amanda drifted off to sleep she thought of the smiling bride she had been in her wedding pictures. Will had been her knight in shining armour waiting for her at the end of that aisle. Amanda had felt so certain that he'd do anything for her, that he'd always keep her safe. The worst part of losing Will was losing that certainty. Because even if she found him and he came home, could she ever claim back that feeling?

10

The doorbell.

Its shrill sound shattered the silence within the house. Amanda's eyes flew open, her heart instantly racing.

The doorbell rang again, just as loud and insistent. Throwing herself out of bed, Amanda managed to tug on a long cardigan over her short pyjama set before she hurried out of her bedroom. She powered down the stairs and into the hallway.

Golden sunlight illuminated the lower floor of the house. Dusk was approaching. How long had she been asleep?

She blinked hopefully at the shadow of a man on the step. Had Will finally returned to her?

Pulling open the front door, Amanda swept her hair out of her face along with any further questions.

'Hey,' Shane smiled awkwardly. He was in his grey suit, his pale blue tie already loosened. In his hands he held two brown paper bags and Amanda could smell the takeaway they contained.

'I guess you were expecting someone else,' Shane's smile fell as he tugged at his tie.

Amanda rubbed at her eyes, realizing that her face must have given away her disappointment.

'No,' she wrapped her cardigan tightly around herself, 'I mean, yes. I hoped you were Will.'

Shane pulled his lips into a thin line and nodded.

'Aren't you working?' Amanda stared at the bags he was holding.

'I was,' Shane raised the bags slightly. 'But then I finished, was starving and figured I needed to drop in on you so, you know,' he shrugged shyly, 'I thought I'd kill two birds with one stone.'

Amanda stepped aside so that he could come in.

'Your Mum said you were here.' Shane explained as he slipped past her. The smell of Chinese food flooded Amanda's senses and her stomach grumbled appreciatively. She realized that she hadn't eaten all day.

'Sounds like you're hungry,' Shane laughed lightly.

'I keep forgetting to eat,' Amanda sighed as she led Shane towards the kitchen and plucked two plates from the cupboards before turning on the percolator.

'How are you holding up?' Shane settled himself on one of the stools.

The percolator boiled loudly as the dense aroma of fresh coffee mixed with the sweetness of the takeaway.

'I just keep going over everything in my mind. The money, the phone, the van.' Amanda emptied the contents of the two paper bags on to their plates. She paused briefly as she watched the fluffy rice tumble out of its plastic container. Shane had ordered her favourite: sweet and sour chicken with egg-fried rice. Had he remembered it was her favourite or was it merely a coincidence?

'That's partly why I'm here.'

'Partly?' Amanda's eyebrows shot up.

'Yeah,' Shane smiled and his green eyes glimmered mischievously, just as they always used to do when they were younger and he was withholding some secret from her. At first Amanda would usually resort to tickling the information out of him, but as she got older she found more effective methods of persuasion. Not that she could use any of those now. Her cheeks burned with shame as she tucked a loose strand of hair behind her ear. 'The team got a hold of the van, did a thorough forensics search on it.'

'And?' Amanda had to remind herself how to breathe. What if there had been blood in the van? Will's blood? What if he was hurt somewhere and she was busy having dinner with her ex?

'And there was nothing.' Shane swiftly put her out of her misery.

'Oh,' pressing a hand to her chest, Amanda sighed with relief.

'It also means we've got nothing to go on,' Shane added carefully.

Amanda eyed the relaxed way he sat at her kitchen counter, the sparkle in his eyes. For so long she and Shane had been strangers and now he was waltzing back into her life as if there had never been those years of separation.

'You don't think he's coming back, do you?' Amanda's voice was hard as she asked the question.

Shane flinched. She couldn't tell if it was in surprise or because he was hurt by the accusation.

'Do you?' he deflected the question back to her.

'You're the cop, you tell me!' Amanda flared.

'You're the wife, you tell me!'

Amanda groaned in annoyance and skewered a chunky piece of chicken with her fork.

'No one knows anything right now,' Shane said quietly.

'I think you just came round here to piss me off,' Amanda narrowed her eyes at him but her tone was playful. 'You used to love pissing me off.'

'It's because you're so easy to wind up. Remember when I made you think our old flat was haunted?'

'You kept moving things and then denying it,' Amanda laughed. 'Like you kept leaving the scissors on the side or closing the curtains at random times.'

'You were convinced the place was haunted. I had to own up before you hauled a priest round to purify it,' Shane was laughing into his dinner.

'You scared me,' Amanda defended herself. 'And you were so believable with your lies. I genuinely didn't think you'd moved any of it. You were that good.'

'Why, thank you.'

Shane was grinning like the roguish boy he'd once been. Amanda could still see him beneath the suit, fighting to get out. She remembered the fun they'd had in their flat. But her memories swiftly darkened when she recalled all the nights he didn't come home, when she'd cry herself to sleep worrying about him.

'Won't Jayne the Pain wonder where you are?' Amanda asked, bringing a blast of ice into the room.

'She hated being called that in school,' Shane pointed his fork in Amanda's direction.

'Then she shouldn't have been such a bloody pain.' Jayne had been the kind of girl who only cared what guys thought of her. She saw all girls as competition and something to be eliminated. And she hated Amanda because of her friendship with John and Shane. Jayne was forever saying wicked, barbed things about her. The kind of things which haunt you past your childhood and into your adult life.

Jayne had been the one to start the rumour about Amanda's

Dad. About how he'd died in a drink-driving accident. But that had never been the case. There had been ice on the road. He'd lost control of his car. The truth did nothing to dilute Jayne's lies. She used her forked tongue to spread vicious rumours about Amanda's father. Somehow Shane had seemed able to forget all of that, look past it. Maybe Jayne had even apologised to him about it but she'd never extended such a courtesy to Amanda.

'How can you even stand to be with her?' Amanda raged, the pain of the memories, of all the scornful words becoming too much. She felt hot and agitated as though her blood were boiling up within her veins. 'She's horrid, Shane, utterly horrid. And you know what she put me through.'

Now there was no mistaking Shane's expression. He looked ashamed, like the little boy who had once stolen from his mother's purse. He opened his mouth and then snapped it shut again.

'I'm sorry,' Amanda raised a shaking hand to her damp eyes. 'It's none of my business who you date. It's not my place to care. I'm just so upset over Will and—'

Shane reached towards her and grabbed her free hand. His skin was so warm, so soft. His touch wasn't as hardened as Will's was.

'I want you to care who I date,' he was staring into her eyes, really staring. It was as if she were suddenly the only light source in the world and if he looked away from her he'd forever be plunged into eternal darkness.

She was suddenly acutely aware of every fibre in her body, of the head radiating away from Shane's touch, burning up her arm. It had been so long since he'd held the power to set her on fire that she didn't think he still could. She snatched her hand away from him before the burn could become unbearable.

'I want to find my husband,' Amanda's voice was barely a whisper.

'And we will find him,' Shane quickly hid behind a mask of professionalism. 'I'm doing everything in my power to aid the investigation.'

Amanda nodded gratefully.

'But just for now, for tonight, can't I have come round as a friend rather than an investigating officer?'

Amanda's lips twitched up into a smile. The house felt so

empty without Will in it. It would be nice to have some company for an evening.

'Sure,' she pushed herself off her stool and headed for the refrigerator. Pulling it open, she reached inside and withdrew two cooled bottles of beer.

'Well, I am off duty now,' Shane cocked an eyebrow at her.

'I'm sure Jayne can slither over here to pick you up later,' Amanda passed him the bottle.

'Yeah,' Shane laughed. 'I'm sure she can.'

*

With the French doors open, Amanda sat beside Shane at the wrought-iron patio table she'd picked up in a sale the previous summer. The sun had almost set, casting long shadows across the lawn.

'Your grass is in impressively good condition,' Shane nudged a nearby patch of almost perfect green blades with his foot.

'Will regularly flouts the hosepipe ban,' Amanda said, her voice mockingly low and suggestive. 'Please, Officer Perton, don't lock me up for it.'

Shane was laughing as he raised his beer to his lips.

'So your husband is house-proud?'

'Very.'

'You keep the place nice.'

'I do my best.' Amanda felt a little buzzed as she drank down her second bottle of beer. She felt warm and relaxed beneath the waning sun and strangely at ease in Shane's company. It was like they were back on the beach, beside a makeshift fire beneath a star-filled sky. They had so easily slipped back into their old dynamic filled with good-natured banter. Why had Amanda avoided him for so long, held him at such a distance?

'Do you often think about our old place?' Shane threw her a sideways look and Amanda felt her heart constrict in her chest. This was why she kept Shane at bay. Because of all of their history. Because deep down there was a part of her that would always love him, that would always wonder what could have been if only they'd stayed together.

And love was like a delicate flower. It needed lots of sunshine and nourishment to grow. Amanda couldn't have let her relationship with Will be damaged by the shadow of what she'd had with Shane.

'You mean the rat-attack flat?' Amanda was laughing, the beer in her system making her giddy and light-headed.

'How could you give it such a nickname?' Shane protested playfully. 'We had rats there *twice*. That's it.'

'Remember when you found that one in the shower? You screamed like a little girl.'

'I did not.'

'You did too,' Amanda giggled. 'You screamed the bloody place down, then you made me go in and corner it before the council showed up. You were always such a bloody wimp.'

Amanda tugged at the label on her half-empty beer bottle. She knew that the rat had been lucky that she lived with Shane and not Will back then. Will would have surely killed it. He'd have been swift and efficient, but he wouldn't have let the rat live to see another day. He was brave like that. Heroic.

Amanda completely pulled the label off her bottle and dropped it down on the table. Or was Will ruthless with the way he handled things?

'You still thinking about him?' Shane noted the distant look in her eyes.

'How can I not?' Amanda put down her bottle, suddenly losing her desire to drink.

'I mean, we've been through everything,' Shane pushed his hand through his hair, leaving it sexily dishevelled. Amanda forced herself not to notice. 'He left first thing in the morning while you slept. You guys hadn't argued or anything.'

There he was, listing events on his long fingers. If Amanda closed her eyes she could almost smell the oaky burn of their beach fire, could feel its heat pressing against her face.

'There was nothing else out of the ordinary, nothing you've not previously reported to the police?'

Amanda straightened in her chair. There was something. She suddenly realized there was. It was like seeing a familiar actor on TV but struggling to pinpoint how you know them. The information was in her mind, she'd just not accessed it before. She'd been so consumed with worry, with shock. Maybe it didn't even matter. Maybe it was nothing.

'Amanda?'

Her heart almost broke upon hearing the tenderness in Shane's voice. She remembered how he'd softly say her name in the dead of night when she'd been lost to yet another nightmare. He'd pull her back from the swirling waves and the jagged rocks with the strength of his voice. Then he'd wrap her in his arms and kiss her so deeply that she forgot all about what was haunting her.

'Amanda, what is it?'

'It's probably nothing.'

'What?'

'I'm pretty sure it's nothing.'

'Let me decide that.'

She reached for her bottle and beer and drained the last of its contents.

'Tell me,' Shane urged, using the voice he usually reserved for when he was trying to pry a secret out of her.

'There was a wrong number.' Amanda hated how lame she must sound. She was really grasping at straws now.

'A wrong number?'

'Yeah,' Amanda raked a hand through her hair, trying to focus on the memory which, thanks to the alcohol in her system, felt hazy. 'The night before Will disappeared, this guy called the house phone. He asked for someone and when I said they didn't live here he got weird.'

'Weird how?'

'Like insistent. Almost threatening.'

Despite the warmth of the evening the memory of the guy's tone left Amanda cold. She shivered and tucked her legs up beneath her, drawing her cardigan in tightly around her.

'Who was he asking for?'

'I...' Amanda groaned. 'I can't quite remember. And then later, when I told Will about it, he...' she smoothed her hands across her knees. 'I thought he'd find it funny. But he didn't. He actually seemed kind of spooked. He went to bed early and we didn't discuss it again. We didn't discuss anything.'

'And you don't remember the name the guy was asking for?' Shane pressed, leaning forwards.

'He had a Scottish accent. Kind of like Will's. But the name...' she rummaged around in the depths of her mind, searching for the answer.

'Like you say, it's probably nothing,' Shane was leaning back against his chair, drinking from his beer.

'Jake Burton.' Amanda blurted, smiling triumphantly. 'He was asking for Jake Burton.'

'Are you sure?' An edge had suddenly crept into Shane's voice.

'Yes,' Amanda scowled at him. 'I'm sure. The weirdo wrong number guy asked for Jake Burton. Told me that he must live here.'

'And what did you say?'

'What do you think I said, I told him he was wrong.'

'And you'd never heard that name before?'

'No,' Amanda was shaking her head. 'Why? Does it even matter? It was just some wrong number.'

'I need to go,' Shane was on his feet and straightening his tie.

'What, now?'

'Yes, I've just remembered that I left something back at the station.' He was powering back through her house, towards the hallway. Amanda had to run to keep up with him.

'What the hell is going on?' she shouted.

As Shane paused to turn and look at her, she wedged herself between him and the front door. She raised her chin and stared defiantly into his eyes. She used to love how in a certain light the green looked to be flecked with soft shades of blue.

'You're not leaving here until you tell me what's going on.'

'Nothing, I just need to go,' Shane took a step forward and reached around her, grasping the door handle. They were standing so close their chests were almost touching. Amanda could feel her breaths becoming laboured, her skin tingling in anticipation.

She remembered what it felt like to be kissed by Shane, to have his hands run down her body, exploring every burgeoning curve.

'Who is Jake Burton?' she asked breathlessly.

Shane was looking to her eyes, his lips parting and his head lowering.

'Who is he?' Amanda repeated stubbornly.

Clearing his throat, Shane straightened and eased back from her. 'I'll come by and check on you tomorrow. Until then keep everywhere locked up tight and secure.'

'Why?'

Shane opened the front door but Amanda hauled him back into the hallway by his shoulder.

'What aren't you telling me?'

Shane had never been good at keeping secrets. John and Amanda used to joke that he had the worst poker face. His lips would pull up in delight if he had a good hand or twitch down if he knew he was on to a loser.

'You can't lie to me,' Amanda warned.

'I know,' Shane smiled sadly at her, letting one hand rest on her shoulder. 'That's why I'm leaving.' He leaned in close to plant a solitary kiss upon her cheek.

'Who is Jake Burton?' Amanda demanded again.

'Do me a favour?' Shane was stepping out the door, preparing to leave. 'Stay off your computer. Don't go running any searches, don't go resurrecting Lambchop. You can't be involved in any of that shit right now, do you understand?'

'Then just tell me.'

'Let me go into the station, iron out some of the facts and then come and check in on you tomorrow, okay?'

'Shane, tell me,' Amanda was on the verge of tears. She wanted to scream 'who the hell is Jake Burton' until her lungs bled. She'd thought the wrong number was nothing, just a weird event, but what if it was the key to everything? What if she'd been looking for Will in all the wrong places?

'I can't tell you, not until I'm certain.' Shane was on the driveway, disappearing into the lengthening shadows of the night.

'Why not?'

There was a time when Shane would tell her anything regardless of his levels of certainty. His heart was as open to Amanda as it was to himself. During their years apart, how many secrets had they stored up from one another? How much had their hearts changed?

'I can't tell you,' Shane was raising his phone to his ear either to call a taxi, or worse, Jayne, for a lift to the station.

'Dammit, Shane, just tell me!'

Shane was turning away from her, leaning into his call. 'Some things once known can never be unlearned.'

'Shane!'

'I won't be the one to break you on this,' he was jogging away from her house, towards the pavement. 'Not until I'm certain.'

11

It was two days before Shane returned to Amanda's house. Two days of him ignoring her calls, two days when Will continued to fail to come home.

Sleep had become a foreign concept to Amanda. At night her house creaked and groaned so loudly that she feared that there was some dark entity lurking in the wall cavities. How had she never noticed these sounds before?

'Just come and stay at mine,' her mother urged. 'It's still your home, you know.'

But Amanda couldn't do that. She still had a job to do, bills that needed to be paid.

It was noon and she was still in her pyjamas. She'd been staring at her laptop's screen for the better part of twenty minutes. The glossy Diowater website was open in her main tab. It still needed a few tweaks until it was complete, but Amanda was struggling to summon up the energy to do even the smallest task.

She'd put her current client off for as long as she could. A bout of summer flu she'd said, coughing and spluttering into the phone. It was too painful to tell them the truth. She didn't need their pity, or worse, their alienation. She just needed their work.

The doorbell rang. It no longer held the hope for Amanda that it once had. Slowly she unfurled her legs and stood up, ambling out of the study. She didn't care that she was still in her pyjamas, didn't care that whoever was on her doorstep was being forced to wait as she made her languished procession through the house.

There was time for the doorbell again as she shuffled into the hallway. Amanda cursed the uninvited caller under her breath. She'd already accepted that she wasn't about to find Will standing in the doorway. Each time the doorbell rang it was for a delivery, or on one occasion for a uniformed guy wanting to read her gas meter.

Throwing open the door, Amanda greeted her caller with a

thunderous look.

'Hey,' Shane was there where her husband should have been. Only he wasn't in a suit. He wore dark denim skinny jeans and a yellow polo shirt. He'd managed to straddle the line between smart and casual, something Amanda knew he'd never have been able to accomplish without Jayne's intervention.

Both Shane and Amanda used to live in oversized hoodies and baggy jeans. They baulked at the idea of wearing something more smart, more fitted. Yet now Shane looked like he'd waltzed out of the pages of an Abercrombie and Fitch catalogue. Even his hair was stylishly gelled and pushed forward in a slight peak.

'Sorry, did I wake you?'

Amanda looked down at her own dishevelled appearance. Her cotton striped pyjama bottoms were crumpled, the vest top she was wearing had a huge coffee stain on it and she'd not brushed her hair since the previous morning. It sat matted upon her head like a most unsightly bird's nest. She stepped backward, feeling ashamed. Shane shouldn't see her like this. No one should. She was a mess in every conceivable way.

'I was up,' Amanda tried to run her fingers through her hair, but it was useless. She needed to do battle against it with her tangle tamer in order to look halfway decent.

'Oh,' Shane eyed her pyjamas.

'All right judgement,' Amanda snapped, feeling hostile. She knew how terrible she looked, she didn't need to see it reflected in Shane's eyes. 'Where's the slick suit today?'

'It's my day off,' Shane peered beyond her, looking inside, angling for an invitation.

'Come in,' Amanda stepped aside and let him breeze past her. She almost choked on his aftershave when he was close to her. Instead of a delicate spray that morning it smelt like he'd bathed in the stuff.

'So to what do I owe the pleasure?' she remained in the hallway, in no mood to entertain a visitor.

'Firstly, I owe you an apology,' Shane looked down at his hands. 'I shouldn't have run out on you the other day.'

'True.'

'Secondly I came here to tell you something. But you have to understand that it's strictly off the record. I'm not here in a professional capacity.'

Amanda cocked her head at him, her interest levels rising.

'Is this about Will?' she pressed.

Shane nodded stiffly.

'About the wrong number?'

He nodded again, though more reluctantly.

'What the hell is it?'

'Can we...' Shane gestured towards the kitchen. 'I'd rather we were sitting when we go over this.'

'Okay...'Amanda didn't like how Shane was behaving. He was stalling and she could see that his palms were slick with sweat. Why was he so nervous?

As she strode into the kitchen and turned on the percolator a fearful thought cut through her like a knife, causing her to double over.

Clutching at her sides, Amanda pondered the awful truth; what if Will was dead? What if that was why Shane was at her house, to deliver the terrible news to her in person?

'Have you found him?' she spun around to face Shane who was climbing onto one of the stools by the counter. Her eyes were wide and desperate.

'No,' Shane lifted a hand towards her and shook his head. 'It's not that, don't worry.'

The flames of panic within her cooled as the percolator shook and produced a fresh batch of coffee. Handing Shane a mug, she sat down beside him.

'Then what is it, Shane? Why are you here? Who is Jake Burton?'

'Woah, that's a lot of questions.'

Amanda frowned. Of course it was a lot of questions. She'd been left alone for two days to do nothing but stew on what little she knew about her husband's disappearance. She'd had to basically sit on her hands to stop herself from searching for Jake Burton, whoever the hell he was. But she wanted to heed Shane's warning, to hang back from the darknet and her contacts there, at least until she knew more. The last thing she wanted to do was invite danger to her doorstep.

'I've spent the last two days working the case,' Shane explained, tightly clutching his mug.

'And?'

'And I did some digging about this Jake Burton you mentioned. It's a pretty generic name, but I remember something coming up when I originally searched for missing persons cases in Scotland, trying to find a link.'

'Jake Burton is a missing person?' Amanda felt herself become stiff with fear.

'He was,' Shane stared into his drink, looking distressed. 'And then it was reported that he was dead.'

'Dead?' Amanda pressed, her voice rising. She felt like things had just got serious. Worryingly serious. 'Why the hell would someone call me asking for a dead person? It must be a different Jake Burton. It's a common enough name and—'

'Amanda,' Shane sighed as he said her name. 'What I'm about to tell you can't go beyond this room, do you understand?'

Amanda could only nod numbly. Shane looked so serious. And so scared. His fear was rubbing off on her. She nervously glanced around the room, half expecting to find someone pressed against the French doors trying to eavesdrop on them.

'And I'm here as a friend,' Shane stressed. 'Because you're not supposed to know any of this. Not yet. No one is.'

'Then why are you telling me?' Was Shane putting his job in jeopardy by telling her such secrets?

'I'm telling you—' Shane sucked in a long breath and then lifted his gaze to look directly at her. In his eyes he was the boy from the starlit beach, the boy she'd make pillow forts with, the first boy she gave her heart to. 'I'm telling you because I care about you. Because even though I should be professional in this, and detached, when it comes to you I just can't.'

Amanda didn't know what to say. Was Shane admitting that he still had feelings for her?

'Jake Burton,' he continued, 'and Will Thorn.'

It felt strange to hear Shane say Will's name, like hearing a child speak the name of a long-dead relative unprompted.

'What about them?'

'They're the same person.'

For a second Amanda was certain she'd just misheard him. 'Sorry, what?'

'Will Thorn *is* Jake Burton. Or at least he was. I found an old photograph of Jake Burton online from when he'd been arrested for a previous conviction. They're the same person, there's no doubt about it.'

'What?' Amanda felt like she was going to choke on her

surprise. Her entire mouth felt arid and dry as if she'd just spent a month travelling through a desert.

'When you said about the wrong number, and the name, something clicked. I remembered seeing the name during my initial searches. So I went back, I delved deeper, made some calls and accessed Jake Burton's criminal record.'

'I don't understand.' Amanda was wilting against the counter, crumbling in on herself like an old abandoned house whose foundations had finally rotted away enough for it to collapse in a dramatic display of rubble and dust.

'Jake Burton was a man with questionable connections.'

'Connections to what?'

'To people who I hope you never have to deal with.'

In movies depicting war Amanda remembered seeing soldiers get caught up near a blast. After being sprayed with shrapnel and debris the world suddenly went silent for them as they'd briefly lost their hearing. Whilst everything around them exploded, they were cocooned in their surreal cone of silence. That's how Amanda suddenly felt. Shane was still talking, she could see his mouth moving, but she couldn't hear what he was saying. She was still recovering from the explosion of learning that Will truly did have another life. And probably another family.

Shane had left his stool, was standing directly beside her and smoothing her hair out of her eyes. Slowly Amanda's hearing was returning to normal. 'Apparently Jake Burton did time in jail up in Scotland and was reported missing just under six years ago. Shortly after he was reported missing, he was reported dead.'

'So he might have another family? A wife? Children?' Amanda could barely breathe. She glanced around her kitchen suddenly distrusting every appliance, every unit. Will had been deceiving her all along. How was that even possible?

'I'm afraid we fear it may be more serious than that,' Shane dropped his hands to her shoulders and gently squeezed them.

'More serious than leading a double life?' Amanda could taste the tears which had fallen down her cheeks. She could feel her body trying to shake, to give into the shock of it all.

'We just don't have all the details yet, I need to dig more into Jake Burton's criminal past,' Shane's hands were now on her face, cupping her cheeks and tilting her gaze up to meet his.

'As soon as I know anything else I'll tell you. But I thought that you had a right to know the truth, Amanda. That Will isn't who he says he is.'

'But why?' It made no sense. He *was* Will Thorn. She'd seen his passport, his birth certificate when they got married. He had an identity. A life. 'Why would he lie?'

'That's what we need to find out,' Shane used his warm touch to wipe away some of her tears. 'But we will find out. You just need to sit tight and be patient, can you do that?'

'How can they be the same person?' Amanda was still struggling to fit it all together. Will Thorn was her husband. But then who was Jake Burton? And why had someone called her home asking for him? Her head ached so intensely that she feared her skull may crack as it tried to contain all her questions.

'I don't know yet,' Shane told her softly. 'But I'm here for you, Amanda. And I'm going to get you answers, I swear.'

'But,' Amanda greedily gulped down air, needing to steady herself. She felt like she could faint and scream all at the same time. Staring at Shane, she wanted to see more than pity in his eyes, she wanted to see answers.

'Who did I marry?' she rasped as she felt the world she knew, the world she had built with Will, come tumbling around her as flimsy and precarious as a house of cards.

12

Amanda slammed her front door closed, a part of her not even caring if she'd locked up properly. There was so much she didn't care about anymore. So many things were losing their meaning in Will's absence.

As she drifted down her driveway, Amanda's gaze swept across her car, parked up neatly in front of the house. Numerous trips down winding country lanes to her mother's cottage had dirtied it. The paintwork was dulled as it lay beneath a thin layer of grime and dust. Amanda's lips trembled as she considered what Will would say if he were there.

'Look at the state of your car,' he'd remark as he stood beside it, slowly shaking his head.

'It's fine,' Amanda would insist. Because to her it was. She didn't mind the dirt which clung to it. All she cared about was that the car was driveable. She'd never been one to shine her machine.

'I'm going to wash it,' Will would already be stalking back inside to seek out a bucket and sponge.

'Really, it's fine.'

But Will liked everything to be perfect. It was as if for him it wasn't enough that their lives were picture-perfect, they had to be immaculate in every way, right down to their cars or how he'd fold over the end piece of toilet paper.

'You treat this place like a show home,' Amanda would lament whenever she caught him straightening towels in the bathroom and picking up a speck of dirt from the floor.

'Because it is a show home. It's a palace and I intend to keep it that way.'

'Homes are meant to be lived in.'

'Homes are meant to be taken care of and cherished.'

'You realize the house doesn't have feelings, right? It can't hear you right now.' Whenever Amanda mocked Will his eyes would crinkle at the corners just slightly. She sometimes struggled to tell if he was humoured by her or annoyed.

Will was always striving for perfection.

Amanda reached her hand out towards her car and dragged a finger along the side of it, tracing a long line in the dirt. She cocked her head and looked at the car more intently. It was dirty enough to warrant a cheeky message on the back like *wash me* or *I like it dirty*. When Will eventually did come home, and Amanda had to keep believing that he would, it'd be funny if there was a message waiting for him on the back of her car, a message prompting him to give it a thorough clean. Because he was coming back, wasn't he? And when he did, everything would just go back to normal, right?

'Not that he'd need any additional incentive,' she muttered to herself as she rounded the end of the vehicle. She knew that the sight of her dirtied car would be more than enough to send Will into a cleaning frenzy. Amanda was holding her hand up, poised to write a message, but she instantly froze when she looked at the back windscreen as someone had beaten her to it.

In blunt lettering was a message waiting for her. Amanda stopped breathing as she read it, her chest tightening.

Where is Jake?

When her heart kicked back in it was working double time, thumping manically in her chest. Panicked, she looked around, searching the window of every nearby home, every cluster of bushes, as though she expected someone to just suddenly appear and claim responsibility for the message.

Amanda stared at the words.

Where is Jake?

Who could have written it? It surely had to be the same person who'd originally called asking for Jake Burton. Were they watching the house? Watching her right now?

Amanda felt cold. The icy sensation plunged right down to her core. Nervously she rubbed at her arms and kept glancing around. She felt so hideously exposed, as if she were standing there completely naked with everything laid out for everyone to see.

Had someone been at her house?

The question boomed through her head accompanied by

another, more primal, response.

Run.

Over and over she thought the word to herself like a relenting foghorn.

Run.

And so she ran.

＊

The sunlight on the ground was mottled as it streaked in through the canopy of leaves overhead. Amanda's feet pounded against the soft ground, snapping twigs underfoot. It was early morning and while most people were preparing to face the urban nightmare of rush-hour traffic Amanda was sprinting through the woods behind her home.

She passed only a handful of people as she ran, most of them out with their dogs. She'd nod stiffly in greeting and power past them. It felt good to be out of the house, to feel the fresh morning air all around her. She loved her early morning runs but now she needed it more than ever, needed to try and outrun the questions that kept snapping at her heels.

Where is Will?

Who is Jake Burton?

Quickening her pace, Amanda liked the pull she felt in her calf muscles. Her lungs began to ache in protest but she ignored the discomfort, pressing harder, moving faster.

She ran through a densely wooded area, expertly jumping over large roots which rose up out of the ground like abandoned corpses slumbering in the early morning sunlight. Amanda sped down a steep incline and almost collided with the grand oak tree at the base of it. But still she didn't stop. She swerved, her trainers briefly skidding on the soft muddy ground. And then she was running again. Hard and fast. She ran deeper into the woods, putting more distance between herself and her home with each fevered step.

Amanda's entire body throbbed as various muscles began to

catch fire. She couldn't remember the last time she'd pushed herself like this. But she wasn't prepared to stop. Not yet. If she was running then she wasn't thinking. And Amanda yearned to stop thinking more than anything else.

She ran down a narrow path. Outstretched branches pressed against her bare arms. Amanda knocked them aside, breathing hard as she kept on running. She tumbled out into a clearing and finally stopped for breath. Skidding to an abrupt halt, she doubled over and placed her hands on her knees, sucking in air.

Eventually she straightened and looked around. She knew the clearing she was standing in. It existed in the centre of the woods, like a foliage-filled heart. In February snowdrops carpeted the ground like freshly fallen snow, and then later in the season bluebells. It was a place of beauty, where the trees cleared to allow the sun to beat down unobscured. The branches of the trees, thick with luscious green leaves, swayed in a soft breeze as they stood circling her.

Amanda was still gulping in the fresh morning air, using it to put out the fires which had started to burn within her through overexertion. The clearing was usually a peaceful place, filled only with birdsong. But for Amanda it currently felt chaotic, just like the rest of her run had been. Her iPod was blaring in her ears so loudly that the music was surely getting seared on to her brain. It was angry music, full of powerful drums, screamed vocals and bluesy guitars. It was the music of her youth: Linkin Park, Papa Roach and Blink 182. She hadn't even deliberately selected the tracks, they'd just played, one after another, as if her iPod could read her mind better than she could.

It was the music Amanda had listened to with Shane. Together they'd lie on his bed, holding hands and listen to his CD player threaten to tear down his parent's terraced house with its booming sound. It was the music Amanda turned up so loud her eardrums threatened to bleed whenever they argued. It was the music her heart was broken to, and also the music that helped mend it.

Popping out one of her pure-white earbuds, Amanda reached into the pocket of her denim cut-offs and silenced her iPod. The angry base of a Linkin Park record was gone and the sudden vacuum caused by the abrupt lack of sound was unsettling. Amanda spun around, nervously taking in all the shadows which loomed at the edge of the clearing.

A twig snapped behind her. Then another. Was she alone? Or had someone followed her? It would have been easy enough to shadow her steps through the woods. With her music pounding in her ears she was oblivious to the world beyond her little bubble. Amanda's chest tightened as if a hand had forced its way down her throat and was now making a fist around her lungs, squeezing them like a stress reliever. Gasping, she leaned forward, her hands on her knees once more. Spots of light danced in her vision. Her legs buckled and she dropped down into the dirt. Amanda shuddered against the pain in her chest and tried to get her bearings. There was a metallic taste in her mouth and she swore she could hear the roar of the ocean even though it was over on the other side of town. And then everything went black.

*

'Hey, are you okay?'

Whoever was delivering the question sounded far away, at the end of a phone call that had poor reception.

'Hey, Miss. Drink some more water.'

Something soft and wet pressed against her leg as she felt cool water sliding down her throat. Amanda spluttered as her senses started to come back to her. She looked around, her eyes wide and distrusting.

She was still in the clearing in the woods. Only now instead of being on her knees in the centre, she was sat on a large log near the edge, close to the canopy of trees whose leaves whispered all around as if discussing what had just happened amongst themselves.

'Miss, are you okay?'

The soft wet thing pressed against her leg again. Numbly Amanda looked down. A small dog with deep brown eyes and brown and white fur was looking up at her, its expression a mixture of adoration and confusion.

'Hey, Rocky, leave her be.'

The little dog glanced away from Amanda back towards the owner of the voice who was asking all the questions. An elderly man with a kind face was staring at her. Despite the season, he was wearing a long khaki coat and jeans. Amanda recognized him as living on the edge of her estate, though it pained her to admit that she didn't know his name, or even if he lived alone.

'Ah, there's more colour in your face now,' the man smiled kindly at her. 'Rocky here found you. You must have fainted in the clearing. Got to be careful not to overdo the exercise, especially when it's so hot out.'

Amanda looked back towards the centre of the clearing. So she'd passed out. Had she really overdone it? Or was there more to it than that? Was everything with Will, Jake, whoever the hell her husband was, finally catching up with her? Was she now having physical reactions to all the stress?

'Drink some more water,' the man urged. 'And Rocky and me will walk you home. You live in them new houses by me, don't you?'

'Uh-huh.' Amanda managed to splutter out her response between swallowing down as much water as her chest would allow.

'I thought I recognized you. I'm Bill Connors,' he extended a rough hand towards her, which Amanda gingerly shook. As she did, she noticed that her own hands were trembling. As were her legs. It felt like her entire body was on a vibra plate and she was powerless to get off.

'You'll be right soon enough,' Bill reassured her. 'My wife was prone to fainting spells. She was a whippet of a thing too.'

Amanda forced herself to smile. Bill was being kind. If he and Rocky hadn't discovered her collapsed in the clearing who knew what might have happened to her, or who might have come along.

'You live with your husband, don't you? Big strapping fella. I've seen him out tending to your lawn. He's pretty house-proud, I admire that.'

Will. He was talking about Will. Amanda tried not to cry, but her body was past obeying her orders. Hot tears slid down her cheeks. Rocky became anxious at the sight and placed his paws on her leg and stared up at her face, his fluffy white tail wagging so furiously that Amanda feared it might fall off.

'Hey,' she knocked away her tears with the back of her hand and then fussed the adorable little dog. His tail wagged with increased fervour.

'Oh, he loves a fuss,' Bill stated with pride. 'He also can't stand to see a lady cry. Proper little gentleman that one.'

'He's gorgeous,' Amanda complimented Bill as she kept rubbing Rocky behind his ears. His soft brown eyes were glued to her, looking at her as though she were the most wondrous thing he'd ever discovered during his walks in the woods.

'I'll have to be careful he doesn't try and go home with you,' Bill joked. 'But we should really get you back to that husband of yours, he'll be worried. That's if you feel up to walking?'

Amanda stood up. Her legs wobbled beneath her as though they might buckle at any moment. 'I'll manage,' she breathed as Bill stepped close so that she could lean against him for support.

As they stumbled out of the clearing together, Amanda looked back at the wall of trees, listened to their whispers and studied the shadows which gathered between them. She used to think oak trees were grand and sturdy, capable of shielding the smallest of creatures from a storm. But now she saw how their long branches and the gnarled roots that sprouted from the ground could conceal countless secrets, could hide even the darkest of deeds.

*

Amanda promised Bill that she'd call her GP right away but only to get him to leave. She appreciated the old man's concern but she needed to be alone. Closing the door on Bill and Rocky, Amanda was surprised by how much she welcomed the icy solitude of the house. Since Shane's visit she'd started to think about how much Will had lied to her. How Will Thorn wasn't even his real name. A part of her still desperately wanted him to come home, but another more fearful part was scared about what additional truths she might uncover in her search for her missing husband.

Fear and anger raged within her, each trying to take hold. The message on her car burned in her mind. Who had done it? Had they followed her into the woods? Where was Will when she needed him in their home, needed him to protect her? She should report the message to the police. Shouldn't she? But it felt oddly foolish to call them up about a cryptic note on her car. Would it even help lead to Will? Maybe she could call Shane. He'd come over, look at the car, make some obligatory notes and assure her that it was nothing. Right? Or was it a clue, a thread to pull at which would lead her to her husband?

Amanda lashed out, kicking at the stool beside her in frustration. It clattered to the floor, banging loudly against the polished tiles. Her husband should have been home with her, should be fretting over her faint in the woods. But Will wasn't even answering his phone. It was disconnected.

'Dammit,' Amanda flung herself and grabbed the stool she'd been sat on. She lifted it off the ground and then threw it towards its partner which lay on its side on the floor. They banged together, metal grating against metal.

'Dammit,' Amanda lamented again, pounding her fists against the granite countertop. Her body felt weary and useless, but the rage within her needed to come out. Holding it all in was taking too much energy.

'Where are you?' she screamed to the emptiness. She couldn't even picture Will in that moment. Was he really off being Jake Burton, sat in the home of another family? It was too hard to believe. Amanda threw her fists against the countertop again.

Will had been the one to propose to her. They'd only been dating a few months. It had been a wonderful whirlwind of dinners, cinema dates and lingering kisses in the back of his car. He made Amanda feel like she was the centre of his universe. When he picked her up he was always on time, always called her when he said he would.

She'd felt herself falling right after their first kiss. She'd felt the power in his embrace but also been surprised by the tenderness. As the kiss deepened, Amanda knew in her heart that this was a man who she could willingly give all of herself to.

'Marry me,' his eyes had twinkled as he said the iconic words as an order rather than a question. It had been a whirlwind six months of dating. Amanda had gazed at the modest ring he'd presented as he stooped down on one knee. It was everything a proposal should be: honest, spontaneous and from the heart. It was everything Shane's proposal hadn't been.

Amanda baulked at the memory and stormed towards the fridge. Reaching inside, her hand hovered over a bottle of beer. Her fingertip tapped its bottle cap but then she changed her mind, grabbing the expensive bottle of vodka leaned up beside it. Amanda rarely drank vodka. Like so many things, it reminded her too much of Shane, of how they'd drink it with John and then take it in turns to spit it out on to their bonfire. It was a dangerous game, but back then that was the only kind they played. Amanda had been oblivious to what was at stake, like her heart.

The clear liquor slid down her throat as she drank it straight from the bottle. It was like an icy fire. Amanda spluttered, lowering the bottle. In a few seconds she'd be feeling the much-needed buzz of being drunk. She carried the bottle with her into the lounge. Grabbing a remote, she turned on her sound system and searched through her music until she found a particularly passionate Linkin Park track. Leaning back against her sofa, Amanda tipped the bottle to her lips and consumed more of its fire. She knew she shouldn't, knew it was dangerous in the wake of her faint. But she needed the release. Needed to stop thinking.

Shane had been drunk when he proposed. After one of their uglier fights, Amanda had retreated to her mother's. She'd been balled up in bed, trying to sleep, when she heard a commotion out on the front drive. Shane had pulled up. Only he'd missed the driveway and ploughed straight into the lawn. Amanda looked out in horror as he awkwardly toppled out of the driver's side of the car, dragging an old ghetto blaster with it. A lead ball of dread settled at the base of Amanda's stomach. She had opened the window to tell him to stop, to go home and sober up, but he refused to listen, he was a man on a mission.

Shane had held the ghetto blaster above his head, its music crackling out and shattering the peace of an autumn evening. His eyes were bloodshot and he slurred all his words as he looked up at Amanda and told her that he didn't want to fight anymore, that he wanted her to marry him. Before she could even respond, he dropped the ghetto blaster, leaned forward and threw up all over himself. Slamming her window closed, Amanda buried herself beneath her duvet just as she heard the front door fling open and her mother run out to see what was happening.

The vodka in her system now started to weave its magic spell. Amanda began to feel wonderfully detached from her life. By the time the bottle was half empty she no longer cared that Will had lied to her, or what his name even was. She shimmied around her living room, truly embodying the sentiment of dancing like no one was watching. Throwing her arms about, she spun, she jumped, she laughed.

But it took just a few more sips of vodka for reality to slam against her like a brick wall. Amanda looked at the framed wedding pictures in her front room. She was suddenly so consumed with hate that she felt like if she opened her mouth she'd breathe fire and turn the images into ash.

'Who are you?' Amanda approached one of the pictures and screamed at Will, hating herself for still finding him so handsome in his suit. 'Who the hell are you?' she grabbed the picture and threw it towards the sofa. The glass cracked as it landed, splintering right down the middle, separating the smiling images of the newly wedded couple with a crude, thick line.

'Who are you?' Amanda demanded again of the picture.

*

In her drunken state, Amanda managed to do several impressive things. She managed to call a taxi, leave her home and look up Shane's address on her iPhone. She'd later have no recollection of doing any of those things.

She shoved a crumpled twenty-pound note into the bewildered taxi driver's hand, as the fare had been considerably less than that. Then she swayed her way towards a smart red-bricked building. According to her iPhone investigation, Shane lived in the house on the far right, the one with the dark green door.

Stumbling up to the door, Amanda pounded her fist against it without a moment's hesitation. She kept pounding until something clicked on the other side and the door was cautiously opened. She almost tumbled in on Shane, who was wearing jogging bottoms and a tight fitting T-shirt, his hair askew as though he'd been sleeping.

'Amanda,' he was quick enough to catch her in his arms. 'God, you've been drinking.'

'What the hell?' Amanda barely registered the long-legged figure on the staircase. She sensed that Jayne was there, openly judging her, but she didn't care. It was Shane who she'd come to see. She looked up at him as he held her in his arms, helping her remain steady on her feet.

'How could I do it?' she wondered hopelessly.

'I imagine you drank your weight in something potent. Probably vodka. You never could handle it.'

'I'm calling the police,' Jayne seethed from the staircase, 'she's a state.'

'No,' Shane ordered sharply. 'I'll handle this.'

'Make sure you do.'

Amanda heard Jayne's footsteps thunder back up the stairs and pound heavily above them. The small hallway she was standing in kept spinning around her. It was like being on a ride. She laughed giddily, enjoying the sensation.

'Okay, let's get you home,' Shane started nudging her back towards his front door.

'No,' Amanda snapped back into the moment. 'How could I do it?' the question tumbled from her mouth again. She started to cry hot, heavy tears.

'You're just drunk,' Shane's grip was surprisingly strong as he guided her towards his car in the driveway.

'No,' Amanda stopped beside the passenger door, staring into the green eyes of the one person she'd once trusted above all others. 'How could I love a stranger?'

Shane blinked at her. His own eyes misting with tears. He opened his mouth to speak but Amanda acted first, lunging forward and vomiting all down the side of his car.

*

Jake rubbed the sleep from his eyes. Billy was in the driving seat, tapping out the rhythm of the song playing on the radio against the wheel.

LONDON – 106 MILES

'Hey,' Jake stretched and looked ahead at the motorway. A few other trucks rumbled along nearby, but it was still pretty quiet. The sky remained dark and dense. Dawn was still a few hours away yet. 'How long was I out?'

'An hour or so.'

'Huh.'

The glow of the streetlights washed over them both as they journeyed towards the capital. Towards their destination.

'How long 'til we get there?' Jake looked at the digital display of the satellite navigation system propped up against the dashboard.

'God knows, turned her on silent a few miles back. She always sounds so judgemental.'

'Ha, yeah.'

'You dreaming about what you're going to do with all that dough when you take it home?' Billy cracked his trademark smile. A smile that could sell you anything.

'Not really thought about it.'

'Come on,' Billy urged. 'You could get a nice flat near the city centre. Nice reliable car that all the other loser dads drive.'

'What about you? What are your plans for the cash?'

'A new life.' The streetlights made Billy's eyes glow wildly as he drove.

'A new life?' Jake laughed. 'I think a new life will cost more than a dozen grand, Billy.'

'I'm serious.' And from his tone Jake knew that he was. 'I'm going to take my cash and make a new life for myself out in Spain. Twelve grand will get me that far.'

'You're really making that money stretch.'

'Mmm.'

'So how long 'til we arrive?' Leaning forward, Jake pressed the volume button on the sat nav.

'Drive two miles and take the next exit,' a clipped English accent prompted.

'Urgh,' Billy moaned, 'that thing bloody grates against me. Such a know-it-all. Sounds like my old maths tutor Miss Hoskins.'

Jake squinted at the little digital screen. 'According to this we should be there in two and a half hours.'

'Oh good,' Billy joked, still smiling, 'I can't wait.'

13

Sunlight burned like fire against Amanda's tightly sealed eyelids. Groaning, she tugged the duvet higher over her head, desperate to block out the blinding power of the sun.

'Oh no you don't.' A familiar voice was chiding her, pulling the duvet away from her, allowing the full heat of the morning to sizzle against her skin. 'Time for you to rise and shine, missy. You've already slept away most of the day.'

Amanda dared to peel open her eyes. For a moment her vision was blurred and then the images around her settled, like an old-fashioned television locking on to a stronger signal. Her mother was sat on the bed beside her, swathed in a bright orange wrap dress. The air smelt musty; of old perfume and stored secrets. Amanda saw the posters on the wall, the purple fabric of the duvet still covering her legs.

'Why am I here?' delivering the question revealed how sore Amanda's throat was, as though she'd spent the previous night swallowing razor blades.

'I'll bet you don't remember,' Corrine pursed her lips, holding in her judgement.

'Remember what?' Amanda coughed. She needed water. And lots of it.

'Shane brought you round last night,' Corrine recalled with a sigh. 'You were in such a state, I had to wash the sick off you before I could put you to bed.'

Amanda looked down at herself as if suddenly distrusting her own body. She didn't remember being hauled over to her mother's, or even throwing up. The previous night was just a calm sea of darkness in her mind; empty and endless.

'Apparently you showed up on Shane's doorstep.'

Amanda felt a fresh desire to vomit. Her stomach clenched and she jerked forward, heaving.

'There, there,' Corrine rubbed a hand over her daughter's back in circular motions. 'I doubt there's anything else to even throw up.'

She'd gone to Shane's house? But why? Amanda felt light-headed. She shouldn't be drunkenly turning up at her ex-boyfriend's house. She should be spending every minute searching for her missing husband. Searching for Will.

Something imploded in Amanda's mind. She pressed a hand to her temple and winced.

'Come on, let's get some food in you. Will make you feel better.' Corrine was helping her off the bed, treating her like she was a little child. Amanda stumbled after her mother, her head throbbing. Each time she thought of Will the pain grew sharper, more persistent.

'You've been through such a lot,' Corrine was saying as she busied herself at the stove. Amanda had been dropped down into a chair at the kitchen table. She watched her mother cooking, hearing her words as though they were being delivered via a filter. She sounded so far away; so distant.

Will.

Amanda pinched her eyes closed and massaged her forehead. There was something she wasn't remembering, some vital piece of information which her hangover was concealing from her.

'I'm certain there's a Jake Burton there.'

Her eyes snapped open, fearful and wide. The wrong number. Jake Burton. Shane's visit and his terrible revelation. Amanda gripped the table for support, fearing she might be destined for another fainting spell.

'Here,' Corrine placed a fresh plate of beans on toast in front of her. The smell made Amanda's stomach churn. 'You need to eat,' her mother prompted.

Will was Jake Burton. That was why she'd ended up on Shane's doorstep drunk and disillusioned. Her marriage was a lie. Will wasn't even who he said he was.

'Shane wasn't mad at you,' Corrine was sliding into the chair opposite Amanda, holding a mug of tea. 'He just seemed worried.'

Amanda blinked at her mother. Is that why she thought she was upset? Because she feared she'd angered Shane? If only she knew the depths of Will's betrayal. How he hadn't even been the man he claimed to be. Opening her mouth, Amanda was prepared to reveal everything, to share the burden of her secret.

'He said he'd pop by later after work to check in on you.'

'Who?' Amanda abandoned her previous train of thought.

'Shane.'

'Oh.'

'I'm afraid we fear it may be more serious than that.' Shane's vague warning tolled in her mind like a bell breaking the eerie silence of an icy winter morning across a desolate harbour. Each swing of the giant instrument powered through her body like a gun shot. Her mother couldn't know about Will's dual identity. Not yet. Not until Amanda knew the knowledge was safe to share.

'Everything is going to be all right.' Corrine was staring at Amanda, watching her like she was some broken china doll who she'd spent hours painstakingly gluing back together. Now she had to wait and see if all the pieces had been reattached correctly; if the doll was still the same as it had once been.

'He's not coming home,' Amanda looked at her hands resting on the table. The blue nail polish she was wearing was all scuffed and chipped. She'd painted her nails over a week ago, when Will was still very much Will Thorn.

'You always stick your tongue out when you do that,' he'd chuckled to himself as Amanda rested her foot on the coffee table and leaned forward to sweep blue paint across her pale nails.

'Do not,' Amanda had protested playfully. Will was leaning back in an armchair, a bottle of beer in one hand. A Netflix show was on the television, one which Amanda was only half watching but she knew that Will enjoyed. As he sipped his beer, he kept throwing her little glances, each one full of adoration.

'I like that colour on you,' he had commented, his voice deep and smooth like the finest red wine.

'Thanks,' Amanda straightened, capping her bottle of nail varnish and admiring her handiwork.

'It matches your eyes.'

Amanda had smiled at her husband, loving the way he completely filled the chair with his large frame. Loving the way he completely filled her life.

'You can't think like that,' Corrine urged, her voice strident with conviction. 'Will is going to come home to you, Amanda. Shane will find him.'

First the phone, then the van. And now Jake Burton. Amanda didn't know who Will was anymore, which meant she could no longer predict if and when he was ever going to come home. But what was troubling her now was why he'd left in the first place, and lied to her as much as he had.

'What if he doesn't come home?' Amanda wondered flatly. 'Does that make me a widow? Divorced? Estranged? What?'

'He's your *husband*,' Corrine insisted. 'The bond you two share cannot be broken easily. Will loves you, Amanda. Whilst I'm open about having had my misgivings with the man, I never doubted that he loved you. How could he not?'

Amanda rolled her eyes. Will couldn't have loved her that much if he'd been lying to her for their entire marriage.

'I know you're worried,' Corrine neatly folded her hands on top of one another. 'But whoever has taken him, Shane will figure it out. He's a sharp boy.'

'He's a man now, Mum.'

'You know what I mean.'

'But that's the thing,' Amanda pushed aside her untouched dinner. 'I'm not sure anyone did take Will. I think he left because he wanted to.'

Corrine didn't offer any objections to the theory.

'And that means it's up to him whether or not he comes back.'

'You're not the kind of girl to sit around and wait on him to come back,' Corrine was standing up, taking her empty mug over to the sink.

'Then what am I supposed to do?'

'That's a question only you can answer,' Corrine said in a sweet, sing-song voice as she began filling the sink with warm water.

Amanda didn't know what she should do. Will was out there, somewhere. And he clearly wasn't coming home. She drummed her fingers against the table. If Shane and the authorities didn't find him, what then? Will surely couldn't just disappear into thin air. He had to be somewhere.

Amanda drummed her fingers faster, their beat becoming more frantic. She had enough to go on, enough information to commence her own search. Only she wouldn't be looking for Will Thorn, she'd be hunting Jake Burton, who perhaps wouldn't be such a ghost online.

Will was still her husband after all and if the tables were turned she knew that Will would move heaven and earth to find her. Or was that just a lie too? Were his feelings all part of some fabrication and none of it had been true?

'Can you get that?' Corrine's request snapped Amanda out of her thoughts. 'The doorbell,' Corrine pointed a soapy hand towards the hallway.

'Oh,' Amanda stood up. She'd been so wrapped up in her worries that she hadn't even heard the doorbell.

She opened the door and found Shane waiting on the doorstep, looking immaculate in his suit.

'I'm getting used to finding you on doorsteps,' Amanda quipped as she let him in.

'I just wanted to check in on you,' Shane's voice was curt, professional. Had Amanda crossed a line when she'd drunkenly appeared at his home? Was their newly flourishing friendship destroyed before it had even had a chance to bloom?

'I'm so sorry about last night,' Amanda quickly gushed. 'I was drunk, and upset, and—'

'Let's go somewhere and talk,' Shane interrupted, placing a firm grip on her arm. Amanda looked towards the kitchen where her mother was merrily humming to herself as she did the washing up.

'Just let me get changed.' Her old bedroom was like a time capsule, the drawers stuffed full of old T-shirts and hoodies, clothes which still fit. She disappeared upstairs before Shane could respond.

*

Ten minutes later and they were climbing down the cliff-side path. Amanda was in front and Shane was keeping pace with her, remembering the route as well as she did. The patch of beach behind her mother's home was empty. A few sandcastles had been abandoned, enjoying their last few hours before the ocean reclaimed them.

Amanda removed her ballet pumps and approached the damp sand, allowing a gentle wave to wash over her feet. The water was icy cold and the sharp sensation it sent through her body helped to banish away the remnants of her hangover.

'I'd forgotten how relaxing this place could be,' Shane, still in his suit, lingered back on the dry sand. Amanda savoured a few more cold waves before walking back to him.

'I still like to come down here and think,' she admitted as together they began walking slowly along the beach.

'How are you feeling? Last time I saw you, you were a bit worse for wear,' Shane turned his head to smile wryly at her. Amanda blushed, feeling like the shy little girl whose skin used to burn whenever she caught him stealing glances at her across the classroom.

'I feel better now,' she drank in the salty sea breeze, letting it cleanse her.

'I get why you're upset,' Shane kicked at the sand. 'The revelation is making you question everything.'

'Yeah.'

'But we'll get to the bottom of it, Amanda. Don't worry.' He said her name so softly, with such tenderness, as though he'd taken the time to repeat it over and over until he could say it just right.

'I just can't believe that he'd lie to me like he has.' Amanda ceased walking. She faced the horizon where the sun was dipping towards the shoreline. Tiny boats bobbed up and down in the distance, preparing for a night out on the waves. Amanda envied the distance they could put between their lives and themselves, how disconnected from the world they must be out on the open water when night fell. They had only the tug of the ocean to lull them to sleep, only a canopy of stars for light. Shane used to talk about hiring a boat and spending a summer exploring the coast together. But like so many of his grand dreams, nothing ever came of it.

'Look, I know things are looking really bad right now but you can't let this shake the foundations of what you guys have. There might be a reasonable explanation for it all.'

Amanda spun round. Was Shane trying to repair her broken marriage? Defending Will? But why?

'You're always so quick to judge, Amanda,' he looked down at his feet, kicking at the sand.

'So quick to judge?' Amanda could scarcely repeat his words to him. 'Shane, my husband ran out on me and lied about who he is.'

'It's what you've always done with guys,' Shane continued, shoving his hands deep into his pockets. 'You place these unrealistic expectations upon them. You think that every guy should be this perfect hero who can do nothing wrong.'

'Every guy?' Amanda stared at him, pretty sure that they were no longer discussing her and Will. Or Jake. Or whatever name her husband actually went by.

'I get that you lost your dad when you were young.'

Amanda unwillingly let her gaze trail along the coastline, towards the cliff where her father had pulled her back from oblivion that fateful day.

'He was such a hero to you. Like that day when you were looking for bird's nests and tumbled over the cliff edge,' Shane was still talking. 'He became larger than life, he became something of a fantasy to you. And when he died four years later, that fantasy became myth. And now you expect all men to live up to this ideal. This ideal you crafted in your mind due to tragic circumstances.'

Amanda's cheeks were slick with tears. Was Shane actually berating her for having worshipped her father?

'And no one is going to live up to it,' Shane's voice was rising, each word electrified with pent-up emotion. 'If your dad hadn't died you'd have grown up and realized he was human, fallible. You'd have seen his imperfections, seen him as just a guy rather than this Greek god you have in your head.'

'What?' Amanda wiped at her cheeks. 'What are you even getting at? Because to me it sure as hell sounds like you're kicking me when I'm down!'

'No one will ever be good enough for you, will they?'

Amanda was stunned. She wanted to yell that Will was good enough. That when she'd met him he was the perfect guy; he'd open doors and pull out chairs for her. She didn't have to moan at him to mow the lawn or repair a broken shelf. Will was a man of strength, of his word. But what if he'd just been trying to live up to her fantasy? What if the real Will, this Jake Burton guy, was nothing like the man she'd known?

'You need to let go of the past,' Shane's hands were now on her shoulders and his face was inches away from hers. Amanda tilted her head to look at the cliff edge in the distance, her hair tangling around her as the breeze picked up.

'You still have the nightmares, don't you?'

Amanda could only numbly nod.

'I never tried to be perfect for you,' Shane's words were almost stolen away by the wind but Amanda just caught them before they tumbled away down the beach. 'I was only ever honest, because I thought that was enough.'

'It was enough.' Amanda looked into his green eyes, remembering how she used to love seeing herself reflected in them. She always thought she was the best version of herself through Shane's eyes. But the lie left a bad taste in her mouth. She pushed him away and stepped back on to the damp sand, where she knew he couldn't follow.

'At least I wanted it to be enough,' she admitted, her voice small. 'But it wasn't.'

'But if you let go of the past you could stop chasing this perfect ideal. You could finally have something real, something true.' Shane stepped towards her, his polished shoes sinking into the soft, wet sand, but he didn't seem to care. He cupped her face with his hands. Amanda drew in a salt-laced breath.

She remembered standing on the beach, probably in the exact same spot, when she and Shane had flirtatiously decided to act out the infamous beach scene in *From Here to Eternity*. He'd grabbed her waist, drew her in close and then pulled her down onto the sand, kissed her so deeply that the butterflies in her stomach escaped out of her and flew off towards the late afternoon sun. It was a kiss that would linger on her lips long after they'd untangled their limbs from one another.

'You were always perfect to me,' Shane was drawing himself towards her, lowering his head. Amanda knew what came next. Their lips would meet and magically they'd turn back the hands of time and be two love-struck teenagers again. But Amanda was no longer sixteen. And despite Will's web of lies, he was still her husband, he still deserved her loyalty, at least until he'd proven otherwise.

Shane was right that she needed to accept that Will wasn't perfect. That no man was. She'd save her judgement for her husband until she'd heard his excuses first-hand, delivered directly from his own lips. Stepping away from Shane, Amanda shook her head, raising a hand to her mouth.

'We can't,' she uttered. Shane was crestfallen. His green eyes shimmered with gathering tears as the setting sun filled the sky with blood. Amanda reached back towards him, leaning up to leave a kiss upon his cheek. A promise of sorts.

'Thank you for being there for me.' She was preparing to take off down the beach, to ascend the cliff-side path two steps at a time. There was something she had to do. Will was out there somewhere and she was suddenly determined to find him, to not give up on him just because he'd shown himself to be less than perfect.

'I always will be,' Shane clasped her fingertips in his as Amanda pulled away. There was longing in his eyes. 'Always.'

14

It'd taken less than half an hour to grab her stuff and head back home. The only source of light in the dark room was the screen of the open laptop. It's soft blue glow made Amanda appear pale and haunted as she leaned over it, her fingers dancing across the keyboard.

She ignored the way her skin tingled from the memory of Shane's touch. All that mattered was finding Will. Jake. Her husband.

Time had lost all relevance. All Amanda knew was that when she'd sat down at her computer it was still dusk outside. Now there was only darkness beyond her windows, darkness which had infected her home since she hadn't even bothered to get up and turn on any lights. But Amanda welcomed the darkness. It felt like any extra layer of protection against what she was currently doing. It provided shadows that she could hide within.

Her laptop whirred as it accessed more data. Chewing on her lip, Amanda studied the screen. She was back on the darknet. Back operating as Lambchop. It was going against Shane's wishes but what choice did she have? She had to find her husband and this was the only way she knew how. She raised one hand to rub at her tired eyes. How long had she been staring at the screen? It was hours, but how many? How far away was the dawn of a new day?

Amanda had tracked people before. Or rather, Lambchop had. She'd hacked her way into bank records, passport control. She'd been able to extract the most slender needle from a stack of hay. At university she'd loved the thrill of the chase, how sat behind her laptop she could almost feel like some sort of superhero. The darknet provided a space for her and others like her to operate beyond the boundaries of the law as unseen as ghosts. Amanda and her fellow hackers haunted websites, extracted the information they wanted by any means. Sometimes they even made the news.

She ceased typing to lean back and drink from her mug of

coffee. The contents had cooled long ago, but she didn't care. She just needed the caffeine rush. The brief pause made her reflective. From behind her computer screen she'd been privy to so much, to a world that people fought to keep hidden. She'd watched confidential military videos, helped aid the people who decided to leak them to the world. Amanda always felt like a digital vigilante, using her skills on the computer for the greater good. She never once imagined that she'd be using such skills to find her own husband.

'You can't be doing this!' Shane, fresh into the police force, had raged when he discovered Amanda's activity on the darknet. She'd just received a neat lump sum for aiding an illegal transfer of money and Shane was demanding she tell him how she'd come by the cash. She'd watched him pale when she explained how the hacking she used to do for fun as a teenager had now become a lucrative form of income.

'This is illegal,' he'd pushed his hands through his hair and paced around the small flat they shared. 'You could go to prison for this,' he gestured wildly at her laptop which hummed innocently in the background. 'We both could.'

'I'm not getting caught,' Amanda insisted. 'I operate on a fake DNS on an IP address which is registered to Florida. And after every big job, I drill through my hard drive and fry it in the microwave before getting a new one.'

'Are you listening to yourself?' Shane threw his hands up in frustration. 'This is madness, Amanda. And bloody dangerous!'

'You didn't used to think it was madness,' Amanda had scowled at him. 'You used to think it was fun, exciting.'

'Yeah, back when we were kids. Things were different then. It was just a bit of innocent fun.'

'Yeah,' Amanda agreed, her shoulders slumping when she looked at the man in the freshly pressed uniform. The man who had become a stranger to her. 'Things really were different then.'

Two weeks later, Shane moved out. The pressure cooker that had become their relationship was too much for either of them to bear. There was no blame placed, just sad looks exchanged as Shane placed down his key, slung his duffle bag over his shoulder and walked out of Amanda's life.

'It's me or this darknet crap,' he'd threatened in the days leading up to their end. He'd come in from a late shift at the station and woken Amanda up, seemingly with the sole purpose of arguing with her. Tired and disorientated, she was in no mood to fight.

'Why would you make me choose?' she'd demanded groggily. 'I wouldn't make you choose between me and being a cop. Besides, I know which you'd pick,' she'd grumbled before dropping back down against her pillows.

'I'm trying to make this world a better place,' Shane had told her righteously.

'So am I,' Amanda turned on her side, keen to go back to sleep.

'I'm trying to become the hero you want me to be,' Shane said so softly that Amanda wasn't sure if she'd dreamt the words.

Her laptop groaned loudly. Amanda shook herself back into the moment, certain that for a few minutes she'd managed to drift off to sleep, coffee mug in hand. She traced her finger over the mouse pad and stared at the screen.

Jackpot.

Lambchop still retained enough goodwill within the darknet community to rustle up a handful of hackers willing to help her find Will. Of course, she wasn't giving them the details of her request, just the name, or rather names, of who she was trying to find. She'd posted for help in numerous chat rooms but been met with radio silence. Until now.

```
Identity fraud is tricky
```

WikiPeakes89 had written.

```
They could be operating under
several names. The best way to
locate them is to use against
them the one thing they can't
change; their face. You want
facial recognition tech. All the
major security systems are using
it, relatively easy d/l. Need
help hit me up. Good to have you
```

Amanda had received several responses, all along the same lines. They suggested she use facial recognition technology. Then all she'd have to do is import a scan of a photo of Will and the internet would do the rest. She knew how to hack the system of CCTV cameras throughout the UK. It was something she'd done before, but it would take a lot of time. The systems weren't all on a central server, she'd need to spend the hours hacking each individual system. It was time she wasn't sure she had. With each passing second she risked getting caught or losing any trace of Will that lingered online. Hence her need for support from the darknet community.

She was in the middle of quickly typing out a response when her doorbell rang. It was becoming something of a regular occurrence since Will left, along with the phone ringing.

'Damn,' Amanda exhaled sharply and locked her laptop screen before getting up, hiding her activity from any visitor. Leaving the study, she noticed that the sky outside was grey and growing lighter by the minute. She'd managed to work all through the night. Her mouth widened into a yawn as she pulled open her front door. Unsurprisingly she found Shane standing before it. He looked polished and fresh in a new suit, the citrusy odour of his shower gel still clinging to his skin. Clearly he was en route to work.

'Sorry to wake you,' he apologised sheepishly. Amanda wanted to laugh and point out that far from waking her he'd just disturbed her from her own work. But she knew that would make Shane suspicious.

'Have you found something?' Amanda thought of all the illegal activity being channelled through her laptop just a few feet above their heads. If Shane had found Will then perhaps she wouldn't have to sink back into the murky mire of the darknet. Perhaps she could retain some semblance of innocence.

'No,' Shane stepped inside, not bothering to wait for an invitation.

'Why can't you find anything out?' Amanda wondered tersely as she went to make herself some much needed fresh coffee.

'It's difficult. I don't have the jurisdiction to just wade

through all the files. I have to wait to get permission and follow due protocol.'

'Tell them I'm his wife and that I have a right to know.'

'It doesn't work like that.'

'Well it should,' Amanda switched on her percolator. 'I'm his next of kin.'

'You're *Will's* next of kin.'

Amanda shivered as though Shane had just poured ice down her back. She sucked in a tense breath and turned away from him, grateful to have the preparation of the coffee to distract her from their conversation.

'I've not come here to make you feel bad,' Shane sighed.

Amanda stridently dropped one hand to her hip as she turned to face him.

'I've come here to warn you against doing anything stupid.'

'Don't worry; I've no intention of topping myself.'

'That's not what I meant and you know it,' Shane's voice was hard, all the former soft edges removed. He was completely different to the guy she'd stood on the beach with, making the memory start to feel false, like a dream.

'Shane,' she sighed as she said his name, thinking of her laptop whirring away, of all her old contacts offering their assistance. Together they'd hack every CCTV camera in the UK if they had to. If something was electrical they could access it. Wi-Fi had made the entire world a hacker's paradise.

'Don't look for him, Amanda.'

She pulled her eyebrows together, trying to suss out if Shane was somehow monitoring her online activity. But that was close to impossible; she hid behind a carefully constructed digital wall of smoke and mirrors. To catch her, you'd need to be as good as her, if not better. And Amanda doubted that anyone in Tremwell Bay was capable of that.

'Don't look for him, don't try to seek him out. Just let me do my job.'

'But that's just it,' lack of sleep had made Amanda irritable. She felt like she was back in the stifling environment of her old flat, arguing with Shane after he'd tumbled in from a night shift his shirt spotted with someone else's blood. 'You're not doing your job, Shane. It's been over a week and my husband is still missing. All you've succeeded in doing is asking more questions, not providing any answers.'

'I'll get to the bottom of it. I promise,'

'I'm *sick* of being in limbo all the time,' The words sounded sharper than Amanda had intended. Shane took a step back from her, rubbing his neck.

'Amanda—'

'Will is my *husband*. I owe it to him to find him. He'd look for me. He wouldn't stop looking for me.'

'Don't do this; don't open up this can of worms.'

'Why the hell not?'

'Because Will might be dangerous.'

'What?' Amanda spluttered on her question. She wanted to laugh hysterically at the implausibility of it. Will was many things, but he wasn't dangerous. He was her gentle giant. He possessed so much physical power but he'd only ever shown kindness and care towards Amanda.

In their first month of marriage a beautiful little chaffinch had flown into one of their upstairs windows and died instantly on impact. It dropped down to the ground causing Amanda to jump from where she was sat reading in the front room. She approached the French doors and looked down pitifully at the fallen little creature.

'Oh, the poor thing,' Will had come up behind her, sounding genuinely aggrieved. He'd placed a large hand on Amanda's shoulder and peered down at the little bird.

'It can't have seen the windows.' One minute the chaffinch had been flying around, full of life, perhaps heading back to its nest. The next, everything had gone dark for it. The fragility of it all had made Amanda gasp for breath.

'I'll go and clean it up,' Will had squeezed Amanda's shoulder. His strong touch bled through her body, blissfully seeping into every muscle like hot oil. Will held that rare sort of magic that just being around him made everything seem better. He went outside and his version of cleaning the bird up involved him giving it a proper burial at the back of the garden.

As Amanda had watched him labour over the small hole, wrap up the tiny bird and then carefully place it within its final resting place, her heart was so full of love for Will Thorn that she thought it might burst. He was so kind, so gentle. So like her father had been.

'He's not dangerous.' The percolator came to the boil and Amanda poured out two fresh mugs of coffee. 'He might have another family somewhere, but that's it. And I deserve to know the truth. But I know with all my heart that Will isn't dangerous.'

'Think about what I've already discovered,' Shane urged. 'Jake Burton had a criminal record. He did time, Amanda.'

'What did he do time for?'

'Theft. Breaking and entering.'

'So petty crime then.' Amanda remarked churlishly.

'—Drug smuggling.'

This silenced her. Amanda's chin dropped to her chest.

'Amanda—'

'No, you don't know enough to judge him,' Amanda angrily thrust a coffee towards Shane, her eyes shining with tears 'Maybe there are things I don't know about Will. Like his real name or who his family are. But sharing a bed, a life, with someone lets you learn a few very real truths about them. Will is kind. Will is brave and he is also sensitive. He's not dangerous, Shane. Whatever he did in his past, he'd have done it for good reason.' In her heart Amanda knew that Will was a decent man despite what his past implied.

'I just want you to be careful.'

'And I just want to find my husband. I'm tired of waiting around for the police to actually do their jobs.'

'Stay away from the darknet, Amanda. I'm begging you.'

'What if it were Jayne?' Amanda challenged. 'Would you just accept that she'd disappeared? Or would you do everything in your power to find her? To bring her home?'

Shane said nothing.

'I have to find him.'

'At least let me confirm why Jake Burton was reported dead. Can you let me do that?'

Amanda closed her eyes and released a long breath. She thought of the money. Of the van. Of the false identity. Then she thought of something her mother always used to say to her when she was growing up. Corrine would plant her bejewelled hands on her little daughter's shoulders and grandly impart her pearls of wisdom.

'My dearest, Amanda. In your life you must always be the heroine of your own story, never the victim.'

She repeated this on a daily basis in the months following Ivor's death. Amanda failed to acknowledge the significance of the sentiment, feeling as though fate had cast her as a victim before she'd even been given the chance to blossom from a girl to a woman.

And Amanda knew that she was still being a victim. She was waiting around on a call that might never come, on a husband who might never return. And it all tied back to a wrong number she'd received. If she wanted to become the heroine of her story she needed to uncover the truth by any means. Amanda's hands tightened around her mug as her entire body became infused with steely determination. She was going to find Will. No matter what.

'Just keep being patient,' Shane pleaded.

Amanda glanced at the chrome clock hanging on the far wall. 'Aren't you going to be late for work?'

'Shit, yes,' Shane followed her gaze and hastily necked the remainder of his coffee and straightened his tie. 'I've got a call with a Glasgow police department scheduled for later this morning,' he explained as he hurried towards the hallway. 'I'm doing everything I can, Amanda. You just have to trust me. And you just have to wait.'

'Okay, I'll wait.'

Shane was now on the other side of the door, outside in the pale morning light. His whole face brightened with relief. Amanda almost pitied him for believing her lie so easily. He'd never been so quickly convinced of her compliance when they were together. But back then he'd known her better than anyone. Her heart clenched.

'I'll swing by later tonight to check in on you again,' Shane offered, leaning forward to place a kiss on her cheek. For a second the gesture felt so natural; Amanda was waving her husband off to work, the sun was shining and it was set to be a beautiful day. But she stiffened as he stepped away, remembering how she intended to spend the next twelve hours locked away in her study doing everything she could to find Will. The last thing she needed was Shane coming over right in the midst of her making a breakthrough. He'd only shut it down. Or worse – arrest her.

Amanda's objection was bubbling up her throat, preparing to depart through her lips, but she was too late. Exhaustion had made her mind sluggish. Shane was already in his car and pulling out of the driveway. All Amanda could do was weakly wave him off and internally chastise herself for not being quicker, for giving him permission to return.

Back upstairs her study was no longer shrouded in darkness. Early morning light warmed the room, pushing away any lingering shadows. Her laptop sat on the desk, no longer whirring, merely patiently waiting. Amanda sat down in front of it and unlocked the screen. Her heart crept up into her throat. There were no longer any shadows to hide behind. If she proceeded, she'd be doing so in broad daylight. She paused for a moment, letting the gravity of her actions settle around her. Once she proceeded with her search there was no going back, the darknet was like a black hole which had a way of consuming all those who came too close. But she had to find Will. Sucking in a sharp breath Amanda logged in.

There were eight more messages waiting for her in the chat room, all offering their immediate support. The final message was from WikiPeakes89;

So, are we doing this or what?

*

The glass shattered in a crescendo of sound. Amanda was just stepping out of the shower when she heard it. It reminded her of when she'd been in college and had fallen over a drum kit in the music room. The cymbal had clattered to the ground so sharply that she'd alerted her entire class to her ungraceful misstep.

Just like then the sound had died almost as soon as it'd been made. Stepping uncertainly out of the bathroom, draped in a fluffy sheet towel, Amanda titled her head and strained to listen for further sounds.

There was a squeal of tyres outside. It sounded close.

Will.

Lately Amanda's knee-jerk reaction was to attribute any sort of strange activity to her missing husband. She ran across the landing, down the stairs, not even sure what she was looking for. But when she burst into the living room she saw it.

A vase was flat against her plush woollen rug, knocked from

its perch on the windowsill by the brick that was beside it. And there was glass everywhere. Amanda instantly recoiled to the edge of the room, thinking of her bare feet. A cool summer breeze swept in through the newly formed hole in the window. Amanda looked at it, still stunned, struggling to take in what she was seeing.

Her stomach knotted, winding her. She knew this wasn't some random act. This was connected to Will. It had to be.

Somehow she drifted back into the hallway and called the one person who she knew she could count on for help.

*

'Did you hear anything?'

Shane was on his knees, looking over the shards of glass which glistened in the sunshine like scattered diamonds.

'I was in the shower.' Amanda felt lame and helpless as she lingered behind him. She'd pulled on some joggers and a T-shirt, her hair still damp down her back.

'Well, there's no message on it,' Shane carefully turned the brick over. 'But I'll take it back to the station to be dusted for fingerprints, it might reveal something.'

'It's connected to Will, I just know it,' Amanda stated tearfully.

'It's probably just kids,' Shane coolly rationalized. 'There's been a string of petty vandalism in the area, always happens this time of year when kids get bored during the long summer holidays.'

'No,' Amanda's voice was shrill, insistent. 'This is to do with the people who are looking for Will.' She pointed a shaking finger at the brick. 'The prank calls and the message on my car. It's all connected, I just know it.'

'Wait, what message on your car?' Shane was standing up and smoothing down his shirt. 'And you just had that one prank call, asking for Jake Burton, right?'

Amanda's gaze dropped to the ground, to her sumptuous rug which was still soiled with dangerous shards of glass.

'I...' she was wringing her hands together, feeling oddly guilty for withholding information from Shane. 'I saw a message on my car before I went jogging the other morning.

And then in the woods I… I blacked out and I guess I didn't remember to mention it,' she shrugged helplessly.

'What kind of message?' Shane was staring at her, silhouetted against the golden light which was pouring in through the broken window.

'It said *Where is Jake*?' Amanda chewed her lip. 'But, I mean, I don't know. I tried to shake it off in case it was just someone messing with me. But then someone keeps prank calling the house and just lingering on the line. And now this,' she gestured towards the brick which Shane had slipped into a clear plastic evidence bag, 'they're looking for Will, aren't they?'

'You didn't mention further prank calls,' Shane furrowed his brow and looked sad. 'I can access the call records for your landline, see where these problem calls are coming from.'

'Yeah,' Amanda wrung her hands together, not knowing what she should do with them. 'That'd be great.'

'And I'm pretty sure this is just kids playing about,' Shane glanced back over his shoulder at the broken window, 'but if you're feeling spooked, you should go and stay at your Mum's place.'

'I've been there more than enough lately.' Amanda was watching him, wondering how much truth his explanation held.

'I know but—'

'Can you just board it up?'

'Yeah, of course. But if you're not feeling safe in your home anymore—'

'I need to stay here.'

'Amanda,' Shane's eyes were still full of sadness as he stared at her.

'He's coming back,' she told him stridently. 'And I intend on being here when he does.'

'How can you be certain that he's coming back?'

Amanda's gaze hardened. 'Because I'm going to find him.'

'You're not…' Shane looked back towards the shattered window. His shoulders sagged as he released a deep sigh. 'The darknet.' His gaze was hooded as he turned back towards Amanda. 'Promise me you're staying away from that shit.'

The window let in all the sights and sounds from outside. A giant crack in the perfect exterior of her beautiful home.

'I'm going to find him any way I can.'

'So this?' Shane fiercely shook the clear bag he was holding that contained the brick. 'This could all be because of some old cage you've rattled?'

Amanda blinked at him. The thought hadn't crossed her mind. She'd assumed that the brick was connected to Will. Jake. It had to be. The summer breeze that slid in through the new opening suddenly carried a considerable chill.

'Just board it up please,' she lifted her chin and gave Shane a level stare. 'I bet this was just kids messing about, like you said.'

'Alright, fine,' he was shaking his head at her, 'but since you insist on staying here I'll still make sure to pop round later. I don't like you being here alone.'

'Okay…thanks.'

'Everything is going to be alright. I'm here for you, don't forget that.'

Suddenly Amanda wasn't sure whose past she feared more – her own or her husband's.

*

Her laptop chirped. Amanda wiped away the last shred of sleep-induced fog that clung to her and focused on the screen. She had a new message. But it hadn't come through to her regular email. Someone was trying to directly contact her through her darknet account.

A sickly feeling crept up her throat as she logged into her Lambchop ID and checked her inbox. One new message. Sender – Turtle82.

Amanda pushed herself away from her desk, her eyes wide in disbelief. It couldn't be the same contact, could it? But the coincidence was too much to ignore. Squeezing her eyes shut, Amanda gripped the edge of her desk and slowly pulled her chair back towards it. She desperately wanted to just delete the message but she couldn't. Turtle82 knew too much about her, about the things she'd done in the past. Mainly because they'd done them together.

```
Lambchop I see you've resurfaced
after all these years. Up to old
```

```
tricks?
  T
```

The message was simple. Friendly even to an impartial reader. But Amanda could read between the lines.

I see you've resurfaced meant that Turtle82 continued to track her, keep tabs on her. Whilst she was trying to find Will through the darknet, she should have known that someone might also be looking for her. As a student there were things she couldn't hack. She was known in darknet circles as being one of the best, or at least Lambchop was. Her own identity was completely separate. She'd sit up late in her uni room while everyone else was out partying, leant over her laptop, its glow illuminating her face. She'd hack into anywhere if the price was right, and Turtle82 was always finding her new jobs, always nudging her in more questionable directions. They were like a ghost that was guiding her, a name on a screen just like she was, nothing else.

Amanda would change a student's A-Level results for a fee. An American's SAT scores. Enabling them to attend the college or university of their choice. She'd illegally move money, disable security systems, wipe CCTV footage. She never considered the moral implication of her decisions, not like Shane would have. Her refusal to acknowledge the damage she might be causing helped to drive a wedge between them. A wedge which became a canyon.

Again Amanda read Turtle82's latest message. Did they have work for her? Or was this a threat? Did Turtle82 know more than the fact that she'd re-emerged within their murky social network? Did they know who she was? Would the next message read 'Dear Amanda'? Her heart almost stopped at the thought. She'd been so desperate to find Will that she hadn't considered the blood she'd be polluting the water with now that she was reopening old wounds... and all the sharks who'd come circling.

'Fuck you, Turtle,' Amanda muttered between clenched teeth as she hit delete and the message disappeared from her screen. She wasn't about to let a ghost from her past get in the way of her finding her husband.

15

```
//search:fx6
  //upload
  //execute
```

Amanda lifted her hands from her laptop. It was done. The scrape was set up. She looked at the picture of Will she'd scanned into her computer. It lay on her desk, his warm smile currently angled towards the ceiling. The man in the picture was the man she was looking for. The man who cared about animals, had a guttural laugh which always made it sound like he was responding to a dirty joke, and had eyes full of kindness and wisdom. Amanda was searching for Will Thorn, not Jake Burton. A part of her still refused to accept that the two identities were one and the same.

This kind of search wasn't entirely new to Amanda. She'd used facial recognition technology before, or at least she'd hacked into enterprises that were using it for security measures. It had been easy enough to clone the software once she'd hacked her way into their networks. And there had been old darknet jobs when Amanda had been hired to infiltrate CCTV networks. Most of them ran on a central grid, similar to telephone lines. Those kinds of jobs were easy and paid good money.

Amanda had helped track down runaway children, those in debt who were trying to out run their problems. And now she was using the tech to hunt her husband. The inner workings of her laptop whirred noisily. She was pushing her current computer to its limits, asking it to work through an insane amount of data in a short time.

As her computer kept whirring away to itself, her fingers twitched over her keyboard. It would be so easy to return to her darknet chatrooms and forums. To put out the call; Searching for info on Jake Burton.

Were Jake's/Will's date of birth the same? There couldn't be too much discrepancy between them. And what about place of birth? Were any of the few stories Will had told her of his life back in Scotland actually true?

'It was a hard place to grow up in,' he'd say with a distant look in his eyes. Amanda knew he'd lost his brother. She didn't want to force him to relive that pain for her. So she kept her questions to herself, assuming that Will would open up to her about his past if he wanted to. But he never did.

Pushing her chair back, Amanda moved away from the desk, thinking of what her little Grandmother used to say: 'A watched pot never boils.'

'Find him,' Amanda ordered her laptop as she slipped out of the room. She intended to go downstairs, to make some more coffee and watch TV. But her feet guided her towards her bedroom, towards her bed. She let her instincts take over as she crashed against the soft pillows, her body finally giving way to exhaustion.

*

It was a sunny day. The light glistened on the water as though thousands of sapphires were floating just beneath the surface. Amanda pushed her hair out of her eyes and strode confidently towards the cliff edge. The wind sharpened as she reached the rocky ground. She paused briefly, sucking in a salty breath and looking out into the oblivion which was the ocean.

She used to entertain fantasies of jumping into the water and just swimming until she reached another country.

'You'd die of exhaustion before you reached anywhere,' John would pop her bubble of an idea with his sharply accurate knowledge. 'That or drown when the current pulled you under.'

'That's why we should get a boat,' Shane had declared, his dark hair flecked with copper streaks thanks to a summer spent outdoors.

'And where will we get a boat?' John had asked with a shake of his head, the gesture more fitting to a grown man than an eight-year-old. 'We can barely find twenty pence to go and get sweets from the newsagents.'

'I'll make one.' Shane had stared at Amanda as he made the promise. 'I'll make one and together we'll set sail and explore the entire coast. We'll find caves full of hidden treasures and swim with dolphins.'

'You're going to make a boat?' John wondered dubiously, not yet realizing that Shane's invitation didn't extend to him, that in a few years their trio would be down to two.

'Don't get too close to the edge,' Amanda's father delivered his warning loud and clear. She waved a dismissive hand towards him. She just wanted to see the bird's nests up close. From down on the beach she'd see the birds swarming at the side of the cliff. Their decision to build their nests so close to such a perilous drop intrigued her. Usually she'd have Shane or John by her side for such an exploration, but they were off on a Scouts camping trip. Her plan was to find one of the pristine baby-blue eggs and keep it as a trophy to triumphantly reveal to her friends when they returned. Especially Shane. Amanda couldn't wait to see the glow of approval in his eyes when she showed him the little egg.

The wind tried to push her back, but Amanda forced her way to the edge. She dropped to her knees and shuffled forwards. A few rocks were dislodged and they went tumbling over the side. Amanda swallowed. She could feel her bones starting to rattle together, but she knew she needed to be brave. Her small hands gripped the very edge of the rocks. She peered down at the sheer side of the cliff. She could make out the little baskets of nests resting on random outcrops. They were filled with soft downy feathers and some contained eggs.

'Yes,' Amanda gushed into the wind. She spotted one nest just a few feet below her. If she stretched, she could just grasp an egg. She strained, sending more stones skittering down around her.

'That's too close.'

She barely heard her father's shout of disapproval over the thunderous roar of the waves beneath her. The water swirled, whipping up white foam and crashing against the jagged rocks. There was no beach beneath her on this part of the coastline, only the icy waters of the ocean ready to swallow her whole.

'Almost...' Amanda stretched her arm out as much as she could. Her fingertips grazed the edge of the little nest, stroking the rough twigs which had been lovingly collected by the mother bird. She pushed herself forward again, determined to claim her prize. Only her hand didn't connect with the nest. It didn't connect with anything. It waved through open air as her entire body tumbled over the edge of the cliff. She saw the sky rolling above her which was swiftly replaced by the frothing waters of the ocean. She was plunging to her death. She tasted metal in her mouth as though she'd just bitten her tongue. She was too stunned to scream. Too stunned to do anything other than fall like one of the stones she'd previously dislodged.

Then something was grabbing her legs, digging in tightly and hauling her back. Amanda was shaking as her father bundled her up in his embrace and fearfully shuffled away from the cliff edge as though the sea might still rise up and claim his little girl.

'How could you be so stupid?' he was berating her and crying at the same time as he sat on the rough grass and rocked her back and forth in his arms. 'You stupid, stupid girl. You could have died.' He kissed her forehead numerous times, refusing to let her go. Amanda continued to shake, her teeth noisily chattering together.

'Oh, Amanda,' her mother came running up to them, her long white skirt billowing in the wind as though she were signalling her surrender to ships out on the water. 'Amanda,' she threw her arms around her little family, the tightness in her grip equally as protective as Ivor's. She'd seen what had happened from the little house with the rose garden. She'd seen her daughter almost plummet to her death.

'Amanda, you could have died,' Corrine exclaimed desperately.

'But I didn't,' Amanda managed to wriggle fear of her parents' embrace just enough to enable her to look up at her father. Ivor's kind face was set against a clear blue sky. His cheeks were slick with tears and his eyes were red, but his smile of relief, and the feeling it gave Amanda in that moment, imprinted on to her soul. 'Daddy, you saved me,' she told him adoringly. 'You're my hero.'

*

Amanda stirred in her bed. Waking up, she touched her cheeks and noticed that they were damp.

'Daddy,' she breathed, the moment from her dream slipping away from her, getting sucked into the darkness of the room. Her hand strayed across the bed, expecting to find the solid form of Will sleeping soundly beside her. She wanted to curl up against him, to absorb some of his warmth. He was always so warm.

'Will?' Amanda huskily called out his name. She needed his arms around her, to be reassured. Her hand moved further across the bed, finding only smooth sheets where her husband should have been.

'Will?'

Sitting up, Amanda flicked on her bedside light. Its garish glow revealed that her bed was empty; the pillows on the far side weren't even indented. The fog of sleep began to clear. Amanda tensed as she recalled how her husband wasn't in the bed, wasn't even at home. He was missing. Or he'd left her. She still didn't know which. She wanted to drop against her pillows and disappear back into her dream, back to a place where her father still existed. Her hand lingered on the switch for the lamp, preparing to turn it off. But then Amanda heard it. A high-pitched beeping. It was brief yet consistent, like a piece of hospital machinery which would beep all through the night. Now that she'd noticed the sound there was no going back to sleep until she'd silenced it. With a groan, Amanda swung her legs out of bed.

Stepping out on to the landing, she wondered if it was the smoke alarm shrilly telling her that it needed its batteries replacing. That was the kind of job that Will always took care of. He prided himself in managing things around the home. The second something broke, like a chair or a mug, he was instantly there fixing it.

Amanda moved towards the sound. It wasn't coming from the landing. She let the noise guide her further away from her bedroom. It seemed to be coming from her study. Amanda's heart clenched as she rested her hand on the door handle to the room. She remembered setting up her scrape, allowing her laptop to remain connected to the darknet while she slept.

Like most hackers she'd set up numerous alarm systems to alert her if someone became aware of her activity and began to track her. What if such an alarm had been triggered? She'd have to shut down the entire search, wipe her hard drive, take a drill to it and then blow it up in her microwave just to be certain that all evidence had been erased. And then she'd have to start all over again as she knew that the scrape of the CCTV network was the only way she'd find Will. Names could be changed. Faces couldn't.

Pushing open the door, Amanda was able to confirm that the sound was most definitely coming from her study. From her laptop to be precise. The device called out shrilly, demanding her attention. Pushing back her shoulders, Amanda made herself as large as possible, prepared to take on her digital foe. She approached her computer and unlocked the screen.

A message was flashing. Blinking like a faulty light bulb. It took a few seconds for Amanda's tired eyes to process what she was seeing. When she realized what she was looking at, she dropped down into her chair in shock.

The message was simple.

```
Match found
```

On the screen behind it were two pictures side by side. The first one was the image of Will which Amanda had previously scanned into her laptop. He was smiling out at her from the screen, dressed in his suit and photographed just before their wedding ceremony. He looked so handsome, so strong. Like the hero out of some fairy tale.

In the accompanying image there was a man walking down what looked like a railway station platform. His head was angled as if he'd just looked up for a second. But in that second he locked eyes with the CCTV camera overhead and it was enough for Amanda's facial recognition technology to pick him up.

The man on the platform was Will. There was no mistaking the glisten in his eyes or the slant of his mouth. There was her oak tree. Her knight in shining armour. Her husband. But where was he? And where was he going?

16

Amanda's heart was pounding, echoing in her ears like an ominous war drum. Her mouth went dry as she let her fingertips move across her keyboard in a flurry. She needed more information, needed a specific time, a date. And within seconds she had it.

Amanda stared at the data, searching the succinct text for some hidden meaning. Will had been caught on CCTV camera twenty-four hours ago on the platform at Glasgow's railway station. Was he going there to see his family? Were they in some kind of trouble? Her mind was a jumble of questions as she fumbled for her phone. She needed to tell Shane, to get him to focus all his resources on Scotland. The image on the CCTV camera was just over a day old; Will might still be in the area.

Chewing on her lip, she scrolled through her contact list and noticed the time. It was just after six in the morning. Looking towards the window for confirmation, Amanda saw that sure enough the sky outside was lightening as a new day began. Shane hadn't returned to her home the previous night like he'd promised. He'd barely stuck around long enough to board up her broken window. Had something come up? Had he felt that his time would be better spent elsewhere?

Jayne.

Amanda thought of the overly made-up face which always scrunched up with disdain whenever she was around. Shane had probably spent the evening with Jayne. Her stomach twisted in dismay and she threw her phone down onto her desk, angry at herself. She wasn't supposed to feel jealously towards Jayne, she wasn't supposed to feel anything.

Postponing her call to Shane, Amanda decided to shower. If she called him now, at such an unsociable hour, it set the wrong precedent. She needed to push Shane back to where he belonged; at a professional distance. Having him around, being so kind to her when Will had revealed himself to be built of lies was getting confusing. And Amanda needed to be focused if she had any hope of finding her husband.

The hot water slid down her back and steamed up the surrounding glass panels. Leaning back, Amanda savoured the sensation of it massaging her aching limbs. She scrubbed at her skin until it felt pink, but she still didn't feel clean or refreshed. She kept thinking of Will out on that train station platform, dressed in jeans and a dark hoody. If he hadn't looked up at the CCTV camera for that split second she would still be searching for him, still thinking him lost. He appeared to be alone, walking with his hands shoved into his pockets. There was no captor by his side urging him to move forwards, no sign of assault on his strong features. Will looked very much like a free man moving around of his own volition. And that made it all seem so much worse.

Heat clung to Amanda's skin as she stepped out of the shower and began to hastily dry off. The sun was now fully risen and sending bright light into the bathroom, making the white surface of the tiles glisten as damply pure as freshly fallen snow.

Despite the presence of the sun, the early hour meant that the air outside was still crisp. Large dewdrops clung to the blades of grass on Amanda's front lawn as she hurried to her car. She wasn't going to call Shane and invite him over, she feared she was reaching a point where she couldn't trust herself around him. Instead she planned on driving over to the station, on meeting Shane there like any regular person would do. No more house calls. No more confusion. And no more speculation about where Will was. Amanda knew now. He was in Glasgow which meant that with or without Shane's help, soon she would be too.

*

'Well, isn't this a pleasant surprise?' John greeted her with a jovial smile as the double doors parted and allowed Amanda into the small reception area of the police station. The air was heavy with stale coffee and sweat. It reminded Amanda of how her local gym smelt first thing in a morning.

'Hey, John,' Amanda forced her sweetest grin, tucking a lock of still damp hair behind her ear. She should have taken more time to blow-dry it properly but she'd been in such a rush. Her heart thudded heavily with each passing second, reminding her that Will might already have left Glasgow, even Scotland, might have eluded her grasp.

Shaking her head, she pushed away the unpleasant feeling that she was actively hunting her husband, and that he was actively evading her.

'Is Shane in yet?' Amanda sounded so much like her former self that she groaned. 'I mean DCI Perton. Sorry.'

'He'll always be plain old Shane to us,' John said with a raise of his eyebrows and a low chuckle. 'And yes, he is in. Up with the birds as always, puts the rest of us to shame.'

Amanda didn't recall Shane being an early riser. She remembered panicked mornings trying to rouse him from a deep slumber so that he could get to college in time for an exam, or avoid missing a university lecture. But her efforts were always in vain. Even if she splashed Shane with cold water he'd just groan and roll over. He could easily sleep the day away, emerging around three in the afternoon bleary-eyed and yawning as though dawn had just broken.

'Can I…' Amanda smoothed her hands down the white lace tunic top she'd hurriedly pulled on over her skinny jeans and swallowed. 'See him?' she eventually finished, cringing. She felt like the needy, emotional wreck she'd once been when it came to Shane, back when everything was falling apart and she'd come and cry to John at the station about how she didn't know her boyfriend anymore. 'I mean, as an official appointment. It's about my husband.'

This made John straighten in his seat. 'Oh, of course, Amanda. I mean, I'll put a call through to him in the office right away. We're all crossing everything that your husband turns up soon.'

'Thanks.'

Less than five minutes later Shane strode into the reception area. Amanda was loitering by a set of plastic chairs, clutching a Styrofoam cup of weak tea which John had insisted on giving her.

'Amanda?' the questioning lilt in Shane's tone was mirrored in his furrowed brow. He wore a pale grey suit and emerald skinny tie, his hair lightly gelled. 'I know I said I'd stop by last night,' he extended a hand towards her and Amanda's eyes flitted nervously back to John who was still behind the reception desk, pretending not to listen to them.

'It's not about that,' she reassured him quickly, talking over him. 'It's about Will.'

'Okay?' the lines in Shane's brow remained locked in place.

Amanda took a step towards him and lowered her voice. 'I've found him.'

'What?' Shane couldn't conceal his surprise as the word tumbled loudly from his lips, causing John to look over with interest. 'Has he come home?' he asked more quietly.

'No,' Amanda was shaking her head. 'But I've found him.'

'What did you do?' Shane narrowed his eyes.

Amanda floundered, wondering how much of her darknet activity she could risk revealing to Shane.

'Dammit, Amanda,' before she could respond he'd read into her silence and was tugging her by her upper arm, pulling her out of the reception and taking her deeper into the bowels of the station.

'Shane,' he pulled her so abruptly that the tea in her little white cup swirled around precariously, almost tipping over the sides. 'Hey, careful.'

He hauled her into the interview room she'd originally been questioned in with such contempt that Amanda feared she was already a common criminal in his eyes.

'What did you do?' he repeated, dropping both hands to the small table but remaining standing. Amanda cowered across from him as she dropped into the vacant chair, beginning to regret her decision to come to the station. She should have told him about her discovery when he stopped by her house, or at least on neutral ground. Here he was very much Shane the cop, not Shane the boy who'd whisper sweet nothings to her beneath the stars.

'I told you, I've found him.'

He leaned towards her, his mouth a tight line. He looked like a panther preparing to pounce.

'Found him how? Where?'

Amanda looked down at her little cup and picked at some of the soft material at its lip.

'I'm waiting,' Shane almost bellowed the words at her. He was mad. Really mad.

'How do you think I found him?' Amanda countered petulantly.

Shane groaned and stepped back from the table, crossing his

arms over his chest. Amanda noticed the bulge in his upper arms as he did so and wished she hadn't. She kept seeing flashes of the boy within the man which she knew was dangerous. She needed to separate the two. This was DCI Perton. He was just a local police officer, partner to Jayne the Pain. He had no hold over her heart. Will did. And she was close to finding him. So close.

'Don't play games with me,' Shane growled at her. They truly had reverted to playing their old parts at the very end of their performance together, when everything was imploding in on itself.

Amanda sucked in a breath and placed her tea down on the table. 'I ran a scrape of CCTV networks using facial recognition tech. It took me a few hours, but I got a positive ID. It's definitely him.'

'And you did this via the darknet, didn't you?'

Amanda was silent.

'Fuck,' Shane smacked his hands down against the table. The sound cracked through the small room like thunder. A storm was breaking between them. 'How can you come to me with this, Amanda? I can't have any part in this, don't you get that? This information that you have is utterly useless as you've not acquired it legally.'

'But it's not useless,' Amanda insisted. They weren't in a court of law. It didn't matter how the hell she came about the evidence all that mattered was finding Will. 'He's in Glasgow, he was caught on CCTV there at the train station just over a day ago.'

'I can't use this,' Shane was shaking his head. 'And I could lose my job just by having this conversation with you.'

'If we go now we might still—'

'I'm not going anywhere.' Shane's voice was hard, distant. 'I actually can't believe that you came here to tell me this.'

Amanda reached for her cup of tea wondering what troubled Shane more; that she'd found Will or that she clearly no longer wanted him dropping by her house unannounced?

'This is dangerous information, Amanda,' he continued. 'I told you to stay away from this, to leave things be.'

'I need to find my husband.' What part of doing anything she could to find him didn't Shane get? 'You'd do anything to find Jayne if she went missing and you know it.'

'Last night,' Shane stared at Amanda long and hard for a second before letting his gaze slide over to the small window in the upper part of the wall. It revealed a square of perfect blue sky. 'I didn't swing by your place as I was busy getting kicked out of my apartment.'

'Kicked out?'

'It's fine,' Shane pushed his hands into his trouser pockets. 'I'll crash at my parents' place until I find a new place to rent.'

'Why did Jayne kick you out?' Her eyes widened in surprise.

'Why do you think?' Shane wasn't looking at her; he was staring down at his polished black shoes.

'She's mad at you for helping me?' Amanda stood up, feeling outraged.

'Not helping you, no.' He lifted his head and looked at her. Amanda saw herself reflected in his green gaze, felt the tug of all their shared memories pull her heart towards his. 'She's mad at me for caring.'

Amanda's lips parted. She wanted to say something, she just didn't know what. Shane was edging around the table, coming closer to her.

Beep.

It was shrill and sharp, cutting through the tension of the moment like a brutal blade. Amanda jumped, failing to recognize the noise. Shane was staring at her like a lost puppy, waiting for her to tell him how to act, what to do next. The beep came again.

'I...' Amanda's hands rummaged in her jeans pockets and she pulled out her phone. There was an alert blinking on the screen. It was just a reminder that her scrape had found a positive match. Amanda sighed, remembering how she'd synced her phone up to her laptop to relay any results, not realizing that there was an obvious time delay.

'Amanda?'

Her hand was shaking as she looked at her phone. 'He's in Glasgow,' she explained, not recognizing her own voice. 'I have to go and find him.'

'No, you can't,' Shane reached for her forearm, his eyes pleading. 'Not like this. Amanda, you're working beyond the law, I can't protect you.'

'Then don't,' Amanda shook herself free of his grip. 'If you truly wanted to help me you'd come with me now.'

'You're not following a legitimate lead.'

'Yes, I am,' she accessed the image of Will on the platform on her phone and waved it in Shane's face. 'See?'

'You can't show me that,' Shane pushed the device away. 'I can have no part in your illegal activity, Amanda.'

'Fine, suit yourself,' Amanda shouldered her way past him, heading for the door.

'If you go to Scotland then you're going alone,' Shane warned, his eyes wide with hurt like a dog who'd just been scolded.

'Then I'm going alone.' Amanda powered through the door, waving briefly at John before dashing out of the station towards her parked car. She didn't have much time if she hoped to catch Will while he was still in Glasgow. The thought of going alone filled her with dread, but she refused to give up. She was going to find her husband. No matter what.

17

Amanda could barely remember driving home from the police station. She was on auto-pilot as she navigated the narrow, twisting streets of Tremwell Bay. Her mind was already two steps ahead; plotting how she'd reach Scotland and what she'd do once she was there.

Back at her house Amanda hurried through the front door and up the stairs, gasping for breath as she burst into her bedroom. She hauled an old overnight bag out of her closet and began hastily filling it with items.

She kept asking herself questions she couldn't answer; how long would she be gone for? What did she need to take with her?

All the while her heartbeat drummed in her ears, marking each passing second.

'Please still be there,' she whispered tensely, thinking of Will as she shoved some jeans and a vest top into the overnight bag. She knew that her husband could already be long gone, having boarded a train at the station and disappeared to God knows where. Perhaps he'd disappeared into the Scottish highlands, out in the wilderness, away from the prying eyes of CCTV cameras, and thus untraceable. Grinding her teeth together, she kept packing, refusing to accept that Will had already moved on. He had to be in Scotland; it was the only lead she had.

With her bag packed, Amanda slung it over her shoulders and dashed out on to the landing. Powering down the stairs and entering the hallway, she saw the figure at the door before they'd even had chance to ring the bell.

'Dammit,' she dropped her bag to floor as her heart sunk. She didn't have time to waste. With a brief glance she looked towards the back of the house, towards the kitchen, and considered stealing out through the French doors and using the side gate to get to her car. But she guessed that the man at her door was Shane and she wasn't about to run away from him. He deserved better than that.

Amanda opened the door to find Shane was staring back at her. One hand lingered nervously by his side whilst the other was held up towards the doorbell.

'I…' he clicked his fingers together as if trying to summon the words.

'If you've come here to stop me then don't waste your breath.' Amanda was doubling back towards the staircase and grabbing her bag. 'I'm going to find him, Shane. I don't care what you say.'

'I'm not here to stop you.' Shane looked pale as sweat beaded on his forehead.

'Then why are you here?' Amanda demanded hotly.

'I'm coming with you.'

The shock of his comment caused Amanda to drop her bag a second time. It landed on her feet but she barely registered the weight. She was staring at Shane, looking deep into his eyes and trying to judge if he was joking or not, if this was all part of some ruse to make her stay.

'You're going to go, I get that,' he was talking quickly, his words running together. 'And I can't condone how you came by the information. But, Amanda,' he sighed when he looked at her, his jaw clenching, 'I just can't let you do this alone.'

'What about your job?'

'I told them that I'm following a lead on something. Because that's what I'm doing, right? If I'm gone any longer I'll tell them I got a sick bug.'

'Won't they wonder where you've gone?'

'I'm often out in the field during an investigation. I just need to make sure I keep checking in with them. Besides, John has my back.'

Amanda smiled sadly, remembering a time when John used to have her back too. It felt surreal to recall when they all would have done anything for one another. Stooping down, Amanda picked her bag back up and gave Shane a long, level look. Perhaps the distance between their former selves really wasn't so great. Because Shane was here, on her doorstep, willing to stand by her. Willing to prove the unconditional aspect of their friendship.

And it was just friendship. Amanda wanted to pinch herself to remind her of that. Jayne had ended things with Shane but that meant nothing. Amanda was still a married woman. Although she didn't actually know who she was even married to anymore. She released a dry laugh at the absurdity of it all.

'What's so funny?'

'I was just thinking that this is easily the most bizarre thing we've ever done,' she was stepping outside and locking up her front door. 'I mean, we're about to chase after my husband, who kind of isn't my husband as he's someone else entirely. It's madness.' She approached her car, breathing in the crisp, sweet air of a summer's morning. 'Are you sure you want to do this?' her hand rested on the door handle but she didn't open it up. 'I mean, I could go alone, Shane. It's no problem. I don't want you risking your job.'

'I'd rather risk losing my job than risk something happening to you.' He sounded so brave, so certain. This was a side of Shane that Amanda hadn't seen in so long that she'd thought it gone. 'That said,' he walked around to his car and popped the door open, 'I really think I should drive.'

'What?' Amanda's mouth fell open with her objection.

'Come on, Amanda, you're a terrible driver. And I'd like to get to Scotland in one piece.'

'I am not a terrible driver,' despite her protest Amanda was going over to Shane's car and dropping her bag into the boot.

'Remember when you knocked over the signpost outside of town?'

'It came out of nowhere!' Amanda was laughing as she climbed into the passenger seat, remembering the night in question. The streets of Tremwell Bay had been slick with rain and Amanda had barely passed her driving test. In her little beat-up Metro she'd driven Shane and John to the fancy cinema two towns over so that they could all watch *Avatar* in its full three-dimensional glory. Driving home, Amanda had been so caught up in chatting away with her friends that she forgot to fully commit to her role as driver. The next thing she knew she'd ploughed her little car straight into the sign for Tremwell Bay which had subsequently rested on her bonnet in a twisted medley of distorted metal.

'You drive then,' Amanda leaned back in her seat as Shane typed their destination into his satnav.

'It's going to be okay,' Shane assured her as he reversed out of her driveway. 'We're going to find him.'

*

There was an art to getting out of Tremwell Bay. You wanted to avoid all the little roundabouts decked out in flowers that got backed up the second more than one car approached them. You also wanted to avoid certain sets of traffic lights which were in seemingly constant use thanks to a steady flow of tourists. There was an art to it all which the satnav wasn't privy to, despite its formal, assured tone.

Shane cursed several times as they remained held in their little town thanks to an abundance of traffic. Almost forty minutes passed before they were out on the motorway, heading north towards Scotland.

They had barely spoken since they left the bay. Amanda pressed her head against the window and watched the passing traffic power by in the neighbouring lanes. The thought of seeing Will made her feel as contorted inside as the town sign which had almost made her car a write-off. A part of her was desperate to get folded up in his thick arms, to breathe in his familiar scent and just let go of all her worry, her anguish. But a larger part of her teetered between anger and confusion. Why had he left her like he had? And who was Jake Burton? Amanda needed answers.

A large lorry grunted by them in the next lane, the straps holding down its cargo flapping in the breeze.

'How about you don't drive like a grandma?' Amanda turned towards Shane, raising an eyebrow.

He gave her a tight shake of the head and kept his eyes on the road ahead. They were in the slow lane. They'd been in the slow lane since they'd merged onto the motorway some twenty miles ago.

'Seriously, Shane, I want to get there today not tomorrow,' Amanda moaned. She was all too aware of the fact that Will might not even be in Glasgow anymore.

'I'm not going to rush, Amanda,' he told her tightly.

'You're doing sixty,' she leaned forward to peer angrily at his speedometer.

'And that's just fine.'

'I should have driven,' Amanda sat back and sighed heavily.

'You weave through lanes like a pinball on acid.'

'Driving is boring,' Amanda rolled her eyes, 'switching lanes keeps it interesting.'

'And dangerous.'

'Since when did you become such a stickler for safety?'

'When I realized I had something to lose,' Shane looked away from the road for a second to let his eyes fall on Amanda. She found herself blushing beneath his gaze. 'Besides, we'll be there well before nightfall.'

'Right, great,' Amanda shifted nervously in her seat. Again she wondered what exactly she was going to say to Will. There was so much she needed to know.

'Are you thinking what you'll say to him?' Shane enquired after a moment's silence.

'I guess,' Amanda resumed watching the passing traffic speed by. She liked to look at the cars and imagine where the occupants were going, why there was the need for such haste.

'Do you think he'll be pleased that you tracked him down?' Shane asked, his jaw tightening.

'I...' Amanda wanted to say yes, of course he'd be pleased. Grateful even. He was her husband so he'd naturally expect her to come after him. But she didn't feel certain of his response. She didn't feel certain of anything when it came to Will anymore. Over the last few days, he'd become a stranger to her. 'I don't know,' she admitted sadly. She could feel a weight pressing against her chest, making each breath laboured. 'I hope so,' Amanda coughed against the pressure.

'If he's got any sense he'll be pleased.'

'Mmm.' Amanda knew that Will Thorn would be pleased to see her. He'd bundle her up in his arms and kiss her forehead and tell her how sorry he was to have worried her. But how would Jake Burton react? Amanda's hands twitched, thinking of her laptop which she'd shoved into her overnight bag before she'd left the house. The internet would be sluggish out on the motorway but she'd have enough of a signal to search for Jake Burton. She glanced at Shane out of the corner of her eye. He was once again focused on driving, both hands resting firmly on the wheel. It seemed like he was rarely off duty, always acting like the cop he now was.

But he was here with her in the car. That had to mean something. That he was okay with some of her methods. Maybe he was okay with her accessing the darknet in his presence? Amanda turned in her seat, wondering how she could get him to stop for a moment, pull off the motorway and allow her to access her laptop. She desperately wanted to keep checking for updates, it felt like a compulsion, one which she'd not had to resist since she was a student. The black hole of the darknet was definitely drawing her in, placing her beneath its shadowy spell. Her mouth opened to ask for a bathroom break when her phone buzzed in her pocket. The vibration trembled through her body as Amanda squirmed in her seat to allow herself easy access to it.

There was an alert on the screen. Amanda sucked in a breath, her eyes wide. The alert was from the scrape she'd set up on her laptop. It had made another positive ID. Amanda looked at the image on the screen, feeling dizzy.

Will was stood putting petrol into a car she didn't recognize. The image was a little blurry. She couldn't make out the registration number of the car, but she knew it was Will who was filling it up, even if his features weren't as clear as they were in the previous picture. He was in the same clothes, one arm casually resting on the roof of the car, just a man filling up with petrol not a husband on the run. He was glancing upwards, unknowingly locking eyes with a CCTV camera overhead.

'Oh my God,' Amanda's free hand was at her throat.

'What is it?' Shane immediately sounded alarmed.

'My um…' Was he going to be mad at her for still using the darknet? Did it even matter anymore? 'My scrape made another positive ID.'

'On Will?' An edge crept into Shane's voice which Amanda couldn't decipher.

'Uh-huh.'

'So where is he? Is he still in Glasgow?'

'Just let me…' Amanda was logging into her laptop via her phone. She needed more details. 'He's at a service station, but I don't know where.'

The internet was frustratingly slow as Amanda waited to be told where and when the image had been taken. She knew the feed between her laptop and phone was slow, the delay could have already wasted precious time.

Finally, the address came up on her screen. Amanda peered at the unfamiliar places, trying to put all the pieces together.

'Well?' Shane was growing inpatient.

'Dunbroch.' Amanda said the name of the place as though it didn't fit properly in her mouth. She'd never heard of it before.

'Dunbroch?' Shane repeated with more ease. 'That's in the

south of Scotland. Small town, pretty rural. I went camping there once with my scout troop.'

Amanda was barely listening as she stared at her phone in disbelief. So Will had already moved on from Glasgow. But why? It seemed like he was running, but from what? From her?

'How old is the image?' Shane pressed her.

Amanda typed things into her phone, groaning at the sluggish connection. Begrudgingly, the device revealed the additional information.

'It was taken three hours ago.'

'Right, okay,' Shane sped up and eased into the middle lane.

Amanda threw him a frantic look. 'What are you doing? What happened to slow and steady?'

'Your husband just became a flight risk. He's moving too much.'

'What?'

'He's in Dunbroch now, but within the next twenty-four hours he could be anywhere in Scotland and that scrape of yours won't find him if he holes himself up on some distant island. If you want to catch him, we need to act fast.'

'So, what, we're just going to drive to Dunbroch?' Amanda blurted. She and Shane used to plan about taking road trips together, about driving off towards the sunset and seeing where the night took them. But they never did it. It remained yet another pie-in-the-sky idea between the couple.

'It's not much further than Glasgow. Do you want to find your husband?'

'Yes,' Amanda responded instinctively.

'Then we need to move quickly.'

'So we're going to Dunbroch?'

Shane nodded as he entered the fast lane. 'So we're going to Dunbroch.'

18

Amanda's phone did not buzz with an alert again. The scrape of the CCTV networks she'd set up didn't make another positive ID. The day was ending as they drove into Scotland, the sun slipping away to reveal a canopy of sparkling stars.

'Just a few more hours,' Shane muttered wearily from the driver's seat. He'd shed his jacket and tie earlier but remained in his shirt, the sleeves rolled up to his elbows.

The drive to Scotland was long. When her laptop chirped in her lap, Amanda almost missed the sound. But Shane caught it.

'Your umm,' he released one hand from the wheel to wave it at her. 'Your laptop just made a noise,' he clicked his fingers and Amanda straightened in her seat. She'd been on the cusp of sleep, drifting away to somewhere blissful, but now she was back on the road, back staring at the rear end of cars as she chased after her missing husband.

'It did?' Amanda wondered groggily as she popped open the device and logged in.

A new message. Her stomach churned when she saw that it was for Lambchop. And as she saw who the message was from, her palms grew clammy: Turtle82.

She'd ignored Turtle's original message, refused to accept that it might contain a thinly veiled threat. Whoever was behind the Turtle82 account they'd been furious when Amanda announced her retirement from the world from hacking. They'd made threats. Threats which her younger self had naively dismissed.

Watching Shane out of the corner of her eye, Amanda opened up the message within her darknet account. If she told him that she was scared, that Turtle had found her again he'd be more than mad, he'd be furious. He'd make her shut down her darknet account completely and without it they were flying blind in their search for Will.

Ignore me all you want but our

153

```
paths    will    cross    again.    It's
fate.
   T.
```

What did that even mean? Amanda frowned at the screen. Was Turtle *following* her? Did they plan on bursting into her life right in the middle of her searching for Will? It was more than Amanda could handle. She hit delete and slammed her laptop shut.

'Everything okay?' Shane wondered as he overtook a car hauling along a beat-up caravan.

Amanda watched the vehicle with suspicion, wondering if Turtle82 was hidden in the shabby caravan, hunched over a laptop and smirking to themselves as they fired off sinister messages to her.

'You ever worry that in your pursuit of honey you stirred up the bees nest too much?' she was too tired to pretend everything was fine. Too wrung-out to make up a convincing cover story.

'This about the darknet?' Shane's gaze flickered over the laptop, quickly making the connection. Amanda couldn't deny that he made a great cop. He was so intuitive and observant. Qualities which she'd ultimately found highly irritating as their relationship entered its death throes.

'I…' a pained sigh fluttered up from Amanda's chest and danced across her lips. 'An old contact is kind of hounding me.'

'Hounding you how?'

'Just some weird messages.' It sounded so juvenile when Amanda said it aloud. So stupid. She was getting stressed out over some *messages.*

'This connected to the stuff you did in college?'

'Uh-huh.'

'I can't protect you from that world, Amanda. You should just shut it all down before anyone can trace you.'

Too late.

Turtle82 was possibly the only hacker Amanda knew who was better than herself. If they wanted to find her they'd always figure out a way. Online no one could stay hidden forever.

'Just shut it all down,' Shane repeated, his tone sharp. 'I mean it, Amanda. We can find Will the old-fashioned way.'

'No,' Amanda surprised herself with the certainty in her

voice. 'I mean,' she smoothed her hands across her closed laptop. Let Turtle82 chase her. Let them send her a thousand sinister messages. She'd delete them all. And then Lambchop. Once she'd found her husband. All that mattered was finding Will. 'Not yet.'

'It sounds like it's getting dangerous, Amanda.'

'It is,' she admitted with a nod. 'But it's nothing I can't handle.'

'Amanda—'

'He's worth it,' she snapped. 'Any danger I'm putting myself in is worth it if it means I find Will. Jake. Whatever. Just keep driving please.'

'Fine,' Shane's hands tightened against the wheel, 'you never would listen to me about all that darknet stuff anyway. Not sure why I'd expect you to start now.'

*

Time seemed to have lost all meaning. Beyond the windows of the car, the world changed. Green farmland divided by ancient oak trees was gradually replaced by still hills adorned with tightly packed heather. The motorways had thinned down to winding narrow lanes which twisted through the other worldly landscape. Twice Amanda looked down on the serene surface of a loch which spread towards the horizon like a miniature ocean.

Within the car little changed. Shane connected his iPod to his stereo, letting the songs of their youth blast through their thoughts. Amanda felt reassured by the passionate vocals and frantic drumbeats which helped her heart keep a steady, nervous rhythm in her chest. With each passing mile she potentially got closer to her husband. But oddly the more they travelled, the farther away from him she felt, like it was not the distance that divided them but more the canyon that Will's lies had opened up. It grew wider with every new piece of information, to the point where it was no almost impassable.

'You goin' to get that?' Shane was glancing at Amanda, his hands tight on the steering wheel.

'Huh?' she blinked, pulling herself out of a stupor. She was lingering somewhere between waking and dreaming. With a yawn she wondered how long it had actually been since she'd had a decent night's sleep.

Shane pointed to Amanda's pocket where her phone was vibrating angrily like a giant hornet.

'Crap.' Rubbing at her eyes, Amanda plucked the device from her pocket and regarded the screen uneasily. Was she that tired she'd failed to notice it pulsating against her thigh? Her mum's details were flashing on the screen.

'It's my mum,' Amanda groaned as she slid forward in her seat to silence the stereo. For a second all she could hear was the rumble of the engine and the gentle rotation of the four tyres beneath her. She knew better than to ignore the call. If she did Corrine would just keep calling, her mother was persistent like that.

'Hey, Mum.'

'Honey, is everything okay?' Corrine sounded anxious.

'Mmm, I'm fine.' Amanda squeezed her eyes shut, wondering how much of the truth she could reveal to her mother.

'Are you driving?'

'Umm, no. Not me.'

'Then who are you with? Are you all right? You've not called me all day.' Corrine was beginning to sound hurt, clearly worried by her daughter's lack of communication.

Amanda threw Shane a look, needing guidance. If she admitted where she actually was she'd just be met with another barrage of questions. Questions she couldn't answer. At this point she didn't even know how long she'd be gone, or what would happen when she found Will. If she found him. The uncertainty of it all caused a leaden lump to settle in Amanda's stomach, weighing her down and making her feel nauseous.

'Shane is taking me camping.'

'Shane?'

Slapping her palm against her forehead, Amanda cringed. It was such a random lie to tell, but sort of half true. She was with Shane. And they were on a road trip. Kind of.

'He knows how down I've been lately, so he's just trying to cheer me up,' Amanda was speaking fast, trying to work her way out of the lie as quickly as possible.

'Well isn't that nice of him?' Corrine's voice was bright with approval. She'd always liked Shane. Her fondness for him was a large part of why she struggled to warm to Will.

'Yeah, it's…' Amanda caught Shane looking at her. When she glanced his way he swiftly returned his attention to the road, a blush creeping up his neck. 'It's very nice of him.'

'When will you be home?'

'In a few days I guess.'

'And what about Will?'

Amanda reached for the dashboard to steady herself, wondering how to respond.

Will is on the run in Scotland, Mum. His name isn't even Will. He's been lying to me all along. The man that I married isn't my husband.

'Shane said the second the police get a lead we'll come straight home. I just can't…' Amanda's hand was on her heart, she could feel every pained beat. 'I sit around all day waiting on a call, waiting on him to walk through the front door and tell me that everything is fine, but it hasn't happened. He hasn't come home.'

'But he will, Amanda.' Corrine must have sensed her daughter's weakening resolve as she offered the words of support.

I'm not so sure, Mum.

'I know. I just need a few days to clear my head.'

'Well make sure you keep calling me, okay? You know how I worry about you.'

'Yeah, Mum. Sure.'

'I love you.'

'Love you too.' Amanda ended the call and shoved her phone back into her pocket. During their conversation the darkness outside had thickened. There were no street lights, no silvery light of a moon to guide them. It was as if the car had strayed into a black hole.

'Where the hell are we?' Amanda peered at the nothingness, hoping that the shadows might briefly part to reveal something to her.

'Apparently just a few miles outside of Dunbroch,' Shane glanced at his satnav. 'We could really do with stopping and getting some petrol.'

'Stop where?' Beyond her window Amanda saw only darkness.

'There should be a service station just up ahead,' Shane

nodded at the digital screen glowing blue on his dashboard. It shone as bright as the Northern Star within the car.

'This is creepy,' Amanda sunk down in her seat. She could feel the reality of her situation punching through the cocoon of her fatigue like tiny poisoned darts. They were in another country, seemingly in the middle of nowhere, chasing a ghost. Will Thorn didn't even exist, not really.

'There was an old truck following us a few miles back,' Shane's eyes glistening mischievously in the light of the satnav.

'Don't,' Amanda warned.

'You were too busy taking a nap to notice. But when it got up real close I got a look at its licence plate.'

'Stop it.'

'It was tough to make out at first, but it kind of looked like it said, Be Eating You. You know, like B ETNG U.'

'Shane!'

He was laughing heartily to himself, the jovial sound filling up the car. Amanda playfully stretched out her arms and gave him a light punch on the knee.

'That's not funny and you know it. That film proper scared me.'

'I don't know what you're talking about,' Shane was still smiling. His hair was rough and unstyled thanks to hours spent running his hands through it. And without his jacket and tie he looked so much like the Shane Amanda had fallen in love with; the guy who was always carefree and full of impossible dreams. 'I was just telling you about this truck I saw.'

'You're just trying to scare me.'

Shane started to sing, taking on a creepy voice, 'Jeepers, creepers, where'd you get those peepers?'

'That's it, stop the car,' Amanda was reaching for the handle on her door.

'But then you're playing right into its hands. It wants us to stop the car. For you to get out. Makes you easy prey.'

'Shane!' Amanda squealed his name. She knew he was just winding her up, but out in the middle of nowhere, in the pitch-black, his method for teasing was proving worryingly effective.

'Ooh,' Shane was looking ahead, leaning forward to scrutinize the darkness.

'Seriously, don't bother. I'm in no mood to be freaked out.'

'No, look,' he lifted one hand from the wheel to gesture

ahead. Amanda looked. Lights flickered ahead in the distance like tiny fireflies. Only she could tell from their linear layout that there was nothing natural about these lights. They were approaching a town.

'We must have reached Dunbroch,' she muttered as she stretched in her seat and ran her fingers through her hair, wondering why she didn't feel more excited to have reached their destination.

'And not a moment too soon, I'm dangerously low on petrol.'

It only took ten minutes for Shane to find the service station. All of the petrol pumps were empty, so he slid the car towards the one closest to the twenty-four hour convenience store where he'd have to pay. The bright flood lights burned against Amanda, feeling as strong as the sun after the darkness they'd come from. She rubbed at her eyes as they tried to adjust.

'I'll just load her up,' Shane was climbing out, letting the sticky air of a warm night enter the car as he opened the door.

'Okay.' Amanda rubbed at her legs, hating how much they ached. Her entire body felt disjointed, as though she'd been taken apart and then put together incorrectly.

'Actually,' Shane was looking back in at her, one hand resting on the roof of his car.

'If you're going to tell me that creepy truck has just pulled in then don't bother,' Amanda was pouting as she tried to suppress a playful smile. This was classic Shane; to harp on about a story until he'd finally reeled her in.

'No,' he shook his head, his expression serious. 'I was thinking it might be worth asking the guy in the store if he's seen your husband.'

'Oh.' Amanda's lips twitched down in disappointment. The game was over, they were back to the grim reality of searching for a man who might not even want to be found. 'Oh,' she forced herself to make a quick recovery, suddenly sounding overly enthused. 'Yes, of course. That's a great idea.'

'What can I say?' Shane shrugged with faux modesty, 'I'm always thinking like a cop.'

Amanda climbed out the car. It felt good to be standing up, to be able to stretch out all her aching muscles. She could feel the fibres in her body singing with release, like a spring that had finally been sprung. Pressing her hands to the base of her spine, she leaned back, savouring the feeling as she worked out some of the knots she'd acquired during the long drive. She watched Shane standing on the other side of the car, his head dipped down in concentration as he filled the vehicle with petrol. His shirt clung to him and his jawline had darkened with the promise of fresh stubble. He looked dangerous yet reliable all at the same time. He'd retained his boyish good looks but was a fine figure of a man. Amanda tucked her hair behind her ear and tried not to stare. It had been a long time since she'd looked at Shane that way; like he was a real guy and not just some boy from her past.

'Sometime this week would be good,' Shane looked up, surprising her, as he nodded towards the gaudily lit convenience store.

'Okay, okay, I'm going.' Amanda reached for her phone and unlocked the screen. It didn't take her long to find a decent picture of Will that she had stored. It was the one from their wedding day which she kept on her front room wall; the one where they were both smiling as though they'd never been happier. Pushing back her shoulders, Amanda boldly strode into the store. The glass double doors slowly parted for her as the cool air conditioning swept against her skin, causing it to prickle.

At the far end behind a bright red counter stood a middle-aged man with a thick black beard and soft blue eyes. His hands were resting on his little pot belly, but as Amanda approached he straightened and smiled at her, revealing slightly crooked teeth.

'Good evening.' His eyes widened just slightly.

Amanda flashed him a nervous smile. 'Hi, um, good evening,' she did her best to mimic his greeting. The stale odour of cigarettes clung to his clothes. 'I, uh,' she pressed a hand to her chest, 'I'm looking for my husband.' She held up her phone towards the store clerk, pointing at Will's smiling face. 'This man is my husband. He's missing and might be in the area. Have you seen him?' Amanda was talking slowly, overly pronouncing every word like she used to have to do with her late Grandmother when the old woman started to lose her hearing.

The bearded man looked at the image on the phone and then back at Amanda. He frowned, eyeing her uneasily.

'My husband,' Amanda repeated, more insistent. She tapped Will's face in the picture. 'Have you seen him?'

Clearing his throat, the bearded man focused on Amanda's phone with admirable intensity. His eyes narrowed as he scrutinized the image before eventually giving a slow shake of his head.

'Ach, no, I've not seen him.'

His accent was so thick that Amanda had to really listen to catch each of the words.

'Okay,' she hid her disappointment behind a gentle smile, 'well thanks anyway.'

Back in the car Amanda closed her eyes and waited for Shane to finish filling up on petrol. She could feel the ache of her heart in her chest. She was so close to finding Will, but then why did she still feel so far away from him? From the truth of it all? When Shane climbed back in he brought a burst of sharp evening air with him which made Amanda's skin bristle.

'God, you took long enough,' she muttered, not opening her eyes.

'I'm guessing the guy in there was a dead end?'

'No, he knew exactly where my husband is,' Amanda replied sarcastically.

'I'll forgive your ratty attitude because you're tired.'

'I don't have a ratty attitude.'

'Yes, you do,' Shane nodded knowingly. 'Whenever you're sleep-deprived you become a monster. You're like a gremlin, only instead of not giving you water in order to keep you cute and lovable I need to ensure you're fully rested at all times.'

'I'm not—' Amanda stopped herself. She could sense the ache behind her eyes, the frustration gnawing at her every conscious thought. Shane was right. She was morphing into a monstrous version of herself because she was teetering on the point of exhaustion.

'There's a little bed and breakfast close by. The guy in the store recommended it when I paid for the petrol. Let's book ourselves in, get some rest and then conduct a more thorough search for Will tomorrow.'

'But what if he leaves while we're sleeping?'

'Look around.' Shane gestured at the small streets beyond his windscreen that were lit by old-fashioned street lamps. 'Will didn't come here as part of a whistle-stop tour. He came here to hide. This place is in the middle of nowhere. It's not like he could be scheduling himself a flight out of the country from here or anything.'

'So you think he'll still be here tomorrow?'

'He better be,' Shane drove forward, letting the satnav guide him to the nearby hotel. 'I refuse to take my chances overnight with ogre Amanda.'

'I am not an ogre.'

'That's exactly what an ogre would say.'

'You're so annoying,' Amanda rubbed at her eyes, managing to smile despite how tired she was.

'Be warned, I may have to book us in at the B&B and engage in conversation which will delay you getting into bed and being able to rest your grumpiness.'

'You're not funny.'

'No, I'm hilarious.'

It was the comeback Shane always used to throw at her when they were playfully arguing beside one of their beachfront bonfires. Against the crackle and pop of the wood they'd taunt one another, John included. It was always in good humour, and as the fire died Shane would bundle Amanda up beside him in a blanket and they'd fall asleep side by side, their bodies intertwined so that you couldn't tell where the one ended and the other began.

Amanda yawned sleepily. Sat in the car she felt that if she stretched out her hand she'd be able to feel the heat radiating off the bonfire, that if she strained to listen she'd hear the gentle rush of the nearby waves. Her eyes slid shut as a contented smile pulled on her lips.

*

If the satnav was still on she'd tell them they'd arrived at their destination, but Billy turned her off miles ago, citing his nerves couldn't take her superior tone any longer.

Jake was driving again. He pulled the truck up into the dirt driveway which led towards the two warehouses. They were both made from sheets of corrugated metal and in the early morning light they looked almost alien. Climbing out, he dropped against the ground, a few tentative blades of dew-soaked grass getting crunched beneath his boots. He strode around to the back of the truck, preparing to throw open its doors, when something grabbed him, pulling him into the shadows.

'What the fuck, man?' Jake raged as he shook off his friend. 'You scared the shit out of me.'

'Sorry,' Billy smoothed his hands down the front of his faded hoodie. His hands were shaking.

'Seriously, you sure you're not high?' Jake demanded tersely.

'I'm not high,' Billy strained to keep his voice low. 'But there's something you need to know.' He leaned away from Jake and looked into the shadows surrounding them. Then, coming back in close, he whispered; 'We're not selling this shit here today.'

'We're not?'

But that had been McAllister's plan. The one he'd fervently insisted they carry out. The one he'd made threats about.

'No,' Billy shook his head, 'we're not. We're going to buy some more shit and take this through the tunnel, into Europe and make some real fucking money.'

'Jesus, Billy—'

'We cut out the middle man, McAllister, and pocket the cash all for ourselves. We'll give him the measly twenty-four grand he was going to give us.'

'I don't think it works that way.'

'Just, trust me.' Billy reached into the seam of his jeans and produced a pistol. Jake clocked its dark shape in the dim light and instantly recoiled.

'What the fuck is that for?' He stared at the gun as though it were a bomb which might go off at any given second.

'Just... take it,' Billy forced the gun into Jake's hands. 'I've got one too. Consider it insurance.'

'Billy—'

'I'm looking out for us on this, Jake. Don't I always look out for us?'

'Yes, but—'

'Just follow my lead. Okay?'

Jake was silent.

'We've got this, Jake. After today, we'll live like kings. Trust me.'

Those were the last words Billy ever said to him.

19

'Morning sunshine.'

The male voice pulled Amanda out of her dream. She sat up in a bed that wasn't her own in a room she didn't recognize. The walls were covered in faded floral wallpaper, the threadbare curtains open to reveal a glorious blue sky and beneath it a collection of grey buildings with slanted slate roofs. Amanda rubbed her eyes and looked down at the duvet she was currently huddled beneath. It bore the same design as the walls; roses on the vine stretching endlessly along the fabric. Each petal and leaf dulled by steady use over a considerable amount of years.

'You sleep okay?' Shane was on the other side of the room, watching her with interest. His hair was damp and his eyes bright.

'I… um,' Amanda glanced at the bed. The far side of it was unmade, the sheets still tucked in tightly to the mattress.

'I slept in the chair,' Shane nodded towards a pink bucket chair in the corner which had probably once been a brilliant shade of red.

'You did?' Amanda wondered groggily.

'I thought I was being a gentleman,' Shane pushed his hands through his hair, shaking out the remaining droplets of water. 'I tried to get two rooms but when only one was available I had to settle for us sharing. I considered sleeping in my car but figured you wouldn't mind me sleeping in the chair.'

Amanda smiled thinly, remembering all too well a time when she and Shane would share a bed, would sleep side by side. He used to always tuck her up in his arms like a child cradling their favourite stuffed toy. He'd hold her tight until they both drifted off to sleep and inevitably rolled over to their own side of the bed.

'Did you sleep all right in it?' the chair looked far from comfortable. It had a rigid back and armrests worn away to reveal the wood beneath them.

'Better than I would have in the bed,' Shane laughed. Amanda froze, wondering what he meant. 'You thrashed about a lot,' he swiftly explained before she could dwell on the meaning of his comment. 'I guess you were having nightmares.'

The cliff. The drop. Her air catching in her lungs. Amanda sighed and closed her eyes. The dream had been so close, so real. She could taste the salt in the air.

'It still bothers you, huh?' Shane carefully sat down on the edge of the bed. He used to hold Amanda during the darkest hours of the night, whispering to her that everything was okay, that it was just a nightmare.

'Sometimes,' she told him a little too briskly as she climbed out of bed. 'But they're just dreams.'

'There's power in dreams, Amanda,' he called after her as she headed into the bathroom.

*

It was hot in Dunbroch. Much hotter than it had been back in Tremwell Bay. The residents of the small Scottish town were in the midst of a heatwave. Though there was an electricity in the air which hinted that there were storms on the not too distant horizon.

Even in her denim cut-offs and lace tunic top Amanda felt overdressed. Squinting against the early morning sun, she wished she'd taken the time to pack some sunglasses. But everything had been done in such haste.

'So what now?' she turned to Shane as they stepped out of the bed and breakfast and on to the small street outside which steeply led up towards the centre of town.

Shane was in the same shirt and trousers as the previous day. Shielding his eyes from the sun with his hand, he peered up the street. 'We need to go in some of the local shops, ask if anyone has seen Will.'

Amanda nodded and chewed her lip thoughtfully. She kept hoping that her phone would come to life with a new alert, that she'd be given another positive ID of Will somewhere specific. But no matter how much she repeatedly checked her phone and laptop no new information came through. The town they were in was so rustic there wasn't a CCTV camera in sight. And there were a lot of tourists. They were already floating up the street in their large sun hats clutching their digital cameras. Will was hardly going to stand out in a town that was accustomed to harbouring strangers.

'Do you even think he's still here?' Amanda wondered despondently.

'It's the only lead we've got,' Shane shrugged as he began making his way up the steep street.

*

Two hours later and Amanda was fast approaching her limit. Her limbs were on fire thanks to the burning sun and the steep streets. And each time she entered a shop there was no respite from the stifling heat since nowhere had air conditioning. It felt like walking around in a permanent furnace.

'I'm so nearly done with this,' she panted as she kept pace with Shane. In each shop it was the same story; Amanda would present her phone and the image of her and Will on their wedding day. People would frown, throw her a bemused look and she knew what they were all thinking – what kind of person has to hunt down their husband? Some people even gave her a pitying look as they studied her, as if she was just in denial and needed to accept that her husband had left her.

In the darkened depths of pubs the regulars would gaze sadly at Amanda over their glasses of whisky and tell her she was wasting her time, that a pretty girl like her should be off living her life.

'We've just got a few more places left to check,' Shane guided her into a small bakery. He refused to be discouraged by their lack of success. The window display was full of cakes and pastries which were all glossed with a sugary coating. Amanda's stomach growled as she studied an egg custard and its perfect yellow surface.

Shane went in first and pulled his cop routine to ensure compliance from the shopkeeper. There was nothing like a police presence to bring out people's most honest natures. Amanda had no idea what he was even saying. She just waited until he gestured for her and then raised her phone up to whoever was being questioned.

In the bakery it was an elderly woman with impressively dark hair which was gathered at the nape of her neck in a loose-fitting bun. She reached for a pair of tortoiseshell reading glasses when Amanda offered her the phone. Taking the device in her leathery hands, she studied the image, her old eyes squinting.

'You seen him before?' Shane prompted her response. The old woman pursed her thin lips and began to nod.

'Yes,' she tapped Will's face with a long nail. 'Yes.'

Amanda's heart danced in her chest as she heard the word yes. It was the first positive response she'd had all day.

'What? Have you seen him?' she immediately fired her questions at the old woman who merely nodded patiently at the couple.

'I've seen him,' the woman confirmed coolly.

'What, where?' Amanda was barely holding herself together. She wanted to reach across the counter, grab the woman and shake all the information out of her. Thankfully, Shane was much more restrained.

'Can you tell us when you saw him?' he wondered politely.

'Yesterday. Such a tall fella, hard to forget.'

'That's him,' Amanda slapped her hands down against the counter. 'Did he say where he was going? Why he was here? Who was he with?'

Shane reached for her hand and gave it a squeeze, urging her to calm down.

'Do you think he's still in town?' he asked the woman levelly.

'Should think so,' she nodded, pursing her thin lips. 'Mrs Morris said he's renting a holiday cottage just outside of Dunbroch. Lovely little place. So close to the sea.'

'A holiday cottage?' Amanda gasped, stepping back from the counter. Questions sprinted through her mind. Why a holiday cottage? Had Will up and left her to go on an impromptu vacation? But that made no sense. She swallowed and forced out the question she feared to ask. 'Was he alone when you saw him?'

To her relief the old woman nodded. 'He was alone, yes.'

Then what the hell? Amanda stormed out of the bakery and began retracing her steps back to the bed and breakfast. She could hear Shane chasing after her as she lamented to herself; 'Why is he holed up in some cottage on his own? I've got to go and see him.' She was almost running when Shane grabbed her wrists and forced her to halt.

'We need to think this through,' he said stoically.

'What's to think about?' Amanda shook herself free from his grip and continued powering down the street. 'He's my husband,' she called back over her shoulder, 'I've got to go to him.'

*

'I'm not going over this again,' Amanda declared as she checked her reflection in the small mirror in the car's visor.

'Amanda, I just—'

'I told you I'm going alone.' When she was sure that her hair looked as good as it was going to she snapped the visor back up and peered beyond the windscreen at the field of long grass which swayed gently in a pleasant breeze.

'It's not a good idea,' Shane told her, sounding like the cop he was back home. 'The situation might be dangerous.'

'How?' Amanda demanded. 'He's my husband for Christ's sake and he's holed up in some little holiday cottage in the south of Scotland. That hardly sounds like dangerous behaviour to me.'

'He's not who he says he is,' Shane continued, undeterred. 'He's a criminal, Amanda. And I only know about the crimes he got caught for. What about other things he may have done? We still don't know why Jake Burton was reported as dead. Think about what he might be running from, you don't want to get embroiled in all this.'

'Whatever his reason for being here, it won't suddenly make us unmarried.' Amanda was watching the long grass sway as if dancing to music that only the vegetation around the car could hear. The B&B and Dunbroch were twenty minutes behind them and they were sat parked up at the edge of a field. They decided not to take the car any closer. The rest of the journey towards the holiday cottage would have to be made on foot. And Amanda wasn't looking for company. The woman at the bakery had been certain that it was the southernmost cottage in town that Will, Jake, had rented.

Amanda had to hope that the old woman was right, that she hadn't guided them towards a cottage full of a happy family spending their holiday by the sea.

'He lied about his name, what else might he have lied about?' Shane's question pulled her out of her own thoughts.

'I won't know unless I ask him.' Amanda moved to open the car door, but Shane tugged her back, just as he had been doing for the past fifteen minutes.

'Let me go inside,' he pleaded.

'Because he'd be so receptive to that; my ex-boyfriend showing up,' Amanda rolled her eyes.

'Amanda—'

'Please, just let me handle this. Despite all the lies, I do know him, Shane.'

'It's not safe, at least let me call for some back-up from the local authorities.'

'And treat him like a common criminal when he's done nothing wrong?' Amanda's cheeks flushed with outrage. The picturesque town wasn't the backdrop for a criminal in hiding. Amanda felt her guard. Will was still her oak tree, her port in a storm. And as soon as she saw him he'd explain everything.

'He left you!' Shane smacked his hands against the steering wheel. 'And he is a bloody criminal. At least Jake Burton is. He left you without saying a damned word, knowing he risked breaking your heart. How could he just up and leave you like that?'

'You tell me,' Amanda countered coolly. As close as she'd got to Shane over the last two weeks and as good as it'd felt to reconnect, she couldn't forget that their love story had ultimately had an unhappy ending. Exhausted by the countless battles they kept fighting in the war that was their relationship they'd both simply surrendered and walked away. It was a decision Amanda often found herself regretting in the small hours of the night when she'd been woken by a nightmare. But she locked those feelings away because she knew no good would come of them.

'Regret makes you weak,' Corrine had said after Ivor's death. Amanda kept asking her mother to take down pictures of her beloved father which were all around the house. Each time she cast her eyes on one, it was like taking a bullet. But Corrine refused.

'To take them down would be saying that I don't want to remember. That I have regrets.'

'But it hurts to see him,' Amanda had wept.

'As much as it hurts me too, it warms my heart at the same time,' Corrine had tenderly traced a finger down a picture of the little family out on the beach the previous summer. The image was all smiles and sunshine, there was no heavy cloud on the horizon foretelling the dark hand fate would soon deal them. 'I loved your father deeply and I regret nothing. I want to look around and see his face every day. It helps keep him alive.'

Amanda wrestled her mobile phone out of her pocket and looked at the picture which she'd been brandishing around town. She and Will looked so happy, like one of those irritatingly perfect couples you see advertising summer vacations. She was wrapped up in Will's strong embrace, gazing into the camera.

'I need to know the truth and I need to hear it directly from him,' she said quietly as she kept staring at the face of her husband who was in very real danger of becoming a stranger to her.

'Just let me go with you. I'll—'

'No.' Amanda cut Shane off. 'You've seriously done enough, Shane. More than enough. You've risked your job to help me. I'm not going to forget that. But I need to do this alone, surely you understand?'

Shane wasn't looking at her, he was staring ahead as if mesmerized by the long grass in the field.

'Go back to the B&B and wait for me there.' Amanda opened her door. Warm afternoon air danced up her bare legs. When Shane made no signs of objection, she climbed out fully and stood up beside the car, peering out across the field. From where she was standing she could just make out the distant roof of a small building. The patter of her heartbeat sped up as she considered how close she was to being reunited with Will. How close she was to meeting Jake Burton.

'I'll call you in an hour or so and you can come and pick me up,' she leaned back into the car and forced herself to smile at Shane, hoping she looked more confident than she felt.

'I won't leave town without you,' Shane told her, his green eyes misty.

'I know,' Amanda's smile widened as it became genuine.

'One hour,' Shane said tightly. 'And then I'm coming to get you. And that's non-negotiable, you understand?'

'One hour is more than enough,' Amanda looked towards the little roof, wondering what Will was doing at that moment. Was he sat in a window bathed in sunlight, head bent down towards a book? Or was he sat in the cottage's small garden looking out to the sea which shimmered distantly on the horizon?

'Any sign of trouble you call me,' Shane ordered. 'And I'll be here right away.'

Amanda nodded, wondering what kind of trouble Shane envisioned occurring? She braced herself for the painful truth that Will was living another life, that he had some Scottish wife stashed away somewhere. She touched a hand to her chest, wondering if her heart was strong enough to handle it. Glancing back at Shane, she knew that she was strong enough because she wasn't alone. Shane was willing to be there at her side, to bear witness to her showdown with Will. He'd even risked his beloved job to help her. The level of his dedication to her made Amanda's knees briefly weaken. She reached for the car to support herself. At the end of their relationship she'd desperately wanted Shane to put her at the top of his list. And now he had.

'You okay?' Shane was instantly peering up at her, his voice pitched with concern.

'I'm fine,' Amanda stepped away from the car and edged purposefully towards the field. 'See you in an hour,' she threw a quick wave over her shoulder and entered the field, letting the grass tickle against her legs. The sun was bright overhead and the air held a sweetness to it. But all Amanda could hear was the steady drumbeat of her own heart as she forced herself to move forwards, to approach the cottage which she prayed contained her husband and all his secrets. Secrets which might possibly destroy them both.

20

Amanda ignored the metallic taste in her mouth and did her best to focus. Sunlight was bleeding in through the windows in the small kitchen, casting ornate shadows upon the bare wooden floors.

But Amanda didn't notice them. Nor did she smell the heady aroma of heather floating in through the open door or hear the gentle rustle of the long grass outside as a cooling breeze brushed its way through it.

All she saw was the barrel of the gun looming inches away from her head. There was only darkness in its depths. And possibly her own death. Her fate hung on the twitch of a trigger. Amanda had known fear like this before when she was eight years old and she'd almost tumbled over the edge of the cliffs near her home. The sun had been shining that day too.

Only now her father wasn't waiting in the wings to save her.

'Why did you come here?' he growled the question at her, each word drenched in angry disdain.

Amanda swallowed, using the second to gather her thoughts. She couldn't risk saying, or doing, the wrong thing.

'I had to.' She squeaked out the words like the frightened mouse she had become.

'No,' he was shaking his head but the hand holding the gun remained eerily stoic, like his muscles were well rehearsed in steadily managing its weight. 'You should never have come here.'

The taste in Amanda's mouth grew sharper. Just as it had that day when she had begun to fall over the cliff edge and saw the sea and jagged rocks swirling beneath her. She defiantly raised her chin to meet his gaze.

'I had to come,' she told him, her voice strengthening along with her resolve. 'I had to find you.'

'It's too dangerous here,' Will's words came out as a roar. Amanda licked her lips and reminded herself to stay calm, to look her husband in the eye. But each time she tried to meet his gaze she found herself locking eyes with the dark abyss which existed down the barrel of the gun he was holding.

The cottage had seemed so quaint when she approached it, as though it had been lifted directly from the pages of a fairy-tale book. It had a wooden blue door and the walls were covered in climbing rose bushes which reminded her of home. Amanda had felt calm, almost serene as she knocked briskly on the door. But the second the door swung open Amanda's illusion of tranquillity was shattered. She noticed the gun before she saw her husband. Her legs shook and she struggled to follow his order when he commanded her to get inside.

In any other circumstance she'd admire the pretty tiles on the kitchen walls, how some of them contained painted images of bottles of wine and thistles. But Amanda kept looking at the gun, not daring to take her eyes off it.

'Why did you leave?' she forced out the question that haunted her the most, unable to stop the tears which began to slide down her cheeks.

'Amanda,' the gun lowered, just a fraction. Enough to give Amanda hope.

'Weren't you happy, Will?' she pulled in a tight breath and lifted her eyes to look directly into his. His gaze appeared cold, detached. 'Or should I say Jake?'

'So he told you?' Will raised one large hand to scratch at his cheek.

'Who?' was he referring to the caller? To the wrong number which had changed everything?

'Your little cop ex-boyfriend,' Will's lips curled in revulsion. 'I bet he relished that.'

Amanda was too stunned to reply. Will rarely spoke about Shane. He preferred to stay mute on the subject of Amanda's ex-boyfriend.

'So now you know,' he narrowed his eyes at her, 'and yet you still come here to judge me?'

'You're my husband,' Amanda kept her voice soft, trying to placate the man she once knew. The gun lowered another inch.

'You don't think I'm a monster?'

'I—'

'After all those things I did? All those people I hurt? People I…' Will broke off, suddenly unable to look at her.

Amanda's entire body went cold as if she'd just been plunged beneath the ice on a frozen lake. She'd ignored Shane when he protested that Will might be dangerous. She refused to believe that her gentle giant would hurt anyone. But now Will was admitting that he was what, a murderer?

She thought of the field full of long grass. Shane was no longer waiting on the other side of it; he was back at the bed and breakfast, giving her the allotted amount of time she'd so stubbornly fought for. And if she ran would Will follow her out and need only one deadly accurate shot to end her? Prior to entering the cottage she'd have never believed that her husband would hurt her. But now everything she knew to be true was crumbling at its foundations which had been built on precarious lies.

'What did you do?' Amanda breathed, her eyes wide and full of fear. Every nerve in her body felt raw as though she'd shatter into a million pieces at the slightest touch.

'You don't know?'

Amanda shook her head.

'Sit,' Will gestured with the gun for her to sit at the little kitchen table made from oil-stained wood. Her body felt stiff as she forced it into one of the spindle-backed chairs. The floral cushion at the base offered little comfort.

Will sat down opposite her, laying his gun on the table and angling the barrel towards her. It made a dull flat sound as he released it from its grip, telling Amanda how heavy and reliable it was.

'I haven't led the best life,' Will began, watching her intently, but there was no warmth in his expression, no flash of the smiling man from their wedding pictures. 'Growing up I got involved in things. Bad things. I did a lot of bad deeds for bad people. But my life here in Scotland… it was complicated. I did what I had to do to survive. But six years ago things went bad. Really bad.'

'How bad is bad? Why should I even believe you? And your name?' Amanda clasped her hands in her lap like she was back at school, rigidly sat upright and waiting to be punished by her old headmistress.

'It's Jake Burton,' Will sighed. 'Pretty much everything else was true I swear.

'Were we true?'

Jake ignored the question.

'I guess you'd say that I got mixed up in organized crime. It

174

started off small; I'd get paid for boosting a car here and there. Then it was breaking and entering. Then it was drug smuggling. And I got caught, did my time.'

Amanda shuddered. This wasn't the man she'd shared a bed with, planned to spend her life with. She was speaking directly to Jake Burton. Will was gone.

'I did what I had to do to make money. And when I got out of jail, there were even fewer legit jobs available to an ex-con like me.'

'And your brother?'

'He was caught up in the same shit I was. Only he didn't play by the rules.' Jake massaged his neck and for a brief second a shadow of regret passed over his face. Amanda swore she saw the birth of a tear glint in the sunlight.

'What happened six years ago?' Amanda wanted to keep him talking. As long as he was talking he wasn't thinking about killing her, at least she hoped not.

'I was involved in a job that went badly. Billy... he—' Will cracked his knuckles. Was he talking about his brother? Amanda didn't dare ask. 'I had to disappear,' there was fire in his eyes when he looked back at her. 'Jake Burton had to go. I had to become Will Thorn.'

Amanda remembered the cocky voice on the other end of the line, how the guy had been so confident that Jake Burton was at her house. And he'd been right.

'The guy who called the house, you think it was what, your boss?'

'Or one of his lackeys. Either way he's coming for me. He believes that we have a score that needs to be settled.'

'But doesn't he think you're dead? Or at least that Jake Burton is?'

'Clearly not any more. I always prayed that he'd never find me. But I guess you can only outrun the past for so long.'

Amanda licked her lips, absorbing all the information. So Will had fled because he thought he was in danger? But he'd left her alone at the house when someone dangerous knew he'd lived there. What if his old boss had turned up and found her there?

'You left me,' her chin trembled as she made the accusation. 'You left me there when I might have been in danger.'

'I thought I was leading the danger away,' Jake glanced down

175

at the gun on the table.

'And now?' What did he intend to do with that gun? Shoot down his old boss? What if more than one guy came to the little cottage? If Amanda had managed to find him then other people would too. The darknet didn't discern about who it allowed to access its questionable sources of information.

'And now you've led the wolves right to my door,' Jake snarled at her.

'I just wanted to find you,' Amanda stated desperately. 'I just wanted to make sure you were all right.'

'Well now we have to leave. I've already stayed here too long.' Jake got up, reached for the gun and shoved it into the waistband of his jeans. Amanda's eyes flickered to the door, wondering if this was her chance to run. She sprung up, about to seize the opportunity when Jake moved around the table to her, grabbing her by the arms. She'd forgotten just how much strength her husband possessed. There was no wriggling out of his grasp.

'Just let me go,' Amanda demanded, flailing against his grip. 'I won't tell anyone where you are. I just want to go home.'

'It's too late for that,' Jake was hauling her towards the door. 'I can't risk you telling that little cop of yours what you know.'

'Please, Will, I won't,' Amanda pleaded, hoping that buried deep down within this dangerous criminal was some semblance of her husband. Jake threw open the door and tightened his hands around her arms. Amanda yelped, feeling her veins start to expand and pound uneasily in her upper arms as though she were having her blood pressure measured.

'It's Jake,' his voice was so cold and unfamiliar when he spoke that Amanda started to wonder if she'd imagined Will Thorn, if her husband had never actually existed at all.

'Please, let me go,' Amanda made one last-ditch attempt to get free. She wanted to run through the field, run all the way back to the little hotel with the faded floral wallpaper and collapse into Shane's waiting arms.

'You're not going anywhere,' Jake tugged her through the door, not bothering to shut it behind them. He pulled her through the long grass like she was a disobedient child, all her pleas for release falling on deaf ears.

Amanda winced against the force being applied to her arms and the way her legs were dragging behind her, kicking up clouds of dirt. Will would have stopped, would have made sure she was okay. At the very least he'd have tossed her over his shoulder in a fireman's lift. But Jake just hauled her along by her upper arms, causing them to stretch and burn beneath the pressure. His face was pinched, his thick eyebrows pulled together. He looked like a man suffering beneath a great burden. She felt his palms grow clammy as they moved. Was he afraid? She'd never seen her husband truly afraid so she wouldn't know.

They walked for five pained minutes and then Amanda noticed the sheer surface of a car's roof glistening in the sunlight. It shimmered like a silver sea. Jake dropped one hand from her to wrestle some keys free from his jeans pocket.

'Jake, just let me go. I'll never bother you again or tell anyone what I know, I swear.'

She heard him unlock the car and swing open one of the doors. He roughly forced Amanda inside, pausing briefly before he slammed the door closed to give her a hard look. Jake Burton looked frighteningly formidable silhouetted against the sun. He was all muscular power and simmering dark rage. His reply to Amanda was curt, leaving her quivering fearfully in the passenger seat; 'You're coming with me.'

21

They drove in stony silence. Jake forced the car down narrow lanes at a frightening pace. All the while Amanda watched him, wondering where her husband had gone.

She's never seen Will scared before. He was always the strong one. The one who listened to the rumbles of a thunder storm as though it were nothing more than fingertips tapping on glass. He was unshakeable. Infallible. But now he was afraid. He wore his fear like an iron mask, narrowing his features.

The car careened towards a tight corner and Amanda clutched at her seat belt as the vehicle swerved and she was thrust against it. Beyond the window she saw the road give way to a sharp incline. A mossy hillside led down into grassy depths. Amanda swallowed, the metallic taste in her mouth sharpening.

'You need to slow down else you're going to kill us both.' She kept her voice level, calm, trying to create some illusion of control for herself as much as Will. Jake. She hadn't even known her own husband's name.

'You've ruined everything.' Jake's knuckles were white as he gripped the steering wheel with unnecessary force.

'I just... I wanted to find you,' Amanda reiterated, feeling helpless. 'Please, let's just go back and talk about this and—'

'He might die now because of you.' Jake's words were sharp and Amanda felt each one pierce her chest.

'Who?' she wondered gently. 'Shane?' the thought made her blood ice in her veins as above them dark clouds began to gather. The warmth of the sun was quickly diminished as they rounded another hill. Shadows lingered in the empty road as the air quickly cooled.

'No, as if I'd care about that asshole,' Jake gave a brisk shake of his head and kept driving. Kept speeding down roads that twisted through the hill landscape like an unsprung coil.

'Then... who?'

A raindrop. It landed on the windscreen in an inelegant splatter. The sky was growing ever darker. A storm was coming.

'Will?' Amanda squeaked his name, then realizing her error

she cleared her throat. 'Jake?'

'Just sit there and be quiet.'

More rain. The road was quickly awash with it. Jake turned on the windscreen wipers but didn't lessen his speed. Amanda tensed in her seat, imagining the car spinning out on the slick road, her and her husband tumbling down a hillside. Over and over until metal and glass collided together and she was nothing but a collection of broken limbs. Is that how Shane would eventually find her – torn and broken and beyond repair?

'Jake?' it was the tone she used back in their home. Back in their marriage. The tone which meant that he'd done something wrong. Perhaps he hadn't picked up the dry cleaning when he'd promised to or he'd accidentally deleted Netflix off the television. Again.

Something in Jake broke. It was a faint twitch, naked to most eyes but not Amanda's. She knew what it meant; that she was getting through to him.

'Talk to me,' she urged as the speedometer slid down from a precarious seventy to a worrying sixty miles per hour. 'Who is going to die?'

Jake stopped the car so abruptly that Amanda was flung against her seat belt, momentarily winded. The brakes squealed as he pulled up onto the side of the road. Rain was bouncing off the roof in an uneven melody.

'Jake?' Amanda reached out a hand towards him and then stopped herself. This wasn't her husband anymore. She needed to remember that. But Jake looked so wounded against the darkening sky outside. His hands were still gripped against the wheel, his gaze locked beyond the windscreen, his eyes wide but unseeing. 'I'm your *wife*. I don't know what this shit is that you're going through, but I'm here.'

Amanda tried to forget how it'd felt when Jake had aimed a gun at her. Tried to ignore her own fear.

'The person who is going to die…' Jake clenched his jaw and kept looking ahead. Amanda didn't speak. Instead she held her breath and silently urged him to go on. '…Is my son.'

A grumble of thunder accompanied the bombshell. It tumbled away from them through the mass of gathered pewter clouds. Amanda blinked. For a brief second she thought that perhaps she was hallucinating. Surely Jake hadn't just said—

'Your *son?*' she repeated, her voice strained. She could feel her throat tightening, her chest releasing each breath in short, panicked gasps.

'Yes,' Jake released one hand from the wheel to scratch at his bristled cheek. 'My son.'

'You have a son?' Amanda hadn't willed her tears into existence, but they were there, running down her cheeks as dense and heavy as the rainfall outside. She could feel the revelation breaking her.

'I have a son, yes.' Finally Jake looked at her and in that moment he morphed back into Will. There was remorse behind his eyes and also pain. So much pain. 'His name is Ewan and he'd be six years old now.'

It was all too much to take in. Amanda fumbled with her belt, her fingers finally finding the clasp and releasing her so that she could crumple forwards, her head in her hands.

'Everything I've done – leaving Scotland, changing my name, it's all been to protect him.'

'And what about his mother?' Amanda felt jealousy twist within her like an eel. 'No, don't tell me,' she snapped before Jake could respond. She pushed open the car door and made to go outside. Jake didn't move to stop her. 'Lies, it's all been lies!' Amanda raged as she left the comfort of the car and let the storm envelope her. She no longer cared about the gun Jake had in his possession. She was blinded by the burn of this most recent betrayal.

A son. Will had been a father. For six years. And not once had he mentioned it.

Looking up to the sky, Amanda let the rain blend into her tears. Her clothes were already soaked as she staggered away from the car, dazed and distraught. Another rumble of thunder hid the sound of a car door closing. She only realized that Jake had followed her out into the rain when his thick arms wrapped around her. There was no pressure in his grip, no malice. He was her oak tree once again.

Amanda couldn't fight the feelings which stirred within her. She fell against him, sucking in a desperate breath. The air tasted of damp earth peppered with the electrical undertones of a storm. Her shoulders shook as she rested against him.

'I couldn't tell you.' She felt his words travel up through his chest before she heard them. His steadily beating heart was so close. So reliable in its constant echo through his strong body.

'No.' Pushing Jake back, Amanda wiped the rain and tears from her eyes and stared at him. 'No,' she repeated, shaking her head. 'You…' she pointed a finger at her husband, at her former pillar of strength who had become a tower of uncertainty. 'You *left* me. And you *lied* to me. For years! Christ! What did I ever do to deserve that?'

'I was trying to protect my son.' Jake reached for her, clasping her hands in his own. His soaked T-shirt clung to his muscles, to the thick bulges of his biceps. Amanda hated herself for noticing how handsome and wild he looked. Out on the roadside in this rugged landscape he could easily be Heathcliff, stepped straight off the pages of one of Amanda's favourite books.

'Were you ever going to come back?' Amanda asked, weakening to his touch. Jake squeezed her hands but said nothing. But his silence said it all. 'So your son is worth saving, but I'm not?' Snatching back her hands, Amanda made for the car. She didn't even know what she was doing anymore, she'd become a slave to her emotions.

'He's just a little boy,' Jake called after her, remaining in the rain. 'And I did this to him. I put him in danger.'

You put me in danger too. Amanda thought as she climbed back into the car. She remembered all the ominous phone calls, the brick through her window and the writing on her car. Whatever wolves Jake was running from, they'd already been to her door, but that didn't seem to trouble him.

'I thought you were safe.' Jake was getting back in the car, throwing sheepish glances her way. 'You were married to Will Thorn not Jake Burton. And it was Jake Burton who had a price on his head. Jake Burton who'd made so many mistakes. I thought that if I left they'd follow after me, that they'd leave you alone.'

'Look, I—'

'The men who called our home, who are hunting me, they will track down Ewan and kill him. I'm not being overly dramatic, Amanda. These kind of men, they don't believe in loose ends and their threats are only taken seriously because they always follow through on them. They rely on a culture of fear.'

'I'm trying to understand all this. So your son is… six?'

It was hard to imagine a miniature version of Jake that wasn't also part Amanda. Did he have his father's dark hair and brooding demeanour?

'He turned six last month.'

'I see.' Amanda ran her hands through her wet hair.

'Amanda—'

'Was any of it ever real?' Snapping her head towards him, Amanda narrowed her eyes.

A mountain of lies. A colossus of a man. This wasn't meant to be her life.

'All of it but my name.'

'I don't even recognize you anymore,' Amanda spat out, her arms protectively crossed against her chest. 'You used to be this guy who looked after me. You were my resident spider-killer, my weird-midnight-noise investigator. And you did it with such charm. You were like one of those guys out of a black and white movie, all morals and chivalry. You were like—' Amanda gasped against the sob which had worked its way up her throat, 'my dad.'

This caused Jake's mask to slip, just a little, enough to reveal that Will was still underneath. Amanda's gentle giant briefly turned away from the road to regard her with sad, tired eyes.

'I still want to be that man for you,' his voice was hoarse. 'I *am* still that man. But...' his shoulders sagged. 'I'm afraid, Amanda. Wasn't your father ever afraid?'

Pursing her lips, Amanda reluctantly considered the question. Her dad had always been larger than life, a hero. She hadn't been around when he took off his cape and put on his glasses.

'No,' she replied stiffly, 'not that I saw.'

'Well trust me, he would have been. Sometimes. He'd have just been hiding it from you, that's all.'

'Is that what you were doing? Hiding your fears from me?'

'Yes. No.' Jake clenched his teeth together in frustration. 'I was trying to be the man I always wanted to be. The man I knew I *could* be. But now...' he was focused on the road, absently shaking his head. 'I'm afraid, Amanda. I'm afraid that I'm going to lose my son.'

'Yeah,' Amanda squirmed in her seat, 'I can see that.'

The road continued to bleed out before them, empty and long like a ribbon unravelling across the landscape.

'Take me back to the cottage,' Amanda confidently raised her chin as she gave the order.

'I need to get to Glasgow. That's where Ewan is.'

'If you truly want to save your son then take me back to the cottage. Shane will be there by now and he'll know what to do.'

'Shane?' the corners of Jake's eyes crinkled but not in a good way. 'The cop?'

'Yes, the cop.'

'No,' Jake shook his head with vigour. 'No way.'

'Ja—'

'He's a *cop*, Amanda. He's probably on McAllister's fucking payroll.'

'You can trust him I swear.'

Jake started driving, he didn't turn around.

Amanda dared to reach over and touch his arm. She saw him tense as the charge from the connection surged through his body. 'Trust me on this,' she urged him. 'I came all this way to help you. I'm not about to lure you into some kind of trap now. We need Shane's help.'

'Fine.' Clenching his jaw, Jake made a sharp turn.

*

The rain had arrived at the cottage before they did. The field of heather was no longer sun-kissed. Instead the foliage was drooped towards the earth, clogged and damp. Jake didn't talk as they drove back, but he didn't speed either. His hands remained tight to the wheel as they navigated hairpin turns and hillside roads.

The door to the cottage was still open when they returned, only the doorway wasn't empty. Shane was standing within it, squinting against the rain into the distance. Jake pulled up beside Shane's car and remained behind the wheel, reluctant to move.

'Jesus, are you all right?' Shane was pulling open Amanda's door, not caring about the rain which was running down his back. 'I know you said to go back to the B&B, but I stayed close and then I heard shouting and a car engine and tried to follow you but was too late and—' as he helped Amanda out his gaze dropped towards the driving seat. 'So you found Will,' he concluded flatly.

'Let's get inside,' Amanda dashed for the door, for the comfort of the cottage.

Shane was close behind, flanking her every step. 'What the hell is going on?' he demanded, his wet hair glistening beneath the glow of the bare light bulb hanging in the centre of the kitchen ceiling. 'Did he hurt you?'

Yes. Amanda could already feel the damage done to her heart. It felt bruised within her chest, on the verge of shattering.

'No.'

'You had me so worried,' Shane's hands reached for her shoulders and stayed there. Amanda offered him a soft smile of gratitude. There was something so comforting about his touch. So familiar.

'I knew you'd be waiting here for me.'

'Of course. Amanda, I'll—'

Shane was cut off as Jake strode into the kitchen. He stooped to pass through the low doorway and then stood beside the quaint little table. His face was streaked with rain, or maybe it was tears. There was no way of knowing.

'Look, I don't know what the hell you're up to, Will, but Jake Burton died five years ago. His family reported his death and—'

'I'm Jake Burton.'

'And he has a son,' Amanda added, her voice barely a whisper.

'A *son*?' Shane's eyebrows shot upwards and he remained protectively by Amanda's side, wedging himself between her and Jake.

'Everything I did, I did to protect my son,' Jake lowered himself into one of the chairs at the table. The delicate wooden structure creaked beneath his weight.

'Does that include marrying Amanda under false pretences?' Shane asked churlishly.

'No,' Jake placed his hands on the table and clasped them together. 'I married Amanda because I love her.' He looked up and his eyes instantly met Amanda's. She felt the magnetism in that look, knew that he wanted to see the weight his words carried. But she looked away and sat down in the chair beside him.

Shane remained on his feet for a few moments. He thoughtfully scratched his neck and then dropped into the chair opposite Jake.

'How does changing your name help you protect your son?' Shane arched an eyebrow at the other man and waited.

'Because it was better for my son if I were presumed dead. Trust me.'

'I think the last thing that I'm going to do here is trust you. So you better start talking.'

'I...' Jake unclasped his hands to stare down at his palms. The trace of old scars lingered amongst calloused fingers. 'Growing up I had no family. My dad was a no-good drunk who drowned in his own vomit when I was thirteen. I lost my mother when I was five. She apparently took her own life. I was put into care, but no one wanted me. No foster home could handle me. I just struck out on my own like most kids like me did.'

Amanda flinched. She'd never known these tragic truths about Jake's life. And they were truths? Weren't they? She'd always just believed he was estranged from his family, not that they were non-existent.

'So my family became my best friend, Billy. I'd have followed him into the depths of hell if he'd asked it of me. And one day he did.'

'Go on,' Shane ordered, though his tone wasn't as hostile as it had previously been.

'Work was never easy to come by. We both drifted from job to job, did a couple of stints out on the oil rigs. Then one day Billy gets this idea for easy money. We just need to get on a flight to Spain. Take a few bags with us. Easy enough.'

'Drug running?' Shane's eyes narrowed.

'It would have been five grand apiece. If we hadn't got caught.'

'So you were arrested?'

'Convicted. Imprisoned.' Jake drew a thick finger across the uneven terrain of his palm.

'How long?'

'Eight years,' Jake shook his head sadly and then met Shane's gaze. 'I'd had previous. Minor shit; a carjacking here, possession of stolen goods there. It was enough to get me a nice meaty sentence. Billy too. When we finally got out, getting work was even harder. No one wanted to hire a pair of ex-cons. And then,' Jake cleared his throat. 'I found out I was going to be a father.'

185

Amanda felt her face growing hot. She was listening to somebody else talk about their life only this was *her* life. *Her* husband. The thought of Jake getting someone else pregnant made her skin crawl. Gripping the edge of the table, Amanda fought to keep her composure.

'Ewan was just a wee boy, just a few months old, when Billy came to me with this job he wanted to do. Twelve grand each. Enough to sort out me and my boy for a good while. I could put a deposit on a flat, get a car. Sort my life out good and proper.'

'So, the downside to the job?' Shane asked knowingly, like he'd heard this sort of story a thousand times before.

'We had to drive a truckload of coke down to a warehouse in London. We did it in the dead of night. Billy assured me it'd be fine. We drop off the goods, go back to Scotland to get our money. Only just before we got there he told me he intended to double-cross McAllister.'

'McAllister?'

'He's the puppetmaster behind most of the drugs that come in and out of Glasgow. A kingpin of sorts. And he's a fucking monster. Before we left, he all but threatened my boy. Since we had a record of getting caught he told us we either come back with a clean sheet or we don't come back at all.'

'What happened?' Amanda's hand fluttered to her chest. It all sounded so very dark. There was nothing dashing or daring about what Jake described. It was just terrifying; people making life-or-death decisions with worrying flippancy. And yet she still wanted to protect Jake. Still felt bound to the vows they had made to one another.

'We drove straight into a trap,' Jake concluded grimly. 'Billy, as always, trusted the wrong person. McAllister learnt about his little plan, had his men lying in wait for us. It was an all-out slaughter. I barely escaped with my life and Billy...' his voice trailed away as he looked towards the window, at the rain which battered against it.

'The drop went bad so you changed your name?' Shane pressed.

'The drop went *very* bad so I changed my name,' Jake agreed with a regretful shake of his head. 'I had some contacts from my time in prison who I could trust to be discreet and just issue me a new passport and such. But I laid low. I intended to let Jake die along with Billy.'

'But they found you?'

'After all these years they found me.' A shadow passed over Jake's face.

'So what do they want? Money? The drugs?'

'They want what all ruthless men want.'

'And what's that?'

'Revenge.'

22

The rain whipped against the kitchen window. The sunshine of that morning felt like a distant memory.

'So your plan was to come back to Scotland and what? Take on McAllister?' Shane's nose wrinkled with a sneer as he asked the question, but Jake didn't notice. He just leaned back in his chair and ran his hands through his thick black hair.

'All I care about is protecting my son.'

Amanda flinched as she got up from the table. She moved to the sink, pretending to be preoccupied with getting herself a glass of water. Her hands shook as she turned on the tap. She could still see the dark depths within the barrel of the gun which her husband had aimed at her.

All I care about is protecting my son.

She wanted to spin around and scream 'what about me? What about the vows we made to one another?' But instead she plucked a slim glass out of a nearby cabinet and filled it with water from the tap.

'This is a fool's errand, you know that, right?' Shane's voice was hard, like he was back in the interrogation room at the police station picking apart a perp.

'They know I'm alive.' There was gravel in Jake's voice. Raising his hands, he cracked his knuckles. 'I need to get to my son before they do.'

Shane's eyes narrowed and his mouth opened as he prepared to take another swipe at the man beside him.

'Let us help,' Amanda offered a little too enthusiastically as she clutched her glass in one hand and leaned against the kitchen counter with the other. She couldn't fight the urge to step in, to come to his aide. Jake *was* Will. At least to her eyes, perhaps not still her heart.

'You. Help?' Jake looked up at her. Behind the furrowed brow and the weary eyes, Amanda had to believe that her husband was still in there. 'How?'

'You're worried about your son, right?'

'Right.'

Amanda was thinking logically, which meant she was back in her comfort zone. It frightened her when she felt like she was being led by her emotions. She confidently returned to the table and placed her glass down.

'But no one knows you're back in Scotland. Do they?'

'No.'

'Then let me go and check in on your son. Make sure he's okay. No one knows my face, I'll be okay.'

'No,' Shane snapped, a hand reaching towards Amanda. 'That's… no. Out of the question.'

'But Wi-Jake can't go himself so—'

'They might know what you look like.'

'How?' Jake demanded gruffly. 'She got one prank call at the house, they won't know what she looks like.'

Amanda glanced at Shane and chewed her lip.

'One prank call?' Shane glared at Jake like he were an unwanted piece of chewing gum wedged beneath his shoe. 'Try multiple prank calls. And a brick through the window. And notes on her fucking car. You put Amanda in danger. You led those bastards right to her door.'

Jake looked over at her and there he was; Will. The mammoth man who was her sworn protective, the grizzly bear she snuggled up to at night. His features softened but a hardness remained in his eyes and his mouth twitched as he battled his inner conflicts.

'They kept hounding you?' his voice was low, softer than before.

'I'm fine,' Amanda forced a weak smile. 'It was scary, sure, but I'm okay.'

'They could have been in the house, seen a picture of you, watched you when you went out,' Shane was listing off reasons she shouldn't leave the cottage on his fingers. Amanda heard every one, felt the icy reality of each revelation sliding down her spine. And yet…

'It's a whole load of what-ifs,' Amanda smacked her palms against the table, drawing the immediate attention of both men. 'Ewan is just a little boy. I'm willing to risk being seen to check on him. My face might still be unknown, whilst Jake's definitely isn't.'

It felt so strange saying his real name, like being a child and denouncing the existence of Santa Claus out loud. It changed everything.

'Well, I'm coming with you,' Jake started to get up.

'Like hell you are,' there was a fire behind Shane's words which startled Amanda. He was on his feet before Jake was, staring down the other man. 'You've put her in enough danger as it is. *I'm* going with her. You'll stay here and do nothing until we get back. You understand?'

Amanda's husband had never liked being told what to do. He was a forceful man, used to giving orders, not following them. But perhaps Jake was different. Cracking his knuckles once more, Jake lowered himself back into his chair and Amanda silently released a sigh of relief, remembering that her husband still had a gun tucked into the waistband of his jeans and she wasn't ready yet to dismiss the possibility that he'd use it.

'I just want to know he's okay.' Jake was looking at her. Pleading with her.

'I'll check in on him,' Amanda promised. 'What was his last known address?'

'A block of flats outside Glasgow city centre.'

Amanda grabbed a pen from the kitchen counter and scribbled down details onto the back of her hand.

'He lived there with his mother.'

Swallowing nervously, Amanda kept writing, refusing to pause and let the implications of that statement sink in.

'Okay… your son's name is Ewan Burton, right?'

'Right.'

'And his mother?'

'Evangeline. Evangeline Burton.'

Amanda felt dizzy. If Shane's hands hadn't gripped her shoulders at that moment she'd surely have crumpled to the floor like a game of Jenga which had just had a crucial piece of itself removed.

'Come on, let's go,' Shane's hands were still on her shoulders, his breath against her cheek. 'If we go now we'll reach the city before it's dark.'

Numbly Amanda nodded and followed Shane towards the door which led out into the rain.

'And you stay here,' Shane pointed back inside at Jake who remained at the kitchen table. 'If you so much as move outside of this cottage, I'll report your return to Scotland to McAllister myself. We clear?'

'Crystal.' Jake didn't look up.

*

The rain had picked up. It pounded Shane's car as they wove round tight bends and steep hillsides. Their new destination had been punched into the satnav. It icily told them that they were about two hours away from Glasgow.

For the first hour Amanda said nothing. She just stared out of her window, watching the rain trickle down the glass as Shane drove with the car stereo on low. He was playing an old Coldplay album like he remembered that it was her go-to CD whenever she was stressed. At times in the past Shane had been able to read her like a book. And now, as the music played he understood that she needed quiet contemplation rather than facing down a barrage of questions.

Finally the clouds above parted and a weak thread of sunlight broke through as the rain slowly diminished.

'You okay?' Shane wondered cautiously, as if now that the storm had passed it was safe to ask questions.

'I'm fine.'

'Look, you're clearly not fine. This whole situation is beyond fucked up and—'

'I said I'm fine.' Amanda folded her arms across her chest.

'Okay, you're fine,' Shane exhaled a sharp breath. 'Getting a real sense of déjà vu here.'

Amanda felt her lips lift into a smile and some of the weight against her chest ease. More times than she could count she'd pout and insist that she was fine to Shane. Usually whilst in the car or in a long line at the supermarket. He'd press her to open up and she'd keep stating that everything was fine until eventually she broke. Because whenever she said she was fine it was always the complete opposite and she was so far from fine that she couldn't even see it on the horizon anymore.

'So he was married before? So he's divorced?' Shane took his eyes briefly off the road to glance at her. Amanda shrugged and let the question linger in the air between them. 'That doesn't bother you?' he pressed.

'I just…' Shrugging, Amanda pushed her hair behind her

191

ears and forlornly leaned back in her seat. 'On the long list of things I'm currently bothered about, that's pretty low.'

'Why help him?'

They sped past a sign which said that Glasgow was forty miles away and the traffic around them thickened.

'Because.'

'Because?'

'Because,' with a sigh Amanda straightened and focused on the still wet road reaching away from them. 'Contrary to recent evidence, Will, dammit, Jake, was a good husband to me. He loves me.'

'You think that's still true?'

'Don't you?'

Shane kept his eyes on the road but his jaw twitched. 'I think you're the kind of woman that a man loves for a lifetime.' His hands tightened against the wheel.

'At the next exit take the third right.' The clipped accent of the satnav filled the space between them.

'Not long now,' Amanda rubbed at her eyes and wondered how someone's life could change so drastically in such a short space of time.

'Yeah,' Shane agreed softly, 'not long now.'

*

It had been easy enough to find Ewan and Evangeline Burton once Amanda had run a search on her laptop and quickly confirmed the details Jake had given her. She also found Evangeline's Facebook page, though she didn't open it.

The rain had completely stopped as Shane pulled into a car park nestled between two austere blocks of flats which loomed up towards the sky like a pair of grey monoliths.

'They are in apartment 328,' Amanda read the information from her laptop which was propped up on her knee. 'Third floor.'

There were scarcely any vehicles in the car park. The car in the adjacent bay was missing all its hub caps, whilst a shiny white BMW was a few spaces to Amanda's left, though whether anyone was in it she couldn't tell since all its windows were blacked out. It looked starkly out of place and its presence unnerved Amanda. She sensed that it'd been bought with drug money, which meant that McAllister's presence could be close by.

The flats themselves were woefully oppressive. Amanda could feel their stark presence bearing down on her, making her feel tiny and insignificant. Each building reached up into the sky but not in a glorified way like an Egyptian pyramid did. These flats weren't trying to touch God, nor were they an example of a nation's splendour and glory. They were cement giants crammed full of windows which looked out on the landscape like vacant eyes. The flats looked like they belonged to some dystopian future.

'Do you think he…' Amanda closed her laptop to squint up at the vast building which easily towered over twenty storeys high. 'Do you think he lived here?'

'Maybe.' Shane had rolled up the sleeves to his shirt and was drinking from the coffee he'd grabbed when they stopped to top up on petrol.

'Mmm.'

'It's a far cry from home, huh?'

'It's pretty bleak,' Amanda admitted.

'Kind of makes a bit more sense why he was willing to take crazy risks for money.'

'I guess.'

Amanda stared at the third floor of the building to the right of the car park, willing Evangeline and her son into view. Her stomach turned. As much as she wanted to see them, to ensure Ewan was okay, she was equally hopeful that they just wouldn't show. That it would be a bust. That Evangeline had gone into hiding after she assumed her husband was dead.

'Pow, pow, I got you.'

A light voice rang out from behind the car. Gasping, Amanda turned and saw a woman striding across the car park, laden down with plastic shopping bags. Around her danced a little boy with thick black hair in a Spiderman costume.

'Amanda?' Shane must have noticed the colour drain from her face.

'That's them,' she gasped, turning back round but keeping track of the couple via the windscreen mirror.

'You sure?'

'I'm sure.' Her heart was racing. She felt like Icarus after he'd dared to fly too close to the sun and now she was burning. Her entire body smarted with the pain. As the little boy's light, helpful voice drew ever closer, Amanda felt only dread.

'Pow, pow, drop down you're dead. I got like you like ten times!' He was circling the woman, flicking imaginary spiderwebs at her from his wrists. He had a shock of dark hair, just like his father, and green eyes that shone with childish delight. Green eyes which Amanda quickly realized he'd inherited from his mother.

'Ewan, stop that,' she scolded as she strode through the car park, shoulders back and chin held high. Amanda stared at her in the mirror, it felt like looking at a ghost.

Evangeline Burton was beautiful. But it was a beauty that had become tarnished. She had the look of a woman who'd been forced to lose her innocence far too young. Her dark hair was slicked back in a severe bun and large silver hoops were laced through each earlobe. Her emerald eyes were framed with thick black eyeliner and heavy lashings of mascara, and her thin lips were ruby red. She had on her war paint and given her strident stance it appeared she was used to doing battle on a daily basis.

Both Shane and Amanda were silent as Evangeline and Ewan passed by the car, oblivious to its occupants. Ewan kept firing webs at his mother and insisting she play along. Evangeline kept ignoring him, maintaining a rigorous pace as she hauled her shopping towards the block of flats. The bags were bulging, the plastic thinning at the handles, yet still she remained upright and proud. She was a warrior.

Amanda couldn't look away even though she knew she should. Even in her faded skinny jeans and oversized hoodie, it was easy to see that Evangeline was glorious. Drape her in a toga and she could easily pass for a Grecian goddess.

'Well, she's rough as a bear's—'

'Don't,' Amanda cut Shane off before he could say something to try and make her feel better. 'She's beautiful, Shane. Don't act like you can't see it.'

'I can't.' She could feel that Shane was staring at her. Really staring at her.

'At least we know Ewan's okay,' she smiled breezily at him. 'I mean, look at him,' she gestured beyond the windscreen to where Evangeline was managing her bags to unlock the main door into the flats. As she fumbled with her keys, Ewan kept

194

bouncing around her, full of boundless energy.

'I bet he thinks he could just scale the wall into their flat,' Shane laughed, his eyes crinkling at the corners.

'He's certainly spirited.' Amanda opened up her laptop. She accessed the device's camera and zoomed in on the little boy, her finger lingering over the relevant key. Just as Evangeline successfully opened up the doors, Amanda snatched her fingers back and closed her computer. She figured that it wasn't how Jake would want to see his son for the first time in all these years. He'd want to see the little boy laughing and breathing in real life, not static in some captured image.

'So he gave up his entire life here to protect them?' Shane was pensively looking up at the block of flats. Evangeline and Ewan were now gone from sight.

'He must really love them,' Amanda whispered, her chest tightening.

'And he just went and did it again. Gave up everything to protect them.'

Gave up me.

Amanda choked on her own thoughts. She felt a lump gathering in her throat as tears streamed down her cheeks.

'Oh, shit, I wasn't thinking.' Shane reached for her, wrapped his arms around her and pulled her against his chest. And Amanda wept.

She pictured Jake walking across the car park with Evangeline at his side, the burden of the shopping divided between them. And when Ewan ran up to his giant father and fired imaginary spiderwebs, Jake played along and Evangeline laughed delicately at them. This was once Jake's life. Amidst the concrete and the poverty, love had flourished like a delicate flower.

This was his life.

The thought reverberated through Amanda as she shook against Shane. He kept his arms locked around her as she continued to cry. Over and over, she asked herself the same question; If this was Jake's life, was she the lie? Was their marriage the part of himself that had been untrue?

*

'So what now?'

The sky was darkening outside as Amanda bit into her fast food burger. Her eyes still ached from all the tears she'd continued to shed as they drove out of Glasgow. She'd have gone straight back to Jake if Shane hadn't insisted that they stop to eat, to gather their thoughts.

'We go back and tell Jake that his son's okay,' she dabbed at her mouth with a napkin.

'You sure you want to go back?'

Amanda considered the question a moment too long. 'Of course,' she insisted. 'I mean, he deserves to know the truth about his son.'

'He doesn't deserve you,' Shane seethed. 'He's a fucking idiot for putting you through all this.'

'Love isn't all sunshine and rainbows,' Amanda looked deep into his eyes, seeking the boy within the man. 'You and I know that better than anyone.'

'Love isn't letting go,' Shane's eyes shone with the tears he refused to shed.

'Eventually we all have to let go,' Amanda concluded sadly as she finished off her burger.

'Then why am I still here?'

Ignoring the question, Amanda reached for his carton of half-eaten fries. 'Mind if I have these?'

Smiling, Shane nodded. 'Sure.'

He watched her shove a handful of fries into her mouth.

'Most girls like to be all coy and dainty when they eat. But not you,' he commented.

'Is that a bad thing?' Amanda's question was muffled by all the food she was chewing.

'No,' Shane smiled broadly at her and gave a light shake of his head as though humoured by some private joke. 'No it's not.'

23

It was dark when Shane pulled up close to the isolated holiday cottage once more. Amanda was surprised when the headlights gleamed against the slick surface of Jake's car. She hadn't expected him to stay true to his word and remain there, especially when he'd proved himself to be skilled at disappearing.

The slamming of the car doors shattered the tranquil silence surrounding the cottage. The ground was still damp underfoot even though the storm had moved on. Amanda could taste the salt on the air, which told her they weren't far from the sea.

'Do you think he's still here?' Shane's hand was already on the front door handle as he pondered whether Jake would be inside.

'I hope he is.'

The darkness from outside had spread into the kitchen. Thick shadows gathered in every corner, but a sliver of light shone out beneath a distant door. Amanda was drawn to it. Pushing open the door, she emerged into a small living room. Wooden beams stretched across the low ceiling and two faded red sofas were angled to face the fireplace. There were no flames within its hearth, just the ash from some long-dead fire. Not even an ember crackled in the dust.

'Hey.' Jake shot up from where he'd been sat on a sofa towards the back of the room. He rubbed at his eyes and massaged his neck as if he'd been resting in an upright, awkward position for quite some time. 'You were gone so long I started to wonder if you were coming back.'

How does it feel to just sit and wait in darkness for someone who might not return? Her mind was screaming the question. She had to bite her tongue to prevent herself from breathing life into it. Stiffly she walked over to the fireplace and stood with her back to it, facing Jake.

'Did you see him?' he asked hesitantly.

Amanda nodded.

'How is he?' Jake furrowed his thick brow.

'He's…' Amanda coughed away her unease. 'He's good. Better than good. He's an adorable little boy, full of life. He was wearing this cute little Spiderman costume and—'

Jake held up his hand to her, signalling that he didn't want her to go on.

'He's fine, Jake. Really.'

'Well, fine isn't good enough,' Jake scratched at the dark bristles upon his cheeks. 'The only way I can ensure he's truly safe is to take the head off the snake.'

'You mean go after McAllister?' Shane was lingering by the doorway, back against the wall, arms folded across his chest.

'Exactly.' Jake reached for his glass and drained the last of its contents.

'Going after McAllister is madness.'

'Maybe. But it's the only way I can make sure my son is safe.'

'You take down McAllister, then what? Someone else rises up to fill his place?'

'My issue is with McAllister.' Jake shrugged. 'I'm not looking to eradicate the sale of drugs up here, just take out the one man who has placed a target on my back.'

'How noble,' Shane scoffed.

'Look, boy scout, I didn't ask you to come up here and help me.'

Jake was on his feet and Amanda could see from his bloodshot eyes that he was drunk. How many hours had he sat and stewed in the darkness self-medicating with whisky? Knocking back glasses until he felt numb towards the pain of fearing for his son?

'Oh yeah, well if I didn't—'

'Look,' Amanda placed herself between the two men. She could feel the angry heat radiating off them both. She pressed a palm against Jake's chest and gestured with her other hand for Shane to stay back. 'Your son is safe. But if finding McAllister will give you piece of mind, then I'll help.'

'You're already in this too deep,' Shane raged through clenched teeth.

'What harm can an innocent little internet search get me into?' Amanda countered sweetly. Her eyes dipped to the waistband of Jake's jeans, to where she assumed he still had a gun stashed. It was in all their best interests for her to diffuse the tension in the room as swiftly as possible by any means.

'You think you can find him?' Jake was backing down, retreating back towards the sofa.

'I found you, didn't I?' Amanda playfully arched an eyebrow at him and surprised herself with her light tone. Jake's entire face crinkled into a warm smile.

'You're resourceful, I'll give you that.'

'Never come between a woman and her computer,' Amanda teased.

*

At the kitchen table Amanda fired up her laptop and commenced searching. Jake hadn't given her much to go on. The man he was after was named Gregg McAllister. Hardly the most unique name in Scotland. He was apparently over six feet tall with a 'Glasgow-smile' scar. Which meant that someone had once taken a knife to both corners of his mouth and crudely extended his grin.

'Do you really think you can find him?' Shane was standing behind her, one hand on her shoulder.

Jake was stalking across the kitchen on the other side of the table. His movements were wild and restless, like a beast that'd spent too long in a cage.

'There's got to be... something.' Amanda's fingers danced their way across her keyboard, firing in every plausible search she could think of. But as she predicted Gregg McAllister was smart. He wasn't about to announce his presence to the world on Facebook.

'Urgh,' grimacing in frustration Amanda kept searching.

'Will this take much longer?' Jake demanded from across the room. He glared at Shane and Amanda sat behind the laptop. It was like a line had been drawn down the centre of the kitchen table; a line which none of them could cross.

'These kind of searches take time,' Shane offered flatly.

'Are you as familiar with those... things... as she is?' Jake was gesturing at the laptop like it was some alien object.

'We've always shared a love of computers,' Amanda felt increased pressure from Shane's hand upon her shoulder as he spoke. It felt protective. Reassuring. 'Remember that old Atari we set up at your parent's house?'

'God, we played it so long that one summer your fingers locked up,' Amanda recalled, laughing.

'And your Mum kept insisting we'd get square eyes. Remember when she hid the joystick?'

'In the laundry basket? Yes! It was so—'

'Can we get back to protecting my son?' Jake's voice thundered through the room as though the storm had returned.

'Yeah,' Amanda shook her head and focused on her computer screen. 'Of course.'

There were so many Gregg McAllisters. And none of them seemed at all likely to be the head of a drug-smuggling operation. There were gym owners. Pub landlords. College students. Oil rig workers. A fire—

Amanda hammered down on her keys, calling up the story.

'Eight years ago there was a fire at a country estate just outside of Edinburgh. An entire wing of the building was destroyed and Kelly McAllister, seven, and her sister Erin, ten, were killed.'

'I remember that,' Jake clicked his fingers at her. 'Billy talked about it when we started working for McAllister. He said it had been a grudge attack from a rival. That McAllister had never been the same since he lost his girls.'

'So that's where he used to live.' Amanda did more searching. As she delved deeper into the story she saw the smiling faces of the pretty little girls who'd died as their faces adorned old news reports. The fact that they'd got caught up in their father's war and paid the ultimate price was heartbreaking. Pushing her tears down, Amanda focused on what she needed to find; an address. A phone number. Anything.

'Weird,' she leaned closer to the screen, wanting to be sure of what she was seeing.

'What?' Shane leaned in too.

'According to these property records, the building wasn't sold on after the fire. Which means that Gregg McAllister may still live there.'

'Makes sense, he adored those girls,' Jake grumbled from across the room.

'Okay, so if I can find the report from the fire service records, I'll get the address.'

'Are you sure about this?' Shane asked, his breath was warm

against her cheek. He was so close she could smell the cologne which he'd freshly applied at some point when she'd been absent from his side.

'She's sure,' Jake answered on her behalf. 'Get me the damn address.'

'Do you really think he'd hurt Ewan?' Amanda ceased typing to look over her laptop at her husband. 'I mean, he knows the pain of losing a child. Why would he inflict that on someone else?'

'Because he knows the pain,' Jake scowled, 'because he knows it's a pain like no other. That's exactly why he'd inflict it on someone else.'

'Okay.'

Amanda found the address easily. She typed it into Google maps to get a better look at it. It looked to be a large house, almost a mansion, with a separate triple garage. It was surrounded by dense woodlands and had a single sweeping driveway leading up to it. In the back garden there was what looked to be a pavilion which could have housed a swimming pool. It was an impressive property. And highly fortified.

High walls bordered it on every side and when Amanda zoomed in she saw the CCTV cameras peering out from every corner, the iron spikes lacing the top of the walls. Heavy gates were closed at the end of the driveway.

'It's not the kind of place you can just drive up to.' Turning the laptop around, she showed Jake the property. Planting his palms against the table, he leaned forward, his movements stiff and uncertain. 'But I'm pretty sure that's his house.'

'Yeah,' Jake agreed gruffly. 'Looks like the place.'

'So you know where he lives, what now?' Shane demanded. 'Are you going to pen him a strongly worded letter and hand-deliver it?'

'I'm going to hand-deliver something.'

'He's a wealthy man up in his castle and you're just—'

'A serf? A peasant?' Jake raged. 'Either I kill him or he kills Ewan. It's that simple.'

'There has to be another way,' Amanda looked at Jake, her eyes pleading.

'There isn't.'

'You take one step out of this place and I'll arrest you.' Shane clenched his jaw and stepped away from Amanda.

'You have no jurisdiction here,' Jake waved a dismissive hand at the other man.

'Try me.'

Amanda noticed Jake's hand twitching, lingering close to the small of his back where his pistol was surely wedged up nice and close to his body, within reach.

'Let's just sleep on it, okay?' She sprang to her feet, her body sagging with relief at the thought of resting. It was exhausting playing peacekeeper.

'Amanda, there's no way—'

'Let's sleep on it.' She cut Shane off and looked deep into his eyes, praying that he could read her expression and understand that it was best to stand down.

'Fine,' Shane conceded and raised his hands up. 'Whatever.'

*

Amanda got the double bed in the cottage's sole bedroom. There had been no argument from either of her companions as she made for it and eagerly tucked herself up beneath the floral covers.

Shane had stretched out in an armchair in the corner of the bedroom and Jake was in the lounge, struggling to fit his large frame across one of the sofas.

Sleep came quickly for Amanda. It carried her away from the cottage on silent wings. She was back on a sun-soaked cliffside, the wind tugging at her hair. The ocean roared beneath her, guttural and menacing.

She moved towards the sheer edge, towards the birds nesting just a few feet from her. If only she could get closer to them. If only—

And then the world slid on its axis. Amanda tumbled over the edge and the wind met her in the face, punched her in the chest. The taste of the salty air was replaced by a metallic tang. Amanda sucked in a shuddering breath. This was it. She was going to die.

Hands.

Not on her legs but her shoulders. Shaking her. Sifting the dream out of her mind.

'Amanda!'

Her eyes opened. Gone was the sunlight and blue sky of the cliff edge. Instead she was in a darkened room, the air clotted with dust and cologne.

'Amanda!'

She was looking into Shane's eyes. He was so close. She could see the white trace of an old scar upon his forehead. Could smell the mint of his breath from when he'd previously brushed his teeth.

'Amanda, you need to wake up.' He sounded alarmed.

Rubbing at her eyes, Amanda shifted so that she was sitting up against the plump pillows on the bed. A single floor lamp had been turned on, its deep red shade bathing the room in rose-shaded hues. If she hadn't been awoken so abruptly she might find the room rather beautiful and serene. But instead her heart was racing and trying to claw its way up into her throat.

'What… what's going on?'

'He's left.'

'Left?' The dream had been so vivid and it was reluctant to let Amanda go. A part of her was still hovering above the angry waves, waiting to be plunged to her death.

'Yes, he's left. Jake is gone.'

'Who's Jake?' She'd been sleeping so deeply. Her connection to the waking world hadn't yet been fully restored.

'Will,' Shane's voice softened. 'Your husband.'

And it all came flooding back to her with the ferocity of a freight train. Her memories smacked against her, knocking the air from her lungs. Jake was Will. And Will was gone. Several tears dropped down her flushed cheeks.

'He's gone?' she was whispering as though she and Shane were sharing some dreadful secret.

'I got up to pee. Went to check on him and he wasn't there. His car's gone.'

'Shit.' Amanda was scrambling out of bed, reaching for her clothes which were stacked up on the floor. She didn't even care that Shane was seeing her in her underwear. Although a part of her which she tried to ignore did hope that he was enjoying the view. 'Where do you think he's gone?' she asked as she sat on the side of the bed and tugged on her skinny jeans.

'Where do you think?'

'Shit,' Amanda repeated as she ceased dressing to cradle her head in her hands.

Jake was surely en route to the McAllister mansion to start a fight he had no hope of winning.

'If he goes there they'll kill him,' her hand fluttered to her throat and lingered there.

'It's highly likely.'

'We have to stop him.' Amanda stood up a little too quickly, felt herself go dizzy.

'He could be miles ahead of us.'

'Or just a few minutes,' she countered hopefully. 'Either way we have to go after him.' Amanda pulled on her t-shirt and then made for the door but Shane remained in the bedroom, his hands thrust deep into his trouser pockets.

'We could just leave him to dig his own grave,' he suggested as she looked back at him.

'Shane, I couldn't. I mean—'

'He left you, Amanda. You owe him nothing. What kind of man leaves a woman like you?'

'You tell me.' Amanda blinked away her tears.

'Look, if we can just—' Shane crossed the space between them in a single stride, his hands reaching for hers.

But Amanda pulled back, retreated into the shadows of the living room.

'We find Jake.' Amanda kept moving, making for the kitchen and then the car. 'We find him and we help him save his son. Beyond that I don't know what happens.'

'If we follow him down this rabbit hole...' Shane was still hanging back. 'Things are going to get dangerous, Amanda. People are going to get hurt.'

'Haven't they already?'

Amanda stared at Shane for a second too long before pushing open the door and stepping out into the brisk embrace of the night.

24

'Dammit, Will.' Amanda clipped her seat belt in place, too tired to care that she'd just got her husband's name wrong.

'We'll find him,' Shane was getting behind the wheel, placing his key in the ignition. As the car roared to life, Amanda reached for her seat belt, freeing herself from her seat and diving back out into the cold.

'Amanda!' she heard Shane shouting to her as she hurried back to the cottage and grabbed the one thing she didn't dare leave behind; her laptop. With it tucked up beneath her arm she raced back to the car.

'Are you really so attached to that?' Shane asked as she climbed back into the passenger seat, breathing heavily after her race through the field.

'We might need it.'

'Do you know the plates on his car?'

Amanda chewed her lip as they pulled away from the idyllic cottage. Her silence was answer enough for Shane.

'Without his plates, or access to his satnav, we can't track him, you know that.'

'Did you check his plates?'

'No.'

'Aren't you supposed to be some super cop?'

'Super*cop* not Superman.'

The car bounced along the rough lane which drew them down towards the main road. In the darkness it was hard to tell where the road disappeared altogether in a sharp drop and where there were just shadows.

'Why would he leave alone in the middle of the night?' Rubbing her temple, Amanda leaned back wearily in her seat. 'Is he deliberately trying to get himself killed?'

'He's not thinking.' She felt Shane's gaze briefly drift over her. 'People do stupid things for those they love.'

'You really think this McAllister guy would harm a little boy?'

'Your husband seems to think so.'

Amanda released a brittle laugh as the atmosphere in the car grew tense. 'He's hardly *my husband*. I'm starting to wonder if he was ever mine at all.' She was full of bravado, pretending she was past caring, but the words stung as she said them.

'What's the most direct route to this guy's mansion?'

'See, we needed this after all,' Amanda replied smugly as she opened up her laptop, bathing the space around her in soft light. She made the relevant search and waited barely a second for the result. 'We could take the motorway.'

'Too obvious. He wouldn't want to draw too much attention. I reckon he'd stick to the back roads.'

'How can you be so sure?'

If it was Amanda, she'd choose speed over stealth.

'I've tracked guys who are running before. I'm a super cop, remember?'

'How many people run in homicide cases?'

'Pretty much all of them. Aside from the dead ones.'

Shane hit the brakes hard as the car slid round a particularly tight corner. In the headlights Amanda saw the craggy surface of a hillside rolling up beside them.

'Who can even drive fast round here?' she frowned as she stared at the empty road through the windscreen. It was nothing more than a trail of cats eyes leading into darkness.

'I'm guessing he knows these back roads. He did grow up around here.' Ignoring a turn-off for the motorway, Shane stuck to the narrow, twisting lanes which kept them bound to the hillside.

A minute passed. Then two. Shane didn't turn on the stereo like he normally would. Nor would he turn on the satnav, which would allow their own movements to be tracked remotely. Instead he just drummed his fingers against the wheel as if listening to music only he could hear. 'I mean, what's he even going to do when he gets to the guy's house?'

'Hmm?' Amanda was pulled out of her own darkening thoughts by the question.

'Jake. When he gets to McAllister's place, what do you think his plan is? Ask nicely to be let in then crack the guy's skull open with his bare hands?'

Amanda shifted awkwardly in her seat. She knew Shane was going to find out eventually. 'He has a gun.'

'A gun?'

The car shuddered as Shane drew his foot back off the gas. He looked at Amanda, eyes wide with a mixture of shock and horror.

'Fuck, Amanda, seriously? Why didn't you tell me?'

'I figured it was best not to bring it up when he and the gun were close by.'

'A gun,' Shane was shaking his head as he kept driving. 'That's... that's not only highly illegal but it's asking for trouble.'

'I know.'

'I mean, possession alone carries a stiff sentence.'

'I know.'

'He could aim that thing at someone and shoot without even meaning to.'

'I *know*. He's not thinking rationally at the moment. He turned the gun on me when I first found him.'

'He *what?*'

This made the car stop. It came to a halt in the middle of the road, headlights still illuminating a string of cats eyes scattered like breadcrumbs towards some unknown destination. Shane leaned forward, tightening his grip against the wheel. 'He held a fucking gun on you?' He wasn't looking at Amanda, he was staring blankly ahead.

'Yes, but he was afraid. I think he was maybe trying to scare me into leaving, I don't know, and—'

'He held a gun on you?' Shane repeated in disbelief. 'Amanda, this guy is supposed to be your *husband* and not only does he run out on you the second there's a hint of danger back home, he also puts your life in jeopardy when you take the trouble to go find him! I'm done. Some people just aren't worth saving.'

Reaching for the gearstick, Shane pushed the car into reverse.

'Shane, please,' Amanda reached for his hand, holding it against the gearstick. Her pulse quickened. Whether it was out of fear or something else she couldn't tell. 'I have to help him.'

'But why?'

'Because,' Amanda looked into the eyes of the boy she'd once loved more than anything. He was so grown-up behind the wheel of a car, dressed in a crumpled shirt with shadows stretching across his handsome face. But the boy was still there.

He looked back at Amanda through adult eyes, but they still held the same hope and kindness as they'd once done.

'Because it's the right thing to do,' Amanda squeezed his hand as it lay beneath hers.

'Argh, Amanda.'

She could see him folding. His shoulders dropped and his head tilted to the left just like it always did when she was about to beat him at a computer game or a particularly heated session of Risk or Monopoly. Shane hated to lose but he was always gracious in defeat.

'I'll get you next time,' he'd promise. And to his credit he certainly tried.

'The whole reason you became a cop is to help people.'

'That and bragging rights,' Shane offered her the whisper of a cheeky smile.

'Help me help my husband and then we'll head home, I promise.'

'And what? Be one big happy family?' Shane was teasing, but Amanda released his hand and turned away. She thought of Evangeline, the urban warrior princess striding through the streets of Glasgow with her buoyant little boy by her side. Amanda already knew that whatever happened, Jake wasn't going to be coming home with her. Will Thorn was gone.

*

An hour passed. It slid by as effortlessly as the darkened Scottish landscape. And with each passing minute Amanda fell deeper into a pit of her own despair.

'What if he took the motorway?'

'What if he isn't heading for the mansion?'

'What if we're already too late?'

She kept firing questions at Shane. Questions he couldn't possibly answer.

'We just have to keep going.' Somehow he still managed to sound vaguely positive, keeping his mood up for her benefit.

'It's been an hour.' Amanda kept scanning the roadside, praying she'd see Jake's car up against it after suffering from a flat tyre or some other misfortune. But she had no such luck. The roadside was empty save for shadows.

'We must be close to him.'

'What if he went back to the cottage?'

'Then we'll find him when we eventually go back. But first we check the roads.'

They approached a petrol station. The first one they'd seen in miles. It shone like a Christmas tree against the bleakness of the empty road. Amanda gazed out at its bright neon lights, at the three cars pulled up at its pumps.

Three seemed like a lot for such a late hour on such a quiet road. Amanda dropped her eyes to check the time on her laptop.

Four a.m.

Then her eyes snapped back to the petrol station and she gasped. Her hands were instantly against her window, banging and pointing.

'That's... that's his car.'

'You sure?'

'Yes, that's it.'

Shane was almost past the petrol station but the road was quiet enough to enable him to stop and reverse back towards the artificial glow of the petrol station. 'Want me to pull in?'

Amanda was bounding out of the car, Shane's question following on the air after her. She ran, moving on impulse not logic towards the parked up silver car which was beside a pump. And there, stood beside it in a lumberjack shirt and jeans was Jake, head bowed, a bright red baseball cap pulled low, shielding his eyes.

'What the hell is this?' she demanded breathlessly as Jake straightened. His expression flickered between surprise and anger as he looked at her.

'Get back in the car with your little cop friend and forget you ever saw me. Forget you ever knew me.'

Amanda felt her knees buckle but she stayed standing.

Forget you ever knew me.

Was that what he was doing? Was their love so easy for him to shake off?

'I want to help you.' She spoke slowly. Forcefully. She glanced nervously at Jake, towards his back. Was the gun with him? If he dared to fire it here the whole place risked going up. Surely he'd retained enough of his senses to know better than to do that?

'You've helped enough. This is on me now.' Jake looked

towards the numbers slowly ticking over on the petrol pump, refusing to meet Amanda's gaze.

'You're going to get yourself killed,' she hissed at him, feeling a heat start to rise in her cheeks.

Jake was throwing away everything. And for what? A fear over something that might not even happen?

'Just leave me be,' he growled the order through clenched teeth.

'I made a promise to you,' Amanda pulled in a long breath, taking any tears she might shed down to the pit of her stomach. 'For better or worse. And this is way, way worse than I ever imagined. But I'm not giving up on you, Will. I'll always help you.'

'Jake,' he grumbled his true name with scary clarity. Amanda scratched at her bare arms. It truly was like Will Thorn had never even existed. But then what did that mean for her, Amanda Thorn? Had she become some barely stable thing which could be scattered against the wind and banished from memory? 'Look, Amanda,' he slotted the pump back into its stand and reached for her. His hands were warm as they connected with her lower arms and protectively rubbed her goose-pimpled skin. 'I know I'm not the man you married, but I still care about you. I still want you to be safe. Go back home. I'll make sure that my past never troubles you again.'

Amanda remembered the first time Will had touched her. Really touched her. There had been three dates. Numerous occasions of grazed hands and feet meeting beneath a table, but no full-on touching. By their fourth date Amanda was going wild with desire. She wanted Will's strong hands all over her, to feel his lips against hers. But he was always such a gentleman. Always picking up the bill, holding a door open for her. Then, at the end of their fourth date, he leaned in to kiss her goodnight on the cheek as they sat outside her apartment building in his car and everything changed.

He kissed her cheek and lingered close to her. So close. Amanda could hear herself panting, could feel her body trembling. It happened quickly. Will's lips found hers and then she melted against him. They were kissing as though it had just been invented. His hands were exploring every curve they could access. And as they kissed Amanda knew that Will's touch had definitely been worth the wait.

'Jake… Jake Burton?'

Amanda snapped back into the moment as two men strode over to her and Jake. She watched her husband's face harden as though he'd suddenly been turned to stone.

'Jake? It is you, isn't it?'

25

'Jake Burton as I live and breathe.'

Amanda sucked in the crisp early morning air, filling her lungs until they might burst and doing everything she could to keep her hands from shaking. Her mind was screaming at her that this was no coincidence, that these men had been lying in wait at this petrol station for God knows how long. Had she just walked straight into a carefully laid trap set for Jake?

The taller man sauntered towards them, both hands thrust deep into his pockets. He was long and willowy like a reed, with a crop of fire red curls sat atop his aging face. When he smiled, his dark eyes crinkled menacingly.

'You know, we've been running up and down these back roads for days now. Looking for you.'

Whilst the tall man tried to adopt something of a casual demeanour, his stocky companion shadowed his every move with his thick hands balled into fists.

'How opportune to find you here,' the redhead released a hand from his pocket to gesture grandly at the surrounding petrol station. Glancing towards the glass-fronted store, Amanda saw that the clerk had gone, the counter was empty. She lifted her gaze to Jake, searching his expression for some sign of how he was going to react.

His features remained set in stone, his head still bowed beneath his cap.

The gun.

Amanda's eyes briefly betrayed her as they flickered towards Jake's waist. Was it still there? How long would it take him to grab it and arm himself? A few seconds? Less? And what then? Amanda imagined the staccato bursts of gunfire disturbing the peace of the night. The sickening sound of a bullet piercing a chest, tearing through precious organs.

But Jake could feel just as easily as these strangers. If he was concealing a weapon, chances were that they were too.

'I'm sorry, I think you've made a mistake.' Amanda applied her sweetest smile and laced her fingers through Jake's. She could feel the tension in his hand, but she kept smiling, leaned against him and traced her other hand up his arm. 'This is my husband, Will. We're up here on vacation.'

The redheaded man's eyes narrowed into suspicious slits as he stared at her. Whilst the stocky man's nostrils flared like a bull waiting to charge.

'Will, is it?' the tall man turned his head to stare back at Jake. 'Well, a rose by any other name—'

'If you gentlemen don't mind, we really need to be getting on our way.' Amanda's cheeks ached from forcing such a saccharine smile, but she had to keep up the façade. She tugged on Jake's hand, urging him back towards his car, away from the petrol pumps.

'Actually, Miss…' the red-haired man furrowed his brow at her.

'Mrs. Thorn.'

'Actually Mrs… Thorn,' he seemed amused by her surname, 'we have some mighty important business with your husband that we need to attend to.'

'And I've been travelling for the better part of four hours and really need to lay my head down at our hotel.' Amanda dropped a hand to her hip.

'Look, Mrs Thorn—'

'You've if you don't mind I'm exhausted and really don't have time for this.'

'We just need a quick—'

'I'll advise you gentlemen not to come between a pregnant lady and her sleep.' Amanda moved her hand to delicately rest it on her stomach. The redhead threw an uneasy glance towards his companion.

'Yes, come on sweetheart,' Jake was finally playing along, helping her into his car, 'we'll have you at the hotel in no time. Then you can rest.' He slammed the door shut and paced around to the driver's side.

'This isn't over,' the redhead called after him. 'We know you're back, Jakey boy.'

'My name is Will.'

He said it with such conviction that for a moment Amanda wondered if it had somehow become true again, if he was once again Will Thorn. *Her* Will Thorn. But as he turned on the engine and drove the car away from the petrol station, his hard expression returned. Jake was back.

'You shouldn't have done that,' he told her tightly as Amanda watched the fading lights of the petrol station in the rear-view mirror.

She wondered what Shane thought was going on? Wringing her hands together, she suddenly overwhelmed with an uneasy sense of betrayal. But Jake was still her husband, wasn't he? She had every right to hold his hand, to introduce herself as his wife.

'Are you really pregnant?' Jake asked as they kept driving. His tone was flat. Devoid of excitement, joy, anything.

'Would it matter if I was?' Amanda countered.

'Well, are you?'

'No.' She clasped her hands over her stomach as the lights from the petrol station were absorbed by the night. 'But I thought saying it might deter them from pushing things.'

'What made you think that?'

'Because maybe they're fathers too. And fathers will do anything to protect their children.'

Jake's jaw tightened but he said nothing. They rounded a corner and Amanda's phone came to life in her pocket, vibrating against her leg. She'd almost forgotten that she had it. Quickly snatching, it she saw Shane's name flashing on the screen.

'Hey.'

'Where the hell are you?' she heard his pain. His despair. His panic. 'What was that back there? Why are you in the car with Jake? Am I supposed to be following you? What's happening?'

'It was...' Amanda paused, gathering her thoughts. 'Those men recognized him.'

'They did? Shit. Well, they drove off in the opposite direction to you guys, so they can't be following you. Amanda, you need to turn around and come back. You're not safe with him.'

'Jake?' Amanda inched the phone away from her ear. 'Shane says those guys took off in the opposite direction so we can go back now.'

'We're not going back.'

'What did he say?' Shane raged through the phone.

'I said we're not going back,' Jake pressed down harder on the accelerator and the car sped down darkened roads.

'You need to take me back!' Amanda demanded. 'Enough of this bullshit, Jake. Take me back right now. Shane says it's safe

214

and he's a cop. We need his help.'

'No!'

'Jake?'

'We're going to get my son.'

Amanda felt sick as Jake navigated yet another tight corner.

'Hey, what the hell? You need to get back here,' Shane was shouting down the phone.

'Shane,' Amanda wilted against her seat and squeezed her eyes shut. 'He wants to go and get Ewan.'

'Like fuck he does! He just wants to put you in more danger! Tell that asshole to let you go!'

'Shane—'

'I'm coming after you and God help him when I catch up with you. Gun or no gun, I'm taking him down. This has gone too far.'

'Tell him to go and wait at the cottage.' Jake sounded calmer but still eerily in control.

'What?' Amanda heard Shane's voice echo her own through the phone.

'If he goes there and waits, I'll take you back there. I swear.'

'I'm not going to just go back and wait while you—'

'I'll bring her back to you,' Jake cut in, reaching across and plucking the phone out of Amanda's grasp. 'And she'll come to no harm. You have my word.'

He ended the call before Shane could protest further.

'We really should just go back,' she said delicately.

'We can't,' Jake gave a brisk shake of his head. 'Those men have seen me. They'll report straight back to McAllister and then they'll go straight for Ewan.'

'So shouldn't we just go back to the cottage, lay low? Isn't this what they'll expect you to do?'

'Yes. That's why we have to get to him first.'

*

In the grey light of dawn the dual blocks of flats didn't look any more appealing than they had during Amanda's first visit. Jake parked up in the central car park and peered out at the tall building ahead of him.

'So this is where you used to live?' Amanda kept her tone

light, almost flippant.

Jake just scratched his chin and continued to stare at the drab structure. Amanda wondered if he was being overwhelmed by a floor of memories. Were they all precious and joyful? Were he and Evangeline love's young dream until it all went horribly wrong for them?

'Not like our home, is it?'

Our home.

Amanda nearly choked on a sob. So he still regarded something as being theirs. 'It... um,' she gestured up towards the flats, 'I suppose it's urban living, which is going to be different to being near the woodlands.'

'You gave me a better life.' Jake was still looking at the flats, not at her. 'A life I never deserved.'

'That's not true,' Amanda insisted, reaching for his arm.

'Yes, it is,' Jake peered at her from the corner of his eye and appeared almost shy. Will had never been shy. He always possessed an easy confidence which Amanda had envied from the moment she met him. 'And this is how I repay you.' He hung his head. 'You were my dream, Amanda. But this,' he slowly raised a hand to point out at the flats, 'this was always my reality. This was where I belonged.'

'Something tells me that both you and Evangeline are better than this place.'

'You saw her?'

'She's stunning.'

This made Jake laugh.

'What?'

'You truly don't see yourself how other people do,' he kept laughing as he rubbed his jawline. 'I guess that's why it was so easy to fall so hard for you.'

Amanda froze. Such a large part of her had started to doubt if anything she had with Will had been real. But here was Jake admitting that it had been.

'You don't make letting go easy, you know that?' Jake was sliding out of the car, so Amanda quickly did the same. He was striding over towards the flat, head bowed beneath the baseball cap he was still wearing.

'What do you mean?'

'When Evie thought I was gone, she'd have just got on with her life. She'd gotten used to saying goodbye to people. We'd both had tough childhoods. But you...' He turned to face Amanda. They were almost at the entrance to the flats. 'You wouldn't give up on me. Not even now.'

'Well,' it was Amanda's turn to be shy. She looked down at her feet and chewed her lip. 'I guess I took my vows seriously.'

'It's because you're a good person, Amanda. Right down to your core. That's why I never deserved you.'

He pushed against the metal door which guarded the stairwell which led up into the building. It rattled in its hinges but didn't budge.

'I guess we need to wait until someone has to get in,' Amanda looked around. The place was deserted. It'd be a good few hours until people started to seep out of the flats heading out to work.

Jake leaned all his weight against the door and pushed it hard.

Nothing.

He shoved it again. The door rattled uncertainly but didn't open. He pushed again and this time it burst open, clattering loudly against the wall.

'Or you could just burst your way in,' Amanda said with a roll of her eyes. 'Let's just add breaking and entering to child-snatching on our daily list of misdemeanours.'

'He's my son,' Jake snapped defensively as he stalked towards the stairwell. 'Besides,' he glanced back, one hand on the stair rail, 'Evie would want me to keep him safe.'

Amanda followed him up three flights. They didn't pass a single soul. The building was oddly still around them. People were tucked up in their beds lost to distant dreams. When dawn fully arrived, alarms would shriek and chime, shattering the tranquillity.

Jake took the stairs two at a time, leaving Amanda struggling to keep up. Her lungs were burning in her chest as she staggered towards the third floor. Jake was already ahead of her, moving down the corridor and eyeing the numbers on the doors. He stopped abruptly halfway down the corridor and when Amanda reached him she bent her knees and lowered her head to catch her breath.

'This is it.' Jake didn't sound quite as certain as he had back in the car.

Straightening, Amanda looked at the faded brass number on

the door; 328. This was it all right.

'Is your plan just to burst your way in or do you at least intend on knocking?'

'I have a key.' Jake briefly fumbled in his pocket before producing a single silver key. Amanda stared at it like it were a dagger which had been pulled from her own back.

'You have a… key?'

Where had it been in *their* home? Tucked up in a box somewhere? Hidden in the garage? In his car? If Amanda had discovered it, she truly would have found the key to Pandora's box and opening the door it led to would have reigned chaos over her life, just as it was doing now.

'I kept it for emergencies,' Jake told her simply as he placed it in the lock and turned. He said it so casually, as if the key didn't indicate some great betrayal in their marriage.

Amanda was so busy reeling over the key's existence that she almost didn't notice Jake open the door and slip inside the apartment. She followed after him, stepping into her husband's former life.

The door led directly into the lounge, which had an open-plan kitchen integrated into it. The room was simply furnished with a fresh vase of flowers on a distant windowsill and toys scattered across the floor.

Two doors led off either side of the room and Jake was making for the one in the far left-hand corner which had a Spiderman poster on it. Amanda wanted to follow but her eyes were drawn to a framed picture beside the modest-sized television. It was slightly faded and had a crease down the centre as if it had once been folded beneath a pillow or against someone's chest, concealed in a pocket.

Jake and Evangeline, arms wound around each other. They both looked so young. So innocent. So happy. They were smiling for the camera and Evangeline's belly was swollen. Amanda couldn't stop staring at it. It was like driving by a particularly brutal car accident, knowing you shouldn't look at the more gruesome elements but being powerless to tear your eyes away.

'Okay, we have to go.' Jake was back in the room, a sleepy boy in blue pyjamas hauled over one shoulder.

'Jesus, Jake,' Amanda's entire body tightened when she saw him with the boy. 'Where's his mother?'

'Mummy's at work,' Ewan grumbled sleepily.

'At work?'

'Reserve your judgement,' Jake whispered fiercely. 'Evie doesn't have anyone to rely on. She must be working nights to take care of Ewan. Slipping out when he's asleep.'

'He's just a boy.'

'She's doing her best.' Jake looked at the boy in his arms and then briefly closed his eyes and released a pained breath. 'I didn't know she'd struggle this much,' he admitted softly. Then his entire posture stiffened and he stared back towards the door they'd just come through.

'Argh!' Ewan screamed, his eyes wide, suddenly completely awake. He thrashed against Jake, his cheeks turning crimson. 'Where's my Mummy? Argh!'

His screams were shrill, like a cat fighting. Amanda was at his side, keeping her voice low and soothing.

'Hey, hey, it's okay—'

'Mummy!' Ewan demanded at the top of his lungs.

'Hey,' Jake gripped the boy beneath the shoulders and held him at eye level. 'You know me, from the pictures, aye wee lad?'

Ewan's chest was heaving, his eyes bulging out of his head. He stared at the man gripping him and nodded breathlessly.

'I'm Daddy, right?' Jake spun around to nod at the framed picture of happiness where he held Evie in his arms. Sniffling softly, Ewan nodded again. 'So you don't need to be scared, little man.' Jake clutched the boy against his chest and kissed the top of his head. 'I promise that I'm not here to hurt you. I'm here to keep you safe.'

Amanda turned away, feeling like she was intruding upon some tender moment.

'McAllister's men could show up at any minute. We need to get out of here.' Jake was addressing her directly, all softness gone from his voice. There was only urgency in his words now.

'Okay, well,' Amanda looked at the boy. He was so small. So vulnerable in his pyjamas, his dark hair still wild from sleep. 'You can't take him like that.' She was hurrying in the direction of Ewan's bedroom, fighting against the sensation that she had become the grossest of intruders. This was Evie's home. Jake's other wife. His first wife. Which made Amanda the imposter.

'He'll need clothes, and maybe some toys.'

'We don't have time for this,' Jake growled at her.

'Daddy is Mummy coming too?' Ewan wondered innocently. He rubbed a hand against his runny nose as he looked up at the man from the photograph who he knew to be his father. Were there other such pictures? Did Evangeline sit with Ewan on rain-soaked afternoons turning the pages of a large photo album explaining to him who his father was? And all the while Amanda had been safe in her lie, happy and oblivious down south.

'Mummy will come later,' Jake softly reassured the boy.

'Okay,' Amanda hurried into the bedroom and spun around, searching for something she could grab. There was a Paws Petrol backpack slumped in one corner. She picked it up and then began opening drawers, reaching for anything that might be useful. Jumpers. Jeans. T-shirts. Pants. Socks. Shoes. What sorts of things did little boys even need? Shouldering the bag, Amanda returned to the main living room.

'Ewan, do you have a... um... favourite toy you want to bring?' she asked gently. Against his father's shoulder, Ewan rubbed at his green eyes.

'Woody.'

'Huh?'

'Woody.' He pointed to a stubby finger towards a toy on the floor. Amanda recognized the Stetson-wearing Sherriff from a Disney movie.

'Okay then, let's take Woody.' Amanda bent down and scooped up the toy.

'And Spiderman.' Ewan's little hand gestured to another figure on the floor.

'Okay, Spiderman too.' Amanda grabbed him with her other hand.

'That's enough toys,' Jake marched out of the flat and Amanda hurried after him.

'Should we leave a note or something?' Looking over her shoulder, she glanced back at the door to flat 328. 'I mean, won't his mother be panic-stricken when she comes home and realizes he's gone?'

'She'll know it was me,' Jake stated with confidence as he approached the stairwell.

'She will?'

Did Jake and Evangeline have a bond that went beyond words? Would she just sense that he'd been there, that he'd taken their son? Because when Will had left, Amanda had no such feelings. She just felt fear, shock and abandonment.

'She'll think it was me or McAllister. And if the place isn't turned over, she'll know it was me. Besides,' he hung his head, looking guilty, 'I put a fifty pence on her pillow. It's something we always used to do.'

Amanda didn't have time to dwell on the significance of that. How such a seemingly innocent gesture could have so much meaning. Jake was already powering down the stairs, carrying Ewan with ease.

When Amanda stepped back onto the car park, the first soft rays of sunlight had warmed the tarmac. It looked like it was going to be a nice day.

After tucking Ewan into the back seat, Jake climbed in behind the wheel but he didn't start the engine. Instead he stared at Amanda as she buckled herself into the passenger seat.

'Can you ride in the back with him?' he wondered, sounding a little sheepish.

'In the back?' Amanda turned round to see Ewan furiously rubbing at his eyes and struggling to stay awake.

'If he gets scared I'd rather he had someone with him.'

'Okay, sure,' Amanda unclipped her belt and did as Jake asked. She settled herself next to Ewan as the car drove out of the car park and began heading back towards the cottage. Back towards Shane.

The flats were still towering ominously in the background when Ewan nudged his way towards Amanda and rested his head against her arm. Then he promptly fell fast asleep.

26

The sun was shining when they arrived back at the little cottage, this time parking on the driveway. Shane's car was there too, glistening in the sunlight. She'd barely climbed out of the car when she heard the front door open and Shane's footsteps crunch against the gravel path which led to the driveway.

'Thank God you're back.'

And then his arms were around her, pressing her against his chest. Amanda hugged him back, breathed in the now familiar scent of his cologne. She didn't want to let go. She bunched his shirt in her hands, holding on tightly. Shane was safety. Stability. Shane was home.

'Who are you?' Ewan's inquisitive voice piped up, ending their embrace. Amanda stepped back from Shane, suddenly feeling self-conscious, like a kid who'd been caught kissing behind the bike sheds at school.

'This is Shane.'

Ewan was out of the car. He cocked his head and looked first at Amanda and then at Shane. Both Woody and Spiderman were clutched against his chest.

'It's okay,.' Jake came round the other side of the car, stretching out his arms. Watching him reminded Amanda of the ache in her own limbs. She'd spent so many long hours cramped up inside a car that she longed to run free across the Scottish headlands, to feel the wind whip through her hair and scrape against her cheeks. She wanted to breathe in fresh, clean air and listen to the distant rumble of the ocean.

'Is this your house?' Ewan asked Shane, still possessively holding his toys close as though he feared one of the adults might snatch them away from him.

'Um…' Shane massaged his neck and glanced at Amanda for support.

'This is Shane's house,' Amanda started, guiding the little boy towards the single-storey building. 'We're going to stay here. Just for a little while.'

'Where's the rest of it?' Ewan wondered as he was ushered

inside. 'And where are all the other houses?'

The boy was full of questions, each one tumbling into the next.

Where's Mummy?

Where are we?

What time is dinner?

Am I going to school today?

Who wants to play with Woody and me?

Amanda admired his curious nature. And his brazen attitude. He wasn't fearful in their presence. He just seamlessly adapted to his new surroundings. As soon as Amanda placed him in the living room, he started playing with his toys, perfectly content. Change was clearly something of a constant in the little boy's life.

'He seems happy enough.' Jake came and stood beside her as Amanda watched Ewan play.

'You can't keep him here. You know that, don't you?'

'He's safer here than being back home.'

'He should be with his mother, Jake. He should be at school.'

'And he'll go back to all that. When it's safe.'

'And when will that be?' Amanda spun around to face him. There was so much anger flooding her system. She was angry at him for leaving. Angry at him for lying. 'You've been out of his life for *years*, Will. You can't just waltz back in and pick up where you left off.'

Jake was looking at her through sad eyes.

'What?'

'You called me Will.'

'Wasn't so long ago that was your name.' Amanda could feel herself pouting. She wished she was strong enough to stop caring, wished she could just roll with the punches like Ewan was.

'I wish I could have stayed as Will Thorn for you.' Jake placed his hands on her shoulders and Amanda tried not to cry. 'This could have been our future. A nice cottage by the sea. A family.'

'If it weren't for all the lies.' Knocking his hands away, Amanda turned before he could see the first of her tears fall. She quickly smeared it away with the back of her hand.

'Hey, Amanda?' Shane was in the doorway. He'd got

changed and seemed freshly showered. Instead of a shirt he wore a long sleeved T-shirt and jeans. His hair was still damp, his cheeks flushed. Amanda looked at him, grateful that he was here. He anchored the whole warped situation with a comforting sense of normality. She'd known Shane all her life. Their histories were forever intertwined.

'Yeah?'

'Why don't you take Ewan for a little walk to get some air? Maybe show him the sea?'

Jake instantly made a grunt of disapproval.

'They'll be safe enough,' Shane insisted. 'There's no one around here for miles. Besides, you and I need to have a little chat.'

'I don't kn—' Amanda was about to protest when Ewan came barrelling over. He threw himself against her legs and locked on tight.

'Ooh, the sea,' he cooed as he looked up at her, eyes bright. 'I'd love to go and see it. Take me. Take me.'

'Okay, okay.' Amanda reached for the little boy's hand and held it in her own. It felt strangely comforting to feel his small palm against her own. 'We'll be thirty minutes, no more.' She should fight Shane on his order to leave but the lure of stretching her legs was too enticing to ignore.

She looked back at the two men who'd had such an impact on her life. They both looked uneasy being so close to one another. She hoped that when she came back to the cottage they were both still there.

'Come on then, Ewan.' He happily bounced along at her side. Since arriving at the cottage, she'd changed him out of his pyjamas into a bright yellow sweatshirt and jeans.

'I'm bringing Woody,' he told her boldly, quickly grabbing one of his toys as they left the lounge.

'Okay, sure, Woody can come.'

'He's a Sherriff so he loves the outdoors.'

'Uh-huh.'

'And he has a horse. Do you have a horse?'

And the barrage of questions continued.

*

Despite the presence of the sun it was cold out on the rugged hills which bordered the cottage. Amanda picked her way along a trodden path with Ewan loyally remaining by her side.

'Do you come here a lot?' he asked as Amanda led him up towards the crest of a hill. The wind buffeted them both and it felt good. Amanda wanted to extend her arms, to spread them like wings and feel the full embrace of nature.

'Not really.'

The ground was thick with heather. Amanda surveyed the landscape around them. From her vantage point she could see the cottage which had been reduced to a tiny dot. South from the cottage were the rooftops of the little village where she'd previously searched for Jake. It crossed her mind that she could take Ewan there to get some sweets at some point. But when? Surely the little boy would be heading back home soon. How long were they supposed to keep him hidden away in the highlands?

'Is that the sea?' Ewan was pointing at the turquoise crest which met the sky on the horizon.

'Yep, that's it.'

He became the leader, pulling Amanda down the hill closer to the sea. She started to hear the distant tumble of its waves, taste the salt carried on the breeze. It didn't take them long to reach the cliffside and an impressive vista of the sea. Where the land fell away, the water took up residence, sweeping away for miles and glistening majestically beneath the afternoon sun. Amanda tried to suppress the swirling sensation in her stomach which started to build up like a brewing storm. Her palms became slick with sweat. Her body always went into flight mode whenever she was near a cliffside.

'I've never been in the sea.' Ewan's eyes were wide as he took it in, moving his head left to right as he greedily absorbed all of the beauty. His wonderment helped to disperse her mounting anxiety.

'You haven't?' This surprised Amanda. To her the sea had been such a huge part of everyday life throughout her childhood. She couldn't imagine growing up without it's infinite presence stretching out towards the horizon.

'No.' Ewan looked down at his red trainers.

'I grew up right by the sea,' Amanda recalled fondly. 'I'd spend hours exploring the coastline or playing in the waves. I'd try and jump them as they came in.'

'You did that with my dad?' Ewan peered up at her, squinting against the sunlight.

'No… with, with Shane.'

Ewan looked back at the sea, at the waves gently crashing against the beach which was somewhere below them. 'I bet when my dad was in the sea he was the fastest swimmer.'

'Yeah, I bet.'

'Mummy always says he's the strongest man in the world. And the fastest.'

'She makes him sound like a real hero.'

'He is. He went away to protect us.'

'What?' Amanda crouched down to the boy's level. 'Didn't your Mummy ever think…' she needed to choose her words carefully. Saying *didn't your Mummy ever think your Daddy was dead* to a child felt too harsh. 'Didn't she wonder why he went away?'

'To save us,' Ewan replied simply. 'Because he's our hero.'

'Okay,' Amanda stood back up while Ewan started playing with Woody, showing off the beauty of the ocean to his toy.

Amanda kept one eye on the boy and another on the path which they'd just walked. It made no sense that Evangeline thought Jake was still alive. How could she have known? Had he reached out to her at some point? But surely to do so would be too dangerous. Everyone back in Scotland had to believe that Jake Burton had died.

Amanda watched Ewan laugh and play with his toy.

She'll know it was me.

Back on the stairwell of the flats, how had Amanda not been quick enough to ask *doesn't she think you're dead?* Because clearly she didn't. Clearly Evangeline always knew that one day her husband would return. It seemed that the key to his old home was just one of many secrets Jake had kept close all these years.

'Can we?'

Amanda knocked her hair out of her eyes and looked down at Ewan. His attention was fully focused on her, his eyes wide and hopeful.

'Can we what?' She'd been lost in her own thoughts.

'Go down to the beach?' Ewan reached for her hand and tugged on it.

'I…' Amanda looked back over her shoulder. The cottage had already disappeared from view. She knew they really shouldn't go any further. But she'd yet to hear the crack of a gunshot echo across the wilderness, so Shane and Jake must be tolerating one another peacefully. And she did want to see the ocean, to dip her toes in the water and feel a connection to home. 'All right, but just for a little bit.'

Ewan was cheering in triumph as they picked their way down the narrow path which led them towards the beach.

*

It was a small beach and they were only having to share it with a few seagulls. A slender strip of sand was bordered by slick dark rocks which reached out into the sea.

'Yay,' Ewan was running through the sand, making directly for the water. Amanda chased after him, catching him just before he made contact with the ocean. 'It's so… big.' He perched happily in her arms, looking out at the waves.

'It's huge,' Amanda agreed. 'If you went in and just kept swimming you'd reach Europe.'

'Wow.'

He started to wriggle. He possessed an impressive amount of strength for such a small child. Something he must have inherited from his powerful father.

'Go in, go in,' he pleaded.

'Okay but take your shoes off first, you don't want them getting wet,' Amanda instructed as she lowered him back down. Ewan instantly obeyed, tugging off the trainers and socks Amanda had carefully dressed him in earlier.

'You come too.' He was looking at her shoes.

'Okay.' Amanda freed her own feet and then approached the water. Ewan was waiting for her, one hand floating in the air. She clasped it and together they stepped towards an approaching wave whilst Woody waited along with their shoes in the dry sand back on the beach.

'Ah, it's cold!' Ewan laughed with delight as the water pooled around his ankles and then drifted away again.

'This time, let's jump the wave. You ready?'

'Ready.'

Amanda watched the white crest of a wave roll in. 'One… two… three.'

They jumped and the wave reached out beneath them. Ewan was laughing and bouncing up and down, loving how the water splashed around him.

'Again, again!'

And they jumped again. And again. Amanda felt like she was six years old, clutching the hand of her beloved father. He'd throw her a quick knowing grin and then tell her to jump. Together they'd bounce over the waves, and back then Amanda had thought that they were both invincible.

'Again!'

Ewan was starting to bounce with less enthusiasm, his eyes becoming slightly bloodshot and his head drooping as fatigue began to take hold of him. But he kept wanting more, determined not to let the fun end.

'Okay, once more.'

'Amanda!'

The sound of her own name being bellowed caused her to freeze. Ewan's hand was still tightly in her own as she turned around. Shane was racing across the beach towards her. Fear quickly swept away any remnants of fun with one foul swoop.

'Shane?' Amanda began retreating from the water, bringing Ewan with her.

'You've been gone for over an hour,' Shane pressed a hand to his chest as he struggled to get his breath.

'An hour?' Amanda looked back at the ocean as though it had betrayed her, luring her into a false sense of security so that she lost all track of time. 'I didn't mean to be so long. We were just… the water… and the waves.'

'Well, Jake is beside himself with worry. He was convinced that someone had come and picked you both off. He's searching up in the hills. We really need to get back to the cottage.'

'Urgh,' Ewan released Amanda's hand and dropped down into the sand. 'My legs ache. No more walking.'

Shane plucked the little boy up in his arms and cradled him against his chest. 'I'll carry you back.' Amanda noticed Shane's gentleness with the child, the way he softened his words around him.

The trio began making their way back up the beach.

'Woody!' Ewan suddenly howled mournfully, squirming in

Shane's arms.

'I've got him,' Amanda dangled the toy in the child's line of sight. 'He's fine, he's coming back with us too.'

*

Ewan was asleep before they made it back to the cottage. Shane transferred him from his arms to the bed and then sat with Amanda in the kitchen. Jake still hadn't returned.

'So what did you need to talk to Jake about?'

'About you.'

Amanda looked up from the fresh cup of tea she had clasped between her hands. It was made of delicate china decorated in purple thistles.

'About me?'

Shane nodded as he took a sip from his own painted cup. 'After all this is over, I need to make sure you're okay. He's agreed to let me report all his identification documents as forged, which will nullify your marriage.'

'So...' Amanda looked back down at her hands. 'It will be like it never happened?'

'I'm doing everything I can to protect you, Amanda. To help you walk away from this mess.'

'But...' she felt her tears weighing down her eyelashes and tried to blink them away. Reaching across the table, Shane took her hand.

'You deserve a clean slate from all this. To be able to think about your future.'

'I had a future and it...' she threw an anguished glance towards the front door. 'It walked away. It left me.'

'You're going to be all right. You know that, don't you?'

'Why do you even care so much about what happens to me?' Amanda knew she was being petulant but she could feel the web of everything closing in around her, constricting her breathing – her impending annulment, Jake's secret family and past. It was all too much.

Shane's mouth opened, he was about to reply when the front door burst open. Jake entered the kitchen, his face reddened by fierce winds.

'You're back,' he gave Amanda an accusatory glare.

229

'Jake, I'm so sorry. I took Ewan down to the beach and lost track of time.'

'Well isn't this cosy?' Jake looked at the pair sat at the table, at their clasped hands and cups of tea. Amanda withdrew her hand from Shane's reach. 'And where the hell is my son?'

'Sleeping,' Amanda told him. 'In the bedroom, he was exhausted after our walk, so you'd do well to lower your voice.'

Jake eased the door closed and ran both hands through his hair. He lingered awkwardly near the doorway as if he'd just rudely intruded into someone else's home.

Amanda stood up and approached the sink. 'Want me to make you a cup of tea? Sadly they don't seem to have any coffee.'

'We can't stay here.' The words tumbled out of Jake.

'What? Why?'

'Because you found me here.' His eyes bore into hers. 'If you found me here, then they can too. We need to move.'

'Jake, I—'

'They *will* come for me. And when they do it will be more than phone calls and cryptic messages. McAllister will be looking to end this. To end me.'

'What makes you so sure?'

'Because no one crosses him and gets away with it. Even if it takes decades, he has his vengeance. He's a patient man. They saw me at the petrol station,' Jake released a deep sigh. 'They are coming for me, for Ewan. Every second that I stay still, they creep ever closer. McAllister knows for sure that I'm alive now. That I'm in Scotland.'

'So where do you want to go?'

'North,' Jake clicked his fingers at her like he was ordering service at a restaurant. 'Find us somewhere remote we can stay. Use your computer.'

'And what then? We can't just stay in hiding forever!'

'I know,' Jake shook his head in frustration and looked to Shane. The realization that they might now share a secret shocked Amanda with the intensity of a lightning bolt.

'What else did you two discuss in my absence?' she demanded, raising her voice, forgetting about Ewan who was sleeping soundly just a few feet away.

'Tell her,' Shane urged.

'Fine,' Jake sighed and then turned back towards Amanda.

'You two are going to go back to England.'

'Look, Jake, I said I was willing to help and I—'

'And you're going to take Ewan with you.'

Amanda blinked. Certain that she must have misheard her husband's request.

'You're the best chance he's got at getting away from all this,' Jake kept staring at her. 'Once I've handled things up here, I'll come back for him.'

'Jake, I—'

'Please, Amanda. Help me save my son.'

27

'Take Ewan to England?' Slowly Amanda dropped back into her chair and pressed her fingertips against her temple, elbows resting on the table.

'He'll be safer there,' Jake insisted.

Releasing an exasperated sigh, Amanda shook her head. 'No, Jake, he won't. This McAllister guy still found you there. Still called the house. Still threw a brick through my bloody window.'

'But he didn't hurt you.'

'Seriously?' Wiping her eyes, she straightened. 'So because I didn't end up soaked in my blood I wasn't in enough peril? Is that it? Is that why you left?'

Jake staggered back as though she'd just struck a blow against his chest. Clearing his throat, he quickly recovered. 'Being here, in Scotland, we're in McAllister's spiderweb, just waiting for him to get the drop on us. He has less power in England. Fewer contacts he can lean on.'

'Yet somehow he managed to harass me. I'm pretty sure he can get to someone no matter where they are if he's got enough motivation.'

'I just need to keep my son safe.'

'You really think the best thing for your son is to take him away from everything he knows? From his *mother*?'

'For now, yes.'

'Doesn't she even get a say in this? Or do you just not care about who you hurt as you tear through their lives like some out of control steam roller?'

'She'd agree with me.'

'Does she even really think you're dead?'

'Amanda—' Shane was reaching for her, trying to calm her down. But his efforts were in vain. She was on her feet, staring down her husband. Refusing to let him wrap her up in yet another lie.

'Because your son didn't look at you like he was seeing a ghost. And back at the flats you seemed pretty confident that

Evie would know it was you who'd been there. And she's supposed to believe you're dead!'

Amanda could feel the veins in her neck straining, the blood pumping furiously round her body, bringing a flush to her cheeks. She was so angry she thought she might explode and destroy both Shane and Jake in a brilliant blaze of fire.

'She knew the risks attached to the job I was taking.' Jake managed to keep his voice level which only angered Amanda further. 'I told her that if things went south I wouldn't come back.'

'And what? She was just happy to let you go?'

'We lived in a different world, Amanda. We didn't have parents watching our backs all our lives, people who cared about us. We were forced to take risks.'

'I took a risk.' Amanda pointed a shaking hand at him. 'I married you and took a fucking risk, and look where it's got me?'

And then all the anger was gone. She deflated like a balloon, collapsing in on herself. She was so very tired. Exhaustion had frayed the end of every nerve.

'I'm just…' she shook with the force of unshed tears as she returned to her chair.

'I'm going to get some air.' Jake opened the door and then he was gone.

Amanda stared across at Shane in the aftermath of the argument. He let an even silence settle between them before clearing his throat as he rolled his neck side to side, working out his own aches.

'You want to go back, forget all this, you say the word.' He placed his offer on the table. An offer which had always been there.

'I know,' Amanda looked to the front door and then to the internal door which led to the living room and beyond that the bedroom where Ewan was sleeping soundly, oblivious to the chaos ensuing between the adults. 'If Ewan is really in danger, I have to help him. He's completely innocent in all this. I don't want him ending up like those girls in that fire.'

'I tried to do a bit of digging on this McAllister guy. I couldn't find much, but if he's involved in drug trafficking like Jake says he is then he's dangerous. Eighty per cent of the homicide cases I work are drugs related.'

233

'Christ. Are there ever… children involved?'

'Very rarely,' Shane massaged his neck. 'If a child gets involved, it tends to be covered up. Like in a house fire. Or a car accident. And it sounds that for a guy like McAllister there's no line of morality that he isn't prepared to cross.'

The fire at Gregg McAllister's home had been very real and he'd lost two children that night.

'Then we take Ewan to England.' Amanda decided.

'He wants to go north first,' Shane nodded at the front door. 'Feels like he needs to lose the heat off his tail.'

'Like those guys at the petrol station?'

'Exactly. I imagine McAllister's got a whole network of people looking for him. Jake's right, this cottage isn't safe.'

'Then I'll have to find us somewhere that is.'

*

Amanda followed Jake into the single bedroom of the cottage. Amongst a wealth of pillows Ewan stretched out his little arms, releasing an almighty yawn.

'She tired you out, did she?' Jake leaned down against the bed. His voice was softer now, had lost the hardened edge it'd had in the other room.

'It was fun,' Ewan mumbled sleepily. 'We jumped the waves.'

Amanda smiled at the sleepy boy, and then glancing up saw that Jake too was studying him, the creases in his forehead softening.

'He's quite the kid,' she commented quietly. 'I can see a lot of you in him.'

'Hmm,' Jake pulled a hand across his face. 'If you can, it's just genetic. I've never been a presence in his life. Never been a father.'

'Do you regret that?'

The question hung between them, hovering over the sleeping boy.

'I regret a lot of things in my life,' Jake was getting up and making for the door but then turned back to Amanda as though something was drawing him back into the room.

'You don't have to let me in,' she told him gently. 'But if you want to, I'm here. We're still married after all.'

Jake cracked a smile and pushed his hands through his dark hair which was already tousled by the brisk sea breeze. 'I don't regret you,' his eyes suddenly locked onto hers and Amanda felt like he'd just given her an electric shock. There was so much intensity in his gaze, the power of countless unspoken words, feelings. 'Or him,' he shifted his attention towards the bed. 'I wish this could have been our life – our family. I tried so hard to keep everything perfect for us back home. I probably tried too hard.'

'You were fastidious, I'll give you that.' Amanda felt an ache in her chest when she thought of her perfect house, of the neat pile of towels in the bathroom, of the tidily arranged cupboards in the kitchen. Had it all just been a part of Will's act? 'Did you think about him when we were together?'

'I thought about him every day.'

'Oh,' Amanda's shoulders dropped and she internally kicked herself. Of course he thought about his son every day, what kind of man would he have been if he didn't? Will, her husband, he'd have thought about Ewan. He was kind and loving. And Jake... Will was still in there, somewhere. 'I mean, yeah, of course you did.'

'I regretted leaving. I wondered what he was doing.' Jake laced his fingers through Amanda's hand and she shuddered at his touch, remembering how good it used to feel to have Will's skin pressed up against her own. 'Before I met you I was in such a dark place. I was running for my life and from it. I'd given up everything. And the darkness was always there, Amanda,' he squeezed her hand, 'you just lit it up.'

Amanda tasted the salt of her tears as she smiled up at him. 'You did what you had to do and you kept your son alive.'

'And I intend to keep it that way,' Jake said sternly, his usual mask of steely indifference falling into place. 'You. Him. You're part of two different worlds, but you're connected, through me. And that puts you in danger.'

Amanda nodded solemnly. She knew how it felt to be in danger, to stare into the face of your imminent destruction. She'd been older than Ewan but still a child and her own father had risked everything to save her.

'You're doing everything you can to keep him safe,' she looked into Jake's eyes, hoping to catch another glimmer of

Will.

'Yeah,' he released her hand, 'well let's just hope that it's enough.'

*

For the second time in less than twenty-four hours Ewan was lifted out of bed and placed in a car to be driven to somewhere unknown. Amanda settled him in the back seat beside her as Jake and Shane climbed into the front of the car.

'We need to take my car,' Shane had told Jake decisively when the larger man eventually returned from sulking in the shadows outside.

'What? Why?'

'It's too easy to run the plates on your rental. No one up here knows me. My car is the safer option.'

Jake didn't fight the decision.

'You found somewhere?' his tone was hard as he flung the question towards Amanda.

'Yeah, there's an isolated holiday cabin way up north. I booked it online under Shane's name. We can all spend a few days there until it's safe enough to take Ewan to England.'

Amanda gave what she hoped was a brisk, efficient nod. She didn't want Jake to see the worry she hid behind a tight smile.

When she'd booked the cabin online there had been a new message waiting for her on the darknet.

From Turtle82.

As she tensely tapped on the mouse pad to open it, Amanda's heart had stopped beating. Her entire body had frozen in anticipation.

        I need you to do one more job
        for me.

Sucking in a breath, Amanda had read the rest of the message;

        From where you've been swimming

```
lately I'd say we're after the
same fish. Help me catch this
King Carp and I'll consider us
even.
   T.
```

The words swam before her on the screen. So Turtle82 truly did know where she was. What else did they know? Were they aware of McAllister? Was he the King Carp?

Amanda had hurriedly confirmed the booking for the cabin. Then, despite her better judgement, she reopened the darknet, where Turtle's message was patiently waiting for her on the screen. Biting her lip, she let her fingers dance across the keyboard as she fired off her reply;

```
One last job and that's it.
We're done.
```

If Turtle82 was out for McAllister and there was some way she could help, then she knew she had to take it. She could remove the shadow which hung over Jake, allow him to feel safe again. To feel free. And then what? A sorrowful tremor shuddered through her body. Would he go home with her, back to their old life? Or was that all gone now? Would he stay in Scotland, with his first wife and son? Amanda didn't even know what she wanted anymore, let alone what Jake wanted.

'Okay.' Jake grumbled, breaking her train of thought..

A light rain had descended by the time they were all bundled up in the car. Ewan continued to sleep with his head resting against Amanda's shoulder.

'How far away is this place?' Jake seemed uncomfortable in the passenger seat. He kept readjusting his seat belt and looking longingly at the steering wheel behind which Shane was placed.

'Two hours, maybe three.' Shane was pulling away from the little cottage.

'Great.'

Amanda almost laughed at how sarcastic Jake sounded. 'It's going to be fine,' she assured him.

'Let's hope so.'

'Where are we?'

'What's for breakfast?'

'Where's Mummy?'

'Can I play with Woody?'

'When can I go for a wee?'

Ewan woke up around an hour into the drive and started firing questions at Amanda like a mini machine gun. She convinced the men that they needed to stop at the next set of motorway services. Shane had opted to stick to the main roads feeling that the need for speed outweighed the need for stealth.

'They won't even be looking for this car,' Shane had insisted when Jake objected.

Morning had broken when they arrived on the service's car park. It wasn't a glorious dawn to a new day. The sky was leaden and a cold rain fell like mist.

'Okay, let's go stretch your legs,' Amanda helped Ewan out of the car. He instantly placed his hand in hers and together they walked towards the services. Doors slammed behind her as the two men also got out.

'Ooh, McDonald's,' Ewan started to bounce up and down excitedly when he saw the golden arches.

'I guess we can get your breakfast there if you like.'

'Yes!' More bouncing.

An egg McMuffin and a Coke later and Ewan was a ball of untamed energy.

'I'd better take him to the toilet,' Jake suggested when the little boy kept squirming. He kept his shoulders slumped, his eyes nervously darting around the place as though he feared being spotted at any given moment. It was a risk to have him out in public but Amanda sensed that he was trying to snatch every moment with his son that he could. Ewan merrily bounced out of the booth and followed his father towards the rest rooms.

'He's a cute kid,' Shane commented.

'Mmm,' Amanda thoughtfully twirled the stirrer in her cup of coffee. 'His mum must be going out of her mind though.'

'Do you think she'd call the cops?'

'I don't know. Maybe. No.'

'No?'

'Jake makes it seem like she's just as aware of the danger McAllister poses as he is.' Picking up another sachet of sugar, Amanda smacked it against her palm, loosening its sweet contents. Then, ripping it open, she dumped a second load of white crystals into the dark depths of her coffee.

'Need the sugar kick, huh?'

'I feel like I'm running on empty,' as if on cue Amanda's jaw widened into an epic yawn.

'You and me both. Tell me this log cabin has a hot tub, open fire and on-site masseuse.'

'I wish. More like two bedrooms, a modest kitchen and a good thirty minutes away from the nearest town.'

'Sounds heavenly.'

'It should be remote enough to let us lay low for a bit. But when can we leave?'

'How long's a piece of string.'

'I'm serious,' Amanda frowned as she sipped at her coffee, the caffeine struggling to push back her mounting exhaustion. 'We can't just stay up there indefinitely. We're like the most complicated episode of Happy Families ever.'

'You keen to get back to your life?'

'To normality,' Amanda admitted. 'I don't get paid while I'm away like you do. I work for myself, remember?'

'I'm off sick. I called earlier today and I gave myself the Novo virus so I've got a few days yet before I need to resurface back home. I couldn't keep up the ruse about following a lead as it's been too long. I didn't want to risk rousing suspicion.'

'Smart move.'

'I like to think so,' Shane smiled mischievously at her.

'But you can go back anytime, you know. You don't need to stay up here. You don't owe Jake, me, anything.'

'I'm not going back without you.'

'You're not normally so resolute about things.'

'I've grown up these past few years, Amanda. I've changed.'

Her lips lifted into a gentle smile as she looked into his eyes. 'Hopefully not too much.'

*

Amanda was running out of ways to pass the time. She was on her eighth game of I spy with Ewan, who remained enthralled by her attempts to play with him.

'Okay...' she looked outside the car. The roads were bordered by trees on both sides. A light rainfall continued to patter against the windows. 'I spy with my little eye something beginning with...' Amanda desperately scanned the space around her. 'W.'

'Window.'

'Windscreen.'

'Wipers.'

'Woody.'

Ewan got it on his fourth try. He clapped his little hands together in delight when Amanda congratulated him and gave him a victory sweet.

'I think you're making this too easy for him,' Shane grinned at her via the windscreen mirror.

'He's just too good at it.' Amanda playfully tickled Ewan and he burst out laughing. The sound was so light, so purely joyful. It felt grossly juxtaposed to the grim reality of their situation. They were en route to a remote Scottish cabin to hide from men who wanted to kill both Ewan and his father. Yet when the little boy laughed you could almost believe that they weren't in peril, that there was nothing to fear.

'Daddy, you go,' Ewan's bright eyes fixed on the back of Jake's head.

'Maybe later,' his father grumbled.

'Daddy, come on, you do one.'

'I said later.'

Looking hurt, Ewan tucked himself against Amanda's side. 'Your dad's just tired,' she told him soothingly. 'Why don't you close your eyes for a bit and then we'll play again in a little, okay?'

'Okay.'

Feeling the weight of the little boy against her Amanda knew that her life was about to change in ways she could never have expected. Sure, she'd seen children in her and Will's future but not like this. This was... Amanda was caught up in the middle of a battle she hadn't even known was being fought.

The cabin was nestled upon a steep hill, within a dense cluster of trees. The drive up had been bumpy with Shane's car groaning in protest as its tyres pushed through the mud.

Under different circumstances, Amanda might have thought the cabin beautiful. It was a long, single-storey structure made of rounded tree trunks, with little glass windows that looked out on the hillside. It was quaint and reminded Amanda of the cabins she'd read about in *Little House on the Prairie* as a girl.

It was the isolation that troubled her. Climbing out of the car, she looked around and saw only green treetops stretching out for miles. The rain had turned from mist to fog, shrouding the road as it fell away from them. They'd passed by the last town some forty minutes ago and that looked to be a small, coastal place. There were no golden arches for Ewan to coo over, no bright petrol station lights to pierce through the gloom.

'Well, it's back to nature,' Shane came and stood beside her as she surveyed the landscape. She breathed in the air; the fresh fir trees and the damp earth.

'Ooh, we're camping,' Ewan was bounding towards the cabin. 'Can we go fishing? Can we climb trees? Can we make a campfire? Can I toast marshmallows?'

'Wherever he gets his energy from, I'd like some of it,' Shane yawned.

Inside the cabin was decorated with the same wood panelling as outside. It smelt of fresh pine, like the woodwork aisle in a hardware store. Amanda felt a pang as she remembered meeting Jake in such a place. How just setting eyes on him for the first time had been enough to make her heart race.

'This place is awesome,' Ewan was running round the circular dining table. The main room was completely open-plan. There was a lounge area to the left with two pale blue sofas and matching gingham curtains. To the right was the kitchen and dining area. All the furniture was wooden, as were the kitchen countertops. Three doors on the far wall led to the two bedrooms and a shared bathroom.

'If this fog clears we should have a clear view down to the

bottom of the road,' Jake was at the windows, peering out from behind curtains he'd already drawn closed.

'Where's my bedroom?'

Ewan was running for one of the doors. Amanda followed after him as he led them into a wood-panelled room which housed two single beds. Both had blue duvets the same shade as the curtains and the sofas. There was definitely a theme going on.

'This is our room,' he told her gleefully as he pulled her in. He placed Woody on the one bed and then stared up at Amanda. She hadn't realised she'd be sharing a room with the little boy but she didn't mind. She was actually quite pleased. 'You'll read me a bedtime story later, won't you?'

'Of course.' Though Amanda didn't have any books with her she had her trusty laptop. She should be able to source some children's stories on there no problem.

'A ghost story?' Ewan's eyes widened and he started to smile. He was like a cheeky little imp.

'No, not a ghost story. I don't think that would be a good idea.' *For me* she thought. She had enough to fear in the shadows without adding ghosts to the list.

'Then an adventure story?'

'Sure.'

'So is this where you're sleeping?' Shane was in the doorway, casually leaning against it.

'I…' Amanda smoothed her hands down her top and turned to face him. 'What's the other room like?'

'Same as this one,' Shane's eyes glistened in amusement.

'Oh.'

'So are me and Jake supposed to be roommates?'

'No, course not, Jake can sleep in—'

'I'm just kidding. Our sleeping arrangements don't matter since we'll be taking turns to keep watch.'

'Let me help.'

'No.' Shane stepped towards her and rested one hand on her shoulder. The other he used to gently graze her cheek. Amanda shuddered at the tenderness of it. 'You need to get some rest.'

'Are you saying I look tired?' she teased.

'No. I'm saying that I'm doing my best to look out for you and that means making sure you get enough rest.'

'Okay.'

'And no hour long walks in the woodlands around here, got it?'

'Got it.'

'I'm serious,' Shane dropped both hands against her shoulders. 'It's best we all stay put in the cabin. The woodlands around here are pretty dense. It'd be easy to get lost.'

'Then stay here we shall.'

'Oh,' Ewan began loudly whining. 'But I want to climb the trees and make a fire.'

'How about instead we watch a movie on my laptop and roast marshmallows over the fireplace in the lounge?'

'Yay!' Ewan bounced around in a circle.

'Netflix has kid's shows, right?' she threw Shane a concerned look.

'Loads. But I wouldn't bank on having a great internet connection up here.'

'Damn.'

'But you'll figure it out.' Shane's hands were still on her shoulders and he was looking deep into her eyes. 'Besides, the kid proper loves you. He'd be happy whatever you do.'

'And you?'

'I'm happy as long as you're safe.'

'We can't risk starting a fire,' Jake declared as he entered the room.

'Why not?' Amanda stepped away from Shane to confront him. 'I told Ewan we'd roast marshmallows on it.'

'The smoke could attract too much attention.'

'Jake,' Amanda tugged at his thick arm, easing him out of the room and away from the little boy. 'I know you're scared,' she lowered her voice as they stood in the centre of the main living area, 'but you need to make things fun for him. He's just a little boy and he's adapting so well to all this but we can't make it a prison for him.'

'I want to protect him,' Jake glanced fearfully at the windows, at the front door. 'But I don't know how to be a dad to him.'

'Just start by letting him have some fun,' Amanda advised warmly. 'We'll light a fire, roast some marshmallows, watch a movie, make sure there's no reason for Ewan to be afraid.'

'He seems to really like you.'

'Well he *loves* you because you're his father. Spend some

time with him. Get to know him.'

'Right now all I care about is keeping him alive.'

'And you've done that,' Amanda reached for Jake's hand and gave it a squeeze. 'We're literally holed up in the middle of nowhere. No one is coming for us. We just have to wait for McAllister to get bored of looking for you.'

'I've been gone for years. Time is irrelevant to men like him.'

'Try to forget about it, Jake. We're here. We're safe. Let's light a fire and have a bit of fun. What do you say?'

'Okay,' Jake dragged a hand down his face and looked towards the empty hearth in the lounge area. 'I'll try and relax, for Ewan's sake. It's just one fire, what harm can it do?'

'Exactly,' Amanda beamed at him. 'Now let's go find some firewood.'

28

The fire crackled in the small hearth. Ewan was sat cross-legged on the floor a few feet away from it, entranced by the dancing flames.

'There's nothing,' Shane opened up a kitchen cupboard to emphasize his point. Amanda peered in at the shelves containing only dust. 'No food. Not a thing.'

'We should have stocked up at the services,' Amanda groaned. Jake was showering after having successfully started the fire, which left Amanda and Shane on dinner duty. Only there was nothing to eat in the cabin.

'Look, it's not dark yet,' Shane looked behind her, at the closed curtains through which some light still filtered.

'It will be dark in under an hour.'

'I'll drive down to the nearest town. Get some food. Head straight back here.'

'I don't know.' Amanda looked over at Ewan. He was still contentedly watching the fire, gasping as a piece of wood snapped before being consumed by flames.

'He needs to eat,' Shane placed his hands on her arms and drew her to him. 'Kids are like gremlins. They need to be fed and watered but not after midnight else they become little monsters.'

'Haha, very funny,' Amanda replied dryly.

'Seriously though, I won't be long. I'll be back before you've even had chance to miss me.'

'You're keen to leave,' Amanda raised her eyebrows at him.

'Well this cabin is more *Deliverance* than *Date Night*,' he gave a half-smile which Amanda remembered seeing across a packed classroom. It was a smile she'd take a mental picture of and then observe late at night alone in bed, knowing that she'd give anything to have him smile at her that way. Shane's smile had been the first sign that he was leaving the friend zone and becoming a much more significant part of Amanda's life. As a teenager she felt as though she could live and die on his smile. 'Plus. I'm starving,' he squeezed her arms and his smile widened. 'I reckon I can find somewhere that sells pizza. Or at the very least fish and chips.'

'Both sound amazingly good right now.'

'Then it's settled,' Shane released her to reach into his pocket and grab his keys. He playfully spun them around his finger as he walked towards the front door.

'Make sure you come back,' Amanda followed, tightly flanking his every step. When he moved outside, she leaned against the door frame, felt the soft dusting of rain against her arms.

'Amanda,' his smile was gone, his expression serious. 'I'll always come back.'

*

'He's gone?' Jake shook the water out of his hair like he were dog as he emerged from the bathroom, a cloud of steam chasing after him.

'Just to get some food,' Amanda raised her hands at Jake from where she was blocking his path towards the front door.

'We don't need food.'

'We do. The cupboards are literally bare. Unless you want to eat cobwebs and dust.'

'When are we having tea?' Ewan ceased being hypnotized by the fire long enough to gaze up at them, his eyes bright and inquisitive.

'As soon as Shane gets back with the food,' Amanda grinned brightly at him.

'I don't like it. I don't want him going out. We should stay up here, away from whoever might be watching.' Jake stalked around her towards the nearest window. He carefully pulled the curtain back and looked outside. Amanda could see from where she was standing that night had descended. Shane had barely been gone twenty minutes and already the day had been eaten away by the darkness.

And it was so dark. With the thick clouds overhead there wasn't even the sparkle of stars or the glisten of moonlight to shine down on the log cabin. It was like they'd been sucked into a black hole where nothing escaped, not even light.

'Jesus, it's dark out,' Jake muttered with disdain.

'All the more reason to stay nice and cosy in here.'

'We should kill the lights.' And he did. He strode around the cabin flicking every switch until the only light came from the flickering fire. Ewan loved it.

'Ooh, are we telling ghost stories now?'

'Not yet.' Amanda sat on the sofa and the little boy immediately jumped up beside her. The warmth from the fire reached out to her in a tender caress. She was still so desperately tired. She could easily just sit on the sofa while the fire crackled and snapped and slip away into a deep slumber.

'Where did he say he was going to get food?' Jake was still hovering near the windows, blending into the shadows.

'Um... the nearest town.'

'The one forty minutes away?'

'That's the one.'

'And when did he leave?' Jake's questions were becoming sharper, more urgent.

'Twenty, maybe thirty minutes ago. Why?'

'Then that's not his car heading up here.' Jake was backing away from the window, anxiously looking around the cabin.

'What?' Amanda left the comfort of the sofa to go and look for herself. It made no sense that Shane would have turned back so soon. Unless he'd found a grocery store nearby, but there was nothing for miles. Amanda had made sure of that when she booked the cabin. Drawing back the blue gingham curtain, she looked out and saw a pair of lights climbing their way up towards the cabin. The road they were on led directly up to the little wooden structure, no diversions. The lights were brilliantly bright and relentless in their ascent, like an owl locked on to its prey and swooping towards them. 'I mean...' Amanda tried to piece it all together. 'That must be Shane coming back, but I thought he'd be much longer.'

'He must have gone to tip someone off.'

'What?' Amanda was appalled by the accusation. Shane had done nothing but support her ever since she'd first told him about her husband's disappearance.

'Do you trust him?' Jake demanded, standing so close that she could smell the generic shower gel which still clung to his skin. 'How well do you even know the guy?'

'I've known Shane since forever,' she stepped back from the man mountain she used to share her bed with. 'I trust him with my life.'

'Well I don't,' Jake was doubling back through the cabin, heading for the sofa. 'We're getting the hell out of here.'

'You're being paranoid,' Amanda spoke quietly, but she couldn't ignore the fact that the hairs on the back of her neck had stiffened. Jake's fear was contagious. She gave a fearful glance towards the little boy sat beside the fire. He was almost lost to the vast shadows in the room, but the orange glow against his cheeks kept him visible.

Jake grabbed her arms and pulled her deeper into the darkness, away from the warmth of the fire. 'I'm not going to take a risk on his life,' he spoke with such urgency. 'If I say we need to leave, then we need to leave.'

'But—'

'And I won't take a risk with you,' his hand was upon her cheek. The sudden warmth of his touch made Amanda feel like she'd stepped into the fire and that her whole body was being consumed by flames. 'I was supposed to protect you.' His eyes shone in the dim light with the tears he was fighting to hold in. 'I let you down, Amanda,' he stroked her cheek and stepped closer to her. 'When I met you I saw the rest of my life in your eyes. I never wanted to leave your side.'

Jake wiped away a tear which rolled down her cheek.

'But I did leave,' his voice was a whisper. 'I left and I ran and still you chased after me. Still you believed in me.'

Amanda's lips quivered. 'You're still my husband.'

'I envy your strength. And your good heart. It was what made it so easy to fall in love with you.'

The fire crackled behind them.

'I'll never stop loving you.' Jake placed his other hand against her cheek and stared deep into her eyes. 'You'll always own my heart, Amanda. But I need you to listen to me, to trust me. I can't let anything happen to you. To either of you,' he glanced at the little boy patiently sitting cross-legged by the fire.

'Fine,' Amanda conceded, her heart pounding in her chest, trying to escape its cage of ribs. 'Let's go.'

Jake moved away from her, taking the heat with him. Once again Amanda was in the shadows of the cabin, in the cold as she watched Jake stoop down and grab his son, lifting Ewan up into his arms.

'Hey!' the little boy protested, kicking against his father.

248

'Quiet,' Jake shouted at him. But Ewan refused to be subdued. He kept kicking and squirming as he remained locked in his father's grasp.

'Hey, hey,' Amanda hurried to the boy's side as Jake made for the front door. 'We're going to play a little game, okay? We're going to see who can be quiet for the longest.'

'We are?' Ewan instantly brightened.

'And whoever wins gets pizza.'

'Pizza!'

'We need to go now before the car gets any closer.' Jake was stepping through the front door, his voice a whisper.

'But it might be Shane,' Amanda hissed at him, lingering at the cabin's threshold.

'I'm not willing to stick around and take that chance.'

'Jake!'

'If it's him he'll go inside, realize we're gone and come out hollering.'

Amanda knew Jake was right. And a strange feral instinct was telling her to leave the cabin, to go out into the cold. Jake was already snaking his way down the side of the building when she made up her mind and left. She hurried after him, keeping her body low. The dense shadows clustered against the cabin kept them hidden from view. She followed Jake into the trees and up a steep incline. The ground was slick with mud and she struggled to keep her footing. A woodland carpet of fallen leaves and scattered twigs made her progress precarious without a guiding light. She could so easily topple over a stone or protruding root.

Behind them the rumble of the approaching car grew louder. Amanda quickened her pace, reaching Jake at the crest of the hill where he'd dropped behind a fallen log with Ewan tight to his chest.

'Get down,' he ordered.

Amanda scrambled to the ground and knelt beside him. 'What now?'

'Now we wait.'

Through the lines of trees, Amanda saw the dual beams of light approach the cabin. After the engine died a door opened. Then another. Whoever was in the car wasn't alone. She felt panic lock around her heart like a vice causing every breath to become laboured.

249

'It... it can't be Shane.' Her voice trembled in the brisk night air.

'Daddy?' Jake clamped his hand over his son's mouth. Tight enough to silence him but not too tight to alarm him.

'Remember the game we're playing?' Amanda whispered to the little boy. Ewan nodded.

It was so quiet amongst the trees. Too quiet. There was no birdsong, no gentle rushing of a nearby stream. There was silence and Amanda's panicked breaths filling it. She was certain that she was breathing so loud she was going to draw the attention of whoever was in that car.

The cabin door opened with a creak and Amanda knelt closer to the ground, praying that Shane was about to come out and shout for her. Perhaps she'd misheard that second door opening? Maybe it was just Shane?

There was no shouting. No one came running out into the clearing by the cabin hollering her name.

A minute passed. Then another.

'We need to move.' Jake was getting to his feet, hugging Ewan to his chest.

'Okay.' Amanda got up, cringed when a twig crunched underfoot.

'I'm going to take us up and over this hill.' Jake was speaking so softly she struggled to catch his words. Her entire body was tight with fear as she stumbled after him in the darkness. She could barely see her hand in front of her face. She was mainly relying on the sound of Jake's footsteps crunching up ahead.

She moved in his wake, silently seethed as a branch scratched at her cheek. She could moan about the pain later. Right now she needed to blend in with the silence all around her.

'The fire's still going, they must have just left.'

The voice carried to them up from the cabin. It was vaguely familiar. It was—

'Dammit.' Jake muttered as he recognized the voice of the red-haired man from the petrol station just before Amanda did. He quickened his pace.

'Let's split up and search the area.'

Amanda's heart plummeted all the way down to her feet. They were like ducks in a barrel just waiting to be shot.

'Jake?' she whispered his name just loud enough for him to catch it.

'I heard,' was the only response she got as he kept walking. Kept moving deeper into the woodland.

Looking back, Amanda felt something within her die when she saw a slim beam of light cutting through the trees, through the darkness.

They had torches.

'Just keep going,' Jake ordered. And so Amanda did. She matched him step for step as they descended through the dense woodland. All the while her heart kept racing, the hairs on the back of her neck stood to attention, painfully aware that they were being pursued.

Back at university Amanda had been fascinated by Einstein's theory of relatively. She was always trying to understand it, to apply it to daily life. And now more than ever she understood it. In Shane's old bedroom, beneath his faded Star Wars covers as they eagerly explored each other's body an hour felt like a minute. Here, in the dark wilderness of the Scottish Highlands being hunted like a deer a minute felt like an hour. Amanda had no idea how long they'd been walking. Had it been ten minutes? More? Less? And how soon was Shane due back? What would those men do to him if they were still there to greet him?

'I need to go back for Shane.' Amanda was saying the words before she'd truly had chance to make up her mind. She turned and her feet slid out from under her. Damp earth slammed against her cheek as she collided with the ground.

'Amanda!' Ewan squeaked in horror. He must have seen her drop.

'What was that?' a voice from below shouted.

'It came from over there.'

Both beams of light cut through the nearby trees, seeking her out. Amanda remained flat against the ground whilst Jake stepped behind a thick tree, cupping Ewan's mouth as tight as he dared.

'You really think they got this far on foot? There's no car here, maybe they just drove away.'

Amanda dared to release a ragged breath of relief as her hands sunk into the cool earth.

'No. You saw the car when it left. Just the one guy in it.'

So they'd seen Shane leave. That was why they'd come up. They knew there was no escape route for them anymore.

'So we keep searching?'

'We keep searching.'

Amanda was hauled up by her right arm. She scrambled to her feet and glimpsed Jake beside her in the shadows.

'We have to keep moving.' His voice was low but the order still contained all the urgency it needed. Amanda nodded, not that he'd be able to see. She followed Jake deeper, higher into the woodlands. The light rain which had previously seemed inconsequential had now soaked her to the bone. Her hair was flat against her head and she could hear Ewan whimpering softly to himself as he clung to his father. Clearly he'd realized that they weren't playing a game anymore.

The beams of light kept threading their way through the trees, refusing to relent.

'Just give it up, Jakey boy,' a raspy voice shouted, rolling up the hillside like thunder. 'We'll search all night for you if we have to.'

All night.

Amanda squeezed her eyes shut in despair. If only they'd just leave. Not only were she, Jake and Ewan in danger but so was Shane. He could be driving back right now, completely oblivious to what awaited him at the cabin. Had he found pizza? Or fish and chips? Was his car now stocked full of food, wafting delicious aromas around him as he smiled to himself and hummed along to his music?

'We need to make for the road.' Reaching forward, Amanda clasped her hands around what she hoped was Jake's shirt. 'If we go back and get to the road we'll meet Shane. He can get us out of here.'

Jake must have agreed as he changed course, brushing against her as he moved past. But then he stopped short as the beams of light crossed through his path just a few feet away. The men were getting closer.

'How do we reach the damn road?' he lamented.

'We just need to pick our way down.' Fumbling in the darkness, Amanda took the lead. Rather than heading back to the cabin they needed to take the more perilous route of going straight down. As the ground steeply inclined beneath her feet she imagined she was back home, navigating the cliffside with

Shane as they made their way down to the beach. They'd laugh and taunt one another as they carefully planted each footstep. It was so often a race between them.

'I'll get there first!' Shane would brag as he hopped from rock to rock.

'First's the worst, second's the best,' Amanda would counter, cementing her feelings by sticking her tongue out at him. But the long-legged brunette boy wasn't looking. He was too busy trying to beat her. 'Hey,' Amanda would hurry, desperate to claim victory. The winner often got the greatest of spoils – like choosing their pizza topping for that evening or what movie they were going to watch. She'd give anything to be safe inside those memories now.

'It's a race,' Amanda hid the tremor from her voice as she quietly addressed Ewan.

'What?' Jake sounded angry. And afraid.

'I'm racing your daddy down to the road,' she continued. 'And whoever gets their first gets first pick of all the food Shane's bringing back.'

'Okay,' Ewan's eyes were enlarged, the word muffled against Jake's hand which remained locked over his mouth.

The slope was getting so steep that gravity was keen to take over and finish her descent for her, but she couldn't let that happen. In the dark she could smack against a tree trunk or worse, a rock. She needed to take care. Each time she dropped a foot down she braced herself for her inevitable tumble into darkness. But somehow she managed to stay standing. Reaching forwards, her hands clutched against the thick trunks of nearby trees for support.

They had to be getting close to the road. Didn't they?

There was so little light that Amanda wasn't sure she could trust her eyes anymore. But just up ahead the trees seemed to part. It was either the road or—

It was a clearing. A little patch of grass within the hillside. Perfect for grazing sheep but currently unoccupied. Amanda pressed her hands against her knees and doubled over, sucking in long, uneasy breaths.

'Are we there yet? Who won?' Ewan's mouth was briefly freed as Jake also filled his lungs with the clean night air.

'No one yet,' Amanda gasped. 'We're nearly there.'

Her legs were like jelly. She wasn't sure she'd be able to go much further.

And then something chirped. Loud and artificial. It broke through the silence like an alarm and Amanda felt herself melt with despair.

Her phone. Her fucking phone was ringing. Linkin Park's Waiting for the End blared out, blissfully unaware of the silence it was shattering.

Fumbling in the dark, she plucked it from her pocket and quickly hammered on the off button, causing Shane's name to disappear from the main screen. The silence that followed was deafening.

'Did they... did they hear?' she wondered desperately. Jake was frozen in the centre of the clearing, his head bent up towards the sky like a hunter checking the direction of the wind. Ewan was still in his arms, his head resting against his father's broad chest.

'Jake?' she hurried to his side, tugged at his arm as he lowered his head to look at her, his face like thunder.

'Oh, they heard all right.'

Sure enough there was a scamper of someone rushing through the trees. It sounded far too close.

29

As they'd descended down the hillside, creeping through the dense vegetation like the hunted creatures they'd become, the rain had relented. Ashen clouds were swept aside by a rough breeze which allowed silvery strands of moonlight to reach the clearing. The open space was bathed in a gentle, eerie light. But the shadows which gathered in the bordering trees were still dense. Still ominous.

'Take him.' Jake grunted the order as he untangled Ewan from his arms and passed him across to Amanda. The boy was muted by fear. He too must have sensed the nervous energy which radiated out from his father and crackled around him, filling the clearing with electrical current.

Amanda gently lowered Ewan to her side; she didn't have the strength to carry him as Jake had. The boy instantly locked his arms around her legs like a limpet.

'Get him out of here.'

Jake wasn't looking at her. His eyes were trained on the shadows just beyond the clearing. In the faint light, Amanda saw him reach around to the small of his back, grabbing at the gun he had stowed there.

'No,' she reached for Jake's arm as a sharp wind stole her protest away from the clearing, carrying it back up into the trees, back towards their pursuers.

'I'll take care of them and then I'll be right behind you. Stay safe.'

'I want my mummy,' Ewan hugged Amanda's leg so tightly that if he were any stronger he'd risk snapping a bone. He gazed up at her through large, misty eyes.

Ruffling his dark hair, Amanda forced the brightest smile she could, hoping the child didn't notice how her hands shook.

'You'll be back with your mummy soon,' she offered, hoping it was the truth rather than just a platitude to keep him calm.

'Go.'

Jake still didn't turn back towards her as he hissed the order.

She heard the urgency in his voice and plucked Ewan's arms from around her legs to take his hand and lead him to the edge of the clearing. Pressing her back against a large tree, she hugged Ewan to her chest and dared to peer over her shoulder and glance towards the clearing.

Dual beams of light punctured the shadows on the far side. They cut through the darkness and found Jake standing in the centre. With his broad shoulders and unruly black hair he looked like he'd been cut from the stones which sat atop the hill. He was savage and strong, perfectly at home in the wilderness.

Amanda held her breath as the tiger turned on those who dared to hunt it.

Turning away from the clearing, she looked ahead into the murky depths of the woodland, at the tangle of branches ahead. The bark against her back was rough and offered no comfort. She wondered how long she could linger there, or if she'd already stayed too long.

A shot rang out. Its loud snap echoed through the trees, causing slumbering animals to stir uneasily. Another shot. Amanda winced at the brutal clarity of the sound.

'I'm scared,' she could feel Ewan trembling against her like a leaf caught in a rough breeze.

'It's okay,' she rubbed his back and held him tight. 'Everything is going to be all right.'

A third shot. Amanda felt it in her bones as the sound vibrated deep within her. She held a breath in her chest and silently prayed that Jake was safe. Crouching down, she kissed Ewan's forehead and wrapped her arms around him. She didn't dare move. She barely dared to breathe.

She waited for the beams of light to press on, to come searching for her. She waited for Jake to shout out that everything was okay, that the danger had passed. But there was only the sound of her own beating heart and blood rushing in her ears.

'Where's... where's Daddy?' Ewan sniffled after a minute that felt like an eternity.

'I...' slowly, carefully, Amanda straightened and peered back around the tree. The clearing wasn't empty. Three figures were strewn on the ground, bathed in moonlight. 'Jesus,' she gasped as she clasped a hand over her mouth and turned away.

'What is it?' the little boy's voice was filled with fear.

'Can you just…' Amanda swallowed down her anguish and confidently placed both hands on his slender shoulders. 'You wait here for a moment, okay? I'm just going to check on your daddy. I'll come right back here to get you.'

'No,' Ewan made a high-pitched protest, tears washing down his cheeks.

'I promise I'll be just a minute. But I can't take you with me, it's not safe. But you're safe here.' Amanda moved away from the tree and pressed Ewan against its bark. 'Stand here, close your eyes and count to a hundred. I'll be back by then.'

'A hundred?'

'A hundred.'

'But that's so high,' Ewan declared woefully.

'Well, do your best, okay?'

Nodding, the little boy squeezed his eyes shut and began to count. 'One, two, three…'

Amanda stole away from the tree and returned to the clearing. The charred afterburn of a fired bullet had singed the air. She looked to the two figures slumped on the edge of the clearing, they were on their backs and seemingly motionless.

Someone spluttered.

Instinctively Amanda dropped to Jake's side. He too was on his back, his hands across his chest as blood seeped out through his fingers.

'Christ, Jake,' Amanda placed his head in her lap and pulled her phone from her pocket. 'Just hold on, okay? I'll get help.'

'No.' Jake croaked, lifting a bloodied hand to stop her.

'Jake, you need help, you need—'

'No one can know you were here.' He coughed and his face contorted in a grimace.

'Jake, you've been shot, you need an ambulance.'

He kept coughing as blood seeped out from behind clenched teeth, staining his lips a dangerous shade of red.

'I… I got them,' he declared, his mouth briefly morphing into a triumphant smile. But as fresh shudders of agony swept through his body his smile promptly fell.

'You've been shot,' Amanda cradled his head in her hands and swept his dark hair out of his eyes. There was a sheen of sweat across his forehead that glistened in the pale moonlight. Choking on a sob Amanda remembered sweeping back Will's hair when he got laid up with flu the previous winter. It was the only time he'd taken to his bed sick and even pale and bunged up he looked handsome, strong. Like he could beat anything.

'Yeah, they got one good shot in. Bastards.' He shook in her arms and she couldn't tell if he was laughing or crying. Amanda held onto him as tightly as she could. It was her turn to be the strong one, to deliver him from the darkness.

'I'm going to get you to a hospital.'

'No,' he protested again, a hand wrapping around her wrist. His touch was slick and clammy. 'It's too late for me. You need to...' he spluttered as blood trickled down his chin, 'take... Ewan. Stay... safe.'

'Jake,' Amanda could feel the heat of her tears upon her cheeks. 'I'm not leaving you here.'

'You... have... to.'

'I didn't chase you all the way up here just to leave you in some bloody woods.' She tried to make a joke of it, tried to smile.

'You fought...' Jake coughed uneasily, 'for me. And I...' he lightly raised his free hand in the direction of the other two fallen figures, 'I fought for you.'

'Jake, please, just hold on, let me try to stop the bleeding, let me call for help.'

'Will.'

'What?'

'Will.' He was looking into her eyes, right down to her terrified soul. 'Let me be your Will. One last time.'

'Hey, stop talking like this. Let me call the ambulance, everything will be fine.'

'The first time I saw you... in that store,' his gaze had become distant, 'you were so... so beautiful. I wanted you. I wanted to... be Will Thorn... for you. I wanted to stay... Will Thorn for you. I let... you down.'

'Look, it's all in the past now.'

'You still came... for me.'

'You're my husband,' Amanda tried to ignore how his breathing was becoming shallower. She focused on the light in his dark eyes, but even that was growing dimmer. 'I would follow you to the ends of the earth. You know that.'

'I... love you,' Will rasped as he squeezed his eyes shut, battling against his internal pain.

'I love you too.' Amanda's tears had become a river that almost blinded her as she looked down at her fallen husband. 'Don't leave me,' she whispered, lowering her head towards his. 'I wish you'd never left me.'

'Never again,' the hand around her wrist tightened, just slightly. Already he lacked so much of his former strength. 'I'll always be with you.'

'Don't go, Will, please.' Amanda bowed her head against his and heard his final breath pass through his lips. 'No,' she shook as she remained with him cradled in her arms. 'No. Not like this.'

'Argh!' Ewan was screaming. His terror bounced off the trees and powered against Amanda, forcing her to release Will. She turned and saw the little boy staring straight at her, his eyes as wide as his mouth as he kept screaming.

'Damn.' She lay Will down in the soft grass and ran to Ewan. 'Don't look,' the second the boy was within her reach she grabbed him and pulled him to her chest in an embrace, blocking his view of the massacre in the clearing, of his fallen father. 'Just don't look, Ewan. It's all right. Everything will be all right.'

'Amanda?' Shane came out of the trees, his clothes damp with sweat. He stared at her, breathing hard. 'I... I was coming back and I saw this car up at the cabin and then I heard screaming—' he was hurrying towards her but he stopped abruptly when he saw the figures in the clearing. 'Fuck.' He froze as if the mud at his feet had turned to cement. 'Fuck, what happened?'

'He...' Amanda wiped at her eyes, smearing her cheeks with the blood which stained her hands. 'He saved us. Will saved us.'

Shane quickly became a cop. He examined each body, checked for a pulse and declared each one dead with a regretful shake of the head. He lingered at Will's side.

'We need to get him out of here.' She was referring to Ewan who was glued to her side, fearful to take so much as a step away from her.

'He managed to take them both down with two shots. One to the throat and a clean one to the head. But he wasn't quick enough. They fired one out and got him in the chest.' There was admiration in Shane's voice as he pushed his hands through his hair and gazed helplessly at Amanda. The cop was gone and he was suddenly as lost as Ewan was. 'What do we do?'

'We need to go.'

'We can't...' Shane gestured to the bodies but didn't look back at them. 'We can't leave them like this, Amanda. We need to call it in, we need to—'

'He said to make it so we were never here.'

'But,' Shane paced over towards her, his hands in his hair. 'The cabin?' he gestured towards the trees. 'It's booked in my name.'

'I can easily change that once we swing by there and grab my laptop.'

'You're not thinking clearly.'

'Yes, I am,' Amanda insisted, her tone level as she summoned an inner strength she didn't even know she had. 'Will wanted me to protect his son, to get the hell out of here and that's what we're going to do.'

'Amanda—'

'Will you help me honour his final wishes?'

Shane looked between her and her dead husband. 'Christ,' his shoulders slumped, 'I'd do anything for you. You know that.'

'Then let's go.' Amanda led Ewan towards Shane's car which was parked not far from the clearing, along the road which they were so close to when they'd run. If only Amanda's phone hadn't gone off, if only a third bullet hadn't found its way into Will's chest.

'Is Daddy not coming with us?' Ewan lingered at the roadside, looking back into the woods. He'd stopped crying and peered up at Amanda, his little forehead crumpled in confusion.

'No, sweetheart,' Amanda smoothed her hands down his cheeks and smiled tenderly at him. 'He's not coming. But we're going to go back to your mummy.'

'Mummy?' Ewan instantly brightened and eagerly clambered into the waiting car.

'Are you all right?' Shane was at her side, anxiously watching her.

'No,' Amanda told him honestly. 'Right now I'm just focusing on existing from one second to the next.'

'What happens when we drop Ewan back off at his Mum's?'

'That's when I fall apart.'

30

The water turned red as it ran down Amanda's legs and swirled around the plughole.

'You need to shower,' Shane had told her as he pulled up outside the cabin.

'There's no time.'

'You'll attract too much attention like that.'

Amanda looked down at herself. At her soiled clothes. Her jeans were caked in mud and her hands and arms were darkened with her husband's blood. Numbly, she agreed to Shane's order, knowing the importance of keeping herself occupied, of not letting her mind dwell on the trauma that she had just witnessed. She entered the pine-scented cabin and wandered towards the small bathroom as though drifting through a dream. Carefully she shed each item of clothes and then stepped beneath the spray of hot water which was raining down into the bathtub. Bowing her head against the stream, Amanda watched the water darken in shade as it rid her of her stains.

How long had it been since Will had stood beneath that same shower? Hours? And now...

Pulling her hands through her hair, Amanda scrubbed out the mud, the blood, the rain and pushed down her feelings of despair. She couldn't think of Will lying out there in the woods, growing cold. She had to focus on navigating from one moment to the next. And right now that meant showering.

'Okay, let's go,' Shane was already barrelling towards the front door when Amanda emerged from the shower, her laptop tucked under his arm. She gave her hair one final rub with a towel and then left the heat of the bathroom.

The only clean clothes she could find belonged to Shane. She'd risked pulling her muddied jeans back on and coupled them with one of his sweatshirts she'd hastily grabbed on her way to the bedroom. But nothing was getting left behind. The rest of own dirty clothes were in her hands, hanging at her side.

Ewan was already in the car as Amanda climbed in and sat

beside him. His head was slumped towards his chest as he clutched Woody tightly against his heart. He was sleeping. The shock of what he'd experienced had clearly drained him. Amanda tugged the boy so that his head was resting more comfortably against the sleeve of her oversized sweatshirt. She gently stroked his hair as her heart became heavy. Her own pain was now going to become Ewan's. He too was destined to grow up without a father, without even the possibility of him one day coming home. And Amanda knew all too well how deep such pain went, how it grew roots which knotted their way throughout your body and soul.

As Shane pulled away from the cabin, she reached for her laptop and opened it up. They were weaving their way through winding roads, flanked by tall, stoic trees as she changed the reservation details for their cabin. Shane's name was removed and in its place—

Will Thorn.

Amanda stared at the screen. The digital trail of breadcrumbs would end with Will if McAllister chose to follow it. Shane, Amanda and Ewan had never even been there, at least according to all accessible records.

'You okay?' Shane had been driving in silence for the past twenty minutes. He glanced briefly into the rear-view mirror, his eyes locking onto Amanda. She hoped that he could see the gratitude that she felt towards him.

'How long until we get to Glasgow?'

'Hours.'

She looked at the little boy sleeping soundly beside her.

'It's okay to talk about it, you know,' Shane urged.

'I can't,' Amanda shook her head sadly and dropped her attention back towards her laptop. 'I'm not sure I'll ever be able to.'

*

A new day dawned and with it came sunshine. The sky blushed a shade of crimson as the car drove away from the rural highlands and joined a motorway. Amanda leaned forward against the passenger seat and peered through the windscreen, failing to see the beauty of a rose-tainted sky. The morning should have brought rain; endless sheets of it.

'He okay?' Shane's voice was hoarse.

Amanda looked at Ewan who was now bundled up in the far corner, still holding tightly to his favourite toy.

'He's still sleeping.'

'We need to think about getting him something to eat.'

Food. Amanda was almost repulsed by the word. In the darkened early hours, Shane had offered her the fish and chips he'd retrieved from the nearby town. The newspaper bundled around the meal was soaked with fat and the smell emanating out from it made Amanda gag.

'Urgh, bin it,' she'd insisted, barely holding back from retching. Shane had obeyed. At the next rest stop he climbed out and took the cold fish supper with him, dropping it into a trash can.

'I can't think about eating,' Amanda sighed. Eating was such a normal thing to do. And how was she supposed to be normal when her entire world was imploding around her?

'He'll need something,' Shane raised his eyebrows, referring to Ewan.

'I know.'

'So I'll stop at the next set of services. Okay?'

Amanda said nothing. She just slid back against her seat. Her body felt so heavy, as though her bones had been replaced with dense lead pipes.

It was busy at the services. People tumbled out of their cars and scurried towards the shops and cafes united in one sleek building, like ants invading a picnic. Ewan had been reluctant to wake up. Amanda didn't blame him. His dreams were surely a more pleasant place to reside than the real world.

'Don't you want some breakfast?' she tried to sound perky. Positive. Instead her words sounded like a strained squeak. But it did the trick.

'Breakfast?' the boy bounced out of the car as though the horrors of the previous night were already forgotten. Or maybe he just hoped it was all some horrid nightmare he'd made up in his mind? His resilience unnerved Amanda, made her think of Will's own childhood in Scotland, of how hardened he'd needed to be in order to survive. She didn't want to see that hardness develop in Ewan but when the little boy grabbed Amanda's hand without being prompted she knew his heart was still open.

Together they went inside, flanked by Shane. The stubble upon Shane's jawline had thickened so that it was beginning to look like he was growing a beard. If Amanda didn't feel so dead inside she'd have mocked him for it. But jokes had no place in this world.

Ewan insisted on a McDonald's breakfast again. He'd clearly developed a taste for them. As he wolfed down his egg-laced muffin, Amanda sipped at her coffee. Each mouthful was horribly bitter even though she'd emptied three sachets of sugar into the little cardboard cup.

'I can't wait to see Mummy,' Ewan grinned as Amanda dabbed at his cheeks with a napkin. He'd managed to get ketchup all over his face.

'I bet she'll be pleased to see you too,' Shane smiled but the gesture didn't reach his eyes which seemed flat and empty. Amanda saw her own grief reflected in them. It felt strange to consider herself so fragile, like a glass version of the woman she'd previously been. She was now glass and lead rather than flesh and bone. Fragile and heavy all at once.

'And Daddy?' Ewan's green eyes flashed between the two adults at his table. Woody was on his lap, mirroring the child's penetrating gaze with wide plastic eyes.

'Daddy…' Amanda placed a hand on Ewan's shoulder. This wasn't a conversation she was ready to have. But she knew she'd never be ready. 'Daddy won't be coming back to the flat. It's going to be just you and Mummy, like before.'

The only saving grace in the mire of such a devastating loss was that Will hadn't been a constant presence in his son's life. He'd shown up for the first time in years just under forty-eight hours ago. In a week he'd become a distant memory for Ewan. Soon all thoughts the boy had of his father would dilute to the point where Ewan wouldn't trust them, would consider them fragments of a crazy dream he'd once had.

And Evangeline?

Amanda did not welcome the conversation she'd have to have with Will's first wife. How would she even start to explain why she had taken Ewan away? Why Will/Jake hadn't come back with her? And how much was it even safe to tell her?

'When we get there, I can do the talking, if you like.' Shane was watching her from across the table, his coffee frozen midway to his lips. He sensed what was wrong, understood the crinkle in her forehead and the pursing of her mouth.

'I… um,' Amanda hadn't thought that far ahead. Not really. It was like an unpleasant doctor's appointment. She knew that it was coming, knew that she'd have to attend, but she'd deal with it all when she got there. To dwell on it before would be to invite unwanted fear and anxiety into her life. And she had more than enough to deal with. 'Let's talk about it when we get there.'

Her hair, having dried in the car, was somewhere between straight and curly. Sort of crinkled. Each strand filled with kinks and spirals that seemed disorderly. Amanda pushed her fingers through it, trying to tame it. She didn't want to appear utterly shambolic when she appeared on Evangeline's doorstep.

'She'll just be glad he's back,' Shane reached across the table and let his fingertips graze the back of Amanda's hand. She barely felt his touch. Taking Ewan home felt too much like letting Will go. He was the only part of her late husband that she had left.

'Yeah,' she agreed absently. 'You're right.'

*

The following two hours passed by in a blur of traffic. Amanda watched the cars speeding by, the sunlight glimmering against their rooftops like they were fish in a stream. Twice she attempted to play I Spy with Ewan but her suggestions were half-hearted. Not that the little boy noticed. He played with his usual level of enthusiasm. He was so resilient for someone so young. It was only in his sleep that Amanda glimpsed the shadow which had settled over him. He would twitch and kick, his face twisting in despair as his breathing quickened. It would last for just a few moments and then the nightmare would release him.

Amanda hoped the dream would fade as time went on. She knew too well the horror of being haunted by trauma in your sleep.

Their arrival in Glasgow came around lunchtime. A blue sky was peppered with puffs of white clouds as the sun beat down on the car park which Amanda now knew all too well. Shane pulled up in an empty corner and killed the engine. He didn't say anything. Like Amanda, his attention was immediately drawn to the hectic scene across from them, where police cars and an ambulance were clustered together, taking up a number of parking spaces.

As soon as Amanda saw the neon stripes of the police vehicles, her stomach plummeted to her feet. It didn't take a genius to hazard a guess as to why they were there. Evangeline had clearly called the police, of course she had, any mother in her right mind would have done the same thing. Will had been wrong to assume she'd know it was him who'd taken her son. She was probably pacing around her flat at that moment, head in her hands as she wept for the boy, wondering where he could be and praying that he was alive.

'Oh God,' Amanda uttered as she took in the array of official vehicles, their blue lights blinking.

'Okay, okay,' Shane was stiffening in his seat, anxiously smoothing out the creases in his top. 'We just need to get our stories straight.' He lifted his hands to tidy his hair and as he flipped down his visor and glanced into its little mirror he froze.

'What is it?' Amanda was gripping the sides of the passenger seat in front of her.

'Ooh, police,' Ewan was up and peering excitedly through his window.

'The police I get,' Shane slowly turned around to look at her. Dark shadows had gathered beneath his eyes making his expression appear more severe than it usually would. 'A kid goes missing, you call in the cops. A patrol car shows up. Maybe two. But the ambulance,' he threw a furtive glance towards the gathered emergency vehicles. 'And there's a first responder there. Why the need for paramedics?'

'You think they're not here for us?' Amanda wondered cautiously. It felt too good to be true. The police had to be there for them, waiting to cart them away in handcuffs. Perhaps they'd already found Will out in the woodlands.

'Maybe not,' Shane nervously cleared his throat. 'Let me go out and investigate. I'll get a read on the situation and come straight back.'

'What... wait,' Amanda's body tightened. She didn't want Shane to go. Didn't want another man she cared for to leave her side and possibly not return. But he was already stepping out into the morning sunshine, remembering that he himself was a cop and pushing back his shoulders and confidently striding towards the block of flats in which Evangeline lived.

'Aww, can we go too?' Ewan pleaded, scrambling to undo his seat belt. He unlocked it and then came to sit on Amanda's lap which gave him a better vantage point to look out at all the cars. He seemed entranced by the cars, but Amanda sensed that he wanted closeness, safety, that the shadow of fear still covered his every move. Whilst Ewan gazed in wonderment at the cars and their flashing lights and bright stripes, Amanda looked towards the block of flats. Shane hadn't been able to go all the way in. There were uniformed police blocking the entrance, along with bright yellow tape criss-crossed over the main door. Shane was now chatting to the police, nodding his head as they engaged him. Amanda watched, holding a breath in her chest. Gestures were made with arms. More nodding. More gestures. But no one was pointing at Shane and shouting. No one was approaching him with handcuffs, telling him that he had a right to remain silent.

'Mummy doesn't like it when the police are here,' Ewan said as he squirmed in Amanda's lap, trying to get a better view of what was going on outside.

'I can imagine she doesn't.'

'But I do,' Ewan declared brightly. 'I usually sit up in my room and watch them, but it's way better down here. Do you think they'll let me sit in one of their cars?'

'Maybe,' Amanda replied tightly. 'Let's wait for Shane to come back and see what he says.'

She didn't have to wait long. With his entrance into the flats barred, Shane was striding back towards the car, still possessing the stance of a man who belonged, of a man who wasn't currently crippled by nerves.

When he reached the car he didn't climb back in. Instead he opened Amanda's door and stared down at her.

'We need to have a word.'

'Oh.' Amanda coughed, trying to dislodge the lump which had suddenly formed in her throat. Shane's body language screamed that something was wrong. His shoulders were too high, his jaw clenched like he was holding something in. Something awful. 'Sweetie, can you just wait here a second?'

'Awww,' Ewan protested as she lifted him from her lap and

placed him back on his side of the car. 'But I want to see the cars and Mummy. Can I see Mummy now?'

'You can in a minute if you sit nice and still like a good boy.' Amanda was smiling brightly at him as she backed out of the car, but the second she turned to face Shane the smile died on her lips. 'Well, what is it?'

'I spoke to the cops over by the door,' Shane jerked his head back in their direction.

'And?'

'They are here for Evangeline.'

Amanda reached for the car to steady herself. So this was it. They were about to be arrested and Shane was somehow managing to put on a brave face. She wouldn't be nearly as composed. Already she could feel her bones shaking, trying to send sorrowful shudders throughout her entire body.

'But it's not like that,' Shane grabbed her upper arm and drew closer to her, lowering his voice. 'She didn't call them.'

'Then who did?'

A sad sigh left Shane. 'The neighbour who found her.'

'What?'

'The cops said it looked like she OD'd.'

'Wait… what…' Amanda felt dizzy. This couldn't be happening. 'So where is she? Is she at the hospital? Then let's go.'

'Amanda,' Shane gave her arm a squeeze and said her name so softly, too softly.

'No,' she gasped as tears fogged her vision. 'No.'

'The cops said she was DOA. There's no sign of foul play so they are treating it as an accidental death. They'll be leaving the scene within the hour.'

Shane massaged his temple.

'It really doesn't add up to me. There's definitely something strange going on, but the cops won't let me near the place, I have no jurisdiction up here.'

'She's…' Amanda rubbed furiously at her eyes as the tears kept coming. 'No, that can't be. What about?' she glanced down into the car where Ewan was pressed against the other window, watching the gathered emergency vehicles with fascination. He didn't know they were there for his beloved mother, or that Evangeline was just a few feet away zipped within black plastic on a stiff metal gurney. Fate had just dealt the boy an unbelievably cruel hand. He was now deprived of not one parent but two.

'Really we need to hand him over to the authorities.'

'But he doesn't have anyone,' Amanda rasped the words as she teetered on the verge of hysterical tears.

'I know but—'

'And what if it wasn't an overdose?' the thought came suddenly to Amanda, desperate and dangerous. She dropped her voice to a fierce whisper. 'What if someone broke in and did that to her?'

She expected Shane to rebuke such a suggestion, but instead the shadows over his face darkened as he bowed his head towards hers. 'It's possible,' he agreed, his voice flat and monotone. 'I've seen this kind of thing before. Maybe McAllister did have a hand in it. Maybe he's trying to draw Jake out, maybe he doesn't yet know...' his voice trailed off.

'And that means we can't just enter Ewan into the system and hope for the best! McAllister might still be hunting him. And once he does find out what happened back in those woods and might want revenge and—'

'Amanda, I know but—'

'He's lost *both* his parents.' Something between rage and grief was coursing through her body, intensifying her tears and making her limbs shake. 'We're all he's got, Shane.'

'Okay, dammit, I know.' Stepping back, Shane racked his hands through his hair. 'But what then? What are we supposed to do?'

Amanda looked around at the gathered police cars, at the ambulance, at the blue sky above. This was Will's world, not hers. But her husband was gone. She'd held true to the vow she'd made for him during their modest ceremony.

Till death do us part.

But Will had left her an enduring legacy. It currently sat watching the drama unfold on the car park. Ewan had his father's dark hair and his mother's brilliant green eyes. He was an orphan, a victim in a very dangerous adult game of cat and mouse. Amanda wasn't prepared to let Ewan or Will down.

'We take him with us.'

Shane blinked and looked at Amanda as though she'd lost what little of her mind she was still holding onto.

'What? We can't!'

'Yes, we can,' Amanda stated confidently. Her brain was already piecing together the elements of a plan. 'We take him back with us. We'll figure something out when we get back.'

Shane paced away from the car and then turned on his heel and stormed back towards her. 'This is madness, you know that right? And dangerous. This is so, so fucking dangerous.'

'He's just a little boy. I can't leave him alone in this world.'

'Argh, Jesus Christ, Amanda.'

'All you have to do is take us back. Take us back home. After that this isn't your problem anymore.'

'No.'

'Shane, just—'

'I mean, this is my problem. I'll be there for you. For both of you. So long as you're sure this is what you want to do?'

Amanda looked up, felt the warmth of the sun on her face. Somehow the world kept turning even though Will was gone. She needed to adapt, needed to be strong.

'It's what Will wanted,' she concluded resolutely. 'We're going to honour his final wish. We're going to keep Ewan safe. I'll protect him with my life if I have to.'

'I won't let it come to that,' Shane was at her side, protectively wrapping one arm around her shoulders.

Amanda lowered her gaze and stared towards the horizon. 'You might not have a choice.'

We hope you enjoyed this book!

Carys Jones' next novel is coming in spring 2017

More addictive fiction from Aria:

Find out more
http://headofzeus.com/books/isbn/9781786690692

Find out more
http://headofzeus.com/books/isbn/9781784978969

Find out more
http://headofzeus.com/books/isbn/9781784978907

Acknowledgements

Firstly I need to thank the amazing team at Aria, especially Caroline Ridding and Sarah Ritherdon. Their guidance helped me turn Wrong Number into the story it is today and I'm so grateful for their continued support.

I also need to thank my friends and family for always being so patient with me and indulging my strange quirks thus enabling me to be the kind of person who lives inside my own imagination most of the time.

Rollo. You don't do much – you just sit and stare at me with your chestnut eyes and keep my feet warm when you lie against them. But you've been there for every sentence, every rewrite. Writing can be lonely at times, thank you for sticking with me for the long haul.

And finally to you, dear reader, I offer my heartfelt thanks. You're the reason I do this – I write my stories in the hope that they will be read.

About Carys Jones

CARYS JONES loves nothing more than to write and create stories which ignite the reader's imagination. Based in Shropshire, England, Carys lives with her husband, two guinea pigs and her adored canine companion Rollo.

Find me on Twitter
https://twitter.com/tiny_dancer85

Find me on Facebook
https://www.facebook.com/CarysJonesWriter/?fref=ts

Visit my website
http://www.carys-jones.com/

Become an Aria Addict

Aria is the new digital-first fiction imprint from Head of Zeus.

It's Aria's ambition to discover and publish tomorrow's superstars, targeting fiction addicts and readers keen to discover new and exciting authors.

Aria will publish a variety of genres under the commercial fiction umbrella such as women's fiction, crime, thrillers, historical fiction, saga and erotica.

So, whether you're a budding writer looking for a publisher or an avid reader looking for something to escape with – Aria will have something for you.

Get in touch: aria@headofzeus.com

Become an Aria Addict
http://www.ariafiction.com

Find us on Twitter
https://twitter.com/Aria_Fiction

Find us on Facebook
http://www.facebook.com/ariafiction

Find us on BookGrail
http://www.bookgrail.com/store/aria/

Addictive Fiction

9 7 5 3 1 2 4 6 8

A CIP catalogue record for this book is available from the British Library.

ISBN (E) 9781786692481

Aria
Clerkenwell House
45-47 Clerkenwell Green
London EC1R 0HT

www.ariafiction.com

Printed in Great Britain
by Amazon